"How about this? You give me advice. If at the end of the month, the business is still sinking under my direction, I will sell it to you at a very fair price."

A ghost of a smile whispered across Mac's face.

For a moment, that smile made him look handsome, desirable. The kind of guy you'd sit down with at the end of a long day, with a glass of wine and a view of the water.

Good Lord. Now she was waxing romantic about the corporate raider who wanted to destroy her family's pride and joy.

Savannah perched on the edge of the desk. "You know, if you agree to my plan, people might start to call you nice and charming."

"That's your best reason for why I should help you? To change public perception?"

"That, and earn a chunk of good karma points. Everyone needs those, even evil corporate raiders."

His gaze locked on hers. "I'm not evil."

She leaned in, closing the distance until she caught the scent of his cologne, something dark and mysterious, like the man who wore it. "Then prove it."

* * *

Nothing

THE TYCOON'S PROPOSAL

BY
SHIRLEY JUMP

Published in Great Britain 2015
by Mills & Boon, an imprint of Harlequin (UK) Limited,
Eton House, 18-24 Paradise Road, Richmond, Surrey, TW9 1SR

© 2015 Shirley Kawa-Jump, LLC

ISBN: 978-0-263-25172-2

23-1015

Printed and bound in Spain
by CPI, Barcelona

New York Times and *USA TODAY* bestselling author **Shirley Jump** spends her days writing romance so she can avoid the towering stack of dirty dishes, eat copious amounts of chocolate and reward herself with trips to the mall. Visit her website at www.shirleyjump.com for author news and a booklist and follow her at facebook.com/shirleyjump.author for giveaways and deep discussions about important things like chocolate and shoes.

To my friends who are always there with a hug or a laugh when I need it most. You know who you are—and you know I'd do the same for you.

You make the hard times easier and the good times even better.

Chapter One

When Mac Barlow was born, people claimed they heard his grandpa say, "That boy is gonna be somethin' when he grows up. I can just see the fire burnin' in his belly." Grandpa Barlow had died twenty years ago, so there was no one to prove or disprove that moment when Earl Ray Barlow held his first grandson. But the rumor had stuck in the family, growing into a legend, embellished by aunts and uncles and siblings, like extra tinsel on a Christmas tree.

Of course, anyone who knew Mac Barlow knew he'd definitely grown up and into those words. His days did indeed revolve around a roaring fire in his gut for more, his life filled to the brim with long lists of things to do, people to call, deals to make. He'd started when he was a freshman in college, starting with a little seed money he'd accumulated working part-time at a car lot while he was in high school. From the day he'd collected his first paycheck, and had grown into one of this year's Thirty Under Thirty touted in *Forbes* magazine.

So when he roared into Stone Gap, North Carolina, on a Sunday afternoon, it was to kill two birds with one stone—attend his brother Jack's wedding and finalize a business purchase that would add to the Barlow Enterprises coffers.

A purchase that was being thwarted at every possible turn by one singularly stubborn woman. But Mac had never met an obstacle he couldn't beat, a deal he couldn't close, which was what had him here, in person, to get Savannah Hillstrand to see the light, literally, and sell to him. Today.

Mac roared down the streets of Stone Gap, a passing figure on a Harley some might think a ghost, considering he was dressed all in black and driving, as usual, at breakneck speed. He leaned into the curve, nearly kissing the asphalt as he turned on to the street where he'd grown up. These moments on the bike, too few for his liking, were when Mac was finally able to shed the skin of the executive he was during the week. No suit, no tie, no one calling him or emailing him or knocking on his door, wanting a decision. Just him, the bike and the road. It was about as close to a vacation as Mac Barlow got.

He passed through Stone Gap in a moment, like the blip it was. Parts of the town were still frozen in time like some antebellum reenactment of the gentrified pre–Civil War days. He barely slowed for the light downtown, hardly glanced at the buildings that hadn't changed in decades. He kept on going, taking the Oak Street shortcut to the highway. Once he hit I-95, the road opened up and he pushed the throttle. The wind whipped past him, fighting the Harley every mile he rode. Ten miles up, he exited the highway and pulled into the parking lot of an office building.

For a meeting that was only going to end one way— with Mac getting what he wanted.

One lone car sat in the parking lot, a pale blue Toyota that had seen better days. Mac flipped out his cell phone and dialed Savannah's cell. While he waited for her to answer, he glanced up at the glass building, which reflected the late-afternoon sun like a prism. Solar panels covered the roof, angled toward the midday light. The Hillstrand sign itself was powered by a quartet of solar panels, and shaped like a rising sun cresting over the horizon. Nice, Mac thought.

Four rings, five, then she finally answered. "Hello?"

She had a pleasant voice. Melodic. All their previous exchanges had been by email. The dulcet tones of her hello surprised him. "Miss Hillstrand, it's Mac Barlow. I'm here for our meeting."

"Of course. I'm glad you made it, and on time at that. I appreciate punctuality." He pictured her on the other end, one of those librarian types with tortoiseshell glasses and her hair in one of those buns. Her emails had always been short and abrupt, all neat and organized the way he imagined she was. "Come on up. I'm in the main offices on the fifth floor."

She gave him the code to the door, and directions for when he entered the building. He keyed in the numbers, then headed up the stairs, bypassing the elevator to climb to the top floor, where the corporate offices were located. Probably one of those overpriced corner spaces that most CEOs inhabited.

As he walked, he ran through the facts in his head. Hillstrand Solar, one of the top solar-power manufacturers in the South, run for years by Willy Jay Hillstrand, a local fixture who had taken the home-remodeling company started by his grandfather and shifted its direction into renewable energy. In the process, Willie Jay had turned the small family business into a behemoth. Mac had seen the notice about Willy Jay dying a few months back and how he'd left the company to his only child, his daughter. Mac had given her a month, then sent one of his managers out to make her an offer she couldn't refuse.

Except she had refused. The first offer, the second and the third.

He'd let her struggle for another month, then sent another inquiry. She'd ignored him. He waited a third month, and she ignored him again.

A saner man would have moved on by now, but Mac needed this particular business. Willy Jay had had his hand in everything a solar panel could juice, from giant commercial factories to small backyard pools. If there was a solar panel anywhere between North Carolina and the southern tip of Florida, chances were it was made by Hillstrand.

And that was an industry Mac needed. He'd begun to shift his business in the past few years from immediately selling off the corporations he bought, to creating a package deal of sorts by combining companies that worked together. He could command a higher price and unload more inventory at once. Hillstrand Solar, with its expertise and command of the alternative energy market, was a gold mine for the right builder, and Mac had several potential buyers already lined up. Paired with the lumber company he had bought last month, a concrete company the month before and the real estate acquisition he'd made this past week, Hillstrand was the perfect bow on an already-strong package.

Savannah Hillstrand, the newly appointed head of the company, was barely treading water, Mac had heard from a number of his connections. She was struggling to hold on to her father's dream. Which meant if she was smart, she'd sell to him.

He had a sense she was beginning to cave when she'd accepted his offer of a meeting today. A Sunday afternoon, the offices quiet, the phones silent, a time when he could make his strongest offer, in person. He could be in and out in an hour, and then on to the next project. At least four other companies were on his list to look at while he was down south.

Okay, and maybe part of him had welcomed the Sunday meeting because it gave him a reason to put off seeing his family while he was in town. He loved his brothers, he really did, but when it came to his parents—well, his father had made disapproval into an art.

Truthfully, his father was the last person Mac wanted to see. He had no idea how to approach him—let alone face him—after the whopper of a surprise he'd run into last week. Dropping a bomb such as, *Hey Dad, I met my secret sibling,* wasn't likely to make him the favorite son at Sunday dinner.

Pushing thoughts of family out of his mind for the moment, Mac opened the heavy steel stairwell door on the fifth floor and walked into a boring, dull gray space. Faux carpeted cubicles blended so well with the gray carpet that it looked more like a boring ocean than an office. He had seen hundreds of offices like this, each about as exciting as watching paint dry. His own offices in Boston were bright, expansive, open. He'd designed them to encourage creative thinking, for his team to be able to collaborate freely and feel energized. Hillstrand Solar felt a lot like walking into a prison.

"Mr. Barlow. We meet in person finally."

He spun around and saw a tall, beautiful blonde standing behind him. No bun, no granny glasses. In fact, Savannah Hillstrand was the exact opposite of what he had pictured.

She wore a tailored pantsuit in a slate gray with a silky pink shirt beneath the jacket. Her hair was in a loose ponytail with a few escaped tendrils curling along her neck and a pencil sticking upwards out of the elastic like a forgotten ornament. She wore a minimum of makeup, just a little mascara and a glossy pink lipstick that kept his gaze riveted on her mouth for far too long.

"Miss Hillstrand." He strode forward, his hand outstretched, his voice businesslike and unemotional. But inside his chest his pulse was skipping a little. Had to be the meal he'd missed or the long hours on the road. "You aren't quite…uh…what I had…expected." He was stammering. He never stammered. What was up with that?

She shook with him, her grip firm and warm. All business. "Well, you sure aren't what I expected, either. I thought you'd be more…corporate."

Corporate—translation: stiff and dull. He didn't know why it bothered him that she'd thought that was who he was. Of course, he'd thought she was a dour librarian, which probably made them even. "You caught me on a weekend," he said. "Come Monday, it's all suits and ties again. Or my version of a suit and tie, at least."

Her gaze raked over him, taking in the leather jacket, the riding boots, the dark jeans, the white button-down peeking out from under the jacket, the only concession Mac made to conventional dress on the weekends. "And what is your version of a suit and tie? Leather chaps?"

He chuckled. "Not at all. Usually dark jeans, a button down and a tie. And a jacket if I'm forced to meet with a lawyer."

She laughed, a nice, rich sound that sent a ribbon of heat through his veins. The leather chaps comment told him Miss Hillstrand had spunk, that was for sure, and that was something Mac found...intriguing. "So, shall we have a seat and talk about my offer?" he said.

"I'm happy to talk to you, but first I want to reiterate what I told you on the phone. Even though I was amenable to an in-person meeting, I'm not interested in any offer you have. I'm not selling." Now the friendliness dropped from her face and she went all cold. "I made it clear that coming here would be a waste of time, but you insisted and I thought maybe face-to-face you would see how serious I am about *not* selling you Hillstrand Solar. Not now. Not ever."

Mac had rarely met a mountain he couldn't climb or a challenge he couldn't win. Savannah was just one more mountain—well, maybe a few curvy hills—and one who simply needed to see that she wasn't going to be able to keep this company running much longer. Profits had slipped as her longer-standing customers began to question the younger generation's leadership abilities. "I am sure I can provide you with an equitable offer. You'll be wealthy enough—"

"I don't care about money."

He scoffed. "I've never met anyone who didn't care about money. Everyone has a price, Miss Hillstrand."

"I don't." She crossed her arms over her chest and raised her chin, as if daring him to disagree. "So you can come in here and try to charm the pants off me with this offer and that offer all you want, but I'm not selling."

"I have no intentions of charming the pants off you." His gaze flicked to said garment. The gabardine curved over her thighs like a second skin, dark and soft and tempting. For a second, he imagined those pants off, nothing but white lacey panties underneath, and her long, long creamy legs...

Holy hell. Where had that come from? Mac shook his head to clear the unbidden image, then directed his attention back to Savannah's face. This was business, not personal, and he had no intention of mixing the two. Nothing good could ever come of that.

He cleared his throat. "I merely want to make you see the wisdom of selling while you can still fetch an equitable price for the company."

"I am not selling. Period. End of sentence."

"Then why bother to meet with me? That's something you have made abundantly clear already in all your emails."

"Because you refused to give up. I told you. If we met in person, then maybe you would finally see that I am dead serious about this. And I am. *Dead serious.*" She eyed him, her green eyes flashing, then took a step back. "Now that I've made my position clear, I have to get back to work. Good day, Mr. Barlow."

She sat down at her desk—if he could call it a desk. It was really just a hoarder's home away from home, one of those gray spaces in the sea of gray spaces, topped with a computer and a thousand pieces of paper scattered around the surface like crumbs. Chaos, that was what he'd call it. Definitely not the neat and tidy librarian he had imagined.

His own desk was usually close to spotless, the offices of Barlow Enterprises filled with little to no clutter, because it seemed the best thinking and ideas came in spaces that weren't overstuffed. He almost wanted to suggest Savannah do a little tidying as a first step to helping her father's company, but that would be helping her save the business, and his intention was to buy it.

Savannah pulled her chair into the desk, then turned away from him.

Well. Seemed Miss Hillstrand was going to be a tougher nut to crack then he'd expected. Mac leaned a hip on the desk across from hers. "You're over your head here. You know it. I know it."

"Are you saying you don't think I'm smart enough to run this company?"

"I'm saying you don't have the experience. You worked here summers during high school, then went off to college for a degree in history. Should we want to execute a repeat of the Napoleonic Wars, you'd be the first one I'd put in charge. But this is business, Miss Hillstrand, not a textbook, and that requires a certain level of…skills."

"Skills you assume I don't have." She raised her chin.

"Skills I *know* you don't have." He'd researched

her—well, his people had—and issued him a report. A report he could quote almost verbatim. Savannah Hillstrand had worked part-time in the factory throughout high school and college, filling nearly every role in production at one time or another. In between, she'd started a small remodeling business, restoring local homes to their former glory. She'd had a modicum of success at that business, but still returned to Hillstrand Solar in between projects.

It was possible that Daddy had financed her hobby of home flipping and just asked her to put in an appearance from time to time to keep up the family-owned business image. Either way, Willy Ray should have made his daughter at least get an MBA before he dropped the company into her lap.

"You don't know anything about me," she said. "Or this company."

"I know plenty," Mac countered. "And the numbers don't lie. Profits have dropped thirty-five percent since you took over. You've lost two of your biggest customers in the last month alone. Your line of credit was yanked by the bank after you were late on your last—"

She wheeled around. The pencil tumbled from her hair and landed on the carpet. "Are you spying on me?"

"Merely doing my research. I like to have all the facts before I buy a company."

"Well, go dig up dirt on someone else." Her cheeks flamed. "Hillstrand Solar is not for sale to your...chop shop."

He arched a brow. "Chop shop?"

"Isn't that what you do? Buy up companies and sell off the pieces? Regardless of how many people lose their jobs because you had to swallow one more little fish in your quest to be the biggest fish in the ocean."

The truth stung a little, but Mac shrugged it off. Many of these companies were better off once he was done. And many of the owners were grateful to walk away with some money in their pockets. Soon, Savannah Hillstrand would be one of them. It was a matter of time before she agreed with him. "You are a fan of the simile, I see."

"I just call it like I see it. Like my dad did." She waved toward the door. "See yourself out. I don't have time to argue with you."

"You don't have time *not* to listen to me." The pencil lay on the carpet, a bright slash of yellow against slate gray. It seemed…lonely somehow. "Every day you insist on running this place is another day you are losing money. Let me guess…about twenty thousand a week?"

She stiffened and he knew he'd guessed correctly. "I have work to do. Work that pays the salaries of the people who work here, people who depend on me to keep that income rolling in."

"Last I checked there was a classified section in the back of the newspaper. They'll find other jobs."

She jerked out of her chair and marched up to him now, her green eyes on fire. "Are you really that cold and callous?"

"I'm neither, I assure you. I'm a realist."

"A realist." She scoffed. "Another word for a corporate shark."

He put up a hand. Her barbs weren't anything he hadn't heard before—and from his own father, at that. But for some reason it bothered him that Savannah thought he was that cold. "Before you condemn me as the devil incarnate, let me make this clear. This isn't about your family legacy or some romantic notion of keeping a company afloat just because you inherited it. This is about business, plain and simple. *My* business is buying and selling. It's smart financial sense for me to buy and for you to sell. You know that, deep in your heart. The company is struggling and it's going to sink if you don't climb in the lifeboat I'm offering."

"But it's my father's legacy. Part of our family history." Her voice wavered a little, her composure wobbled, a momentary break in the businesslike facade of Savannah Hillstrand. "He would be heartbroken if I sold it off."

"And like I said, this isn't personal." He said the words, but there was something in him that was bothered by the tears welling in her eyes, that forlorn pencil on the floor. It had to be being back in the Stone Gap, because never before had Mac been so bothered by the decisions he made. Or the condemnation of one stubborn CEO. Stubborn and beautiful, he amended.

"The best time to sell is before the company runs itself into the ground," Mac said, his tone growing gentle. "I understand you are trying to keep it afloat, and I admire you for that. I really do. But it's better for you to give it a chance to keep on going with me than to watch it dissolve in the next few months." He hesitated. "Look, I'd like to make you a fair offer based on the financials. Why don't we go over the books together?"

Then he could deal with columns and numbers, instead of this heartbroken woman who wanted to hold on to an already-fading family legacy.

Her face fell, and Mac felt like a jerk. "I'm not say-

ing you're right, because I don't think you are. But…"
The fight had gone from her shoulders, the fire in her
eyes extinguished. For a second, Mac wanted to take
it all back, get on his motorcycle and leave town. But
then he remembered his own mantra about this not
being personal and steeled himself against that look
in her eyes.

"Maybe it would be worth at least hearing you out,"
Savannah said. "In case—and I mean that as a very
slim just in case—I have a change of heart in the future."

"It's always better to be armed with information
before you make a decision." He was winning the argument but it wasn't giving him any kind of satisfaction. Why? This was what he lived for—the pursuit,
the capture, the success. But this time he didn't want
to win so much as he wanted to…

See Savannah Hillstrand smile again. Crazy thoughts.

She nodded. Then her gaze cut away. "My father's
computer is this one."

"*That* mess is your father's workspace?"

She smiled ruefully. "It's organized chaos."

"You got one word right," he muttered. "He doesn't
have his own office?"

"My father never liked offices. He wanted to be with
the people who worked so hard for him. So he opted to
have a cubicle just like everyone else." She ran a hand
over the back of one of the chairs, almost as if Willy
Jay were sitting in it right now. "He said he did it so
he never forgot what was important."

"And what was that?" Mac asked. Because, for some
reason he couldn't fathom, the answer to that question
was impossibly important to him right now.

Savannah lifted her gaze to his, her deep green eyes reminding Mac of the dark, mysterious woods of North Carolina, where everything was lush and full. "That none of this was about business. It was personal. It was…family."

Chapter Two

Savannah took the elevator down to the fourth floor, then went into the break room and stood in the darkened space for a long time beside the picture of her father, taken years ago at an employee picnic, before he'd gotten sick.

She had known this day would come, known it from the moment she had sat in her father's chair and realized she had no idea what she was doing, but a part of her somehow had kept thinking maybe Mac Barlow would give up and she would find some miracle CEO knowledge in the back of her brain.

Not that she hadn't thought about selling the company. Every time an offer came in from Mac Barlow, and the couple others that she had fielded from her competitors, she'd weighed it against the worries on her shoulders. From the day her father died, Savannah had been grieving and overwhelmed. Stepping into her father's shoes had been a Herculean task. She'd loved her father dearly, but he had been the one person who knew how this company ticked. He'd always promised to take her under his wing and show her the ropes, but the heart attack that killed him had come while he was still relatively young and not ready.

Not that Savannah had ever really planned to be a part of the company. Her father had asked her time and time again to be a part of his dream, but her heart had led her in other directions. Savannah had worked in all facets of the company at one time or another, but had never been the one in charge; never *wanted* to be the one in charge. It wasn't until she'd actually sat at her father's desk that she'd realized how many millions of decisions had to be made on a daily basis. Tiny decisions that could alter the course of the profits, and big decisions that could send the business off a cliff.

And it was too late to ask him how to handle it all.

Now, four months later, she still hadn't really found her groove. She was trying, but it was far harder than she'd expected to live up to her father's example. To keep his Hillstrand Solar family together.

And that was what it was—her father's family. Not hers. *His* dream—not hers. But she'd made a promise, and whatever it took, Savannah would keep that promise.

Now Mac Barlow wanted to break up the family. And he refused to give up, no matter how many times she told him no.

The problem was he had a point. When he'd talked about the company sinking and the lifeboat he was offering, she'd finally admitted the truth to herself. Her four months of floundering around like a fish out of water had done their damage to the bottom line. Thus far she'd held off laying off any employees, but truth be told she was losing money and customers at an alarming rate, and she wasn't sure how to recover.

Maybe Mac was right. Maybe the company would be better off in his hands. But the people who worked here…

She leaned against the counter and took in several deep breaths. She needed a plan. Some time to think. She hadn't taken off so much as an afternoon since her father died—hence being here on yet another Sunday— and that had left her feeling even more snowed under by a growing workload.

What she needed was a trip to the old house. A few hours along the water, where the air was clear and the worries seemed far away. Some time sanding down the damaged deck or scraping off the old paint on the dining room wainscoting. In those moments when she was deconstructing and rebuilding, uncovering and restoring, she found a kind of Zen. There was something calming about taking a house that was ready to crumble at the slightest gust of wind and bring it back to its former glory. Even now she itched to be there, to take a few minutes or a few hours to breathe life into those old, familiar walls. There she knew she could make some decisions. Maybe even come up with a plan to save everyone's job going forward.

Except how was she supposed to do that? She could save historic homes, but she had no idea what to do when it came to saving her father's legacy.

Promise me, you'll keep it running, Willie Jay had

said before he died. *Those people depended on me, and now they're gonna depend on you.*

She touched the picture of her father. "Oh, Dad, I wish you were here." She desperately needed a mentor, someone to help her navigate the choppy waters. Someone who had turned around companies before. Someone who knew how to make their profits grow.

Her father smiled back in the perpetual image of him standing in the center of a long line of Hillstrand Solar employees on a bright summer day. The photo had been one of his favorites. He had his arms stretched over the shoulders of the employees closest to him, all part of the circle. He had loved this company, every single inch of it, and loved every one of the people who worked here. No matter what decision she made, she had to make sure the employees kept their jobs.

Because they mattered to Willie Jay. Mattered more than anything else in his life. And maybe, just maybe, if she could keep that legacy alive, she could feel as though she'd mattered to her father, too.

"I'll find a way to make this all work out, Dad," she whispered. "I promise."

His smile seemed to waver, but maybe that was just the tears in her eyes. She swiped them away, drew in a deep breath, then pulled a soda out of the fridge and headed back to the fifth floor.

She caught a glimpse of herself in the glass on the stairwell door. Good Lord, she looked the way she felt. Trying hard to be a sharp, sophisticated executive and failing miserably. A nice, neat suit, topped by a head of hair that looked as if she'd just rolled out of bed. At some point today, her long hair had gotten in her face while she worked, and she'd tied it back in a ponytail without a second thought. Just as she had a hundred thousand times on a job site. But here, with Mac Barlow, she'd wanted to be taken seriously, to be seen as a determined and capable CEO.

Nothing about that messy ponytail screamed *force to be reckoned with*. No wonder Mac kept saying she was in over her head. That was exactly the look she was sporting this afternoon.

She tugged out the ponytail and ran a hand through her long blond curls. She tugged the wisps of her bangs over her forehead, then did a quick glance to make sure the rest of her was shipshape. She wasn't flirting with the guy, she reminded herself. Even if he did look like a cross between a bad boy and a millionaire. It would help her make her case. That was all.

On the short flight up to the top floor, she'd decided two things—she wasn't going to sell to Mac Barlow no matter what he offered her. But before she told him that, she was going to see if she could find a way to get ideas from him as to what she could do. Somehow turn the conversation into one that gave her much-needed advice. Maybe then, if she could implement his thoughts, she could turn the company around herself. And send Mac on his way.

She needed a mentor, and she had one right here. The trick was getting him to give her concrete advice without realizing he was doing it.

She pasted a smile on her face, then strode across the office. Her steps faltered when she saw Mac sitting in the chair her father had always occupied, his attention riveted on the computer screen before him. Her father's computer, the one she had been sitting at just moments before because it made her feel close to her

dad, who she still missed as though she'd lost a limb.
She wanted to yank Mac Barlow out of the chair. Instead, she forced that smile to stay in place and hoped
it didn't look as fake as it felt.

*Okay, play nice. Try to engage him in a conversa-
tion that gives you what you need.*

"We got off on the wrong foot, Mr. Barlow," she
said as she approached the desk. She held the soda in
her hand toward him. "And I wanted to give you a…
peace offering."

He flicked a glance at the bottle. "I don't drink
soda."

"Oh." She took the bottle back, unscrewed the top
and screwed it back on again. So much for that peace
offering. "I'd like to talk to you about the company a
little more."

He kept clicking through the bookkeeping program,
hardly giving her the time of day. "Miss Hillstrand, if
this is another attempt to talk me out of—"

"Of course not," she lied. Best to find a way to get
him chatting about what he did, how he had become
so successful, or at the very least, how he envisioned
making Hillstrand Solar a good investment for his enterprise. Surely, running one business was like running another, and from that conversation, perhaps she
could extract a few secrets to success, if there was such
a thing. Give her a bathroom to restore or a kitchen
that needed to be gutted and reconfigured, and Savannah was in her element. But here, at her father's desk,
with dozens of people looking to her for leadership and
answers—she might as well have been running blind
into a wall. Well, it was time for her to find her focus.
"I merely thought you'd want an insider's perspective.

I've worked here practically since I could walk, and I'd love to give you some feedback. To help you make... a better decision."

"And what decision would that be?" He swiveled in the chair. "Are you trying to talk me out of the purchase again?"

"Certainly not." She screwed and unscrewed the bottle cap again, then chided herself for showing her nerves. A strong CEO never wavered, never showed doubt. Maybe if she played the part, it would eventually suit her. "I just wanted to get an idea of what you planned to do with the company, how you thought you would get it back on its feet if you bought it. Because we both know you can't just flip it if it's struggling."

Mac returned to the computer and moved on to the next screen, peering down the list of receivables. "I rarely share my plans with other people."

"I'm not other people. I'm the owner. And this company is like—" damn the catch in her throat "—family to me. I want to make sure it is taken care of and that everyone will be okay. That the family, so to speak, will remain intact."

It wasn't the company that was family, Savannah realized as she said the words. She knew the people who worked at Hillstrand Solar, of course. It was that the company, every last chair and slip of paper, was a part of her father. Willie Jay and Savannah had been like two peas in a pod, her mother had always said. He'd been her protector, her mentor, her hero, and without him in her life, a yawning cavern had opened in Savannah's heart. Along with the sense that she'd never quite made him proud, never quite shown him what she could do. Taking care of the company filled that cavern. A little.

Mac scanned the list of jobs in production, then returned his attention to the receivables, probably doing the math to see if their monthly sales were up to snuff. She waited.

Finally, he let out a breath and pushed back from the computer. "I understand that need to want to protect everyone's jobs, but sometimes that isn't feasible."

"But many of these employees have been here as long as my father was here. They depend on their paychecks. They're honest and trustworthy and hardworking—"

"I'm not interviewing them, so save the résumés." He waved toward the computer screen. "I'm looking at the bottom line. I make all my decisions based on the numbers. And the numbers are clear. You can't support the amount of overhead you have."

The sinking feeling in Savannah's gut told her that Mac was right. Her father had been a great leader, but he had also been a softy, reluctant to fire anyone. "There must be a way to bring in more revenue."

"There is. More sales. But your sales staff is already stretched pretty thin, and your biggest accounts have gone to your competitors. It takes time to woo them back, time to build up the sales again, time to get that money rolling in."

"It's easier to keep the bees you have with a strong hive than to go out and capture more." She gave him a sad smile. "Something my dad used to say."

His gaze met hers. She swore she saw a softening in his eyes, a connection between them. "My parents are big on sayings like that. Must be a Southern thing."

"You don't hear those sayings much up in Boston?"

He scoffed. "Not at all. Sometimes I miss…" He shook his head and the moment of connection, if there had really been one at all, disappeared. "Anyway, your hive right now is…weakening. It's not completely fallen apart, but it's got some structural damage from the last few months." He brought up the accounting program and started leading her through the reports she'd already pored over herself. Every percentage he gave her, every figure he pointed to, told her the same thing.

She drew up a chair and perched on the edge. The numbers on the screen blended together, a confusing jumble that she barely understood on her best day. There were so many working parts to a business this size. Too many, it seemed, for one person to control. At least this particular person.

But if she didn't sit in her father's chair, then who would? Certainly not Mac Barlow, who would sell it off in pieces, dismantling the last remaining bits of Willy Jay Hillstrand. She was the only one who loved her father enough to keep it moving forward, to keep the legacy going.

When Mac had finished reviewing the reports with her, and thus depressing Savannah even more, she pushed back and let out a sigh. "Then what would you do if you were me?"

A grin quirked up the side of Mac's mouth. It was a nice grin, made his eyes light up, softened everything about him. He went from being the evil corporate raider to…a guy. Just a guy. Okay, just a very handsome guy.

Which was the last thing she needed in her life. She'd fallen for more than one Southern charmer, only to realize charm didn't equal gentleman. Savannah had sworn off dating, at least for the foreseeable future.

"I see what you're doing." The grin widened. "Are you asking me to help you rebuild your company so that you can keep it running?"

"And out of your evil clutches." She smiled. Maybe if she asked him nicely he'd help her. Be the mentor she needed. Okay, so maybe she was being way too Pollyanna here, but Savannah was desperate for some guidance. Might as well be honest. "Yes, I am doing exactly that."

"And why would I help you?"

"Because there is more to life than tearing down companies, Mac Barlow." She leaned toward him and caught his blue-eyed gaze. She wanted to believe the nice guy she had glimpsed really existed. That he could be persuaded to help instead of destroy. "How about building one up instead?"

"You are reading me wrong, Savannah. I am not in the business of building things. I make money, plain and simple. As quickly as possible. I don't nurture struggling firms along," he said. "I buy, I sell, I make a profit and I move on."

Yet he hadn't sold the three firms he'd bought in the past six months. Nor had he said he was going to. And then there was the one tiny company he'd bought several years ago and restarted, a company he still owned as far as she could tell. She'd done her research on him, too, and she'd found it interesting that Mac was shifting gears. Why, she wasn't sure, and he clearly wasn't about to explain. But the information opened a tiny window of trust and hope for Savannah. Maybe there was a chance—a teeny one—that given enough time, she could convince Mac that his relentless pursuit of Hillstrand Solar was a waste of time. "Wouldn't you like to do a good deed for the day?"

He chuckled. "Do I look like the Boy Scout type to you?"

"Maybe the renegade Boy Scout."

That made him laugh again. She liked it when he laughed. It seemed to ease everything about him, and make an already-attractive man ten times more attractive. Not that she was interested in him, of course. Just his brain.

Uh-huh.

Amusement lit his features. "And what is this good deed you want me to do?"

"Just offer me some business advice."

"That undermines my intentions."

She shrugged. "Call it corporate goodwill."

He scoffed. "You haven't been a CEO for very long, Miss Hillstrand. In business, there is no such thing. Everything is driven by—"

"Money, yes, I know. You said that already." She took a sip of the soda. She may be too late for all this, and in the end forced, as her father used to say, to sink the ship in order to save the passengers. But she had to at least try, or she'd hate herself for letting the company fall apart. "You already own several other green companies. Maybe those could partner with mine and—"

"That…wouldn't be a good idea. I'm not trying to build a green empire here, just do what I do best. Buy and sell."

She worried her bottom lip. "Okay, then how about this? While you are here in town, you meet with me, talk about the business, give me advice I can implement, and I will give it one month. If at the end of the month the business is still sinking under my direction, I will sell it to you at a very fair price."

He considered her, his face dark and unreadable. Mac should have been a poker player, because nothing in his eyes or set of his mouth gave away what he was thinking. A long moment passed while she stood there trying not to fidget with the soda bottle.

"Help you. This week."

"Yup."

"I am supposed to spend time with my family while I'm here in Stone Gap."

So Mac Barlow was from Stone Gap. His corporate bios she'd found on the web had mentioned the state, but not town he hailed from. She hadn't lived in Stone Gap very long—only the past couple of years—but never had she thought that corporate raider Mac Barlow could be related to the nice Barlows she had met, including Luke, who ran the local auto-repair shop. "I didn't realize you were related to the Barlows who live here."

"Let me guess. You thought there was no way my charming brothers could have anything in common with someone like me, a coldhearted bastard who is all about the bottom line."

A mind reader, too. "Well…if the description fits."

He laughed. "I assure you, we are related. And as much as I love my family, I'd rather limit my time with them. My family is perfectly great, but there are some…issues I'd rather not address right now and my brothers have a way of ferreting out anything I don't want them to know." A ghost of a smile whispered across Mac's face.

For a moment, that smile made him look handsome, desirable. The kind of guy you'd sit down with at the end of a long day with a glass of wine and a view of the water. The kind of guy who would decorate the Christmas tree with you, then turn off all the lights in the house so you both could lie underneath it, bathed in the glow.

Good Lord. Now she was waxing romantic about the corporate raider who wanted to destroy her family's pride and joy. She really needed to focus on something other than his quick smile. Because even a lion could smile—right before it devoured you whole.

She wanted to hate him. She really did. And a part of her sort of did. But the part that had been intrigued by that smile wondered if perhaps a beating heart lurked beneath the button-down shirt and leather jacket.

She perched on the edge of the desk. "You know, if you agree to my plan, people might start to call you nice and charming, too."

He chuckled. "That's your best reason for why I should help you? To change public perception?"

"That and earn a chunk of good karma points. Everyone needs those, even evil tycoons." She grinned, softening her words.

His gaze locked on hers. "I'm not evil."

She leaned in, closing the distance until she caught the scent of his cologne, something dark and mysterious like the man who wore it. "Then prove it."

A long, hot moment passed between them, his stormy eyes unreadable. He got to his feet and put out his hand. "Okay, Miss Hillstrand, you have a deal."

She took his hand. He had a warm, firm grip. It had been a long time since she had been touched by a man—clearly too long given the undeniable jolt of electricity she felt at the contact. "Great. We can start tomorrow morning, bright and early."

"Why wait? Let's grab something to eat and I'll give you my CEO 101 talk."

"Are you asking me on a date?" She said the words as a joke, but a part of her—a crazy part—hoped he'd say yes. That part was disappointed when he released her hand.

What was she thinking? Why would she want to date the man who wanted to dismantle her father's dream? Okay, yes, Mac Barlow was handsome and had that smile—and it had been a *long* time since she'd been on a date—but still, he wanted her company, not her.

"Lesson number one—multitask as much as possible," Mac said. "I wasn't planning on leaving here and wasting time at a restaurant. Multitasking means eat at your desk, take meetings over lunch, skip breakfast to—"

"Skip breakfast? Now I *know* you're insane." She laughed. "If you want to get on my good side, bring me pancakes and bacon."

"I'll have to remember that." He smiled again, and she wondered for one crazy second if he was remembering that because he was interested in her or because he was going to make his next offer at an IHOP. "So, do we have a deal? We start tonight. Order in some takeout, clear a space on one of these desks and see where it goes from there? With the company, of course."

"Of course." She paused a second. "Actually, if it's okay with you, I'd love to meet anywhere but here. I've been in this office pretty much all weekend." Outside her window the sun had begun its descent, dropping over the Stone Gap landscape like a blanket of gold. How long had it been since she'd been outside instead of chained to a desk all day? "It'd be great to get out and breathe some fresh air for a little while."

"I don't like to waste time, Savannah—"

Goodness, she liked the way her name rolled off his tongue. "Work can wait a bit. At least for a little while." She reached for her purse and slung it over her shoulder. She had been here too many hours and had forgotten what was important. Maybe by being around the places her father loved, she'd find some of what had made him tick, what had made him such a great leader. She'd forgotten all that in these past few harried months, and in her gut Savannah knew that the key to turning things around started with getting back to the basics.

"Work never waits for me," Mac said. "So I'd rather—"

"Listen, you've had a long day of travel already. Wouldn't it be nice to have a quiet meal in a relaxing spot?" she said. "My father believed in enjoying life. Leaving at five, taking the weekends off and, most of all, working a little fun into your day. I've forgotten all that these past few months, and it's time I did just a little of that. It's called refilling the well."

"I call that recess." Mac shook his head. "This is business, not school, and regardless of how your father ran things, you should be here 24/7 until things turn around."

"I agree with you. And I will be. But first I need to…recharge. My father did it almost every day, and it made him a great leader." She took a step closer to Mac, until the blue in his eyes revealed little flecks of gold. Her heart fluttered and she had to force herself not to inhale another whiff of his tempting cologne. *Business only.* "Why don't you come with me, let me show you what really mattered to Willie Jay Hillstrand. And where he found his best inspiration."

"I assure you, I can learn all I need to know from the files right here."

She shook her head, and felt a bittersweet smile stumble on her lips. "No you can't. And I forgot for a while that I couldn't, either."

He assessed her for a long moment, those blue eyes unreadable, except for a small hint of amusement. "I don't know. I have work to do, yes, I should eat, but—"

"Listen, I know this great place that makes fabulous steaks. It's right on the water, and it's quiet. We can eat, and promise not to talk business until dessert is over."

Mac scoffed. "Not talk business? I don't think I know any other topics of conversation."

"And that, Mr. Barlow," because she was afraid if she called him Mac, she might expose the way his touch had tripped her pulse, "is exactly why I can't sell Hillstrand Solar to you right now." *Or ever,* her mind whispered. "My father knew the importance of life outside the business, and that's what made him so successful and made everyone who works here so happy. Unless you understand that, you can't understand me or the company." She bent down, scribbled an address on a piece of paper. "So if you want to help me, then meet me at the Sea Shanty in an hour."

"I'd rather—"

She handed him the slip of paper. Firm, in control, a whole other Savannah than she normally was in these offices. Maybe if she drew on a little of the skills she used with stubborn subcontractors and late delivery trucks, she could handle the CEO chair that still felt as wrong as a pair of shoes two sizes too small. "That's my deal, Barlow. Take it or leave it."

Chapter Three

The meeting with Savannah Hillstrand lingered in Mac's mind, along with the image of the strong, intriguing blonde. He'd agreed to her dinner meeting tonight, but only to talk more business, he told himself, not to get to know her more.

His first impressions of her had been wrong, something that doubled his interest, because if there was one thing Mac had little experience with, it was being wrong.

She was stronger than he'd expected, not at all scared or intimidated by his attempts to purchase her company. She had stood toe to toe with him, literally and figuratively, and challenged Mac to do the craziest thing...

Help her save Hillstrand Solar.

With that interesting little carrot at the end—that if

it didn't work, and she failed, he could still buy it from her. He could be a horrible person and give her bad advice, advice sure to bring Hillstrand Solar to ruin, but a part of Mac was…intrigued by the idea of helping her. Turning a company around instead of just flipping it to the next buyer could be an interesting twist to his usual practices. A challenge of sorts.

Either way, he intended to use the week to convince her that, in the end, selling was the best strategy. If he paid a little more in a month because of the help he gave her, so be it. She'd have the satisfaction of knowing she hadn't ruined the company, and he'd still have that last piece to the bigger puzzle he was assembling.

He had an hour until he was supposed to meet Savannah, an hour he could spend working—or he could bite the bullet and see his family. Part of him just wanted to hole up in a coffee shop and spend the sixty minutes checking email on his laptop, but a twinge of guilt told him he hadn't come all this way just to work. He had missed his brothers and mother something fierce, and it'd be nice to see them.

His father, not so much. Especially after that conversation in Atlanta with his Uncle Tank. His real name wasn't Tank, of course, but he'd gotten the nickname because John Barlow was a barrel-chested guy with a larger-than-life personality, and the nickname had followed him from childhood on up. The younger brother to Bobby, Mac's father, and the one who had always been the jokester, the prankster, but who also had gotten into more trouble than a loose pig at a county fair. When he'd first told Mac the story about Bobby's misdeeds, Mac had dismissed it as yet another joke. Then a little digging had unearthed some truth—truth that redefined everything Mac thought he knew about his family.

And about his father.

Now that trouble was threatening to catch up with the Barlows if Mac didn't find a way to head it off. But that meant talking to his father, something Mac had learned long ago to avoid doing.

You have another brother, Uncle Tank had said, explaining that he had known the boy for some time, staying in contact by posing as a friend to the family, something he'd done as a favor to Bobby. *I talked to him and he said he wants to meet the rest of his family. Soon.*

Meeting them meant exposing the truth. Exposing his father as a cheater. Despite the hard feelings between himself and his dad, he didn't relish telling the others what Uncle Tank had told him. In fact, Mac had no idea how to say the words. How to confront the man he hadn't talked to in almost a decade. Was there ever a good time for that kind of thing?

A moment later, Mac was in the driveway of his old childhood home. He stood there a moment, taking in the long open porch, the big front door still painted the same cranberry color as always. There were new annuals in the flower beds, and a new American flag hanging from the pole, but mostly the house had stayed unchanged, like a snapshot of the past. A part of Mac liked knowing it would be the same, year after year. He gave the old homestead a nod, then walked up the front steps and into the house. In an instant, his family poured into the hall like water overflowing a dam to see him.

He took off his helmet and grinned. Damn, it was

good to see them. "I heard one of you is getting married, and I'm here to talk you out of it."

Jack was the first to clap his older brother on the back. Still trim and fit from his time in the military, Jack had the shortest haircut of the three of them. "Sorry, Mac, you're too late. I'm already in love. Might want to talk to the other one. He just got engaged five seconds ago." He nodded toward Luke.

Luke was engaged? Of the three Barlow boys, Mac would have listed Luke as least likely to get married. He arched a brow in Luke's direction, and his brother started grinning like a fool.

Mac shook his head in mock regret. "I go away for a few years and this is the kind of craziness I come home to?"

"It's the best kind of craziness, so hush up and enjoy your family," his mother said. Della wrapped him in a hug, dragging him toward the dining room table. It was Sunday—family dinner day. Except Mac hadn't sat at the family dinner table in years, and he wasn't so sure he wanted to today, either. He could see his father, standing to the side of the table, his face as unreadable as a hieroglyphic.

A mixed bag of emotions ran through Mac. He'd missed his father, but at the same time, dreaded seeing him. And now the knowledge that Bobby Barlow had fathered a child with another woman had given Mac a whole new set of reasons to be angry at the man. All he knew was that he couldn't deal with this today and definitely not at the Sunday dinner table.

Mama placed a kiss on his temple as if he was five years old again. "It's good to have you home, Maxwell."

Mac covered his mother's hand with his own. He'd

missed her simple touch, her ever-present love for her sons. Despite everything that had happened in the past between Bobby and Mac, Della couldn't hold a grudge if it was glued to her palm. He loved that about his mother. "Good to be back, Mama."

Jack gestured toward one of the seats at the table. "So, you gonna stay awhile or what?"

Mac's gaze went to his father. Even now, even at thirty, Mac wanted that nod of approval. Ridiculous. He should be well past that need.

"Of course he's staying," Mama said. She pulled out a chair and practically shoved Mac into it. "Plus it's Maddy's birthday—"

"Who's Maddy?"

"Stay home for more than five minutes and you'll get caught up," Jack said.

"Maddy is Luke's daughter. With Susannah Reynolds," his mother explained. "It's a long story, one that I'll share after dinner. And now, Luke is marrying Peyton, Susannah's sister. So they're going to be a family very soon."

Mac glanced around and saw a little girl shyly holding hands with Peyton. To their right stood Meri Prescott, the former beauty queen now engaged to Jack. He remembered both Peyton and Meri from when they were kids, especially Peyton, who had vacationed sometimes at the same lake as the Barlows. And there were his two brothers, smiling like loons. "Is there some kind of marriage plague going on here that I missed?" Mac said.

His mother smiled. "You came home just in time for all the celebration."

"Wasn't sure you would," his father muttered. "Haven't heard hide nor hair from you in years."

Mac ignored the barb. Unlike his brothers, he'd never really gotten along with his father. Maybe it was something about being the oldest, the one who set the pace, laid out all the expectations. No matter how far Mac climbed or how well he did, his father rarely had an *attaboy* or so much as a nod for the achievement. And when Mac had announced he was leaving home the day after he graduated high school, it had turned into a fight about Mac abandoning his responsibilities and his family.

The final torch to the feeble bridge between father and son had been one of Mac's first business purchases, a small family-owned used car lot that Mac had turned around and sold to an investor up north, who'd taken the inventory and left the lot vacant for years, a barren spot in downtown Stone Gap. It wasn't until a few years later that the lot was taken under new ownership and management, and saw life again. Bobby had blamed Mac for ruining the town, ruining his friend's life and ruining pretty much the entire world. In the years since, Mac had spent as little time at home as possible.

But now he had a whole other reason for not wanting to talk to his father. A secret that could not only destroy what little relationship Mac and Bobby had left, but dismantle the entire Barlow family.

Besides, with his brothers looking so damned happy they might just burst, and the mouth-watering aromas of his mother's home cooking filling the air, Mac wasn't about to retread old ground or unearth buried bones. "You know I wouldn't miss seeing Jack's last gasp as a single man, Mama," he said. "I even wore black for the occasion."

"You are incorrigible," his mother said. "But I love you anyway."

"She's just saying that." Jack, in the seat beside him, clapped Mac on the shoulder. The three boys all had the same dark hair and blue eyes, but Jack was the leanest and tallest of the three by about a half an inch. "You know she likes me best."

Mac looked around the assembled group, joined by the two women and Maddy. The whole world seemed to have changed in the years since Mac had lived in Stone Gap. His younger brothers were all grown up, getting married, settling down. "Well, damn. You're all here at once."

"So where's your date?" Luke asked.

"What date? I didn't bring anyone with me."

"That's because no one wants to put up with his workaholic self," Jack laughed.

The familiar argument, back again. From the day he'd gotten his first job at eleven, his brothers had teased him about working too much, playing too little. Mac just hadn't seen the need for video games or skateboarding on sidewalks. Not when there were things that could be accomplished, goals to be met. "I'm not a workaholic."

Jack arched a brow. "So you came to town just for my wedding? Not for anything work related?"

"Well—"

"Exactly." Jack shook his head. "One of these days, big brother, you'll slow down long enough to live your life."

"Mac's living his life. Up there in the city far from

all of us. Doesn't slow down long enough to call and say how-do-you-do," Bobby said.

"Dad, I've just been busy."

"Living the big corporate life. Sucking up the little guys and slapping them down like ants."

And that right there was the crux of everything wrong between his father and him. Bobby didn't understand Mac's approach to business, didn't see that sometimes buying a company and shutting it down was a good thing. "Dad, we've been over—"

His mother popped to her feet, cutting off the sentence. "Let me get you a plate and dish you up some food. That way your brothers won't eat your helping."

For a moment, Mac wanted to stay at this table, surrounded by the family he'd seen too little of since he'd left for college. But that itch to complete the To Do list, to move on to the next thing, the bigger thing, like some mountain just out of reach, nagged at him. He'd been chasing that feeling for years and had yet to find anything that tamed the quest for more.

He took one look at his father's face, still impassable and cold, and got to his feet.

If Mac stayed a second longer he was bound to say something he shouldn't. Something such as, *Where do you get off judging me for how I run my business, Dad, when you were screwing up your own life?* Yeah, probably not appropriate Sunday-dinner talk. "Sorry, Mama, but I can't stay. Just popped in to say hello. I have a meeting to get to."

"On a Sunday?" His mother shook her head. "Why are you working on the Lord's day? Even He took a break, you know."

"That's because His work was done, Mama. Mine

never is." Mac pressed a quick kiss to his mother's cheek, then grabbed his helmet off the sideboard, swung it back onto his head and buckled the chin strap. "I'll be around, staying at the Stone Gap Hotel, and here through Saturday for Jack's wedding."

"Then gone again." The cold statement from his father wasn't even a question.

"My life is back in Boston, Dad. Not here."

"Your life is where you make it, son." Bobby shook his head. Clearly disappointed. "And there's nothing wrong with making a life right here. You don't have to conquer the world and trample the little people to have a life."

Mac bit back his frustration. No matter how far he rose in his career, how many milestones he achieved, his father never looked at him the way he looked at his other two boys. Maybe Bobby couldn't understand why Mac would leave Stone Gap, why he'd want something more than what this tiny little speck of a town had to offer. Mac had long ago given up trying to argue the point. His father was never going to see him as anything other than the one who'd let him down, let the town down. One business deal and Bobby refused to forgive or understand.

And now Mac had his own reasons for not forgiving or understanding his father, who came across as the great family man, the pillar of Stone Gap. When the truth was something else entirely.

"I'll be back," Mac promised. Then he headed out the door, got on his bike and started the engine, letting the roar of the Harley drown out the tension he was leaving behind.

Before heading to the address Savannah had given

him, Mac stopped over at the Stone Gap Hotel to check in and get his room key, because chances were good if he got back late tonight, the eighteen-year-old front-desk clerk would be asleep when he returned. He stowed his small bag of belongings in the room, then grabbed his laptop and a notepad before heading back down to the bike. That was all he'd need for his evening with Savannah Hillstrand. Eat, conduct a little business and leave.

No lingering to get to know her, to see if he could make her laugh or coax that dazzling smile from her again. This was all work and no play, and the sooner he could get back to his room to tackle the long list of emails and reports he needed to read, the better. Then, hopefully, this knot of stress in his chest would ease.

He was just latching his helmet when a car carrying familiar occupants pulled into the hotel parking lot. His little brothers, here to check up on him. Mac tucked the helmet under his arm and waited while they got out of Luke's car.

"What are you two doing here?"

The younger Barlows leaned against the hood, their arms crossed over their chests. "We're on a fact-finding mission," Jack said. "As in finding out why the hell you ran out on dinner?"

"I told you. I had a meeting."

"At dinnertime. On a Sunday." Jack rolled his eyes. "The only day you know Mama's going to expect us all around the table."

"You missed a hell of a pot roast, too," Luke added.

"And don't forget the apple crumble for dessert," Jack said. "That was amazing."

"Had myself two helpings since I didn't have to

share with Mac." Luke patted his belly. "Too bad you missed it for a *meeting*, big brother."

Mac scowled. He was back in town for barely a few hours and already they were giving him a hard time. "For one, the time for Sunday dinner is more like late afternoon—"

"So we have time to watch the game. Priorities, Mac." Jack grinned.

"For another, I don't think Dad really cared if I was there or not." Mac shrugged as if it didn't bother him at all, and as if there wasn't other untouched issues between him and his father. Issues he didn't want to share with his brothers, not until he figured out how to drop this secret sibling bomb with as little collateral damage as possible. "So I figured I might as well get some work done."

"What is up with you and Dad anyway?" Luke asked. "It seemed like you were trying your damnedest to avoid him."

"More than you usually do," Jack added. "Dad's mellowed over the years, Mac. You could try cutting him some slack—"

"I'm not having this conversation. I told you. I have a meeting—"

"No, you have a serious itch to avoid your family today. Which is what I bet you plan on doing all week. We had some very fun family activities planned for the week, too." Jack grinned. "You know, group trips to the zoo, maybe grabbing some funnel cakes at the fair, a little brotherly bonding in the backyard..."

Mac snorted. Despite his frustration with his brothers, he found a smile curving across his face. "Funnel cakes? The *zoo*?"

"That's the plan," Luke said, pushing off from the car, a gleam in his eyes. "All with the customary big-brother torture, followed by a cold ocean dunking and topped off with a day of us arm wrestling you into admitting we're stronger than you."

"Smarter, too," Jack added.

"Definitely smarter." Luke nodded, then wagged a finger at Jack. "And better looking."

"Damned shame. You could have been so much more," Jack said, reaching forward and clapping Mac on the shoulder. "If only you'd been born second or third."

Mac shook his head. "It's too bad you two are so delusional. You do know what Mama says, don't you? That she should have stopped having kids after she had the perfect one." Mac put out his arms. "Voilà. Perfection."

The three brothers laughed at the familiar joke. Their mother loved them all equally, but when pressed, would tell each boy that he was her favorite. Mac had missed this camaraderie, the gentle ribbing by people who knew him best. For a second, he considered turning down Savannah's offer and spending the week with his brothers instead. Then he remembered what he had learned from Uncle Tank, and knew if he did that, he'd inevitably feel compelled to confess to Jack and Luke. The truth would come out over some beers or basketball, because if there was one thing Mac had never been able to do, it was keep a secret from his brothers.

The only one Mac should talk to was his father. Then let Bobby handle it from there. It was, after all, his mess, not Mac's. Maybe there was a way to encourage Bobby to come clean, to tell the family the truth before it exploded, which it surely would at some point. A secret that big was impossible to keep quiet forever.

Bobby Barlow, the pride of Stone Gap, had another son. A product of an affair that had been kept hidden for two and a half decades.

Another Barlow brother, who had contacted Uncle Tank, the one who had been the go-between for the child and the mother, probably to keep Bobby out of the mix. Uncle Tank, who had stopped speaking to Bobby years ago, had called Mac, and said only two words, "Fix this." As if Mac could even begin to figure out what to do. An illegitimate son, an *affair*—all that was a hell of a lot harder to repair than a broken tailpipe or a company with too much overtime. Eventually, Mac knew someone was going to figure it out. If the truth didn't come blasting into town on its own first.

Because Colton Barlow, Bobby Barlow's secret son, had made it clear he wanted to get to know his other family—and do it soon.

Fix this.

That was something Mac would tackle another day, after he had all this business with Savannah squared away. He needed time to think, time to figure out the best way to talk to his father.

Just…time.

"Listen, as much as I'd love to go have funnel cakes," Mac said to his brothers. "I have plans for tonight. Why don't I stop by the garage tomorrow?"

"As long as you promise us something," Luke said.

"I'll be at Jack's wedding. I already promised that."

"This isn't about the wedding. That's a nonnegotiable anyway, because your tux is already rented." Jack grinned. "We need to talk to you about planning the family reunion next month. It's also Mama and Dad's thirty-fifth anniversary, and we wanted to make it special. Which means you have to be here for it. Nonnegotiable number two."

"There's a family reunion next month?" And his parents' anniversary? God. This just kept getting worse and worse every second he stayed here.

"Jeez, Mac, don't you read your email?" Jack threw up his hands. "Yeah, I sent you an invite like three weeks ago. The entire Barlow clan, descending on Stone Gap."

"Lord, help us." Luke grinned.

A family reunion next month meant the other Barlow, the one no one knew about, would want to come if he got wind of the event. Now Mac *really* needed to find a way to talk to his father.

"I'll, uh, think about that. I'll have to check my schedule," Mac said.

"Check your schedule?" Jack scoffed. "Family is the only thing you need on that schedule, you workaholic."

The word rankled. Twice in one day they'd called him that. "This workaholic is trying to go someplace. If I can ever get out of here." Mac fended off the rest of his brothers' questions and slipped onto the seat of his bike.

Jack sighed and threw up his hands. "I give up. You know, one of these days you're going to realize you actually need your family."

"I never said I didn't need my family." Mac settled the helmet on his head and buckled the strap. Just maybe not parts of his family, such as a father who hadn't been as true as he claimed to be.

"You didn't have to say it," Luke said, disappointment clear in his expression. "It's written all over your face." Then his brothers climbed back into the car and headed out of the lot.

Mac revved the bike, felt the power of the engine rumble beneath him. He loved his brothers. He really did. But sometimes he wondered if they lived in a fantasy world. They seemed to think a few family dinners would be enough to settle everything. If that was the case, he and his father would have mended fences years ago. But now, with the information about Colton, that broken fence had become a yawning, impassable canyon.

As soon as he could, Mac was leaving Stone Gap. And it would be a long time before he came back.

He thought of Savannah Hillstrand and all her talk about the business being family. How her father had treated every employee like a relative. Maybe some people were honestly like that, but Mac doubted it. Or maybe she was just some Pollyanna who thought the world was filled with rainbows and people singing "Kumbaya."

He wound his way to the outer edge of Stone Gap, past the beachfront mansions that outdid each other with more windows, more balconies, more square footage, then down around the edge of the bay before finally coming to a stop in a dirt parking lot. The ocean breeze rolled in from the Atlantic, sweet and crisp. He inhaled and wondered how long it had been since he'd been on the water. Too long, for sure.

His gaze shifted away from the deep blue ocean and over to a small wooden shack. No bigger than a trailer, the place looked ready to crumple with the slightest breeze. The Sea Shanty was, indeed, a shanty.

This was where Savannah Hillstrand wanted to have steaks? This...*dive*?

When she'd proposed the dinner, with no talk of business until after dessert, he'd balked. That wasn't how Mac ran his life. He worked as much as possible, as often as possible. But as he'd wound his way down the roads toward the address she'd given him, and caught the scent of the ocean dancing in the air, he'd begun to feel a...longing. For what, he wasn't sure, but he knew it had come wrapped in her words. What was it about this woman, who believed in family and vacations and lazy days, that had so intrigued him?

All purely professional interest, of course, even if she did have green eyes that lingered in a man's mind. He just wondered how anyone running a business, particularly a struggling one, could be so...positive and upbeat.

He heard laughter and turned. Savannah Hillstrand stood to the right of the Sea Shanty, talking to an elderly man and laughing at something he had said. A little fissure of jealousy ran through Mac. Insane. He had no claims on Savannah, nor did he want any. This was business. Nothing more.

Then why did his gaze travel over her lithe frame, now out of the severe pantsuit and looking summery and beautiful in a dark green sundress? She had a little white sweater draped over one arm, and her hair was down and curling along her shoulders. She'd changed, done her hair, and a part of him wondered if—well, hoped—that was because she knew she might be seeing him.

He closed the distance between them just as the elderly man went inside the building. At the sound of his riding boots on the dirt, Savannah turned.

A smile curved across her face. "You made it."

"You sound surprised."

"A little, yes."

"Don't be. When I say I'm going to do something, I do it. I'm not one for spontaneity." Though he was having a lot of spontaneous thoughts about her right now. It had to be the surprise of the sundress, the expression on her face, the scent of the ocean in the air, because he was having trouble thinking about anything other than her. "And for me, this—" he waved at the glorified pile of wood that was passing as a restaurant "—is a semitruck full of spontaneity."

"Hey, who knows, Mr. Barlow, in the process of you helping me with the company, I might end up being a bad influence on you."

He laughed. "That I doubt."

"Come on. Let's get a table out back before the sun sets." She waved at him to follow her down a shell-lined path that circled around to the back of the Sea Shanty. The path led to a small deck topped with white plastic tables and chairs and framed by lattice panels on either side. Clearly, it wasn't the ambience that drew people to this place.

It was definitely the view.

"Isn't this amazing?" Savannah said as they slipped into two chairs. She waved toward the ocean lapping at the rocky shore below. "Every time I look at this view, it… Well, as silly as it sounds, it reorients my soul."

Reorients my soul. Mac considered those words as he took in the panorama before them.

A vast blueness stretched before him, further and

broader than his eyes could see. It rippled with tiny peaks of whitecaps, like a dusting of stars in the water. In the distance a sailboat cut through the water quickly and easily. Above his head a trio of seagulls called to each other before one dropped down and scooped a fish out of the shallows. Mac's heart slowed and his chest expanded as he drew in one deep breath after another like a man who had gone too long in stale air. The salty, tangy breeze was refreshing. Restoring.

The same ocean was right outside his offices in Boston, of course. But he rarely saw it heading into work early and leaving late. The air there was filled with the smog from commuters and the stink of diesel from the busy harbor.

Across the bay he saw one lone house, a two-story white Georgian style with a long wooden dock jutting out into the water, topped with chairs to catch the view. It was a peaceful image, like a painting spread across nature's canvas.

A sense of something Mac didn't recognize settled in his chest. Then it hit him—he felt calm, relaxed. When was the last time he'd felt like that? With no worry over an impending deadline or stress about a deal falling through?

The sound of the water lapping over the rocky shore seemed to whisper *relax, relax*, and every cell in Mac's being ached to do that very thing. For a moment, he imagined himself at that house across the way, sinking into one of the two Adirondack chairs facing the ocean and just…being.

"Beautiful, isn't it?" Savannah said. "My dad loved this place. He and my mom would come here as often as they could. It was just a short boat ride for them, so they'd pop over for dinner all the time."

"Short boat ride?"

"Yup. That's my dad's house over there." She pointed to the Georgian he had noticed a moment ago.

"That's where your dad lived? How did he afford a waterfront home?" The moment of relaxation flitted away. Mac made a mental note to take a second look at the company's finances. If the CEO had been financing a big mortgage, that kind of practice would have to stop. "Because I thought Willie Jay had a house a few miles from Stone Gap, too. In Juniper Ridge."

"We do. The house in Juniper Ridge is small, the same house I grew up in and that my parents bought when they first got married. My mom and dad never really wanted or needed a big house. The one on the beach has been in our family for a long time. My dad was frugal in other parts of his life, so he could afford to keep this house." She brushed her bangs off her face and wistfulness filled her features. "It means a lot to our family. Almost everything important in our lives happened over there. And someday I'm going to find a way to get all that back."

Her eyes clouded and grief settled over her like a cloud. Then she worked a smile to her face and turned away from the view. "Anyway, I'm starving. Do you want to order an appetizer?"

"No," he said, before he got too distracted by that look in Savannah's eyes, and how much it made him want to leap in and fix whatever was bothering her. He was trying to buy her business, not build a relationship. No smart decisions could come from connecting with

Savannah on a personal level. "I think we should get to work as quickly as possible."

Because if he didn't, Mac had the distinct feeling he'd get off track by the curiosity to know what Savannah had meant when she'd said she wanted to find a way to get all that back.

And why it mattered so much to him to see that she did just that.

Chapter Four

By the time the steaks arrived, Savannah had lost her appetite. Everything Mac had told her about running a business in the short space of time since they had sat at the table sent one clear message—she was in over her head. He'd given her his CEO 101 talk, and she'd realized pretty fast that he was right—a degree in history and some experience remodeling homes didn't qualify her to sit in Willie Jay's chair. Not that she hadn't known that from the first day, but talking to Mac cemented the truth in her heart.

She understood the basics of what Mac said, about receivables and payables, about the impact of sales on their bottom line, but as he started delving into the minutia of the monthly general ledger—deviating from their no-business talk the instant dinner was set on the table—her eyes began to glaze over and the hope she'd had that she was up to turning Hillstrand Solar around began to dim.

He ran a finger down the screen of his laptop, skipping over the figures he'd downloaded earlier. "If you shift to a just-in-time inventory system and reduce the production workforce by two, you should be able to implement additional lean manufacturing—"

"Wait," she said, putting up a hand. "Did you just say I should fire two people?"

"I said reduce the production workforce." Mac pointed at a number on his screen, flanked by a percentage on the right. "You have too much overhead."

"Reducing the workforce is just a fancy way of saying fire people. I'm not doing that."

"Part of doing business is separating the wheat from the chaff, so to speak, and getting the most return on your investment. By eliminating two of these positions—" he pointed to a line item for the shipping and receiving department "—you can increase your monthly cash flow by several thousand dollars, which will help tide you over until sales increase."

"These are people, Mr. Barlow, not stalks of wheat. And not just numbers."

"These *people* are one of the things keeping you from being profitable. Sometimes, you have to sacrifice one thing in order to gain everything."

Gain everything. Like a successful company again. Like a thriving legacy to her father. Savannah's gaze went to the Georgian house across the water. From here it still looked elegant, almost regal, but she knew up close that the family home was in a serious state of disrepair. Inch by inch it had decayed in the years since her father had started his company, when he'd poured himself into building that solar business one panel at a time. He'd go to the house on the weekends, but he'd relaxed instead of worked on the house, procrastinating on the damage wrought by the relentless ocean breezes. Someday, he'd said. Someday he would restore the place to its former glory.

Just before her father died, she'd secretly started working on it for little bits of time here and there, thinking she could renovate the house and get it ready as a surprise for her father. It would have been the crowning achievement of her remodeling career so far, and a way to show Willie Jay that Savannah could indeed make a living from rehabbing historic properties. Then her father had died and left her the company, along with a heavy, solemn promise to keep it running.

She stood at the proverbial fork in the road. She could sell the company to Mac Barlow right now, walk away and have the money she needed to fund her home-renovation-company dreams. Or she could do what it took to keep her father's dream alive.

Either option sucked.

But in the end there really was only one choice to make. She'd made a promise, the only one her father had ever asked of her, and she couldn't break that, no matter what happened.

Savannah tore her gaze away from the house and refocused on the computer screen. Her steak had grown cold. The wine Mac had ordered was untouched by either of them.

She knew Mac was right about the overhead, even though she wanted to argue. What choice did she have, really? Let the entire company die just to save two jobs? Maybe, when business picked up, she could hire everyone back, but even thinking that made Savannah nauseous. How could she possibly do this? How could she possibly send two loyal employees packing? "Which two...uh, which two would you suggest?"

Mac thought a second, flipped to another screen and read some data there. Savannah waited, her heart thumping in her chest, hoping he'd say she didn't need to fire anyone, after all.

"Jeremy Reynolds and Carla Mueller," Mac said. "Jeremy is the highest-paid employee you have in that department, and Carla is the newest."

She thought of Jeremy's lopsided smile and Carla's cheery attitude. "But you haven't even met them. You don't know what they are like or how much they love working for the company or anything else about them except what you're reading in some cold, data-filled report."

"I know numbers, Miss Hillstrand. And that's what I focus on. Not people."

For a while earlier she'd thought Mac Barlow had a warm side to him. There'd been a moment when they'd been talking about the water and the house when she thought she'd read something almost...wistful in his face. But clearly she had been wrong. This man was about as warm and fuzzy as an ironing board. "Business is all about people, Mr. Barlow. Without those people, Hillstrand Solar wouldn't be where it is today. Did you know that Carla made dinner for my mother every single night for three weeks when my dad got sick and after he died, just to make sure she ate? And that Jeremy took up a collection at work to help offset the medical bills? He even stayed late several nights to make sure the finished orders got out the door so we didn't suffer any disruption in business while my father was gone. Those are the people who built Hillstrand Solar, and I can't fire them just because their salaries are too high or their experience level too low."

"Then be prepared to make other, more painful cuts," Mac said, then took a sip of wine. "You have a simple equation here. Too little money coming in, too much money going out. You have to find a way to reverse that tide."

That was what she had been trying to do for months. With no success. "If I increase sales—"

"That will help long term, but not in the present." He grabbed a pad of paper out of his bag and started jotting numbers on a fresh page. "Let's say you sell a thousand solar panels to a company that wants them next week."

She looked at the first number he put on the page— the total profit on a sale that large. "That would be great. That kind of sale could take us over this hump."

"It would. Once the sale is completed. First you have to order your materials," Mac jotted another number. "Build the panels. Pay your employees for working." He put down more numbers. "Then ship the panels to the customer." Another set of numbers were added, then he did the math and subtracted those totals from the profit and drew a circle around the net gain. "And then wait to get paid. Even if they pay right away, you're still looking at forty-five days—best-case scenario— between order placement and receiving the income. In that forty-five day period, you have paid for a significant amount of materials, met at least three payrolls and kept the lights on in the building. Where is that money coming from if you have negative cash flow?"

"I was thinking I could take out a loan or try to get another line of credit…"

"Your line of credit was already maxed out. And as for a loan…" Mac shrugged his shoulders. "Banks are much more leery of handing out cash since the recession. And they would be less likely to want to take a risk on an untried CEO with a struggling company."

He was right, damn it. It wasn't anything she hadn't already figured out on her own. But she'd kept thinking, hoping, there was another option. Some miracle that would come along and solve everything. Savannah took a long sip of wine. Then another. Jeez, at this point, maybe she should just down the whole bottle. It couldn't possibly make things any worse. "Then what do I do?"

"Fire two employees. That's two paychecks taken out of payroll effective right now." Mac shrugged, as if it was as simple as marching in on Monday morning and saying *you're fired*.

She shook her head. "No. I won't do that. Not to Jeremy and Carla."

He let out a frustrated sigh. "There really is no other way—"

"There has to be. You're a smart man." She waved at the screen. "Give me another option."

"Why are you being so stubborn about this? Part of being in the big office means making the big decisions—the ones no one else wants to make."

"Would *you* fire the people who helped your family through some of their hardest times imaginable? Or would you find another way?"

He held her gaze for a long time, then let out a breath

and turned back to the screen. "You are one stubborn woman."

"I know. You told me that already. Twice now."

"That's because you're twice as stubborn as anyone I've ever met."

"And that's why I'm not letting you tell me to give up. There has to be a way to save this company and to save everyone in it." She refilled her glass of wine, and took another sip. Her nerves began to calm a little. She might not have any answers yet, but Savannah had no doubt that between her and Mac, they could cobble together a workable solution.

"Business isn't a Disney movie, you know," Mac said. "You can't necessarily make it all come out perfect in the end with happy people riding off into the sunset."

"It doesn't have to be a tragedy, either." She pushed her still-full plate to the side and nodded to the waitress to take it away. She didn't want to eat right now. She wanted to sit here until she had another option, one that would let her tackle Monday morning with some kind of purpose. "So let's find a way to make this work."

"Let's?" He arched a brow. "You and me working together? Because so far it seems like we've been at cross-purposes."

"We're not at cross-purposes, Mac. We both want Hillstrand Solar to make money. We're just at cross-*methods*." She tapped the screen. "I say we find a way to make those methods work together."

He sat back in his chair and studied the screen while he sipped the rest of his wine. He seemed to like the challenge she'd given him, welcome it even. "Normally, I'd say you have two options. Cut the overhead to increase profits, or sell and cut your losses. Salvage what you can and maybe walk away with something."

"And I'm not willing to do either."

He let out a long sigh. "What you want is a creative solution to a difficult problem. That's not really my area of expertise."

The condensation on her wineglass cooled Savannah's palms. "It was, once."

"What are you talking about?"

She looked him in the eye. "Ten years ago you bought back a company you had sold. The new owners had moved the location, then left the former location like a ghost town. You bought it, nurtured it back to health and, as far as I know, never sold that business or the location again."

He arched a brow and leaned back in his chair, his jaw slack. "How do you know that?"

"I do my research, too, Mac." It was the one fact she'd stumbled across that had given her hope he would work with her instead of just try to force her to sell. The one item she had held on to when she'd scheduled this meeting with him. She'd prayed there was still a little of that spirit inside Mac Barlow, and that maybe, just maybe, he'd do the same for Hillstrand Solar.

"I'm impressed, Savannah." He refilled his glass, then nodded toward hers.

She shook her head. The last thing she needed to do was get drunk with Mac Barlow. She was already feeling tipsy, and regretting that she hadn't eaten anything for dinner. "Thank you. And thank you for not calling me Miss Hillstrand. That always makes me feel old."

He chuckled. "You are far from looking like an old

woman. Although, I have to admit that when I first set up our meeting, I pictured someone more…dowdy."

"Dowdy?" That made her laugh. "Why would you think that?"

"You've been very professional in all our conversations and email exchanges. You just seemed less…" He shrugged. "Relaxed. Less like you are right now."

"Ah, that's because I'm on the water. When I'm over at the house—" her gaze went to the Georgian just a short boat ride away and a longing filled her "—it's like I'm a whole other person."

"Out of the suits and into a bikini and flip-flops?"

It had to be the wine she'd drank, because she felt her cheeks heat and a flirty smile curve across her face. "I would say a bikini and flip-flops are pretty much as far from professional as I can get. Wouldn't you agree?"

A grin flickered on his face. "Depends on the bikini."

Were they flirting? Was she attracted to Mac Barlow, the very man who was trying to buy and dismantle her father's dream? "I haven't had a lot of bikini time in the last few months."

"Pity." Mac's grin flickered again, almost as if the smile was so unaccustomed to being on his face it had trouble staying put. "Everyone should take time to enjoy the water when you live near a view like that." He waved a hand at the deep blue Atlantic, its gentle waves seeming to beckon them closer.

She took another sip of wine, noting her head had that happy floating-in-clouds feeling. Definitely no more wine for her tonight. "It's still light out. Maybe we should head across the bay, and at least dip our toes in the water."

"I thought we were here to talk business." He gestured toward the laptop and pad of paper.

"You're the one who said everyone who lives near a view like that should take advantage of it. You're living here for a week. So…you should take advantage."

His gaze met hers, hot and intense. "Of the water, you mean."

An undercurrent rippled between them, tempting and dark. It had to be the wine, she told herself, not the way this man had roared into her life with that leather jacket and that dark hair that begged her to touch. "Of course that's what I mean."

Mac held her gaze awhile longer. "Me, too. Of course."

Mac didn't know what had made him agree to get in a little boat and zip across the bay with Savannah. The sun was beginning to set, but the air was still summer warm, hot enough to tempt him to kick back and take a swim.

Okay, yes, he did know. The more time he spent around Savannah Hillstrand and her amazing smile, the less he thought about business. In the back of his mind he was wondering how he could make her smile again, how he could make her laugh. And this house, the one with the tempting Adirondack chairs, brought out her biggest smile, which had made him ache to feel the same. As if merely being with her, on the water, would imbue him with the peace he saw in her eyes.

When was the last time he'd done something like this? Zipped away from work just to take a walk? He thought, but honestly couldn't remember a time since he'd hit eighteen when he'd taken off early and hit the beach or a park or anything remotely resembling a vacation spot. He'd traveled, of course, but always for business, with every spare moment spent in his hotel room on his laptop, analyzing numbers, creating projections, working deals.

Savannah had sat at the rear of the small metal boat, starting the engine then navigating across the bay like a pro. He had to admit it was pretty damned sexy to see a woman who could operate a boat with confidence. The wind caught her hair, whipping the blond tresses around her shoulders. Coupled with the sundress and her bare feet—she'd kicked her shoes to the side when she got in the boat—she looked like a completely different woman from the one he'd met just hours ago.

A tempting woman. A woman who made him forget about business and bottom lines. The kind that could distract him from the whole reason he was here.

That was a very dangerous combination.

She docked the boat beside a short pier, threw a rope onto a cleat and was climbing out before he could help her. "You surprise me," he said as he stepped onto the dock.

"I do?" She slipped her shoes back on to her feet, and started walking toward the house. "How?"

"I guess I didn't expect you to know how to start an outboard or dock a boat."

"I have a lot of skills you aren't aware of, Mac." A slight smile played at the edge of her lips, and a tease lit her eyes.

Damn. He liked the way she said his name. "If we keep changing the subject like this, it's going to feel like we're on vacation together."

The suggestion heated the air between them. Made

him imagine taking Savannah to an island getaway, just the two of them, laughing and toasting and…

More. A lot more.

"I'd call this…recess," Savannah said. "Not a vacation."

She was right, but he didn't want to give up that vacation image in his head. Not yet.

"That's a vacation house," Mac said, pointing at the white two-story house presiding over the dock.

"It used to be," Savannah said softly. "And maybe someday it will be again."

Behind them, there was a splash. Both of them turned at the same time toward the bay, just as a fish disappeared beneath the surface. Savannah turned left, Mac turned right and their cheeks nearly brushed. Hot awareness roared through Mac of Savannah's skin, her perfume, her entire body. His breath held for a second, neither of them moving, as if they were afraid to disrupt the moment.

"It was a…a fish," he said.

"Must have been trying to get away," she said, her voice as soft as a whisper.

He could feel the movement of her mouth in the air between them, feel the warmth of her breath against his skin.

His gaze traveled along the curve of her neck, the ridges of her collarbone, the swell of her breasts beneath the dark green cotton dress. Her mouth opened, closed, another breath passing between them, then he drew in the dark floral scent of her perfume, his mind filling with only her. With wanting her.

"We…" Her words trailed off.

"Yes," he said, and he wasn't sure why, because in

that next moment he was leaning in, brushing his lips against hers. Her lips parted, soft, sweet, hesitant. She paused only a second, probably caught off guard, then her hand came up and rested gently against his arm. Her feathery touch opened a door inside Mac, a door he'd kept shut for a long, long time. He turned, sliding one arm around her, then deepened the kiss.

She opened to him with a little mew, and he nearly came undone at the sound. Then her hands were tangling in his hair, and his arms were going tight around her waist, and the kiss turned from something sweet to something dark, hot, insistent.

Savannah stumbled back, breaking the contact. "That…what…what was that?"

"An accident," he said, because it was, wasn't it? "I'm sorry."

Her eyes were wide and glossy in the waning light. She gave him a short nod. "I agree. Maybe it's best if we just don't…don't do that again."

Every fiber of his being wanted to do that again. That and much, much more. Instead, he nodded. "Agreed."

He turned away, back toward Willie Jay Hillstrand's house. Even in the dim end of the day, Mac could see the peeling paint, the missing shingles, the sagging porch. It had once been a proud and majestic house, he was sure, but after years of abuse from the salty air on the Atlantic seaboard, the home had begun to edge into decay.

"You should sell this house," he said, because it was easier to focus on dollars and cents and sensible decisions than whatever the hell he'd just been doing. "Keep the cash, reinvest—"

She spun toward him, the softness in her eyes replaced by fire. "Do you sell everything you come across? Is there anything you think is too special to get rid of?"

"Everything is replaceable, Savannah."

"No, Mac, that's where you're wrong." Her gaze went back to the house, to the one place in the world that he suspected held all her best memories. He watched her heart break a little when her gaze lingered on the sad frown in the rotting porch, and he felt bad for saying what he'd been thinking.

She pointed across the yard to a small white replica of the beach house that sat atop a tall wooden pole. "Do you see that birdhouse? My dad and I built that when I was nine. It's not very fancy and, frankly, I did a pretty lousy paint job on it, but it's home to this pair of bluebirds who nest there every year. If you look closely, you can sometimes see the babies poking their heads out."

"What does that have to do with selling this house?"

"It's one of the many, many special things about this place. It's a memory that I can't relive and can't get back. But every time I see that birdhouse, and every time I see a new family taking root inside those walls, I think of my father. Of how he built that with me to give us something to look forward to every summer. A story to follow. Those are the kinds of things that make a house more than a property you can sell for a price. It makes it a home. Not everything is replaceable. And not everything has a price tag."

In Mac's world everything had a price, a value. The land they were standing on, the house that she got all emotional about, even the boots on his feet were all commodities. A new birdhouse could be bought in a store, installed at another address. The sooner she learned that, the sooner Savannah Hillstrand would quit holding on to a business out of sentimental value and see the sense in affixing it with a price and unloading it to someone else.

And with that his mind shifted back into business mode. This was a break, a temporary one, over almost as fast as it had begun. Monday morning they'd both be back to work, no more beaches, flip-flops or bikinis in sight. And no more kisses. Especially no more of those.

And that made him disappointed as hell, then, a second later, mad at himself. What was he doing? He was supposed to be convincing her to sell so he could move on to the next project, the next business and get back on the road. Not get involved with her on an increasingly personal level. "We should probably keep this short, so we can get back to—"

Savannah reached over and grabbed his hand, cutting him off midsentence. Almost as quickly, she let go again, as if touching him was akin to brushing against a hot stove. But the touch had already had its effect. His heart leaped and something tightened in his gut. All those great resolutions he'd had a second ago flew away in the breeze.

"It's Sunday, Mac," she said. "It's a gorgeous evening. Let's take some time to enjoy Mother Nature before you get back to work. Refill that well, like we agreed."

Every time she said his name, it was with a little lilt of laughter in the middle of the syllable. As if she saw him as someone who could let loose, have fun, be the kind of guy who stood on a dock and cast a line into the depths of the sea. Still, the idea of just being for anything longer than a few seconds made him...

anxious. As though he'd miss something or lose something if he wasted a few hours. "I don't waste time."

"Who said it was a waste of time?" She grinned, then beckoned him toward the water's edge with a crooked finger. "Come on, let's take a walk."

What would a short walk hurt, really? And maybe he could continue to plead his case for selling while they walked. Yeah, that was why he'd gotten in that little boat and crossed the bay. Because he wanted to talk business. Not because he wanted to see what Savannah looked like barefoot on the sand. Or wondered what she'd feel like in his arms, what her lips would taste like. He had those answers now and damned if they didn't make him want her even more.

As if reading his mind she kicked off her sandals and left them on the beach. Her toenails were red, a stark contrast against the pale sand. "You want to leave your boots there, too?"

"I'm fine."

"You'll be uncomfortable as hell and risk ruining some pretty kickass riding boots, which I bet were custom made for you."

"How do you know these were custom made?"

She quirked a grin at him. "You look like the kind of guy who always buys the best of the best. But I think—" she tapped a finger on his chest, and once again, his pulse went into overdrive, and he wanted to sweep her into a second kiss, a third "—that there's a beach bum in you somewhere. I saw the way you looked at this house."

He laughed. "A beach bum? I'm far from that."

"You're halfway there with the Harley. And I think—" she tapped his chest a second time "—that despite all your talk about bottom lines and profit margins, there's a fun guy in there somewhere. And that's the kind of person Hillstrand Solar—and I—need to help us out of this situation. So follow me, and let the sand get between your toes. You'll be a better leader for it. I guarantee it."

"I don't think sand is going to help me do anything."

"If you truly want to help me and my company, then I think you have to think like the man who started the business. Let go, relax. Be a regular guy, like my dad was." She cocked her head and studied him. "If you can't get in touch with his world and my world, then how are you ever going to truly get in touch with the heartbeat of Hillstrand Solar?"

She walked off, her skirt swirling around her knees as she padded barefoot down the beach. Mac watched Savannah for a few moments, then followed along behind her.

But he kept his boots tightly laced.

Chapter Five

Savannah was at work before the sun rose, fully expecting to arrive before Mac did. But when she walked in the nearly empty building, she found him at her father's desk again, immersed in a set of spreadsheets on the computer. He was wearing dark jeans and a pale blue button-down shirt that stretched across his broad back and muscular shoulders.

Oh, my.

She dropped her purse on the desk in the next cubicle, then peered over the wall panel at him. "How did you get in?"

"I used the code you gave me yesterday. I like to get an early start." He waved at the computer. "I hope that's okay with you."

The clock on the wall ticked a pair of sleepy hands past the six. "It's only half past six. What time did you get here?"

"Sometime a little after five." He shrugged. "Maybe a little earlier."

"Five in the *morning*?" She shook her head. There was a very short list of things she'd be willing to get up that early for, and working on a computer was not on that list. "Did you sleep last night?"

"I don't sleep much."

"You don't take vacations, you don't sleep, you don't like breakfast… What do you do with all those hours in the day, Mac Barlow?"

His blue eyes met hers, direct and clear. "Work."

Mac was exactly as he'd been painted on the internet: a consummate workaholic. Except none of the internet sites had mentioned those piercing blue eyes that could distract a woman in two seconds flat.

"I don't know how you stay indoors, in those meetings and at the computer and on the phone every day. I'd go stir crazy." She stretched her back, already dreading another day at a desk. Every ounce of her itched to be outside, to do something constructive. To demo or build new or paint. Anything other than what she was supposed to do here five days a week. And lately, all seven days.

"I don't even notice the time," Mac said. "When I'm in my office, hours can go by before I realize how long I've been working. I get immersed in a project, and time just slips away."

"I get antsy if I'm indoors for more than an hour. Which is why I love remodeling homes. It gets me outside, doing something hands-on." She pulled up a chair beside him and glanced at the screen. "What is that?"

"I'm creating a spreadsheet we can use to analyze

the workflow in the plant. You said you wanted a creative solution for saving money, and I think this might do it."

"How is this going to save money?"

"If we can reduce bottlenecks and increase output, then you'll increase profits." He pointed to different sections on the digital page. "Without letting anyone go. You'll have to also increase sales, and reduce waste in every inch of the operation, but—"

"You found a way for us to do this?" Had she just said *us*, as in working together with him? She blamed it entirely on her excitement that there actually might be a good way out of this mess.

He put up a hand. "I'm not a hundred percent positive it's going to work. Remember, I don't normally do this. I need to spend the day down on the production floor, analyzing the process and making sure that my figures stand up. And there's going to be some other difficult cutbacks that you will have to make, but—"

"But no one has to lose their job."

"*Maybe* no one has to lose their job," he said. "I'm not promising anything."

"Maybe is better than definitely." She grinned, and for the first time since she had stepped into her father's shoes, she began to see sunshine on the horizon. She listened as Mac explained his thoughts on creating a leaner, more efficient operation, jotting notes as she did. The next couple of hours passed quickly, and when the production employees reported for work in the plant on the first floor, Savannah followed Mac downstairs.

She touched his shoulder before they opened the door to the first floor. "Thank you."

He gave her a curious glance. "For what?"

"For listening. For helping. For being here before the rooster crows, just to work on this." She smiled. "I appreciate it."

"It's my pleasure."

The way he said *pleasure* sent a little thrill through her. She reminded herself he was talking about business, not anything…else. "Whatever made you get into this in the first place?" she asked.

He thought a second. "I guess I've always been a guy who likes a challenge. Who likes to find something I want—"

And that sent her mind down another path entirely—

"—and do what it takes to get it," he finished.

"That…that's a very good trait to have." She wondered what it would be like to be the woman he pursued with that kind of drive.

Oh, that was not a good road for her to journey down. Not at all. He was just another charming Southern man with a great smile. "Let's, uh, see how production is going," she said, and pushed through the door before she could let things get any more personal.

They walked through every inch of Hillstrand Solar. While Mac made notes, Savannah stopped and talked to every employee, many of whom had been there almost as long as she'd been alive. These were the people she felt most comfortable with, the ones who had been part of her extended family. She made sure to introduce Jeremy and Carla to Mac, thinking if he put a face to the names, he'd be less inclined to recommend firing anyone.

"So good to see you, Savannah," Betty Williams said, drawing her into a quick hug. Betty had been one of Willie Jay's first employees. Now in her early sixties, she was the grandmother of the plant, the first one to bring in brownies for a birthday or to circulate a get-well card for someone out with the flu. "You're like our own ray of sunshine. Always have been."

"Aw, thanks, Betty." Savannah returned the embrace. "How's your new grandbaby?"

"Perfect as ever," Betty said. She reached in her back pocket and pulled out a cell phone. "Have I shown you the pictures of her in her new walker?" She started scrolling through the photo app, and Savannah gushed about each picture of the blue-eyed, blonde cutie.

"Excuse me, Miss Williams, I need to talk to Ms. Hillstrand for a moment." Mac took her arm and tugged her away from Betty. "What are you doing?"

"Looking at pictures of Betty's granddaughter. She just learned to roll—"

"You don't interrupt the employees when they're working. In fact, you shouldn't be down here treating the production floor like a high school reunion. Let them do their jobs and you do yours."

Her temper flared. "High school reunion? I'm talking to the people who worked for my father."

"Who work for *you* now. And every second you spend talking to them is a second they don't spend earning money for the company. That's costing you and this company thousands of dollars every month. When I talked about a lean operation, I meant lean for everyone, including you. No wasted time."

She bristled. "Taking five seconds to look at pictures of Betty's granddaughter is not costing me thousands of dollars."

"No, but when you couple it with talking to Joe

about his knee surgery and Scott about his car, and what's-her-name about the cataract in her mother's eye—"

"It's called being nice. Building rapport." She propped her fists on her hips. "Something you don't seem to have much of."

"And how do you know what kind of rapport I have with anyone?" He took a step closer, so close she could see the flecks of gold in his eyes, see the tiny section of stubble he'd missed when he'd shaved this morning.

"Because I've seen the rapport you have with me. Except for those few minutes on the beach, you've been…"

"I'm what?"

"Difficult and stubborn."

"I prefer to call it focused and driven. Both good qualities in a CEO."

Translation—she could use a little more of that. Okay, so maybe Mac was right, but she refused to admit it to him. "My father believed in building relationships with the people he worked with."

"And is that what you are doing?"

"Of course. Plus I've known most of these people since I was a little girl, so it's only natural to—"

"I meant with me."

"Building a relationship with *you*?" Her gaze went to that patch of stubble again, to how it made Mac seem more vulnerable, more approachable. The idea of a relationship with him flickered into a thought, an image, a memory of that holy-hell-soul-scorching kiss last night, but then she pushed the thoughts away. "Why…why would I do that?"

"Because it seems to be the thing you do around

here." He waved toward the busy plant bustling with employees working the assembly lines and the shipping department. "I have to admit, I'm a little...disappointed since you didn't do that with me."

"I tried. On the beach. You weren't interested."

"I never said I wasn't interested."

The words hung there between them, laden with meanings that could go either way.

Her breath caught, her gaze dropping again to that missed patch, then she lifted her eyes to his and realized he couldn't possibly be serious. Why would she think he was? Mac Barlow was only interested in her bottom line, not in her. He couldn't possibly be jealous that she had asked the employees about their lives and hadn't asked him. Or think that the night on the beach was anything more than just that, a walk on the sand.

She shook her head and let out a little laugh. "Whatever. You just told me not to waste the company's time talking to people about anything other than work. So I won't make the mistake of doing it with you." She turned on her heel and headed through the door, then up the stairs. Maybe climbing five flights would be enough to make her forget the way Mac drove her crazy.

For the next three hours, Mac worked with numbers and equations, fiddling with this formula and that one, jotting notes on a pad by his side and keeping his nose to the proverbial grindstone. Focusing kept him from wondering what Savannah Hillstrand was doing at this very moment and why a woman who broke every rule he lived by intrigued him so much.

His cell phone rang, and he started to let it go to voice mail, then noted the unfamiliar number on the

screen. Might be the owner of that garage-door manu-
facturer he was hoping to look at later this week. Mac
hesitated only a moment, then he pressed the Answer
Call button and put the phone to his ear. "Mac Barlow."

There was a pause on the other end. "Uh, Mac, is
it? This is Colton. Your, uh…"

It took only a second to make the connection with
the name. A stone sank in Mac's gut. A part of him had
been hoping Uncle Tank had been kidding, that there
wasn't really anyone named Colton Barlow wanting to
turn Mac's life upside down. But now the man was on
the other end of the phone, a living, breathing human
being. "I know who you are."

Another pause. "I wanted to meet you. And Jack
and Luke. I'm thinking of coming to Stone Gap—"

"That wouldn't be a good idea." Not before Mac had
a chance to talk to his father. Not before he figured out
how the hell he was going to process the fact that his
father had screwed up and screwed up big.

"I have a right to know my family." Colton's voice
hardened.

"You have a family." A mother, a stepfather and a
sister from what Mac had heard.

"I do. And I've gotten close to our uncle's family.
He was…a good friend to my mother over the years. I
never knew he was my father's brother until recently."

The words *our uncle* grated on Mac's ears. He didn't
know this guy Colton, didn't know him at all. And here
he was coming along and throwing a monkey wrench
into everything Mac thought he knew about his own
life. About his *father*. Now it seemed Colton was making himself right at home, whether he'd been invited

or not to do so. "Whoa. Wait. You visited Uncle Tank? Met his *kids*?"

Colton laughed. "For one, those kids are grown men like you and me. For another, Uncle Tank is my uncle, too. He was the first one in this family to accept me. And I've known him for years. I just didn't realize we shared a biological connection until my mother told me."

"No one knew you even existed before two weeks ago. You have to give us time."

"I understand this is a shock to you and to your family—"

"Hell, yes, it's going to be a shock."

"I appreciate that. And I have no desire to ruin your lives. But I went my whole life not knowing my real father, Mac, or the fact that I have brothers. Three of them. Can you imagine finding that out now? What would you want to do?"

Mac wanted to say *run for the hills*, but that wasn't the truth. "Probably the same thing you are doing."

"I've waited almost thirty-two years to meet my father," Colton went on, his tone as clear and direct as Mac's. "And I think that's enough time. Don't you?"

There was no doubting Colton's determination. In a weird way, Mac respected his half brother for not backing down, not allowing anyone, Mac included, to stand in his way with the family he wanted to meet. Not that Mac could blame him. Had the roles been reversed, Mac would have probably just shown up in Stone Gap. Undoubtedly that would be Colton's next step if Mac didn't find a way to stall him.

"You have to give me time to talk to them," Mac said. "This is the week of Jack's wedding and I can't—"

"I'll call back end of day tomorrow. And I *am* coming to town, Mac, whether you talk to them or not. I'm not trying to be a jerk, but this is my father, too. *My* family. I've waited long enough to meet them." Colton severed the connection.

Mac cursed and put down the phone. Twenty-four hours. That was all he had to upend his family's life, because once Mac told Bobby that Colton was on his way to town, Bobby would have to tell the others. The Barlow boys were adults; they could handle this and rebound. Bobby—well, his father had made the mistake and, frankly, Mac didn't care much right now what this did to Bobby's life. But his mother?

This would devastate Della. All her life his mother had called her husband her one true love. They'd had almost thirty-five years of marriage together, with that anniversary just around the corner. Not to mention finding out just before Jack's wedding? No matter how Mac sliced it, the outcome was crappy.

A knock sounded on the wall behind him. He turned in his seat to see Savannah standing in the doorway, lit by the sunshine coming through the windows behind her. Breathtaking. That was what she was, even in business clothes.

The dark fabric of her navy pantsuit offset her blond hair, up again but this time in a bun fastened by some kind of clip. A few tendrils had escaped, dusting the tempting curve of her neck. Even though the suit's cut was severe, it only seemed to accent Savannah's curves, as if her real self was trying to escape the structure of the outfit. She'd paired the suit with bright red heels, a little rebellious streak of color. He wondered about those heels. Imagined her wearing them—and only them.

"I was about to go to lunch," she said. "I was going to ask you to go, but you said you always eat while you work, so I'm just stopping in to say I'm heading out."

Mac's cell sat a few inches away, reminding him of everything he was avoiding. He covered the phone with his pad of paper, then turned to Savannah. His gaze flicked to those red heels, then back up to her deep green eyes. "Actually, I could use a break. Why don't I join you?"

She arched a brow. "Oh…sure. That's fine."

Damn. He'd simply assumed she wouldn't mind him tagging along. Maybe he was reading her wrong. "Unless you wanted to go by yourself."

"No, no, I'd love the company. As long as you promise one thing." She put up a finger and a teasing expression lit her face. He liked her like that, with that little half smile on her face. He liked how quick she was to forget a disagreement, how quickly she shifted back into that friendly tease that so attracted him.

"What's that?"

"No business talk until after we've eaten." She arched a brow as if daring him to disagree.

"But it's a prime opportunity—"

"To build a relationship. A professional relationship," she clarified. "So you don't have to worry about me asking you about your mother's cataracts or your brother's new puppies."

"That's perfect," he said, gathering his jacket and keys, but leaving his cell phone behind. For the first time that he could remember, Mac wanted that moment of…peace. The same peace he'd seen in Savannah's face last night on the beach. "Because the last thing I want to talk about right now is my family."

Chapter Six

Mac's comment only intrigued Savannah. Why didn't he want to talk about his family? As far as she knew, the Barlows were great people. One of the brothers was running the family garage, while the other had a carpentry business. Both businesses were located here in Stone Gap. She'd never heard anything bad about any of his family. Of course, that could be because they were all the exact opposite of Mac.

Though, sitting across from him in the sunny Good Eatin' Café, Savannah had to admit Mac didn't look much like a corporate raider. More like a bad boy trying to reform. He had on a pale blue button-down and dark blue designer jeans, but he'd traded his riding boots for a shiny, expensive pair of men's dress shoes. His mahogany hair had a few wayward waves that gave him a rakish air, and when he flashed one of his rare smiles…

A part of her melted.

Professional relationship indeed. She was thinking about him in ways that had nothing to do with work. Had been ever since that kiss.

Vivian Hoffman, the gray-haired owner of the Good Eatin' Café, came bustling over to their table. She bent down and gave Savannah a quick hug. "So glad to see you here, honey, and with a man, no less. 'Bout time you got your dating legs under you again."

"Uh, Miss Viv, I'm not dating—"

"Nice to see you again, Miss Viv," Mac said. "It's been a while since I've been here."

Vivian studied him, then the older woman's pale eyes widened and she pressed a hand to her mouth. "Well, in all my days, it's Maxwell Barlow. Good gracious, I thought you had disappeared off the side of the earth. It's been a forever since you've been in here."

"Not quite off the side of the earth," Mac said, with a warm smile. "I've been working up in Boston."

"And are you here for your brother's wedding?" Miss Viv asked.

Savannah watched the exchange, intrigued. Miss Viv was a sort of good-neighbor barometer. If she liked a person, chances were that they were good folks, as her mom used to say. The kind everyone would love to have coffee with. Miss Viv's stamp of approval on Mac Barlow said maybe he wasn't as big a shark as Savannah thought. Or maybe Mac had been gone so long from Stone Gap that Miss Viv didn't know the man he had become.

"Yes, ma'am, I am," Mac said. "The wedding is next weekend."

"Wonderful, just wonderful." She put a hand on

Mac's shoulder. "The Barlows have always done Stone Gap proud."

Something in Mac's face shifted. "That's what I hear."

Vivian handed them two menus. "I'll be back in two shakes for your order. It's so nice to see you again, Mac, and to see you, Savannah, with him. If he's a Barlow, he's a good catch. So don't let him go. There's a hundred women in Stone Gap who would gladly snatch him up."

"Oh, I'm not—"

"And as for you," Miss Viv turned to Mac. "You should call yourself blessed if this woman gives you the time of day. She's way out of your league, Mac, but maybe you'll get lucky and she'll feel pity for the likes of you." Miss Viv grinned, then headed off to the kitchen.

Savannah wanted to crawl under the table. Good Lord, that had been embarrassing, like being called out in algebra class and caught passing notes to the cute boy in the second row. "I'm so sorry," she said. "I didn't want to leave her with the impression that we were together, but she interrupted before I could tell her."

Mac grinned. "Well, according to Miss Viv, being with a Barlow is a good thing."

"And what about being with this particular Barlow?"

"The jury is still out on that." He picked up his menu, his face unreadable, the playful mood gone.

A few minutes later they'd placed their orders. The regular lunch crowd began to filter in, sliding into familiar booths and seats. Savannah said hello to a few people, then turned her attention to Mac. As intrigued as she'd been by his comment about his family and the mysteries in his eyes, she reminded herself to stick to safe topics. Ones that didn't make her think about kissing him.

Uh-huh. Considering she'd thought about kissing him a hundred times already, that resolution was already weak. "So, you said you started doing this because you like a challenge. Plenty of jobs offer a challenge. What was it that drew you to buying and selling companies specifically?"

He arched a brow. "I thought this was a working lunch."

"It will be. After we eat. You promised me no talk about Hillstrand Solar before we eat, and I promised no asking about family. So that leaves the field pretty wide-open to other kinds of questions."

"Personal questions."

"Aren't all questions personal in one way or another?"

He considered that. "Maybe so. But personal questions lead to personal relationships. I thought you wanted to keep this professional."

"I do…but I also sort of changed my mind."

"Changed your mind? Why?"

She didn't want to admit the truth. That she liked the way he smiled. That when he'd said *yes, ma'am* to Miss Viv it had sent something warm and dark through Savannah's gut. That a part of her itched to run her fingers through that dark hair and trail kisses along the muscular lines of his neck, his shoulders. "Because that's the way I do business, Mac. Surely you recognize that by now. I can't work with people I don't know, and I still don't know you."

He considered that, his blue eyes as mysterious as a stormy sky. "There's not much to know about me."

"I think there's a lot to know about everyone," Savannah said. "To me, people are like old houses. Layers and layers of paint and wallpaper covering up all those years of scuffs and height markings and memories. Sometimes you have to really work to get to the best part—the heart of the home, so to speak."

"And is that how you see me? Covered with peeling paint and bad wallpaper?"

She laughed. "You? You're covered in barbed wire and poison ivy."

"Hey, I'm not that bad."

"You have your moments." She grinned, then crossed her hands on the table. "Okay. So tell me, what made you get into this kind of work?"

Mac waited to speak until after a waitress had dropped off two glasses of ice water. "When I was in high school I really wanted to own my own company. I know, it sounds crazy, but I guess I was never much for working for other people. I had worked in my dad's garage, but my dad and I didn't work well together. Think oil and water. So I quit there, and got a job at a local car lot. The place was a disaster. The owner was great at sales but terrible at managing people or keeping up with the books and day-to-day. You'd ask him about his receivables, or his annual projections, and he'd have no idea. I loved analyzing those kinds of things, so I started learning about it and handling more of that aspect of the business for him. I really liked the challenge of selling cars and did pretty good. Saved every dime I made, which back then was a pretty good sum."

"Was that Charlie Beecher's place?" Savannah asked. "My dad bought me a used Taurus from there when I turned sixteen. I named it Sylvia and drove that thing for years, until it died one afternoon on route 404. I loved that silly car."

"You named your car?" A grin played on Mac's lips.

"Doesn't everyone?"

He chuckled. "No, not everyone."

"You should try it. Like that motorcycle of yours? I'd call it Beast, because it roars like a lion."

"Beast, huh?" Mac considered that. "I like that name."

"And I bet the Beast will like it, too."

"We'll see about that." Mac chuckled again. "Anyway, yes, it was Charlie's lot. Probably him or his son sold your dad that Taurus. Charlie was a great guy and terrific with his customers. He sold a lot of cars, but he just wasn't much for anything related to the financial aspects of a business. Like managing his invoicing and operating on a budget. As a result he was barely skating by financially, and when I bought the business from him a few years after I started working there, he was teetering on the edge of bankruptcy."

"And then ten years later you bought it back from the company that you'd sold it to." It was that small fact that had surprised her about him. The one that had given her hope that maybe Mac Barlow had a sentimental side, and she could use that to sway him to save Hillstrand Solar.

Mac nodded. "I did."

"Why?"

The one-word question seemed to stump him. He drew in a deep breath, fiddled with the unused straw beside his water glass. "It's complicated."

"Is that code for you don't want to talk about it?"

"Yes." He punched the straw against the table, releasing it from its paper cocoon, and dropped it into the water. "So, what made you want to work in the solar-industries field?"

A change of subject. Okay, that was only fair, she decided. "I originally didn't want to work at Hillstrand at all. I just worked there in the summer, earning extra money helping my dad out. That kind of thing. When I was young, I really liked spending time with my dad, and going to work with him was one way to do that. Eventually, it turned into a part-time job." She shrugged. "I guess I never really thought he meant it when he said he wanted to leave the company to me."

That was the short answer she gave everyone, especially the employees who'd been surprised to see her step into Willie Jay's shoes immediately after the funeral. It wasn't the truth—more a version of the truth—and a version that made the whole surprise of being in charge easier to take.

"Then what did you really want to do?" Mac asked.

"Exactly what I'm doing."

He snorted. "Right. Tell me the real story."

"What makes you think I never wanted to be in the CEO's chair?"

"If you want something, your entire life revolves around it. I spent every spare minute learning about how businesses worked, saving my money, writing up plans. I learned every aspect of business management from the ground up. You said yourself that you just sort of fell into this when your dad died."

"I said I didn't think he really wanted me to run it. Nor did I think he'd die as young as he did." She'd thought she'd have years, many, many years to build her remodeling business and cement her career before her father passed along the Hillstrand mantle. She'd also thought he'd find a successor, someone with the right business acumen and instincts. Someone other than her.

The waitress brought their salads. Savannah's was loaded with chunks of fried chicken, blue cheese and dressing, but Mac's was a veritable vegetable garden with the dressing on the side. Even in his food choices, Mac Barlow was lean.

He speared up some lettuce and ate it. "I researched you, too, this morning."

She laughed. "I doubt you found much about me on the internet besides a few embarrassing pictures from high school soccer games. For the record—" she wagged a forkful of chicken at him "—I was thirteen and had no sense of style."

"You were cute at thirteen. And seventeen. I saw the picture of you at the junior Christmas dance that the local paper ran."

Her face heated. What was she, back in high school again? Flattered because the cute older boy found her pretty? "My mom made me that dress. I remember agonizing over the color."

"Blue looks really good on you," he said.

She glanced down at the dark blue pantsuit and felt the heat in her cheeks multiply. He thought she looked good? Why did that make her so happy? "Thank you."

He speared up some more salad and ate it. "I also found out that you've been remodeling houses for a few years. There was even an article in a local paper about one of your projects."

"The Honeysuckle Lane house." Damn, she'd forgotten those were out there on the web. If she told Mac that her true love lay in renovating old homes, would he ever see her as capable of being CEO? She doubted it. "It was just a…hobby." She turned her attention to her salad so that he wouldn't read the truth in her eyes.

"A hobby?"

"Mmm-hmm." She took a bite of chicken.

"You've renovated over a dozen homes. Spent months on that Honeysuckle Lane project. That sounds like more than a hobby to me."

"The Honeysuckle Lane project was complex, that's all."

"So you're a hundred percent dedicated to Hillstrand Solar right now?"

Why did hearing those words make her feel as though she was being strangled? This was what she wanted—to save her father's company and keep it going long into the future. "Yes, of course."

He eyed her for a moment that seemed to stretch into an hour, then forked up some more salad. "Good. Because I expect you to be giving a hundred and ten percent this week. It's going to take that and more to get this company back on track."

"You can count on me. I can't think of another place I'd rather be." Then she thought of the sagging porch at the beach house, the way the entire house seemed to be grieving, just as she was. How her parents had loved that house, and how her mother hadn't been able to bear returning because she said it was too sad without the love of her life there.

"No other place," Savannah repeated.

But it was a lie.

Mac Barlow was a single-minded man. He would focus on a project and stay on top of it until he reached the end, regardless of the complexity or length of time involved. That kind of laser attention was what had enabled him to buy and sell company after company over the years, generally to great success and profit, but with very little downtime in between.

But for some reason he was far from focused when it came to Hillstrand Solar. Ever since that kiss on the beach and then today's lunch—where he'd sat across a table from Savannah and talked about everything pretty much *but* the specifics of the company—Mac's mind had been on the smile on her lips and the way her green eyes had seemed even greener whenever she wore blue. And how much he wanted to kiss her then, and wanted to kiss her still.

When his mind wasn't on Savannah, it was on his family. On the bad news he was going to be forced to deliver tonight. He hated being in a position where his hands were tied and the decisions were being made by another. That was not the balance of power that Mac Barlow liked.

He shut down the computer a little after five, then popped his head into the cubicle next to him where Savannah was working on realigning the sales territory. They were the only two left in the office, the rest of the staff having left a few minutes ago. But Savannah, true to her word, had stayed to work, tackling the mountain he'd given her.

He'd assessed the strengths of Hillstrand Solar's three salesmen and given her a plan for redistributing the customers to take better advantage of each salesman's expertise. It was a project he expected would take her the better part of the night and tomorrow, but a good one to also give her a better snapshot of Hillstrand Solar's customer base.

He watched her work for a moment and for the thousandth time wondered why he had let himself get talked into helping her, instead of either giving up on acquiring Hillstrand Solar altogether or giving her one last offer, take it or leave it.

But then he saw her, a pencil once again nestled in the clip of her hair, another in her hands. His gaze traveled down the back of her neck, along the delicate skin dusted by a few stray tendrils of hair, then over her shoulders, down the curve of her spine, to the nipped sides of her waist. Savannah was a hell of a beautiful woman, and his mind wandered to thoughts of falling into a king-size bed with her, kissing, touching, exploring.

Would she curve into him? Would she let out that soft little sound again when their lips met? Or would she rebuff him and tell him he had read her all wrong?

She turned just then, as if she sensed him behind her. "Mac. You startled me."

"Sorry." He cleared his throat and took a step forward. As if that would dismiss those thoughts. It didn't. If anything, getting closer to her made him want to touch her more, to draw in the scent of her perfume. "I…I was going to leave early."

She glanced at her watch. "Early? It's after five. For most people that's past quitting time."

"Five, for me, is pretty early. But I have, uh, some family business to take care of tonight." Definitely not a subject he wanted to share with Savannah. Heck, with anyone.

"Okay, no problem," she said. "I'll see you in the morning?"

"Sure." Why did he feel disappointed that she'd dismissed him so easily? It wasn't as if he was dating Savannah or expecting to share another meal with her. He started to tell her that he wanted to stay, wanted to talk to her, but that would mean opening up about the family problems that were nagging at him. Building a connection with Savannah. It wasn't a smart move, even if it was the move he wanted to make. Instead, he just said, "Uh, see you."

"Okay," she said, but her attention was already back on the computer. Mac slipped out of the room and headed down to his bike.

He stowed his laptop in the bag at the back, then settled the helmet on his head. He switched out his shoes, tucked his jeans into his riding boots and started the Harley. It sprang to life with a low purr, rumbling beneath his body like a crouched tiger. A moment later he was on the highway, roaring away from Hillstrand Solar and toward the house where he'd grown up.

The trip only took a few minutes. He'd been hoping for more time, more distance, but he knew the longer he procrastinated on this, the worse it would get. Colton's words rang in his head as he made the final turn toward home.

I am coming to town, Mac, whether you talk to them or not. I'm not trying to be a jerk, but this is my father, too. My family. I've waited long enough.

Which meant Mac could put this off no longer. The driveway of the Barlow home only held one car, his father's beat-up Ford F150, a truck that had seen better days but still ran like a dream after almost two hundred thousand miles. Mac let out a sigh of relief that neither his brothers nor his mother were there.

He parked the bike and headed to the house. He

knocked once, then put his head inside the door. "Dad? You here?"

"In the back," Bobby called out.

Mac made his way through the house, past the dining room that had hosted too many Sunday dinners to count, past the "man cave," a converted parlor that held leather sofas and a big-screen TV for watching football games, then into the kitchen. His father sat at the scuffed chrome and laminate table, a dismantled radio spread on a sheet of newspaper before him. "Your mother wanted me to fix that kitchen radio. Thing's about old as me. I told her I'd buy her a new one, but she likes the one she already has."

"Mama's always been like that. Why buy new when the one you have is working perfectly?" Mac rested his hands on the back of the opposite chair, then let out a long breath and pulled out the chair to sit.

His father looked up at him before going back to the radio, unscrewing the circuit board from the main housing and then holding it up to the light to look at the connections. Mac sat, trying to figure out the best way to say what he'd come to say. Minutes ticked by with only the sound of Bobby working on the radio filling the kitchen.

"You come here just to watch me?" Bobby said.

"I wanted to talk to you."

Bobby twisted the screwdriver into the side of the radio and began disconnecting the top from the bottom. "So talk."

Mac blew out a breath. "I had an interesting conversation with Uncle Tank the other day."

Bobby snorted. "Every conversation with my brother

was always…interesting. How's he doing? Haven't talked to him in a long time."

"Yup. You seem to have a habit of not talking to people who disagree with you."

Bobby sighed. "Is that what this is going to be about? Because it's almost suppertime and your mother is going to be home from the grocery soon, and I don't have time to dig up all that crap again."

"No, Dad, this is different crap."

Bobby stopped working on the radio and raised his gaze to Mac's. "What do you mean, different?"

Now or never. Mac steeled his frame and looked his father in the eye. "When were you planning on telling Mama about Colton?"

Bobby's face went white. His hand trembled, the screwdriver rat-a-tatted against the metal frame and for a second Mac almost felt bad for him. "How…how do you know…" He shook his head and cursed. "Tank. I'll kill him."

"Actually, Colton is the one who went to Uncle Tank. Colton said his mother recently told him their family friend was actually his uncle. He's met Tank's whole family, too." Mac paused a beat. "Now he wants to meet us. On Jack's wedding weekend. Do you have any idea what that is going to do to everyone?"

The thick Adam's apple in Bobby's neck bobbed up and down. "Meet *us*?"

Mac stared at his father. "When were you going to tell Mama? The rest of us?"

"I…I…" Bobby hung his head.

Mac felt a moment of sympathy and a second of regret at seeing his father broken and sad, but then he pushed it away. Bobby had brought this on himself by choosing another woman over Della.

"I…I don't know," Bobby said after a moment.

"Well, you better figure it the hell out, Dad, because Colton has no intentions of waiting." Mac got to his feet and pushed the chair back under the table. It shuddered into place with a protesting screech. "And I have no intentions of being the one who gets to tell your wife of thirty-five years that you were cheating on her. Maybe still are, for all I know. How could you do that?"

Bobby's eyes welled and he shook his head. "It's complicated, Mac."

"Complicated? That's the word you have for it?" Mac shook his head and cursed.

"Let me explain. It was a long time ago and…"

"And what, you weren't happy being married to the love of your life? Because that's what you and Mama call each other."

The tears threatened to spill out of Bobby's eyes. "We are. We were. It's…complicated."

"No, Dad, it's not. It's wrong." Then Mac turned on his heel and headed out of the house. Even the roar of the wind in his ears as the bike tore up the streets of Stone Gap wasn't enough to silence the tornado of thoughts in Mac's head. Maybe nothing was loud enough to drown out those moments in the kitchen when his father had confirmed that everything Mac thought he knew about his parents and his childhood was a lie.

Chapter Seven

Savannah brushed the bangs off her forehead, then stepped back to survey her work. She only had another half hour before the sun set completely, but she'd gotten far more demo accomplished than she'd expected. The bones of the front porch were in a mountain beside the old house, filled with timbers and shingles and the first few floorboards she'd ripped off. The fresh pile of lumber she'd ordered this morning sat on the front lawn, waiting.

She should have been working on the sales-territory realignment, but as the end of the day had ticked away, Savannah had grown anxious and worried about the company. And most of all, powerless, because Hillstrand Solar was still struggling, and turning that ship in a new direction was a slow, painful process. She'd felt stifled by the walls around her, the recirculated air filling the cubicles.

Five seconds later she'd been in her car, heading for the beach house. She'd followed the twisting dirt road, then parked on the side of the house and grabbed her toolbox from the trunk. She missed her pickup truck, but figured if she'd gone home to load the old Chevy, she would have lost too much daylight. Her toolbox and tools were still in the trunk of her car from a temporary porch repair she'd done after a storm a couple months ago.

She'd changed into some shorts and a T-shirt she kept at the house, then set to work. By the time she'd dismantled most of the porch, her head felt clearer, her shoulders less tense and her mind had stepped back from the razor edge of stress she'd been riding for months.

Just as she was about to get back to work, she heard a low roar, then a crunch of tires. A moment later, Mac and his Harley swung into view. Her breath caught at the sight of him, sexy as hell with the black leather jacket and the riding boots. He made bad-boy businessman look good. Very, very good.

Ever since that kiss she hadn't been able to think of much else but him. His smile. His eyes. His touch. She told herself she didn't want that kiss—the complications it came with—but truth be told, she'd wanted it more than she'd ever wanted another kiss before. There was something *electric* about that moment when they had turned at the same time, something that had awakened a deep need in Savannah's gut. She'd barely been able to concentrate at work, knowing he was only a few feet away. And now...

He was here. And Lord help her, but she was a weak

woman right now, with all the willpower of a mouse in a cheese factory.

Mac kicked out the stand, then swung off the bike, removing his helmet at the same time. Once his blue eyes met hers, Savannah's heart trilled.

"What are you doing?" he said.

"Thinking."

He arched a brow. "Thinking? With a crowbar in your hand?"

"That's how I do my best planning." She wiped her bangs away again with the back of her hand and let out a sigh. As excited as her body might be to see him, she knew better than to think he'd come by on a social call. He was probably here to discuss more business stuff with her. As much as she wanted to save Hillstrand Solar, right now she couldn't stand to look at another spreadsheet or read another report. She needed open spaces, ocean breezes, hard work to clear her head and help her refocus in the morning.

"When I didn't find you at the office I figured this was where you'd be," he said.

"Listen, I know I said I'd go over that sales-territory thing tonight," she began. "But the numbers and names started swimming in front of me, and I just needed some fresh air and something…constructive to do."

"Or deconstructive." He nodded toward the pile of debris.

"Yeah. That's even more satisfying sometimes." She gestured toward the remaining floorboards. "Anyway, I was only going to work for another half hour or so, then get back to the sales-territory thing."

Okay, so she'd had no such intention. What she wanted was several hours working with her hands, watching the fruits of her labor change what was dying into something new and vibrant. She doubted she could get the entire porch rebuilt tonight, but maybe just the first few timbers would give her that sense of satisfaction. And then she could breathe and think and concentrate on the business. Because after the past few months, Savannah desperately needed a way to decompress, to find her…center again. And being here with the tools and the wood and the work did that for her.

"This demo thing…does it really help relieve stress?" Mac asked.

"It does indeed." She glanced at his face, and saw the tension in his features, the set of his shoulders. Apparently she wasn't the only one who needed a little time outside the office. She held out the crowbar to him. "Try it and see. Help me rip out the rest of the floorboards."

. He gave the tool a dubious glance. "You sure you want me doing this? It's your family's home and—"

"If you screw anything up, I'll let you know. Start on that end and work toward me. We'll meet in the middle." She grabbed a claw hammer from the toolbox and headed for the far side of the porch. "If you can leave the boards mostly whole, I'm going to build a storage chest out of them later."

"Really? I'm impressed."

She laughed. "Don't be. My carpentry skills are pretty rudimentary. I can frame a wall and build a box, but anything more complex and I have to call in an expert. I'm awesome at demo, though." She raised her hammer and flexed her biceps.

He chuckled. "Okay, we'll see about that, Hercules." He hung his jacket on the front door knob, then rolled up his sleeves and settled in at the other end of the porch. Her heart skipped again at the sight of his exposed forearms, this new, relaxed Mac Barlow.

Mac already had finished removing two boards before Savannah recovered her senses and stopped staring at him. The man was too damned handsome. And distracting. She'd come out here to clear her head, not fill it with images of Mac Barlow taking her upstairs and running his hands over her naked body.

Savannah got to work, and once she was immersed in the repetitive motion of prying up the boards, pounding out the nails, then adding the wood to the pile, she almost forgot Mac was there. Almost, because he was always in her peripheral vision and thus always in her peripheral thoughts. Not to mention that each board she removed brought her closer to meeting him in the middle of the porch.

Fifteen minutes later they pried off the last two boards. Savannah and Mac balanced on the joists beneath the old floor, then gave each other a quick high five. It was a satisfying feeling to see the old, damaged boards gone, and the porch ready for a new life.

"That was awesome, I have to say," Mac said, sending the board sailing onto the pile on the grass. "What can we demo next?"

Savannah laughed. "The sun's going to set pretty soon. I think we can just get started on laying the new floor and maybe framing part of the new roof before we'll have to quit. If you're up for that, that is."

"Sure. Whatever you want. You were right. This kind of work… It feels good. Satisfying."

She laughed. "I had the exact same thought."

"It's been a long time since I've done anything like

this." Mac followed her down the steps and over to the new pile of wood. "And back then it was just small projects with my dad. My brother Jack is the one who loves building things."

"And you love tearing things down." She dipped her head. "Sorry. That was out of line."

"I don't tear everything down," he said quietly. Then, before she could ask him what he meant by that, he gestured toward the wood. "How are we going to cut the boards for the new floor?"

"I brought along my saw." She pulled a chop saw out of her trunk, then set it up on a sawhorse she'd found in the shed earlier. Savannah unclipped her tape measure from her tool belt and thumbed toward the porch. "I'll measure and you can cut."

He grinned. "Do you know how incredibly sexy you look with that on?"

She blushed. He thought she was sexy? "With sawdust in my hair and cobwebs on my shoulders and—"

Mac closed the distance between them. "Incredibly sexy."

"Thank you." Her gaze dropped to his lips and a slow warmth spread through her belly. He'd undone the top two buttons on his shirt, giving her a too-brief glimpse of his chest. She wanted more. She wanted to see all of him. Wanted to touch all of him.

A moment passed. Another. The world was quiet, save for the call of a few birds and the low distant *glub-glub* of a passing motorboat. Savannah heard nothing, saw nothing except Mac. Her throat was tight, her pulse running at double speed. His cologne whispered between them, dark and tempting, and it took everything for Savannah not to haul his body against hers.

He tipped a finger under her chin and lifted her lips until they were just below his. It was sexy and sweet and made a part of her melt.

"You can start an engine, drive a boat, operate a chop saw and rebuild a house," he said. "Is there anything you can't do, Savannah Hillstrand?"

"Run a company." Her eyes watered. It was the truth. She could fix a lot of things, but she couldn't fix Hillstrand Solar.

"That can be learned," Mac said. "You already have passion for the business. That's important."

She had a *promise*. That wasn't the same as passion, but she didn't correct Mac, because if she did, he might see it as an opportunity to convince her to sell. And right now, doing the work that she truly loved, far from the offices and spreadsheets, it wouldn't take much before she was signing the papers over to Mac.

Nor did she want to discuss business with Mac's finger on her chin. Then again she didn't want to work, either, with him touching her. Getting too close to him was like getting too close to quicksand. Savannah worried she'd forget that he was supposed to be the enemy and get swept into something that was nothing more than a fantasy.

With great reluctance she stepped away and nodded toward the porch. The air seemed to chill a bit. "Right now I'm passionate about laying a floor before the sun sets. Do you know how to run that thing?"

He nodded, then crossed to the sawhorse and connected the chop saw's plug to a waiting extension cord. "I think I've got it under control."

"Okay. Good." She headed back up to the porch and started working before Mac Barlow could see another moment of vulnerability or read the desire in her eyes. How long had it been since she'd been to bed with a man?

Far too long, that was for sure. The past four months had been a whirlwind of caring for her father, then taking over for him. There'd been no time for dating, and no one beating down her door for a date. Savannah had worked so long in a man's world—construction and production—that she found most men were intimidated and felt more comfortable treating her like one of the guys instead of a girl. The few men she had dated had been big on words, not so good at actions that rang true.

But not Mac Barlow. He treated her as an equal, and then, in too brief snippets, like a woman to be desired. It was a heady sensation. Intoxicating.

Savannah cleared her throat and concentrated on the tape measure. It took three tries before she read the measurement right, but once her mind refocused, the rhythm of work got her back on track. To what was important—saving the company and saving the house. Restoring what was falling down, before it was all lost. *Promise me.*

That was what mattered, Savannah reminded herself. Not a fleeting attraction to the man who ultimately wanted her to give up the company.

She called out measurements, Mac cut the wood, and she hammered the new boards into place. One after another, laying in the fresh boards like a row of teeth in a wide, happy smile, watching the porch come to life again, giving her the satisfaction of seeing one thing her father loved being restored to its former glory.

A little at a time.

* * *

The last floorboard went in just as the sun began to disappear behind the trees on the western side of the property. Savannah turned on the porch lights, then headed inside and returned a moment later with two beers. She handed one to Mac, then the two of them sat on the top step and watched darkness steal over the bay. The scent of fresh-cut wood heightened the salty tang in the air with a homey scent.

Mac rested his elbows on his knees and drew in a deep breath. He hadn't felt such a sense of satisfaction in a long time. His shoulders ached, and he had the beginnings of a sunburn on his arms and face, but every inch of him was sated by the feeling of good, hard work. "Thanks."

Savannah glanced over at him, surprised. "For what?"

"For the beer, but mostly for letting me help you." He drew in another breath. What was it about newly cut wood that carried that scent of new beginnings? Fresh starts. Hope. They were all feelings alien to Mac for far too long. "I needed that today."

"Bad day in corporate-takeover world?" She bit her lip and shook her head. "I'm sorry. I keep saying things like that and I shouldn't. You helped me, and I appreciate it."

"What I needed today wasn't about work. It was… personal." Even as he said the last word he could feel himself closing that door, the one that divided him from the people in his life. Outside of his brothers, Mac had few friends. Almost no close friends. Something about being the man at the top created an automatic dividing line, and the guys he used to shoot hoops with or play a few rounds of golf with suddenly saw him as an outsider. Then his days had become consumed by work, and except for working lunches and dinners, and the occasional run through Boston Public Garden, there wasn't much time for hanging out with buddies. And certainly not enough time for heart-to-heart conversations about the ups and downs in his life. Especially not the latest monkey wrench.

He couldn't go to his brothers with this thing about Colton. Not yet anyway. Nor did he really want to drop that information in their laps, as it had been done to him. They were moving on with their own lives, marrying great women. The last thing Jack and Luke needed was to be saddled with another stress. Some would argue Mac didn't need it, either, but the monkey wrench was there, nonetheless, expecting him to *fix this*.

"Do you want to talk about it?" Savannah asked.

"Yes. No." He let out a breath. "I don't know. I don't tell people my personal problems."

"Okay." She leaned back on her elbows, the beer dangling from her fingers. She didn't push him, didn't seem the least bit bothered that he didn't want to open up. Which had the inverse effect...

He wanted to let her in. What was it about Savannah and her easygoing attitude that drew him to her? Led him down roads he'd always avoided?

He debated letting the subject drop. But there was no more work to distract him, and the thought of going back to his hotel room and turning on his computer didn't fill him with the same sense of relief it normally did. This whole thing with Colton was too big to dismiss with hours of work, even with an entire house renovation. The subject needled at his every thought, hung heavy on his shoulders. He needed to talk about it, figure it out. But this wasn't a business problem he'd debate with his CFO or a lawyer friend. This was Mac's life. The life he'd thought was based on one truth and turned out to be based on a lie.

"Oh, look," Savannah said softly, pointing across the yard at the birdhouse her father had built. Time had weathered the paint job a little, but the bird's home, sitting atop a high pole, was a damned close match to the main house. "The mama bird is feeding the babies."

A bright blue bird with a rust-colored chest was perched on the edge of the house, while a smaller hungry mouth extended from the opening and snatched at the worm in the parent's beak. A loud chorus of hungry chirps came from inside the birdhouse, and soon two more heads pushed their way out, each wanting a piece of the worm. A moment later the mama bird flew off, probably to bring back another treat for her hungry brood. The babies chirped a while longer, then settled back into the box.

"I love seeing the new family every year," Savannah said. "It's like they're part of my family, too."

"Is it the same birds that return every year?"

"Sometimes. And sometimes the parents die and the fledglings find a mate and return to this birdhouse. I love that their family is constantly changing."

A constantly changing family. He had that right now. If there was one thing Mac had always counted on, it was the steadiness of the Barlow family. He knew whenever he came home to Stone Gap, his parents would be living in the same house, and his brothers would tease him with the same jokes. There was something…comforting in that, as much as he said it annoyed him. But now those dynamics were changing, and he wasn't sure what to do about it or who to turn to for advice.

He glanced over at Savannah, at this woman who would do pretty much anything for the father she had loved, and who got sentimental about a pair of birds. He wondered what she'd have to say if she unearthed a secret sibling. Would she welcome them with open arms or want to bury the truth and pretend it didn't exist? He wanted to know—wanted to know all that and more about this intriguing, beautiful woman beside him.

Never before had he gotten personally involved with someone whose company he was trying to buy. He'd especially never kissed the owner of one of his potential purchases. Or thought about sleeping with her every five minutes. This thing—whatever it was between himself and Savannah—seemed like more than he'd had in a long time. It wasn't just about being attracted to her. It was something bigger. Something with deeper roots. Already, he felt as though she wasn't just a fellow business owner. She was also a…

Friend.

Okay, so maybe he didn't kiss his friends like he'd kissed Savannah. And maybe he didn't picture his friends naked a thousand times a day. But one thing was true—Mac Barlow, indomitable millionaire CEO, could sure use a friend right now. He took a long pull off the beer, then let out a breath.

"I have a brother I didn't know about," he said.

The words came out surprisingly easy, considering Mac wasn't a man who shared much—if any—of his private life with people. But there it was, the fact that he had kept concealed from the brothers who shared his DNA and the mother who loved him dearly. Told to a woman he had known for a handful of days.

"Really?" Savannah turned to look at him. "That'd be enough to throw anyone for a loop."

"I just found out a couple weeks ago from my uncle. He and my dad don't talk—a family argument gone wrong years ago—and he told me I needed to tell my family about my half brother." For the hundredth time, Mac wished Uncle Tank had just called Bobby, instead of handing off the task to Mac like a relay baton. "I haven't told my brothers or my mother yet, but I confronted my dad this evening. That's where I went after work, to see him."

"How'd that go?"

"It sure wasn't sunshine and roses. He didn't explain, but he also didn't deny it." Mac took another drag off the beer. "Turns out my whole childhood was a lie."

Savannah seemed to think about that for a minute. "I don't know if the whole thing was a lie. One part, maybe. But the rest was your story."

"Bookended by this other brother and another woman." Mac sighed. "My dad never told anyone."

"Maybe because he didn't want you to look at him the way you are probably looking at him right now." Savannah shrugged.

"And how is that?"

"Like he destroyed everything you thought you knew."

Savannah was right. That was exactly how Mac was feeling. It was as if the world he'd grown up in, the world he had known as well as his own name, had turned out to be a figment of his imagination. He wasn't born to two people deeply in love. Hell, he wasn't even the oldest. There had been another, older than he was, and another woman who had had Bobby's heart. It turned out the Barlows' solid marriage, which had served as an example to the three boys, had been built on shifting sand.

"But that's exactly what my father did. My mother, my brothers—they're all going to be devastated when they find out."

"They might handle it better than you think." She took a sip of beer, then set the bottle on the step below her. "People make mistakes, Mac. They screw up, and they hurt the ones they love. Nobody's perfect, and learning to accept that the people we love and idolize are imperfect is part of life."

"My father didn't just make a small mistake. He made an entire family. Do you know how this is going to break my mother's heart? Their thirty-fifth wedding anniversary is coming up. How the hell am I supposed to tell her before that?"

"You don't."

Mac shook his head. "Somebody has to. My half brother said he was coming to town to meet the family, and I can't just let him show up without giving them fair warning of what happened. I need to make a plan, find a way to break this news without it doing too much collateral damage."

"No, you don't." She laid a hand on his, a hand of friendship, of comfort, connection. "This isn't a business you can fix up and flip. It's not a company that needs help increasing its bottom line. It's life. And life is messy and complicated and sometimes very painful. You clean up the messes *you* make, but you don't have to clean up the messes other people made."

"What, you're saying trust my father to tell everyone?" Mac shook his head. He couldn't even imagine that disaster. Bobby with his gruff and direct way dropping this bomb into Della's life. Into his sons' lives. "I can't do that. He's not the most touchy-feely guy in the world."

"And you are?"

That made Mac laugh. "Point taken. But still, my father delivering news like this would be like throwing a bowling ball into a china shop."

"Yes, but it's *his* news to deliver." She took another sip, then set the bottle down again. "And that means you have to do something you don't like to do."

"What's that?"

She grinned. "Give up control and let someone else handle this."

"I'm not trying to control this."

"Really?" A bigger smile curved up one side of her face. "Because I hear a man saying that he has to be the one to tell his mother and brothers. That he doesn't trust his father to do it. That it's all up to him to deal with this, rather than letting the one who made the mistake deal with the aftermath. This is crappy news for your family, I agree, and no matter how it's delivered, it's going to have ramifications. But it's not your information to deliver."

Savannah's words eased the tension in Mac's shoulders. She was right. He wasn't the one who had stepped out on his wife. He wasn't the one who had created another child. He wasn't the one who had to undo the damage that was going to be done. "So you're saying I should be support staff instead of CEO?"

She laughed. "I'm saying exactly that."

He shook his head. "I don't know. I don't much like to be the one in the backseat. That kind of thing makes me...uncomfortable."

"I don't think you can learn how to be a good leader until you learn how to be a good follower." She got to her feet and put out a hand to him. When he touched her, it was like sending fire through his veins. Her smile warmed something deep in his gut, made all the tension melt away. "And with that, Mac Barlow, I have the perfect project for you."

Chapter Eight

Maybe Savannah just liked seeing Mac Barlow sweat.

Early the next morning, she'd had him meet her at the old house again. The sun was barely rising in the sky, which gave them a good two hours before the offices at Hillstrand would open and she'd be needed at Willie Jay's desk.

They'd left last night without another of those soul-searing kisses, mainly because she'd kept her distance, telling herself it was for the best. But then she'd spent the night tossing and turning, her fitful dreams filled with a dark-haired man whose eyes were as blue as the ocean on a sunny day. She'd woken up an hour earlier than she'd needed to, and had known it was because a part of her couldn't wait to see Mac again. And, yes, see him sweat. Maybe enough that he'd take off his shirt, and give her something else to fantasize about.

Oh, she was bad, very bad. But that didn't stop her from checking him out every five seconds, even as she told herself this was just about working on the house and teaching a buttoned-up CEO a lesson or two in being a good worker bee.

After they'd parked their vehicles and returned to the beach house's backyard, she said to Mac, "We're here this morning because I want you to learn how the products work from the inside out."

"You really think that's necessary?" Mac said. "I can look at the monthly reports and—"

"And nothing gives you a sense for what we do like actually handling the product. And seeing it in action." Not to mention following Savannah's directions. It was going to be fun to turn the tables on Mac Barlow.

"Are we working on the porch roof today?" he asked.

"Nope. I have another project for you. One where I'm the expert and you're the apprentice."

He gave her a dubious glance, but followed her out to the shed where a quartet of solar panels had sat for months, waiting for installation on the roof of the beach house. She could have called in some of the crew from Hillstrand Solar to do the job, of course, but that wouldn't have been half as much fun as putting Mac to work—and telling him what to do. Besides, she wanted to do as much of the beach house renovation on her own as she could. This one was personal—and she wanted it to have that personal touch.

"Here's the plan," she said. "We're going to install the mounting brackets on the roof—"

He glanced up at the two-story peak of the house. "*That* roof?"

"Yup." She bit back a grin. "You scared of heights?"

"Nope. You?"

"Of course not." She grabbed one end of a ladder, and Mac grabbed the other. They carried it around the house and propped it against the side, anchoring it well in the grass. Mac cast another doubtful look upward. Savannah patted him on the shoulder. "The view is worth it, I promise. Let me get the hardware and some tools, and we'll get started."

She returned a moment later with a pile of mounting brackets, a tool belt and a handful of screws. From her trunk, she'd pulled out a couple of safety harnesses she still had from the days when she'd worked installation. She slid one on herself, then gave the other to Mac.

"I really need this?" he said.

"Better to be safe than sorry. Besides, I need your brains to help me with the business. They won't do me any good if they're scrambled on the driveway."

He laughed and stepped into the harness. She helped him cinch it tight, trying not to think about how very close the action brought them. "Gee, you really know how to instill confidence in your crew," he said.

"If you're not a little bit afraid, then you're going to make mistakes."

"Very true. That's a saying that can be applied to most everything in life," Mac said. "Every big decision I make is always accompanied by a little fear."

"Really? You just seem so…confident when it comes to business things."

"I don't know if I'd call it confidence so much as a willingness to take risks. And risks always come with potential pitfalls, so that's where the fear comes in. Maybe there was something I missed in my due diligence, or the market for that type of company might bottom out, or I might end up losing money… There are a lot of factors to worry about."

"You haven't made too many mistakes," she said. "Your company has become pretty successful in a very short period of time."

"I've made mistakes," Mac said quietly. "And every decision I have made is influenced by those mistakes."

She wondered what he meant by that, but he had already turned away and grabbed the pile of mounting brackets. She let the subject drop and started climbing the ladder with Mac close behind. Savannah scaled the metal rungs with the quick movements of someone who had done so a thousand times, then secured a rope to the peak, attached it to her harness and settled herself on the eastern side of the house, where the trees were sparse and left a large window for the sun to land on the roof. The perfect location for the solar panels.

For a moment, Savannah couldn't move. She looked at that sunny spot and thought of the last time she had been up here. Six months ago. So much had changed in six months. Too much. She bent down and pressed a hand against the rough, warm roof and closed her eyes.

"You okay?" Mac said.

"Yeah." She straightened and brushed the dirt off her palms. "I was just thinking about my dad. The last time I was up here was with him. We were discussing where to install the panels. It was the last time he and I were out to the house together, and one of the last great days we had together. He had his heart attack six weeks later."

Mac put a hand on her shoulder, a comforting, sweet touch. Those were the moments that tempted her to open her heart to Mac. When he was there with a smile, a touch, a word that said he understood and he cared.

"I'm sorry," Mac said. "He sounds like he was a great man."

"He was." She smiled, but the smile wobbled. "One of a kind."

"Then let's get these panels installed. Then he can look down from heaven and see that you are continuing his legacy."

Savannah's gaze landed on that sunny spot again. *You're a great daughter,* her dad had said. *You've always made me so proud to be your father.*

"Am I? With the way the business is struggling and the house is falling apart—"

Mac put a finger against her lips. "You are doing fine, Savannah. He'd be proud, I'm sure."

"I hope so." She glanced again at that sunny spot, then decided Mac was right about one thing. The best thing she could do was keep moving forward, keep fulfilling those promises she had made. She handed a second rope to Mac, which he clipped on to the harness with a carabiner.

He gave the connection a shake. "You sure this is safe?"

"As long as you do what I say, it is." She grinned. Mac's face was a little pale, and he gave the ground far below them a leery glance. She bit back another laugh. The first-timers were often nervous and worried about falling. Even big, strong, tall Mac Barlow was no different. Apparently the CEO was used to being at the top of the business world, but not used to being on the top of a house.

"You're clipped in now," she said. "Even if you slip,

you should be fine. Now, let's start setting the mounting brackets. And remember, I'm in charge."

He chuckled. "I bet you like that."

She grinned. "More than you know, Mr. Barlow."

Savannah explained where to put the brackets, how to find the best place for the screw holes and how to add a sealer around the holes after the brackets were in place. They worked together in the sun for a half hour, the whine of the screw gun the only sound breaking the early-morning peace. Once the brackets were installed and the panels attached, Savannah sat back on the roof and propped her elbows on her knees.

"This is a pretty dangerous job," Mac said, mimicking her position, though still moving a bit gingerly. After thirty minutes on the roof, he'd gotten slightly more confident. "I'm surprised your dad had you doing installs."

"He didn't want me to do it. In fact, he forbade it. But I talked some of the crew into letting me tag along and before they knew it, I was scaling the ladders."

"You have some kind of death wish?"

She laughed. "No. I didn't do installs because I wanted to take risks. I did them for this." She waved a hand at the view before them, the vast blue ocean, the trees that seemed to form undulating green carpets on the southern side of the house. Birds soared above it all, disappearing in black slashes against the sky. "Every view from a roof is different, but they are all breathtaking. Once I finished working, I'd sit on the roof for as long as I could, just taking in the world. Looking out at all this would remind me that in the scheme of things, my problems are pretty small."

Mac's gaze followed hers, and for a long moment he

was quiet. "It is pretty humbling, isn't it? You see this wide expanse, and you realize that people are rather insignificant."

"As are whatever problems we seem to think are so huge. There are hundreds of people just in the space we can see right here." She waved at the tree-covered area, dotted with vacation homes. Within those walls, there were families laughing over breakfast, widows mourning lost loves, dreamers picturing a rosy future. Other lives tumbling along rocky paths. "All those people facing their own challenges and triumphs. Some have harder challenges than others, some celebrate greater triumphs. But we're all in this together." She shrugged and felt her face heat. He probably thought she was being silly, given how cut-and-dried he was. "Anyway, not to wax all philosophical, but that's what I think. It must be the thinner air up here."

"Don't apologize, Savannah." He shifted on the roof to touch her chin, waiting until she was looking at him. She leaned into the touch a little more, craving it, craving him. "I think that's good advice. Wise advice, actually. Something most of us have trouble remembering."

His hand was against her jaw, his touch light but hot, as if a slice of the sun was sliding against her cheek. Her gaze met his, those blue eyes of Mac's seeming to fill the space in front of her until all she thought about was him. What was it about this man that mesmerized her so? She was supposed to keep him firmly on her Enemies list, but every time he touched her...

Her brain misfired and she started wondering what it would be like to take him to bed. To be with him, here and everywhere. Just looking into his eyes made the office seem a thousand miles away, the rest of the world on some distant planet.

That was dangerous. Distracting. She'd made a promise, and falling for Mac would definitely not be keeping that promise. Regardless of how her body melted when he touched her, or how her lips still tingled with a remembered kiss.

"Uh, we should get down," she said. "We have to get to work. I have that meeting with the sales staff in an hour."

"Yeah." His hand dropped away. "You're right."

Disappointment filled her, which was crazy. This was what she wanted—yet it still made her ache with regret. She turned away before Mac could read the truth in her eyes, reminded herself the install was done—so she gathered her tools and got down from the roof.

Because she was right about one thing—the thinner air had her mind running down very nonsensical paths.

Mac was in his sweet spot. Or should have been, at least. An hour after they'd left the beach house, he sat at the desk in the cubicle at Hillstrand Solar, multiple programs open on the screen before him. Accounting, sales, website—he had it all running at the same time.

But his mind was on Savannah. She was in the conference room finishing up their earlier meeting with the sales staff about the realignment of territories, and every time he tried to focus on work, his gaze wandered to her.

She'd stopped at her apartment in town to change before coming in to work. He kind of missed the shorts and T-shirt she'd been wearing this morning, the easy ponytail she'd had in her hair. On the roof she'd looked relaxed and happy. He'd liked that about her. Liked the casual Savannah so much more than the work Savannah.

Here, she was wearing yet another pantsuit—which made him wonder if the ones from the days before cloned themselves while she slept—and her hair was back in that clip, all neat and tidy, no stray tendrils to lure him closer. The happy, relaxed look had disappeared from her face. Beneath the matching jacket her shoulders appeared tense, her posture ramrod straight. It was as if she had become someone else the minute she stepped into this building.

Mac pushed away from the desk and headed into the conference room. Savannah glanced up when he entered, and a smile bloomed on her face. For him? He sure hoped so. Because just seeing that smile made an answering one curve across his face and wiped away all the stress that had plagued him moments before.

He knew he shouldn't get involved with her. Knew he should keep it just about the business. Already, he was finding himself wavering about his plan to help her for a week and then talk her into selling. He had no other plan, because he knew realistically he couldn't stay here forever helping her, but he also didn't want to go back to Boston.

The thought of walking into the office and not seeing Savannah in one of those damnable pantsuits hit him like a punch to the gut. This was crazy. He barely knew the woman. But a part of him—a growing, vocal majority—wanted to get to know her much, much better, especially after that incredible kiss. Even if it was a mistake. Getting closer to Savannah Hillstrand would only further complicate an already-complicated proposition.

But when that smile lit her eyes and she held his gaze for a long moment, *complicated* didn't sound like such a bad idea.

"How's it going?" Mac asked.

"Great. The staff is on board with the new sales territories you and I proposed today. I think everyone's excited about the changes." She glanced over at the trio of salesmen, who nodded agreement. "That's all I had, guys. Unless Mac wanted to add something?"

"No, no, I'm good."

Savannah said goodbye to the salesmen, and they filed out of the room, talking as they left about the new customer assignments. They seemed excited, which Mac took as a good sign. Savannah clearly had handled the meeting well, and done a great job tidying up after he'd left to go back to the books. He liked the way she'd tweaked his idea for realigning the territories. She had a good way of reading people—maybe there was something to her building-personal-relationships theory, after all—and she intuitively knew what would work for them. Those skills had helped her create a stronger territory strategy than he'd suggested, a step above the scattered way her father had done it.

Savannah stacked the papers before her and tapped them into a neat pile. "Did you need something from me?" she asked Mac. Her voice was all business, her posture as severe as the pantsuit. This wasn't the Savannah who'd had him climbing across the roof a couple hours before, teaching him how to install a solar panel.

His gaze lingered on her lips. Why hadn't he kissed her again today back at the beach house? They'd been alone, no one in the world but them. He'd been trying to keep things from getting too personal, but right now that seemed like a moronic idea. Because every time he saw Savannah Hillstrand, he wanted, no, *craved*, personal.

"Mac?" she prompted again.

Oh, yeah. He was supposed to have had a reason for coming in here. A reason other than *I was staring at you and couldn't concentrate on my work.* "I, uh, saw that they're predicting rain for early tomorrow. I was wondering when you were going to finish up that porch roof."

"After work today, I hope. I'll only have a couple hours, but I can get a good start on it in that period of time. Though I won't be able to finish it without a crew and—" Then she waved a hand, cutting off her thoughts. "Unless there's something else we should be working on for Hillstrand Solar tonight?"

"No, no, we're good. I did have some more ideas for turning things around that I wanted to run past you, though." Okay, so he had no such ideas. He'd barely accomplished anything this morning. All he knew was that he didn't want to go back to work yet, and he wanted a reason to keep on talking to Savannah.

"Sure, sure." She gestured toward the chair at the head of the conference table, then pulled out one for herself.

It was all very businesslike and distant, which was how Mac usually liked everything in his life. But after that incredible kiss the other day and the tender moment on the roof this morning, businesslike left him feeling…deflated. As if he'd missed something really incredible. He wanted to get back to those moments when Savannah was laughing and happy. Relaxed.

"Let's not talk here," he said.

"Okay. We can get coffee—"

"Let's get away from the office entirely." As the words left his mouth he had to wonder who was saying them, because that sure as hell couldn't be Mac Barlow suggesting they play hooky. "And get that roof on before it rains. I figure if we start now, we can be done before dusk."

"Are you saying you want to take the day off?" She arched a brow. "Are you feeling sick or something?"

He laughed. Yes, he was sick, but only with longing for more of what they'd had this morning and last night. He wanted to sit on the roof with her again and watch the boats drift by and the seagulls dive for their lunch. He wanted to watch the sun dance across Savannah's features, and wanted to hear her laugh again. "Just tired of being cooped up," he said, instead of the truth.

"That roof is a pretty big job, even for two people," she said. "We can start on it, but to do it right, and do it in one day, we really need a crew. I don't think I can get any of the subcontractors I've worked with in the past out on such short notice."

"Don't worry about that. Let me make a couple phone calls, and I'm sure I can get you all the help you need."

And that was how Mac ended up on the beach an hour later with his brothers and Savannah. At the time he'd called Jack and Luke, he'd thought it was a good idea. Until his brothers acted like brothers and made him wonder what kind of insanity had caused him to bring his family together with the woman he kept trying to convince himself he was most definitely not interested in.

Chapter Nine

Savannah liked the other Barlow brothers from the very first second she met them. Jack was the more studious of the two, with his military bearing and his detail-oriented nature. He took charge of the roof after consulting with Savannah, and had laid out a step-by-step plan for getting it done in the time allotted. Luke was the most relaxed of the three, a true devil-may-care, come-as-you-are kind of guy. It was clear they loved Mac, and loved teasing him mercilessly, which left the usually serious Mac in a state of perpetual discomfort.

That was the part of the afternoon Savannah liked best. Seeing Mac a bit off his game.

"So, big brother, Jack and I are taking bets on what made you do this today. Jack thinks you just found out you have two weeks to live. I think you're in love." Luke sent a wink in Savannah's direction.

She blushed and turned back to the chop saw, where she was cutting the lumber for the roof framing. But she held off turning on the noisy machine until Mac answered. Not because she was curious. At all.

Mac scowled. "Why would you think either of those things?"

"Because you're outdoors. In the middle of the day. Instead of at work. You're either dying, insane or crazy head over—"

"I'm just helping Savannah. Nothing more." Mac nodded toward the other cut pieces of wood at his feet. "Now make yourself useful and grab those so we can get this roof on before you two idiots talk the day away about complete nonsense."

Luke smiled at Savannah as he walked by, heading for the porch. "Don't let Mac's bark fool you. He's a big softy at heart."

From his place on the porch, Jack scoffed. "Mac's about as soft as concrete."

"Exactly," Mac said. "So quit teasing me about my impending death."

"Or impending leap over the *love* cliff." Luke drew out the word and patted his heart. "It happens to the best of us, Mac."

Savannah fired up the saw and chopped the wood, rather than listening to the rest of the brothers' teasing. There was no way Mac was falling for her. Heck, they barely knew each other. And they were work colleagues. That was all. He was merely here to help her finish a project that needed to get done before the rain. That kiss… That had been an aberration. As had all the other touches since then. His refusal to even entertain the idea of falling for her made that clear.

She carried the cut wood over to where the three men were working, each armed with a hammer and a handful of nails. Jack, the most experienced of the three, directed the placement of each timber. "Here's the next set," she said.

Luke stepped away from where he was standing beside Mac. "Why don't you work on the installation for a while with this big idiot here, and I'll go cut," he said to Savannah. "Mac's all thumbs and needs someone to make sure he doesn't accidentally hammer his finger or something."

Mac scowled. "I'm fine. I don't need you to—"

"Sometimes, big brother—" Luke clapped Mac on the shoulder "—you do need me and Jack to tell you what to do." Then he glanced at Savannah with a devilish smile on his face. "Good luck with him. He can be a pain in the ass sometimes."

"Oh, I know that already." Savannah grinned at Mac.

"Gee, thanks." But a smile toyed with the edges of his mouth.

"Anytime. I'm here all week." But secretly, she was glad to change places with Luke. She'd been watching Mac work all afternoon, his dress shirt draped over the fence, leaving him in just a white T-shirt. His biceps strained at the edges of the fabric, and a fine sheen of sweat had plastered the material to his chest, outlining every inch of his amazing chest. Quite frankly, she was surprised she remembered to breathe every time she got near him.

One of the brothers pulled a portable speaker out of Jack's truck, and they turned on some pop music while they worked. The four of them developed a quick system, with Luke cutting the lumber while Jack, Savannah and Mac hammered the pieces together. When the roof was framed, Jack and Mac climbed on top and installed a few pieces of plywood that would serve as the basis for the new shingles. It went by too fast, Savannah thought, far too fast.

"That looks great, guys." Savannah stepped back and surveyed the finished frame. Straight, sturdy and done with a minimum of waste. They'd gotten a lot done in a short period of time. "You made a tough job much easier."

"If you want, we can get the roofing paper and shingles on tonight, too," Jack said. He glanced at his watch. "We have a couple hours of daylight left."

"But first, we're starving," Luke said. "Mac, why don't you take Savannah into town and grab us some pizzas?"

Mac gave his brother a glare. "I can do that, but Savannah doesn't need to—"

"Oh, for God's sake, someone tells you to go spend thirty minutes in a vehicle with a pretty girl, and you're going to argue?" Luke waved toward Savannah's truck. "Go on, you two, fetch us food. The conscripted labor is going to stay here and take a nap."

Mac muttered something about bossy conscripted labor as they headed to Savannah's truck. She climbed in the driver's side, then turned to Mac. "You don't have to go. I can pick up the pizzas if you want."

"Nah, it'll be nice to get away from my brothers for a while."

She noticed he didn't say it would be nice to spend thirty minutes with her. She tried not to let that sting. "They mean well, I'm sure."

"They do." He chuckled. "And that's the problem."

Savannah put the vehicle in gear and pulled out of the driveway. In the rearview mirror she saw Jack and Luke sending Mac a thumbs-up. She liked Mac's brothers, a lot. "I was an only child, so I would have loved some well-meaning siblings."

"And I have one too many."

She knew he was thinking about his newly discovered half brother. Savannah was still surprised he'd opened up about that with her. Had he done it because it was easier to share that information with a near stranger? Or because they really were building some kind of relationship here? "You never know. He could be as great as Jack and Luke, and your family could be better for bringing him into it."

"I don't see how that's going to happen," Mac said.

"You never know. Your brothers put up with you, after all." She flashed him a grin.

He turned to her in the seat. "Are you agreeing that I'm a pain in the ass?"

"If the description fits…" She grinned again, then turned right on to the street that led to the pizza parlor.

He chuckled. "The same could be said for you."

"How exactly am I a pain?" Savannah parked the truck in the pizza place's lot, then turned off the ignition and looked at Mac.

He grinned. "As we have already established, you're stubborn."

"Some would call that tenacious."

"Strong willed."

"I call that determined."

"Bossy."

She laughed. "That's the pot calling the kettle black, if you ask me."

"I'm not bossy." He considered that a moment, then gave her a conciliatory grin. "Okay, maybe I am used to telling people what to do and having them do it. But that's not quite the same thing."

She arched a brow.

"You're also..." He shifted closer, and the air in the car stilled. "Beautiful."

Her breath caught and her heart stuttered. "That's... that's not a criticism."

"I know that." Mac captured her chin with his hand, then trailed his thumb over her bottom lip. Unbidden, her mouth dropped open, waiting, hoping, wanting. "But I couldn't find any other criticisms."

"You're just buttering me up."

"Maybe..." He traced her lip again and she fought the urge to moan. To lean in to him, to give into the constant temptation to be with the last man on earth she should want. "Maybe not," he finished.

The tension in the truck was more intense than that evening on the beach when he'd kissed her. How she craved another kiss, but she knew it would only complicate things. "We...we should get the pizzas."

Mac's eyes clouded, and he dropped his hand and drew back. "Yeah, we should."

The moment had been broken, and Savannah told herself that was a good thing. But as they walked into the pizza parlor, as remote as two strangers, she had to wonder if maybe she was fooling herself.

Three large pepperoni pizzas and a double serving of cheesy breadsticks turned out to be exactly enough food to feed three hungry Barlows and one hard-working Hillstrand. The pizzas and breadsticks were devoured in a few minutes, with the four of them taking up spaces along the front porch to enjoy the cool early-evening air.

Savannah had sat on the top step, just as she had the other night when it had just been the two of them. Mac considered joining her, then figured the rebuff he'd gotten in the car was a clear message. One he should have taken a long time ago—not to mix business with personal.

But as he watched her eat and listened to her joking with his brothers, a steady wave of longing washed over him. He wanted Savannah to be laughing with him, talking to him instead of Jack and Luke. What was wrong with him? He shouldn't be this attracted to Savannah. Yet, despite what his common sense told him, she lingered in his mind, dancing at the fringes of his every thought.

It wasn't just that she was beautiful. It was because of all the things she'd considered criticisms—because she was headstrong and stubborn and determined and smart. Because she was in over her head, but refusing to just give up and drown. He respected that, admired it, even.

But she'd made it clear she wasn't interested in him. Not that he could blame her. He was, after all, the enemy. The one intent on buying her father's company and selling off the pieces to the highest bidder. Yet, at the same time, he was caught in this weird paradox of helping her salvage the company so he couldn't buy it.

Clearly, he defined the words *glutton for punishment*.

After they ate, Mac worked alongside his brothers and Savannah as they fastened the shingles to the new roof. Luke and Jack did their best to tease Mac out of his quiet, pensive mood, but eventually they gave up and talked mostly to Savannah. An hour later the roof was on, and the four of them had cleaned up the debris on the lawn. Throughout the work the other three carried on an easy conversation. Savannah fit right in with his brothers, as if she'd always been part of his family. Something that felt a lot like jealousy kept tickling Mac whenever Savannah laughed at something Jack said or shot Luke a smile.

Insane. She was a colleague, nothing more. He shouldn't care who she talked to or who made her laugh.

Still his gaze kept straying to her long, toned legs, to the intoxicating smile that filled her face. He thought about kissing her, touching her. He wanted her. Half of him wanted to haul her into the house and up the stairs to one of the bedrooms. The other half was exercising restraint and throwing up a big yellow caution flag. Then his gaze traveled along those endless lean legs again, and coherent thoughts disappeared.

Jack clasped Mac on the shoulder as the four of them walked over to Jack's truck. "One new roof installed, and three large pizzas consumed. A good day overall, I think."

"Yeah, a good day," Mac said. For a brief moment he debated telling his brothers about Colton—because it was clear their father hadn't—but in the end decided to take Savannah's advice. Colton was Bobby's mess. Let his father do the cleanup. And it had been a good day, Mac realized. One he didn't want to tarnish with the *guess what, we have a half-brother* news.

"Thanks a lot, guys," Savannah said. "I really appreciate the helping hands."

"No problem. Looks like we finished just in time," Jack said. "A storm's about ready to roll in."

The sky had darkened in the past few minutes, the fluffy white clouds turning gray and threatening. The humidity had risen to sticky level, and there was a heaviness to the air that spelled a good old-fashioned thunderstorm.

"It wasn't supposed to rain until tomorrow," Mac said. Not that most days he cared what the weather was like. But a part of him had been looking forward to sitting on the porch with Savannah and watching the sun set.

"And all weathermen are supposed to be right," Luke said to Mac. "Even the great and powerful Mac Barlow can't control the weather."

He scowled. "I hate when you call me that."

"Then I'll call you the weak and ineffectual Mac Barlow instead." Luke grinned. "In fact, that might suit you even better. Considering you have two brothers who make great—" Luke patted his chest "—and powerful—" Jack flexed a bicep "—look good."

Mac rolled his eyes. "They have drugs for these kinds of delusions, you know."

Jack gave Luke a gentle slug in the arm. "Come on, troublemaker. Let's get out of here and leave Mac alone before he has a stroke. He's been gone awhile. He's not used to us ganging up on him."

"That's true." Luke turned to Mac. "Just imagine how bad we'd be if Mama and Dad had another son. One more Barlow, and we'd be a small gang. You'd never stand a chance, big brother."

Jack and Luke said their goodbyes, then hopped in Jack's truck and pulled out of the driveway, still laughing as they left. Mac watched them go, then kicked at a stray stone in the driveway. The comment about another brother had stung more than his brothers could have imagined. "Damn it. I should have told them about Colton."

"They'll find out soon enough, I'm sure," Savannah said. "Your dad is going to have to do something soon."

"He hasn't for thirty-plus years. Why would he start now?"

Savannah gave Mac a sympathetic look. "People change, Mac."

Did they? Thus far he hadn't seen much of that in his own life. His father was still obstinate and opinionated, and their rift stood as strong as the day Bobby had told Mac that no son of his could be so cold. Then again, Mac himself hadn't exactly made big advances in the change department, either.

He watched the disappearing tail end of Jack's truck. Both his brothers seemed happier, more at ease. Jack had lost a lot of that rigidity he'd developed in the military, and Luke had become more responsible. They'd changed—and had fuller, more complete lives because of that. Women who loved them. Futures to bank on. Whereas Mac had this week, then a return to his offices in Boston and more of the same—rinse, repeat, day after day.

For years that had made him happy. He'd told himself he felt fulfilled. Except after today, listening to Jack and Luke brag about their fianceés to Savannah, Mac had to wonder if his life was as full as he'd thought. Because right now there seemed to be a yawning cavern in his chest every time he thought about returning to Boston.

The storm clouds began to crowd the sky, blotting out the last rays of sunshine. A low rumble of thunder trembled in the air. "We better get cleaned up and get out of here before the storm starts," Mac said.

Savannah nodded. "Looks like it's moving in fast."

A minute later the storm was there, a vicious wind kicking up and bending the trees. The clouds burst and rain dropped in sheets from the sky, drumming a steady, heavy beat. Savannah and Mac rushed toward the house, gathering up empty pizza boxes and the last of the supplies as they went. They charged up the stairs and burst through the front door. He took the supplies from her hands, set them on a bench, then shut the door.

"You're soaked," he said to Savannah. Her hair was plastered to her head, her T-shirt riding along her body like a second skin. Desire flamed in his gut. "Let me... let me get you a towel."

"You don't have to—"

But he was already gone, pulling open the linen closet beside the hall bathroom he'd been in earlier today, and taking two big fluffy beach towels from the stack. He returned and draped one over Savannah's shoulders, drawing it closed. She might look sexy as hell all wet like that, but she could also catch one heck of a cold. "There. You want the second one?"

She shook her head. "No, no. You need it."

"I'm fine. Here, you're shivering." He unfolded the second towel, and ignored her protests, wrapping it over the first one. He brushed her bangs off her cool, damp skin. "You should get out of those wet clothes."

"I'm—"

A bright light flooded the hall, followed by a sharp crack outside the house. An angry wind battered the windows, rattling the panes and shutters. Savannah crossed to the front window and peered out at the yard. Her hand went to her mouth. "Oh, no!"

Mac came up behind her. "What?"

She pointed out the window. "My father's birdhouse. The lightning hit it and now it's…"

Her words trailed off, but Mac could see the damage himself. The lightning had struck the pole at just the right angle, shearing the small wooden house off and sending it crashing below. The rain was coming down too fast for the ground to absorb the water, and the birdhouse was starting to sink in the now muddy yard.

Mac dashed outside before Savannah could stop him. The storm whipped at him, the sky dark and threatening like a furious god, but Mac ignored the angry rantings of Mother Nature. He ran toward the birdhouse and scooped it up, careful not to jostle the contents.

A second later, Savannah was there, wearing a rain slicker she must have grabbed before she ran outside. She held a second one out to him but he shook his head. He couldn't hold the birdhouse and put on the jacket.

"What are—?" Her words were snatched by the wind, so she raised her voice and said it again. "What are you doing?"

"I've got to get this up on something high, until we can fix the pole." Inside the birdhouse, he could hear the nervous chitter of the baby birds. He spun in the yard, heedless of the rain pouring down on his head, his clothes. "There. That shed."

Mac carried the birdhouse over to the shed to the east of the house, then nestled it in the elbowed space where the roof met the walls and created a shelved overhang. More worried chirps came from inside the box. He peeked inside, and saw the baby birds, all intact, if not a little wet and scared. "It's okay, guys, almost all set." Mac turned to Savannah. "We need to secure this or it's going to get blown down again by the wind. Where are your tools?"

"In my trunk." She patted her back pocket, found her keys and held them up.

"Stay here, and I'll get them."

"I can—"

"No. Stay here." Lightning cracked again in the sky and thunder boomed. "I'd tell you to go inside but I know you won't."

"Because I'm stubborn." She grinned.

"You are indeed." He held her gaze for a moment, then took the keys. He liked that about her, liked that she had braved the storm with him, and thought enough of him to bring a second jacket. "I'll be right back."

"Not without this." She held out the jacket again.

He gave her a grin, then slipped it on and flipped up the hood. "Thanks."

A moment later, he returned with a hammer, some nails and a couple scrap pieces of wood. The storm whipped at him, tried to snatch the wood from his hands, but he planted his feet and set to work. Mac hammered the scraps into place on either side of the birdhouse, creating a brace to hold the box in place. "All set," he said, shouting to be heard above the roar of the wind. "Hopefully the mama bird doesn't mind we moved them a bit. Now, come on, let's get you out of the storm before you catch a cold."

They were just heading back to the house when Savannah stopped. "Mac, wait. Did you hear that?"

Mac paused beside her, listening between thundering booms. And then, there it was, a faint, weakening chirping sound. "I think one of the babies fell out."

A few minutes later, they found it nestled deep in the grass, trembling, its chirps getting softer by the second. The bird's dark eyes were wide and round, and he quaked at the sight of the two towering humans. Savannah shrugged out of her coat and draped it like a tarp over Mac as he bent down, slid his hands across the wet grass and carefully lifted the bird. Except for being wet and scared, it looked none the worse for wear after its tumble.

"It's okay, buddy," he said. "We'll have you back with your brothers and sisters in a second."

With Savannah shielding him and the bird from the storm, they made their way back to the temporary home for the birdhouse. Mac raised the baby bird to the opening and opened his palms, then waited until the bird heard its siblings inside. The fledgling's attention perked and a moment later it hopped through the hole and back into the nest.

"Mission accomplished," Mac said.

"It is indeed," Savannah replied, her gaze soft on his and a smile playing across her lips, even as the storm roared around them. "Now come on inside, Mac. It's time for me to take care of you."

Chapter Ten

It was the way he handled the baby bird that had sealed it for Savannah. All the reasons she'd had for not getting involved with Mac Barlow disappeared the second he cradled that fledgling, then carefully guided it back into the birdhouse. Mac had been so tender, so gentle. And he'd done it all without a second thought.

To her, that spoke volumes about the man he was. His first instinct had been to save the baby birds, heedless of the storm. It shifted her view of him. Maybe Mac Barlow wasn't as focused on his return on investment as he made himself out to be.

She'd gotten little glimpses here and there at the man behind the suit, so to speak, and every peek she got enticed her more. Now, seeing him standing in her hall, soaking wet with his T-shirt molded to the planes and valleys of his chest, enticed her in a whole other way.

"As soon as the storm ends," Mac was saying, "I'll fix that pole for you and reset the birdhouse where it was before."

"I still can't believe you ran out into the storm like that."

Mac shrugged. "It was no big deal. Probably some leftover sense of duty from when I was in the Boy Scouts."

"You. Were a Boy Scout." It wasn't even a question.

He laughed. "Why is that so hard to believe?"

"I don't know. You're just so…" She grabbed one of the towels and pressed it into his hands. "Stubborn."

He swiped at his hair, whisking away some of the water. "Some call that tenacious."

She laughed at her own words being turned against her. "Strong willed."

"I call that determined." He smirked.

She took the second towel and raised it to wipe the water off his arms, but Mac turned it back into her hands and pressed it against her own damp body. "Bossy."

"That one I'll take." He let his own towel tumble to the floor and picked up the other end of hers. "But sometimes someone needs another person to tell them what to do."

"I don't need anyone to tell me what to do."

"Even when you are—" he took the corner of the towel and wiped her forehead, her cheeks, then slid it along the curve of her jaw "—soaking wet and run outside in the rain again anyways?"

"Even when."

He lowered the towel from her jaw, rubbed the soft pebbly surface against her arms. A delicious rush of goose bumps chased after his touch. Her lips parted, and her breath caught.

"You are soaking wet." His gaze locked on hers, his eyes dark, mysterious pools in the dim light of the hall.

"So are you."

"Maybe—" a heartbeat passed "—maybe we should get out of these wet clothes before we catch cold."

"There are, uh…" She had to struggle to string words together because she knew what saying them meant. What door they would open. Did she want that? She raised her gaze to his. Yes, oh, yes, she did. Very much. "Clothes upstairs. In the…bedroom."

"That could get complicated," Mac said, as if reading her mind.

"I know," Savannah whispered. She knew and she didn't care. She wanted complicated. She wanted Mac Barlow. She wanted to ease this fiery ache deep in her belly. She put out her hand, and when his slid into hers, she knew she'd made a choice.

Whether it was the right one or not, Savannah didn't care. She would worry about that later. Much, much later.

The storm lashed against the house, rain pattering on the windows, dark clouds blotting the last of the sun from the sky. Mac hardly noticed. All he saw when he stood in the small bedroom at the top of the stairs was Savannah and the double bed behind her.

The air hushed in the room, anticipation charging the space between them. A small bedside light cast a soft amber glow over the room.

Savannah stood before him, her eyes wide, her lips parted, as if begging him to kiss her. He reached up both hands, cradled her face in his palms and brushed a tender kiss against her mouth. She leaned into him, and the kiss deepened.

He pulled back, his chest heaving. "We…we can stop. If you want. If you think—"

She shook her head. "I don't want to stop."

He hesitated only a second, then reached down, grasped the hem of her T-shirt and raised it over her head, breaking the kiss only long enough to slide the fabric between them. It fell to the floor with a soft plop. At the same time, Savannah reached for his shirt and tugged it off and over his head. He ran his fingers along the valleys of her shoulders, down her arms, then up her waist, lingering at the edges of her breasts, still hidden behind a simple white bra. He hooked one finger under each of the straps and slid them down, exposing the swells of her breasts.

Then he lowered his mouth, trailing kisses along her jaw, her neck, down the center of her chest. He shifted right, kissing the top of her breasts, while slowly peeling the satin cup away and following its path with his mouth. When he captured one nipple in his mouth, Savannah gasped and arched against him. She tangled her hands in his hair, anxious, needy, wanting.

He scooped her up and laid her on the bed, pausing only long enough to shed his jeans and boxers and kick them to the side. Savannah's mouth curved into a sexy, slow smile when her gaze landed on his body. "Very nice," she said.

"Oh, I disagree. I think it's you who looks very nice. Very…" He leaned over, unbuttoned the clasp on her shorts and tugged them down when she raised her hips. "Very…" Exposing white lacy panties. "Very…" He slid a finger under one side, and pulled them over her hips and down her legs. "*Very* nice."

The bedside lamp's soft light kissed Savannah's skin with gold. She lay there, one arm above her head, a half smile playing on her lips, looking like a goddess. He slid onto the bed beside her and trailed his hand along the smooth, tempting valleys of her belly. "You are the most incredible woman I have ever met."

A blush filled her cheeks. He liked that. Liked that a simple compliment could leave her a little disconcerted. "I'm just an ordinary girl."

"You are far from ordinary. You can drive a boat and run a company and build a roof. And you can keep me on my toes. That right there puts you in a class of your own."

She laughed, then raised up on one elbow, draped an arm around his neck and drew him in for a kiss. "That should merit hazardous duty pay."

"I'm not hazardous."

She ran her hand down his back, finally circling around to the front to stroke his erection. He let out a low moan and nearly dissolved in her arms. "Everything about being with you is hazardous to me."

He thought the same thing about being with her. It wasn't just her hand on him. It was the way she looked at him, the desire in her eyes, as if there was no other man in the entire world Savannah wanted to be in bed with.

No, it was more. It was the connection between them. A connection formed that first day when she'd turned the tables on him, then cemented on the roof when he'd opened his heart to her. He needed that, craved that, craved *her*.

Her green eyes were wide and luminous. "I don't want to stop, Mac."

Still, he hesitated. This wasn't just a casual fling anymore, but he wasn't quite sure what it was. Either way, the last thing he wanted to do was hurt Savannah. "This could change things."

"This *will* change things," she said, then kissed his neck, her breath warm against his skin. "And I'm okay with that."

By the time she kissed his neck again, he was a goner. He rolled over on to her, and returned those kisses, starting a long, slow, sweet journey from her lips to her belly. She arched against him, and when he slid his fingers inside her, she moaned his name and started stroking him in return. The storm raged outside, while inside the small white-and-blue bedroom, another kind of storm began to build.

Mac fumbled on the floor for his jeans, and tugged out his wallet. It took an interminable amount of time to find and then slip on a condom. When he returned to Savannah, she grabbed him and pulled him down to her, searing his mouth with a kiss that damned near took his breath away.

When he entered her a moment later, it was like filling the last piece in a puzzle. She fitted perfectly against him, matching his rhythm with her own body. He kissed her neck, her lips, everything he could reach, unable to have enough of her, even this close, this joined.

Then the storm took over between them, and she began to gasp. His strokes sped up, and the rush began to build. She clutched at his back, calling out his name, and he exploded just seconds later, holding her tight for one, long breathless moment.

When he finally rolled to the side and pulled Savannah into the crook of his arm, Mac realized two things. One, that making love to Savannah Hillstrand had indeed complicated things. And two, that he was never going to be the same again. As much as he told himself in the afterglow that he was okay with that—

Mac wasn't so sure he was.

Savannah lay in Mac's arms and wondered if it would be rude to get up right now and run out of the room.

It wasn't that the lovemaking had been terrible. It had, in fact, been earth-shatteringly, soul-satisfyingly amazing. It was the realization afterward that she had just gone to bed with the one man in the world she was supposed to keep at a distance. The one man who wanted to take away what mattered most to her. That she'd let a tender moment with some baby birds drive her to make a spontaneous decision made her realize she wasn't thinking clearly at all.

She had said she was okay with how making love would change things. What she hadn't realized was how much it would change the dynamic, and how much she would crave making love to Mac Barlow again— not five minutes after they'd finished.

That was dangerous. That was getting hooked on him, falling for him. Doing that would muddle her mind, confuse her decisions. She was supposed to be saving her father's company, not falling for the corporate raider who wanted to dismantle it.

"I...I should go make us a snack," she said, because saying, *I have to get out of here before I make another foolish decision*, sounded rude. Before Mac could agree or disagree, Savannah disentangled herself, grabbed a clean T-shirt out of the dresser drawer and headed downstairs.

There was almost nothing to eat in the fridge, and very little in the pantry. Her parents hadn't stayed at the beach house in months, which meant no one had restocked the groceries. She found a box of crackers, a suspiciously old looking can of artichokes and a new jar of peanut butter, along with two water bottles in the bottom drawer of the refrigerator.

Savannah pulled a plate out of the kitchen cabinet. When she did, she saw a photo of her parents, tacked to the side of the refrigerator. Her dad, beaming that wide smile he'd always worn, one hand holding a fishing pole bearing his latest catch, the other arm draped over her mother's shoulders. The two of them laughing at something silly her father had said. The picture had been taken at the end of April, only a month before the heart attack that eventually took his life.

She could see the trusting look in her father's eyes, the one that seemed to say, *I left it in your hands, kiddo, because I know you'll take care of what I built.*

That meant not sleeping with Mac Barlow. Not letting him into her heart, or into her life, any more than was necessary. What had she done? Oh God, what had she done?

"I was worried you were harvesting the wheat or growing the tomatoes yourself for a sandwich."

Savannah turned at the sound of Mac's voice. He stood there, in just a pair of dark blue plaid boxers slung low on his hips, looking like some kind of underwear model, and heaven help her, she wanted him all over again. Warmth spread through her body, sparked desire in her veins. This was wrong, so wrong. Why did she keep fantasizing about the man? Why couldn't she seem to keep him at a distance and just concentrate on her job?

"I've been searching through the cabinets. There, uh, isn't much to eat down here," she said, holding up the crackers and peanut butter. "Sorry."

"That's okay. I wasn't really that hungry." Mac nodded toward the window. "Looks like the storm let up."

The clearing skies provided the excuse she was looking for. A reason to leave and deal with what had happened in that bedroom later. Like in a month or a year or…never. "We should get back to town while there's a break in the rain," she said. "I have a lot of work to catch up on."

"Yeah, me, too."

An awkward silence filled the homey kitchen. Savannah handed Mac one of the water bottles, then replaced the crackers and peanut butter in the cabinet. "I'll, uh, get dressed first."

Because if they went into that bedroom again at the same time and got dressed together, she knew the limits of her willpower and knew it would only be a matter of seconds before she'd be all over him again. As it was, just standing in the same room with a bare-chested Mac made concentrating almost impossible.

She hurried up the stairs and then pulled on her clothes. As she was leaving the bedroom, Mac was coming up the stairs. "The space is all yours," she said. "Don't worry about cleaning up in there. I'll do it next time I come here."

And after she'd had enough time to process all of

this, and after enough time had passed that she wouldn't walk in that room and crave more of Mac Barlow.

He laid a hand on her arm. "Hey, are we okay?"

We? Did he think there was a *we*? Or was it just a slip of the tongue? And why did she keep looking for a bridge between them? "Of course. It's all fine."

"Everything about you says differently."

"It's just…uh…awkward afterwards, you know?" Awkward wasn't even the word for it. "Now we have to be all professional in the office and get back to work saving Hillstrand Solar. Or…whatever happens."

He tipped her chin until she was looking at him. "Do you think I'm still trying to buy the company?"

"Aren't you?"

"I'm helping you, Savannah, like I promised. All of this is a…temporary lull in our regular lives."

"That doesn't answer the question, Mac." As she said the words, she knew the answer already. He'd deftly avoided the truth and she had been a fool— a total fool—to fall for him. A temporary lull? The words stung.

"If the methods we're trying to save the company don't work out," Mac said, his voice going all serious, all hints of *we* erased now. "Then, yes, I'll make you a fair and equitable offer."

The old Mac Barlow, the one she had met that first day, was back. The man she had seen tenderly lift the baby bird into the birdhouse had disappeared. Tears welled in Savannah's eyes, but she willed them away. "Of course you would," she said, her voice wavering a little. "I wouldn't expect anything less." Then she barreled past him and down the stairs before he could see the truth in her eyes.

* * *

Mac rode too fast down the still-wet roads, heedless of the slick pavement. All he wanted was distance. Distance between himself and that beach house. Distance between him and Savannah. And most of all, distance between him and the truth.

That for all his talk about wanting to help her, in the end he really wanted what he had come here for—a quick and easy acquisition that he could turn around as soon as the ink was dry.

He thought of the days he'd spent helping her on the beach house. It had been nice, really nice, seeing something come together. Building something. It reminded him of when he'd been a kid building tree forts with his brothers, setting up campsites in Boy Scouts, erecting towering piles of blocks in his living room.

Those days at the beach house had been a vacation from his reality, though. It wasn't as if he was going to give up everything he had built and go into remodeling homes for a living. In the end, he was good at one thing—finding struggling companies, buying them up and turning them around for a profit.

But that didn't ease his guilt about Savannah Hillstrand. He never should have slept with her. Even now, the image of her laying in that bed, one arm above her head, a warm, inviting smile on her lips, made him want to turn around and go right back to her. Instead, he gunned the engine, leaned into the curve and headed toward his father's house.

He hadn't listened to the voice mail on his phone left there earlier by Colton. He already knew what it would say. His twenty-four hours were up and either the Barlows had learned about this new member of the family or they would find out when Colton showed up in town. No way was Mac going to let that happen.

He pulled into the driveway, shut off the engine, and cursed his timing. His mother's car sat beside his father's truck, so close their side mirrors almost touched. Damn.

Mac stowed the helmet, then headed up the stairs and into the house. As soon as the front door opened, his mother popped her head out of the kitchen. "Maxwell! I'm so glad you're here. I'm just finishing up dinner, if you want something to eat."

"I had some pizza earlier, Mama."

She pouted. If there was a contest to show love with food, Della Barlow would win, hands down. "Okay, but if you change your mind, there's a nice baked chicken with your name on it."

"Thanks. Maybe I'll grab some." But he had no intentions of doing that, or staying long enough to share a meal with his parents. No way could he sit here through dinner and pretend everything was okay. Or sit across from his father and not read him the riot act. "Where's Dad?"

"Out in his workshop. When you see him, tell him dinner will be done in a few minutes."

"Will do." Mac passed through the house, pausing to give his mother a kiss on the cheek, before heading out the back door and down to the converted shed his father used for storing his tools and whatever the project of the day was. Ever since Bobby had retired from the garage, he'd taken up woodworking, mostly making things such as jewelry boxes and a new mailbox.

His father sat on an old wooden stool in the shed, sanding the top of a small table. He looked up when

Mac entered. "Mac. Didn't expect to see you here." Bobby's face shifted from surprise to wariness.

Another storm was on its way and Bobby needed to deal with it—now—and before it showed up unannounced.

"I came to share a voice mail with you." Mac pulled out his phone and pressed the Play button beside the message from Colton. A second later, his brother's voice filled the speakers, sounding surprisingly a lot like Jack and Luke. "Mac, this is Colton. I'm coming to town in a few days and stopping by to finally meet our dad. I know you don't want me butting in your life, but it's my right to know who my father is. Maybe we'll get to meet. In fact, I hope we do. I'd really like to know my brothers, too."

The message ended and Mac tucked the phone back in his pocket. He gave his father an expectant look.

Bobby cursed and pushed off from the bench. "He really wants to do this?"

"Sounds like it."

Panic flooded Bobby's eyes. Everything was about to hit the fan in a very big way. "Did he say when?"

"Dad, you heard the same message I did." Mac let out a breath. "What does it matter? Whether Colton is arriving Tuesday or next Sunday, you still have to tell Mama, and then Luke and Jack."

"Tell Mama what?"

Damn. Mac closed his eyes and cursed. He'd left the door to the shed open. He turned, hating himself for not thinking, and saw Della's face, a little wary, a little curious. "Tell you—"

"Mac, don't." Bobby got to his feet and put a hand on his son's arm. "Don't."

He wheeled back to his father. "You can't keep pushing this under the rug, Dad, and you need to deal with this *now*. Not a week from now. Not thirty more years from now. Right this minute."

"Tell me what?" Della asked again, her voice smaller now, her words quaking.

Silence thickened the air in the shed. Bobby stood there a long time looking at his shoes. Mac shifted his weight, wishing he hadn't come here now, not when his mother was home. The last thing he wanted to see was his mother's heart broken.

"Aw, hell, Della." Bobby sighed. "I have to tell you something. Something I should have told you years ago."

"Tell me what?" The third time the words were just barely a whisper.

"Remember that trouble we went through a couple years after we got married?" Bobby said to his wife.

"Yes." Her gaze darted from her husband to her son. "It was a long time ago."

"Thirty-three years, to be exact."

"We'd been married such a short time," she said. "We were so young and foolish, and Lord knew we should have been smarter and waited because neither one of us was much ready to be married."

"No, we weren't. And some of us didn't act like we were married, either. And it turns out there were… repercussions to the stupid choices I made."

Mac watched his mother take in those words, turn them over in her mind. He could see her processing it, hoping it meant something other than what she thought, then as the realization hit her, he saw the hurt and anguish fill her face.

"What are you talking about, Robert?"

"I…I should get out of here," Mac said. No way could he stand here for one more minute and watch his mother's world get destroyed.

"No, you stay," Della said, her voice firm now. "Because apparently everyone knows something I don't know."

Bobby toed at a pile of sawdust on the floor. He didn't say anything.

"Robert? Tell me."

He raised his gaze to his wife's, and in his father's eyes, Mac saw genuine regret. "You knew about Katherine."

The name was like a verbal slap, and Della's eyes welled. But she held her ground, chin up and gave a short nod. "Yes, yes, I did."

Bobby turned to his son, apology written all over his features. "I told your mother years ago that I…I stepped out on her. I was young and stupid when we got married, and as much as I thought I wanted to settle down, the actual settling-down part scared the hell out of me. So I kept on acting like I was a single man. I was working in Atlanta at the time, running parts for one of those auto-supply chains, and I met this woman named Katherine."

Mac's mother stood like a rock, her face as unreadable as granite. "We went through an awful time after I found out about that," she said. "I left your father. Moved back in with my parents for six months."

"While I got my head screwed on straight." Bobby looked at his wife again. "And realized I had already married the best woman in the world."

The sweet words didn't soften Della's features. Her

lips thinned and she met her husband's gaze head-on. "So what don't I know?"

More silence. In the world outside the converted shed, a dog barked, someone started a lawnmower. Life went on. Mac waited. Della waited. Bobby ran a hand through his hair, then finally realized the words had to be said and he started to speak.

"Katherine… She had a son." Bobby cleared his throat. "*My* son."

In that moment Mac felt just as bad for his father as he did for his mother. He knew his parents loved each other—*that* he'd never doubted—but he could see the fear and guilt in the hunch of Bobby's shoulders, the tremble in his voice. Mac's mother just stayed where she was, swaying a little.

"A…a son?" The words squeaked out of her.

Bobby nodded, his eyes downcast. "His name is Colton. And he wants to meet me, meet the boys."

Della's lips thinned again. She didn't say anything for a long, long time. Mac wished he had left before this. That he didn't have to watch pain flicker across his mother's face, or hear the regret and guilt in his father's breaths.

Della turned to Mac. "And you knew about this?"

"I just found out a few days ago. Colton somehow found his way to Uncle Tank," Mac said, because he wasn't about to add more to the story with telling his mother that her brother-in-law had known for years; "and Tank called me. I didn't know what to do, so I talked to Dad and…" Mac put out his hands and didn't finish the sentence.

"I see." Those two words chilled the room. Della looked from her husband to her son, then back to her husband. "It is best that you meet your son, Robert. He deserves that."

"And—" Bobby drew in a breath, let it out in one long shaky exhale "—where will you be when all this happens?"

Della's eyes welled, and her hands trembled at her sides. Instead of answering him, she turned on her heel and walked out of the shed.

The next day, Savannah sat at her father's desk and went through the motions. She'd tried to fill his shoes—had for months now—but they never felt quite right. She looked at the list of recommended changes and cuts that Mac had left her, and decided the only way to get the hang of this job was to do it. And keep on doing it, day after day, like she had been. But this time with more commitment to the job. No more running out to repair something on the beach house. No more distractions. Just putting her nose to the proverbial grindstone.

Maybe then if she spent enough time in the offices and on the plant floor, being the CEO at Hillstrand Solar would become second nature. It had to—because her only other choice was to sell and watch the company be parceled out like cake at a wedding.

She headed down to the plant floor, found Betty at her usual station and pulled her aside. "Hi, Betty. Do you have a second?"

"Sure, sure. Oh, wait. Let me show you the cutest picture of my grandson. He was blowing bubbles on the back deck and it was just the sweetest thing ever." Betty pulled out her phone and started scrolling through the photo app.

Every second you spend talking to them is a second they don't spend earning money for the company.

Savannah glanced down at the plan in her hands. A plan that would surely fail if the CEO failed to implement all its strategies, too. Yet another piece of advice Mac had given her—that the road to success started at the top, which meant she needed to be a better role model and act like a boss, not a friend. "Actually, Betty, let's save that for break time. I need to talk to you about relocating a few things in the shipping department. If we bring the packing table closer to the box storage and set up a better-designed mailing station, we should be able to get packages out the door faster. I also want to set up a pallet right beside shipping so as soon as an order is packaged, it can be loaded with the others and be ready to be brought to the trucks."

Surprise lit Betty's eyes. "Sure, sure. I can get Jeremy to help me move that table and set up the pallet."

"Thank you. And please do it today. We are trying to make every step of the operation leaner and faster."

Betty gave Savannah a long, assessing glance. Savannah expected some resistance, a little anger at the change in tone, but instead a slow smile curved across Betty's face. "Your daddy would be proud, Savannah."

The words caught Savannah off guard. "He would? Why?"

"You're acting like a boss. I think that's awesome."

"Thank you." The unexpected praise warmed Savannah and for a moment, she wished her father were here to see the company beginning to take shape again.

"By the way," Betty went on. "That Mac Barlow that you brought in as a consultant or whatever, he's doing a great job, too. All of us were talking, and he's a pretty sharp tool in your toolbox. He's a little hard to get to know at first, but once he loosens up, he's downright pleasant. And easy on the eyes." Betty grinned, then gave Savannah a little salute. "Right. Back to work. I'll get right on moving that table, Miss Hillstrand."

As Betty walked away to accomplish the tasks Savannah had given her, a small measure of hope filled Savannah. Maybe she could do this, after all—turn the company around and lead it the way it needed to be led. It was only one task, but it was a big step in the right direction.

The door to the plant opened. Savannah turned and saw Mac lit from behind by the midday sun. It outlined his tall, lean figure, made the jeans and boots look even more dangerous. His dark hair was a little mussed from the ride, and she ached to run her fingers through the wavy locks.

Damn. Why did he have to look so good? And why did her heart still skip a beat at the sight of him? He was all wrong for her—even if her body disagreed.

Instead of heading toward him, she took the coward's way out, spinning on her heel and ducking into the staircase. With any luck, he hadn't seen her.

Before she reached the second floor, she heard a heavier tread coming up the staircase behind her. Mac. Damn. He *had* seen her.

He took the stairs two at a time and caught up to her a few seconds later. "Hey, you have a second?"

She turned and stopped on the staircase, one hand on the cold metal railing, her back against the concrete block wall. A part of her wanted to say no, she had no time for the man who had broken her heart the day before, but the other part, the masochistic part, wanted to see what he had to say. If he was going to say, *I'm sorry, I was an idiot, let's try this again.* "Sure."

"I, uh, need to talk to you about the ordering process for the brackets. I think I found a supplier who is much cheaper, but requires more lead time for production. What's your drop-dead turnaround on something like that?"

Work. That was all he wanted to talk about. Why was she surprised? Everything she'd read or heard about Mac Barlow had said he worked nonstop and had almost zero personal life. Those brief snippets of time working at the beach house and then again in the bedroom must have been a blip, an anomaly. Her heart fractured a little more.

"You know, this really isn't a good time," Savannah said. At least she'd said it without dissolving into a crying mess. "I'm just heading out for lunch."

"Great. I'll go with you and we can—"

"No, Mac, we can't. You may be able to easily divide work and personal, but—big surprise—it turns out I can't. So, let's just work separately today. I need…time and space." She turned and headed up the next flight, then pressed on the door to the fourth floor. She didn't need anything to eat or drink, she just wanted to get away from him and took the closest exit toward that.

Instead of reading her mind, Mac followed her into the break room. It was the middle of the workday, so the room was empty, dim, quiet. Leaving the two of them alone.

"Listen, Savannah, I know I didn't end things in the best way yesterday."

She spun around. "Didn't end them in the best way? That's an understatement."

"Business is separate from personal to me," he said. "And, yes, maybe that wasn't the best time to bring up buying the company, so I apologize for that."

"Your mind is *always* on work, Mac. I'm surprised you didn't try to apply lean manufacturing to our love-making. Maybe work on your laptop while we were together." The sarcasm whipped off her tongue at a record pace. But she didn't care. She just wanted him to back away, leave her alone. Quit breaking her heart.

"You really think I'm that bad?"

She took two steps closer to him. "I think you're a whiz at business. That all your success is right within those spreadsheets and reports and plans you love so much. But I think when it comes to personal relation-ships, you've struck out, and so instead of actually forming a relationship, you retreat to work. Your safety zone."

He shook his head. "That's not true."

"Oh, yeah? Then tell me, how long did anything personal last between us? Twenty minutes? Thirty?"

"This is different, Savannah. We are working at saving this business together, and that is not personal. Not at all."

She shook her head and cursed the tears that sprang to her eyes. "That man over there—" she pointed to the picture of her father, the one that seemed to stare back at her with hope and trust that she wouldn't screw this up "—believed that business was personal. He had hundreds of friends. Dozens of people who loved him. Who mourn his passing. And even if I sell Hillstrand Solar to you and you tear down the building and wipe away any trace that it ever existed, people will still mourn. Because they loved *him*, not a business."

Mac took in her words, spent a second digesting them. "Then why are you trying so hard to save this place?"

"Because this business was a part of him and it's—" she sucked in a shaky breath "—it's the only way I have to hold on to him. To keep the promise I made to him before he died."

"I understand promises," Mac said quietly.

"Do you? Do you really? Because it seems to me all you understand is dollars and cents."

"Before you start condemning me," Mac said, taking a step closer, invading her space, "ask yourself this. Are you running this place because you want to, because it's the right thing to do, or because you're too afraid to let it go and strike out on your own?"

"What are you talking about?"

"Those houses. I drove by a couple of the ones you restored. They were absolutely beautiful. You did an incredible job, and it showed in every shingle, every windowpane. Because you were passionate about that—because that was personal to you."

"What do you care?" Why was he driving by the houses? Giving her such a hard time? He wasn't part of her life or her future. He'd made that clear. "None of this is personal to you, Mac. None of it. And is that what you want to leave behind? A bunch of bottom lines and lean manufacturing reports? Or do you want to make a difference in people's lives, really get to know them? Make it personal?"

He shook his head. "That isn't part of business."

"You're wrong," she said. "It's part of everything. Or it is for me."

Then she walked out of the room before the tears

spilled over and onto her cheeks, and let him know how very personal all this had become in a few short days. How she had fallen for him in a big, big way. It was those silly baby birds and the moment on the roof and that kiss—all those moments that had stacked up in her mind and in her heart and told her she was dangerously close to the edge of falling in love with the man who ultimately wanted to take away her father's dream.

Instead of going back to her office, Savannah got in her car and headed for her mother's house. It was a sunny day, and as she turned the corner to the small house where she'd grown up, she expected to see the same sight she had seen for the past few months—the flowers on the walk wilting in the sun, the house buttoned up and shades drawn, her mother somewhere inside that darkness.

Instead, she saw Grace Lee on her hands and knees, her floppy straw gardening hat shading her face, while she dug in the earth of the front yard and planted annuals in the beds. Her mother turned at the sound of the car in the drive, then got to her feet to welcome her daughter. "Savannah! What a lovely surprise."

She drew her mother into a tight hug. It had been a couple weeks since she'd been here, because she'd been so caught up in work. But now she noticed her mother's eyes were brighter, her skin flushed with color. "You look good, Mom. I'm glad you're outside today, working in the yard."

"I thought it was about time," Grace Lee said softly. "Don't you?"

Savannah hugged her mother again, and this time, let the tears in her eyes spill over. All those months her mother had withdrawn from life, mourning the husband who had been her best friend. For months, it had been as though Savannah lost two parents. No matter what Savannah said or did, Grace Lee had stayed in her darkened house. That had been a big reason why Savannah had started working on the beach house, thinking if that was fixed, maybe she could get her mother interested in going back there. But now her mother had pulled herself out of that pit. It warmed Savannah's heart. "Yes, yes, I do."

Grace Lee drew back and swiped away the dampness on Savannah's cheeks. "Oh, honey. Don't cry. Come on inside. Let's have some cookies and milk."

Savannah rolled her eyes. "Mom, I'm not five anymore."

"I know. But you look like you had a bad day, and nothing helps a bad day more than cookies and milk, no matter how old you are."

Savannah laughed. "You are right about that."

Grace Lee dropped her gardening hat on a bench by the front door as they went into the house and down the hall to the cozy kitchen. A plate of fresh-baked chocolate-chip cookies sat on the table. The scent of chocolate filled the air, and Savannah grabbed the biggest cookie off the top of the pile. She sank her teeth into the soft, chewy dessert and her mouth watered. Delicious. Her mother had used her grandmother's secret recipe. "These are awesome, Mom."

"Thanks. I've been busy the last few days." She poured two glasses of milk, then sat across from her daughter.

"So...what happened?" Savannah asked.

Grace Lee shrugged. "I just woke up one day and realized that your father would never want me to lie in that dark bedroom, day after day, missing him. I started small. Just cleaning the house, then I moved on to baking, and then today, I went and bought the flowers to plant. It's not much, but—"

Savannah's hand covered her mother's. "It's a lot. I'm so glad for you."

"Thank you." Grace Lee's eyes were watery but her smile was strong. The two shared a long moment, hands clasped, a renewed sense of hope filling the kitchen. "Now, tell me all about you. How is it going at the company?"

"Good."

Grace Lee cocked her head. "Your voice says the opposite."

Savannah sighed. "It's been tough, Mom. I'm doing my best, and Mac Barlow is helping me. Sort of."

Savannah had told her mother all about Mac back when he'd made his first offer, and kept her in the loop in the months since. They'd discussed Mac's offer on the business ad nauseam. Her mother had always said it was Savannah's choice, though Savannah could see that the thought of selling off Hillstrand Solar made her sad.

When Savannah told her mother that Mac had been working at Hillstrand for the past few days, Grace made a little face. "I thought he wanted to buy the company."

"I talked him into helping me for a week to get Hillstrand Solar back on track. He's had some great ideas to reduce waste and increase productivity." And already Savannah could see the changes helping. Not in huge ways, but she knew these little things were going to add up quickly to better cash flow and a smoother operation. And less stress for Savannah.

"So the company is doing well again?" her mother asked.

"It's getting there, but yes. I've got confidence in the future."

"And how about you? How are you doing?"

"I'm fine, Mom." Except for that little broken heart thing today. Okay, so maybe it wasn't so little, and maybe she was still sitting on the edge of a sob fest, but she'd get over that. Eventually.

"I meant how are you doing in the job?" Grace Lee's fingers intertwined with her daughter's. "I know your father asked you to take over, but really, honey, that was too much to put on you."

"It's fine. I'm fine."

"You say that enough times, I might even believe you." A soft smile stole across her mother's face. It was the kind of smile only a mother could have. The kind that said she understood and saw past all the little lies Savannah was telling herself. "You don't have to do this. We can find someone else to run your father's company, and let you do what makes you happy."

Savannah shook her head. "I promised Dad. It was the last thing he asked of me."

"I know that. But it was wrong of him to do so." Grace Lee put up a hand before Savannah could argue. "Your father was a wonderful man, and I loved him dearly. But he loved that company just as much, if not more. And he asked that of you, knowing it wasn't what you wanted. Because he knew you wouldn't say no."

"Mom, we had this conversation—"

"And we're having it again, because you keep dismissing me. I think your father always hoped you'd love that company as much as he did. But you don't."

Savannah let out a long sigh. "No. I don't."

Finally saying the words, admitting the truth, filled her with a relief that went bone deep. She'd gone too long pretending to be something she wasn't, and at least here, with the cookies and milk and her mother's kind, understanding eyes, she could be honest.

"Then stop doing it."

"It's not that simple, Mom. If I step down, who's going to run the company? And if no one runs it, then I have to sell to Mac Barlow. He's just going to split it up and sell it again. And all those people will lose their jobs."

Grace Lee sighed. Then her face wrinkled in a bittersweet smile. "I wish your father was here. He'd know what to do."

"Yes, he would." That was the irony in the moment, that the one person who knew what to do had died and, in doing so, had created this conundrum. Her father would step in and take over, doing whatever it took to keep Hillstrand running and keep his "family" employed. But when she looked at herself, had she really committed like she should have? She'd let herself get distracted by the beach house, by her own wants and needs. Instead of what was important. Savannah got to her feet and gave her mother a hug. "Thanks, Mom."

"For what?"

"For the cookies—" Savannah plucked three more off the plate "—and the advice. I know what to do now."

Grace Lee put a hand on Savannah's arm. "Do what makes you happy. That's what your father would really want."

Savannah just nodded instead of saying the truth.

Because if she did what made her happy, she'd head out to the beach house and immerse herself in sanding and painting and repairing. But that wasn't what her father would do, and that wasn't the way to bring a happy ending to everyone else. As for her own happy ending, it could wait.

Chapter Twelve

Mac wrestled with the bow tie, then finally gave up and tossed it on the counter. Stupid things. He'd never been able to master them. Too many loops. He was standing in a tux shop with his brothers at the tail end of the day, with only two days to go until Jack's wedding.

"Why am I wearing this thing again? I thought you were having a simple wedding."

Jack grinned. "I am. We just made you put on the monkey suit to torture you."

Luke laughed. "And it worked."

"Wait. I don't have to wear a tux on Saturday?" He glared at Jack, who just stood there grinning like the Cheshire cat.

"Nope. Just a white dress shirt and a dark pink tie. We're wearing khakis, but you can wear your jeans, for all me and Meri care. We just want people to have fun."

They'd dragged him off to the mall, shoved him into the dressing room at the rental shop and made him try on not just one, but two tuxes. "Has anyone told you two that you are terrible brothers?"

Luke grinned. "Every day. It's our special talent."

"Oh, it's a talent all right." Mac tugged off the tuxedo jacket, undid the shirt and pants, then handed them to the salesman. A few minutes later he was dressed in his own clothes and heading out of the store with his brothers.

His brothers. Two out of the three. He glanced at Jack and Luke, and knew he couldn't keep this secret another second. Given how Bobby had handled telling Della, maybe it was best that Mac delivered the news. Mac couldn't imagine his mother having to do it, and really, in the past few days he'd felt himself growing closer to his brothers, building that bond he had missed. Part of that was being honest with Jack and Luke, rather than keeping a secret. "How about we grab some dinner and a couple beers?" Mac said. "I'm buying."

"Then I'm coming," Luke said with a grin.

"Me, too." Jack climbed in his pickup truck, with Mac taking shotgun and Luke sliding into the backseat.

They drove across town to a greasy spoon roadside diner that served amazing burgers and a long list of beers. Sometimes, Mac realized, it didn't matter how much money he had—the cheapest, simplest food was better tasting than the fancy five-star meals. Just walking in the place brought back memories for Mac. He and his family had eaten there often when he was young—the boys always ordering the same giant double-patty cheeseburgers. Being here again filled Mac with a sense of belonging, of home. Comfort.

The Barlow boys tucked into a booth in the back corner, and once the three were on their second beers, Mac decided it was time.

He steepled his fingers on the table. "I have something I have to tell you guys."

"Uh-oh," Luke said, elbowing Jack. "That's Mac's serious face."

"Maybe he's about to tell us he's madly in love with Savannah." Jack grinned.

How had this conversation gotten turned around so quickly? "I am not—"

"He should be. Hell, I'd be in love with her if I wasn't already in love with Peyton." Luke turned to Jack, completely ignoring Mac. "She can swing a hammer and operate a chop saw. That screams *sexy* to me."

"If she watches football, too, she's a total keeper." Jack turned to Mac. "So tell us, is she a Seahawks or Packers fan?"

"Neither. Maybe. I don't know." Mac let out a gust. His brothers frustrated him no end. And they'd raised his hackles with all that talk about Savannah. Not that it should bother him what another man thought about her. But it did bother him. A lot. "That isn't what I wanted to talk about."

"Okay. Serious faces." Luke glanced at Jack, and the two of them mimicked Mac's pose with the stern looks and steepled fingers. "Shoot."

Now that the moment was here, Mac wasn't quite sure how to handle it. Maybe it was best to do it the way he had with Savannah—fast and without a lot of preamble. He took a deep breath. "Dad had an affair when he and Mama first got married, and it turns out we have another brother."

Jack's jaw dropped. Luke blinked. Neither of them said anything for a long time.

"Another…" Jack shook his head. "Wait, for real? You aren't kidding?"

"Have I ever been the jokester in the family?" Mac asked. "No, I'm not kidding."

"Whoa. That's unbelievable." Luke rubbed at his jaw. "Where is he? How did you find out?"

Mac told them what he knew about Colton, starting with the phone call from Uncle Tank, then finishing with the conversation he'd had with their half brother. "Dad told Mom last night."

"How'd that go?" Luke asked.

Mac arched a brow. "How do you think?"

Jack let out a low curse. "Damn. This is going to destroy her. We should go over there, make sure she's okay. Dad, too."

"Why do you care how Dad is doing?" Mac said. "He's the one who screwed up. The one who ruined everything."

"No, Mac. Dad made a *mistake*," Jack said. "A big one, I agree, but a mistake nonetheless. Everyone makes mistakes. It's the job of the family, of the people who love him, to accept and understand."

"And forgive," Luke added.

Mac scowled. What was wrong with his brothers? How could they be so quick to accept this and move on? "Doesn't this bother you guys?"

"Well, yeah, but what good does that do?" Jack said. "It's done. Colton is coming to town to meet us, and that's it. He's our half brother. The only right thing to do is to accept him."

"And what, welcome him with open arms?"

"Well, yeah." Jack glanced at Luke, who nodded agreement. "It's not Colton's fault he was the product of an affair. And unless he's just like you—" Jack gave Mac a grin "—I say we let him into the clan."

Mac stared at his brothers, dumbfounded. He'd expected them to be rocked by this news, yet instead they had decided to embrace it. It reminded him of what Savannah had said on the roof. *All those people facing their own challenges and triumphs. Some have harder challenges than others, some celebrate greater triumphs. But we're all in this together.*

It was the view that he took that would make a difference going forward. He could continue to be bitter and resent Colton's entrance into his life, or he could take the road his brothers had chosen and embrace the change. *We're all in this together.*

"Well, if you want to meet him, I'll give you his number," Mac said. "I know he really wants to meet you guys."

"Thanks," Jack said. "I'll give him a call today. Maybe he can stop by before the wedding. Meet everyone, since we'll all be in one place."

"Lord help you if he's just like Jack and me," Luke said with a grin. "Because then the teasing will commence—"

"And won't stop till you're crying uncle," Jack added. Then Jack reached out an arm, hauled Mac across the table and into a tight three-man Barlow hug. *We're all in this together.*

Yeah, they were. And that felt good. Damned good.

* * *

Friday morning, Savannah was at work before the sun rose. She opened the report Mac had prepared on making Hillstrand Solar a leaner operation, and started jotting notes on the steps she could take right now to implement the rest of the changes. But with every note she made, her steps seemed to weigh more and more, her heart growing heavier. It seemed as though she was slogging through mud.

Her mother's words kept echoing in her head. *Do what makes you happy. That's what your father would really want.*

A hundred times, Savannah glanced at the picture of her father on her desk, as if doing that would suddenly give her the right answers. Then she'd look around the company, at all the desks of all the people whose lives would be impacted if Hillstrand Solar were sold off, and that got her to go back to work. Regardless of what made her happy, these people were counting on her to do the right thing. Her father wouldn't have asked her to run the company if he didn't think she was the right person for the job. Would he?

So she kept on making lists and jotting notes and moving forward. This was her life, and she needed to accept that and make it work. Otherwise, these desks would be empty, these people unemployed and it would all be her fault.

A little after seven, Mac came into the office. He had an extra large coffee in one hand and shadows dusting his eyes. "Morning."

Concern for him filled her, even though she told herself she was still mad at him. But that didn't stop her from caring about him or worrying that he looked like he hadn't slept more than a few minutes. "Late night?"

"Out with my brothers. I forget they're younger than me. And more experienced at the drinking thing." Mac grimaced.

Savannah laughed and reached for her purse. She pulled out a bottle of aspirin and shook two pills into her palm. "Here. This should help."

"Thanks. The hotel didn't have any, and I forgot to stop at the pharmacy on my way over here." He knocked the aspirin back with the coffee, then sank into his chair. He rubbed at his temples, then took another sip of coffee and focused on her. "Okay, so what's on the agenda today?"

She pulled out one of her lists. In the corner of the page, she had unconsciously doodled a drawing of the beach house. Savannah grabbed a pen and scribbled it out, then refocused on the words before her. The entire page was filled already. Just looking at all those bulleted items made her feel overwhelmed, almost depressed. She was finally getting the company back on track, and it made her want to cry. What was wrong with her?

"We have a meeting with the bankers at lunch to renegotiate the loan terms," Savannah said. "And two of our suppliers are coming in this morning to discuss cost-cutting options. And we have a staff meeting after lunch. Plus we are supposed to do an inventory analysis and—"

"Okay, that's enough for now." Mac gave her a weak smile. "I'm a little off my game this morning."

"I can tell." She knew how that felt. Heck, she'd been feeling as if she'd been working with half a brain ever since she'd stepped into her father's role. "Well, if you want me to handle all this—"

He put up a hand. "Before we get started on everything today, I want to ask you something."

She drew in a deep breath and pretended she felt calm. "Okay, shoot."

"My brother's wedding is tomorrow afternoon. It's a casual event, nothing too fancy. But I wanted to see if you would like to go with me." Then he gave her a sheepish grin. "Also, my brothers told me that if I didn't invite you, they would tie you and me together and haul us to the wedding themselves."

He was inviting her to a wedding? After everything? "Do you really want me to go?"

His eyes met hers. "That's why I'm asking you."

But he wasn't asking anything more of her. Just to be his plus one. She wanted more, a lot more. She had ever since that first kiss, and didn't know how to turn off that feeling. To stop caring about him. "I don't know. I mean, we're working together and not really having a relationship, and it's a wedding and... It's probably not a good idea."

"You're probably right. It's probably a terrible idea. But I still want to go with you." Mac got to his feet and took her hand in his. She loved the feel of his palm against hers, of how easily they seemed to fit together. "In fact, you're probably right about a lot of things, including me. I am gun-shy when it comes to relationships. I can flip a business in five minutes flat, but when it comes to dating, and actually being with someone, being a hundred percent there, I...suck. I'm terrible at it. I'm so used to my world of numbers and reports, and then I met you."

"And what did that change?"

"Everything. Every damned thing I thought I knew." He ran his thumb over the back of her hand and let out a long breath. "Listen, Savannah, I'm leaving on Sunday. I have to go back to Boston, back to my business up there."

"What about Hillstrand Solar?" she asked, when she really wanted to ask, *What about us?*

"You have everything under control here, and you have my number if you need help. Or advice. Or someone to create a spreadsheet." He grinned.

"Wait. You don't want to buy the company?"

He shook his head. "I would buy it if it was for sale. But you've made it clear it's not. So now that we have that off the table, would you go to this wedding with me and have one spectacular day together, before I have to leave?"

It was just a date. A last date, at that. A way to say goodbye. Something in her heart broke a little. She considered saying no, that it would hurt too much to say goodbye after the last song played, but then she thought about the aching days ahead after Mac had roared out of her life, and decided she wanted one more day. One more day with his family, with him, with the man who had helped her rebuild a porch and rescued the baby birds and saved her father's dream. It would be enough. Wouldn't it? "Okay, I'll go with you, Mac."

A smile broke across Mac's face. "That's the best news I've had all day."

She laughed. "It's only seven in the morning."

"And at midnight, it'll still be the best news I've had all day." He leaned in and pressed a long, soft, sweet kiss to her lips. He drew back, holding her gaze for a moment. "Now, let's get to work. You have my business brains for the rest of the day. Use and abuse them."

They made their way through the list, getting far more accomplished than Savannah expected. When Mac was in work mode, he was efficient and organized, whipping through one task after another. He stepped back and let her handle most of the meetings, only intervening when she asked his advice. He was gearing her up to run Hillstrand Solar on her own, and clearly showing he trusted her to do so. Then why did the thought leave her feeling deflated?

After the meetings ended for the day, Savannah and Mac went down to the production floor. Several of the employees greeted Mac by name, pausing to talk to him from time to time. He kept the conversations brief, and mostly work related, but a few personal topics snuck in.

"You seem to know an awful lot about the employees," she said as they headed for the staircase doors, and then up the stairs toward the fifth floor. "You asked Jeremy about his new puppy and even looked at Betty's latest grandchild photos."

Mac shrugged. "What can I say? You rubbed off on me a little."

"I did? But I thought you said that wasting time talking to the employees was a waste of resources and money."

He stopped on the landing and looked over at her. "I did. But then I realized I was a little envious."

"Envious? Of what?"

"These employees love you, like you're part of their family. I didn't realize how much I missed feeling that way until I saw it here."

"You used to feel that way? At your company?"

"No," he said softly. "When I worked at the car lot. Charlie and his son treated me like one of their own. They were like my extended family."

"But you bought that lot, sold it off."

"Because Charlie wanted to retire and his son didn't want to run the business. Charlie was about as good with his retirement planning as he was with bookkeeping and other business tasks, so when I bought it from him, it gave him a nice sum to start his golden years." Mac shrugged. "I thought he'd be happy, and he was, for a long time. But then he called me one day and said he missed the old lot. Missed being able to go there and see his customers. He was too old to go back to work, but he wanted a purpose."

"So you bought it back." All the things she'd read in her research on him began to make sense. She could see now why he had bought back one company and sold the others. The car lot had meaning, and was a tie to people he cared about. Maybe, like the car lot, Hillstrand Solar meant more to Mac Barlow than even he realized. Maybe it had that personal connection that he tried so hard to avoid.

"I did buy the lot back," Mac said. "And hired a friend of mine from high school to run it. He lets Charlie come in and putter away, talk to the customers, sell a car or two, all he wants. Charlie's happy, just busy enough to give his days meaning, and the car lot goes on, bringing someone else a little money."

"That was a good thing to do, Mac."

"It's something I don't do enough of." He shook his head. "Not nearly enough."

"Well, maybe once you get back to Boston, you

can do things differently." Though just thinking about him leaving and being hundreds of miles away made her heart ache. Every time she thought she had Mac Barlow figured out, he added a new dimension, a new question. What he'd done for Charlie with his car lot…

That spoke of a man with a heart. A man who had relationships and maintained them. Not the cold, callous businessman he kept pretending he was.

She put a hand on his arm. "I think that was a really nice thing for you to do, Mac. And I'm glad you found a little of that here at Hillstrand Solar."

He gave her a bittersweet smile. "I'm going to miss this place."

This place. Not miss her. The words stung so much that she had to look away for a second. Every time she thought she had him figured out, he changed the equation. "I should probably go," she said, because it was easier to leave then ask the questions in her heart. "It's late and I have some work I want to get done before I go to sleep."

A moment later, she left. The briefcase beside her was full of reports and tasks, and for a second she debated leaving it all behind and heading to the beach house. But in the end, Savannah did what she had promised her father she would do, and went home to keep working. And pretend she wasn't in love with Mac Barlow.

Chapter Thirteen

The three Barlow boys stood in the front parlor of the Barlow family home, dressed in shirts and ties and khakis, looking as nervous and uncomfortable as they had when they were kids and their mother dressed them up for Easter church services. Bobby sat on the sofa, a little pale and about as relaxed as a steel rod. Della stood in the doorway, worrying her hands in her apron.

The doorbell rang. Mac started to head into the hall to answer it, when Bobby waved him off. "I'll get it, Mac."

The boys hung back with their mother while Bobby stepped into the hall and pulled open the front door. There was a long moment, a murmur of conversation, and then Bobby entered the room with a tall man beside him.

Colton Barlow had the same blue eyes as the other

Barlow men, but his hair was a few shades lighter and a little longer. He was maybe an inch taller than Mac, and looked, for all intents and purposes, like the kind of guy who would drop what he was doing to play a game of pickup with his friends. In other words, he looked like a hell of a nice guy. The kind of man Mac would be friends with under different circumstances.

Mac stepped forward. "Colton, I'm Mac. Nice to meet you finally."

Colton shook with him, a firm, friendly grip. A nervous smile wavered on his lips. "Same here."

Bobby watched his sons interact, a mixture of worry and panic on his face. He glanced at Della from time to time, but she remained silent.

Jack was next to welcome his half brother. "I'm Jack. The nicer one."

Colton laughed. "Nice to meet you."

Luke ambled over and stuck out a hand. "Don't believe anything the others tell you. I'm Luke, the charming and smart one."

Colton grinned. "I don't know. My mother might debate that with you." The room stilled. Colton shook his head. "Damn it. I'm sorry. I shouldn't have mentioned her. I know this is all…complicated and difficult, and I just made it more so."

"It's okay," Della said, pushing off from the doorway. She stood before Colton, her gaze skipping over his face as if she was making sure he had the familiar Barlow features. The entire room waited, silent, breathless. Then she gave a nod and a small smile.

"You're part of this family now," she said. "It's a messy family. We make mistakes, we forgive each other and then we move forward." Then she put out her arms and gave Colton a hug. "So let's move forward, Colton Barlow."

It was as if someone had deflated the tension with a giant pin. Within seconds, Luke and Jack were kidding with Colton, while Bobby asked him about his favorite sports teams. The conversation went in fits and starts, like a car having trouble going down the road, but after a while it began to smooth, and Colton settled in to the Barlow home as if he'd always been there.

Mac headed into the kitchen, ostensibly for a glass of water, but really for a moment to process everything that had happened, and to take a moment for gratitude that something that could have destroyed the family he loved had merely caused a hiccup. Not that every day going forward would be smooth and trouble-free, but it was off to a promising start.

Mac leaned against the counter, watching squirrels run around the yard. There was a sound behind him and he turned to see his father standing in the kitchen.

"We got any soda in the fridge?" Bobby asked.

Mac didn't understand why his father would ask him, since Bobby was the one who lived here, but then he realized it was his father's way of making small talk. Mac pulled open the fridge, then handed his dad a bottle of cola. "Big day today."

"Understatement of the year." Bobby screwed off the cap, but didn't drink. Instead, he let out a long breath and leaned against the counter beside Mac. "I should apologize to you."

"You don't need to apologize, Dad."

"Yeah, I do. To you, your mother, your brothers. I should have told you all a long time ago about Colton."

Mac rolled the glass between his palms. It had been

a long time since he'd stood this close to his father, and he didn't realize until just now how much he'd missed that. "How long have you known?"

"About ten years. Katherine had him and never said a word. Then one day she leaves me a voice mail at the shop, telling me she'd had my son, raised him herself with the man she married a year later. She gave me Colton's information in case I wanted to make contact." Bobby shook his head. "I called Tank, asked him to be sure she had money and whatever she needed for him. I'd send money to Tank, and he'd deliver it. Tank was mad as hell at me, because I dumped that on him and tried to forget she ever called. I was just so damned afraid."

"Of what?"

"Of losing all of you." Tears welled in Bobby's eyes. His big, strong father looked as weak as a new blade of grass. "Of all of you hating me. Especially you, Mac."

The words surprised Mac. Of everything his father could have said right now, that would have been last on the list. Their relationship had never been smooth, never as easy as the one Bobby had with Luke and Jack. A part of Mac had always envied that. "Why me especially?"

"You were the firstborn. I always made a big deal out of that. My oldest son, the one who's made me so proud. The leader of the pack, you know?" A watery smile crossed Bobby's face. "And I felt like I let you down as a dad."

"You didn't let me down, Dad." Mac's heart softened. All the years of arguments with his father, all the times they'd gone without speaking no longer mattered. He made a silent vow to get back to Stone Gap a lot more often. He saw the struggle in Bobby's face, the love and concern for his sons, his wife, and his determination to do the right thing by all of them. Mac's brothers were right. Their father had made a mistake, but not one that couldn't be forgiven or understood. "I'm the one who let *you* down."

"You? You've made me damned proud, Maxwell. You've gone a hundred times further than I ever dreamed."

Mac stood beside his father, a little taller than Bobby now, and decided it was past time they talked about the hard stuff. "Then why have you been so angry with me all these years?"

"Because I was selfish." Bobby picked at the label on the soda, tossing the pieces into the sink. "I wanted you to stay here, with me, and run that garage. I always imagined it would be me and all my boys working there. Then y'all went off and did your own things. Jack with the military, Luke with whatever made Luke happy at the time and you with your business, all the way up there in Boston."

"I never loved the garage like you did, Dad." Mac had hated the grease under his nails, the constant smell of motor oil, the endless tedium of replacing brake pads and rotating tires. To him there had been no challenge in that, nothing that had made him want to charge out of bed and get started on his day. In fact, now that Mac thought about it, he'd lost track of that challenge in the past couple years. He was caught in the same thing he'd tried to escape by leaving the garage—an endless tedium of buying and selling. This past week, when he'd taken the Hillstrand Solar problem and configured a new solution, had been one of the most exciting weeks he'd had in a long time.

"Not to mention we butted heads like two battering rams every day we worked together," his father added.

Mac chuckled. "That we did."

"We're a lot alike, you and me." Bobby took a sip of the soda, then put it on the counter between them. "We both like to run our own ships. Cast our own destinies. I never was much for working for someone else, which is why I opened the garage. Made my own hours, answered to no one but myself."

"That's me, too." Mac shook his head. The two of them, more alike than either of them had ever realized. No wonder they'd argued so much.

"I was wrong for giving you such a hard time about selling Charlie's car lot," Bobby said. "I always thought you did it just to make the bucks to get you out of town, away from here. Away from me."

Mac shook his head. "Dad, I—"

Bobby put up a hand. "But then I talked to Charlie the other day. I was down at the garage, helping Luke diagnose a sputtering Chevy, and Charlie walked on in. Haven't seen him in forever. I knew he worked in town, back at his old lot. I thought it was because he was so heartbroken about selling that he took a job for the new owner. Then he told me who owned it now." Bobby laughed wryly. "I never in a million years would have thought you'd do what you did."

Mac shrugged. "I was just trying to help him out."

"You didn't help him out. You gave him a purpose." Bobby studied the floor for a moment. "You know, I was mad at you for years. After Charlie sold the business to you and retired, he walked around this town like a broken man. He had nothing to occupy his days, nothing to do. I blamed you, told you that you ruined his life."

Mac sighed. He put the water glass beside his father's soda bottle, both drinks still virtually untouched. "I didn't know it would impact him that much when he sold. He was the one who offered the business to me, Dad. His son didn't want it, and Charlie wanted more time to spend with his wife."

"Did you know she died six months after he sold the business?"

Mac nodded. "Hell of a tragedy."

"But Charlie told me that in the end he was glad you bought it from him. He had six months with her, day in and day out, before she died. If he'd still owned the lot, he would have spent every day there and had to leave her alone. It gave him the money, but most of all, the time he needed."

"I'm glad." Neither of them had had a crystal ball at the time Mac bought that lot, but in the end, it had been a way of giving Charlie something he hadn't even known he needed. It wasn't a happy ending, but it wasn't as sad an ending as it could have been.

"You did a good thing, Mac," his father said, unwittingly echoing Savannah's words. Bobby put his hands on both of Mac's shoulders, and met his son's gaze. "A good thing."

"I just did what was right, Dad." He covered one of his father's hands with his own. "I learned that from you. You were always fair in business, always treated your customers right. And you ran it like family. Sometimes I get so caught up in the dollars and cents that I forget that."

Someone else he knew treated a business like a family. Savannah had insisted on that, made him promise not to let anyone go. The people who worked for her father loved her, welcomed her as one of their own. And welcomed him simply because he was with her. It had been a new feeling, Mac realized, walking through the doors of a shop and being seen as a friend, a helper, not a marauder out to make off with the spoils of his new purchase.

"Let me give you a piece of advice. Something I wish I'd learned a long time ago." Bobby glanced toward the front room, where his other sons and his wife were all laughing at something Colton had said. "There's no amount of money that can replace family. No mountain you can climb that will ever be more important than what you have at home. If you find a job that satisfies your soul and lets you take care of the people you care about, then that is enough."

"And that's something I think I lost along the way." Mac let out a long breath. Taking his father's advice would mean a lot of changes in Mac's life. Was he ready for that? "Anyway, it's about time we joined everyone else, don't you think?"

Bobby draped an arm around his oldest son's shoulders. "Yes, it is. Long past time."

The two of them went into the other room. Mac joined the circle of brothers, who were asking Colton about his work as a firefighter. Out of the corner of his eye, Mac saw his mother cross to his father.

She put out her hand, offering it in the space between them. He glanced down, his eyes welling again. She gave him a nod, and he slipped his hand into hers. Her knuckles whitened for a second when she gave his fingers a squeeze, but then the world righted itself again and the Barlow family healed.

Savannah tried on so many dresses, her bedroom looked like a dressing room at Macy's during prom season, with clothes piled on the bed, the floor, the chair. Finally, she settled on a pale yellow silk sundress that had a trail of white flowers running along the hem. She paired it with white wedge-heeled sandals, then curled her hair, leaving the tendrils down along her bare shoulders.

Precisely at one—not that she was surprised he was on time—Mac rang her doorbell. She grabbed a clutch, checked her reflection one final time, then took a deep breath and opened the door. "I'm ready."

But was she? For one last date with Mac? And then a goodbye?

"You look…amazing," he said. "Breathtaking."

Heat crept into her cheeks. "Thank you." He looked good, too, wearing khakis and a white button-down shirt he'd paired with a dark pink tie. Desire surged within her, but she tamped it down. This was just a date, nothing more. One afternoon together.

Mac took her hand as they headed down the stairs. She curled her fingers around his, the feeling bittersweet. He was leaving after this and she was clearly a masochist for agreeing to go to this wedding. Seeing him all day, knowing he was going to be gone in the morning, and that she was going to be left behind with a broken heart to run a business she didn't want to run—

Yes, masochist described her perfectly.

He strode down her walkway, then pulled open the

passenger's side door of a restored crimson-red Thunderbird. The car glistened in the sunlight, as perfect as the day it had rolled off the assembly line. "I thought this would be better than my motorcycle."

"It's a gorgeous car." She settled into the leather seat and buckled her seat belt. "It's in perfect condition, too."

"It's my brother Luke's latest project. Like he doesn't have his hands full already, raising a kid and planning a wedding." Mac shook his head, then turned to her with a grin on his face. "So do me a favor when we get to the wedding and tell him I bumped it in a parking lot."

She laughed. She loved how these brothers teased each other. She'd never had that growing up, and wondered if Mac knew how lucky he was to have so many great brothers. "You wouldn't do that to your brother, would you?"

"Hell, yes. They both tease me enough. It's about time I gave back a little of what I got." He put the car in gear and pulled away from the curb. The engine purred like a contented cat. "Let Luke sweat it for a second, then I'll tell him I made it all up."

"Deal." She cast a curious glance at Mac as they drove. "You seem different today. More...relaxed."

"Had a hell of a morning. But a good one." He told her about his half brother coming over to the house, the awkward beginning to that, then the conversation with his father about the car lot. The mending of old wounds, the start of new relationships. "Jack invited Colton to the wedding, and I think he's going to come. Uncle Tank and the cousins will be there, too, so it won't be a total shock for everyone to meet Colton. My mother was the one who surprised me the most, though."

"How so?"

"She forgave my dad. Welcomed Colton with a hug. I'm not saying it wasn't hard for her, because you could see in her face that it was, but she took the high road." Mac turned right, then switched lanes to avoid a puttering sedan in the right lane. "I asked her later why she did that, and she said, when you have something that has worked for thirty-five years, why throw it away over one broken piece? You fix what's wrong and you move on." Mac shook his head and smiled. "That's always been my mother's philosophy. Fix what doesn't work, and move on."

That was a good philosophy, Savannah thought. But one that sounded easier to say than to implement. So much seemed broken in Savannah's life right now, that she wasn't sure where to start to fix it or how to move on. "She sounds like an amazing woman."

"She is." Mac covered Savannah's hand with his own. Again, he was touching her, and she wondered if she was reading his signals wrong, or if it was simply that his good mood extended to a little hand-holding. "My mother's going to love you. So just be prepared. She'll probably invite you to Sunday dinner, which is the final stamp of approval for the Barlow family."

"That would be nice," Savannah said, then tugged her hand out of Mac's and twined her fingers together. She couldn't keep pretending everything was okay, because it hurt too much. And she couldn't keep letting him touch her, because it made her heart ache. "But you'll be gone Sunday, so there wouldn't really be much point in going, would there?"

The truth sat in the small interior of the old car, reminding them both that this trip to the wedding was a sort of undefined thing, not really a date, not really a goodbye. *Just a masochist-for-the-day thing.*

Mac moved his hand to the steering wheel. They stopped at a light, and Mac didn't say anything until it turned green and the car inched forward. "What if I didn't leave Sunday?"

She held her breath while she watched the houses of Stone Gap pass in a blur. "What are you saying, Mac?"

"That maybe I'd like to move my operation down here. Spend some more time with my family." He shrugged. "Get to know Colton. Rebuild things with my dad."

Once again, he hadn't mentioned her. Or anything between them. She swallowed hard and forced a smile to her face. "That would be great, I'm sure. For you and your family."

Not for her. Because if he moved to Stone Gap, she'd have to see him all the time, knowing that there was nothing between them. Nothing but one unforgettable afternoon, and a few tender moments. Moments that clearly mattered more to her than they ever had to him.

The curse of a small town was how close everything was. They had already reached the church parking lot, and that effectively ended the conversation. Maybe that was a good thing, because Savannah didn't want to hear again that the only reason Mac was staying was related to his business and family.

They got out of the car and walked inside the cozy church. Pink ribbon scalloped between the rows and twin tall vases of white flowers flanked the altar. There was an excited hum in the air among the guests, an anticipation of the special day to come.

Mac slipped a hand under her elbow and led her down the aisle, then up to a tall, beautiful woman with dark hair and warm eyes. "Savannah, I want you to meet my mother, Della. Mama, this is Savannah."

"Oh, my, you are so beautiful!" Della drew her into a warm hug. It was an instant connection, as if she had known Della all her life. "So nice to meet you."

Savannah liked her immediately. Della had a welcoming smile, and an easy way of talking. "It's wonderful to meet you, too. Mac has raved about you."

"That's because he's my favorite." Della placed a palm on Mac's cheek and gave him a wink. He shook his head and chuckled. "At least, he is when it's just him."

"That's a standing joke with me and my brothers," Mac explained. "We're all convinced we're each the favorite. But she tells us all the same thing."

"That way you're all nice to your mother all the time." She smiled at him with clear love for her oldest son. "Now shoo, Mac, and leave me here with Savannah. Jack is pacing up a storm in the back there, so go calm him down."

A moment later, Mac was in the back of the church with the rest of the groomsmen, and Savannah was sitting in a pew. She recognized a few people from town and chatted with them and Mac's mother while she waited for the wedding to start. She liked Mac's mother—liked his entire family, in fact. She would miss them when Mac was gone.

True to her word, Della invited Savannah to Sunday dinner, but Savannah demurred. She didn't have the heart to tell Della—or the strength to say it out loud—that this was just a one-day thing, and then Mac would be out of her life.

At exactly two, Jack stood at the front of the church,

flanked by his brothers. All of them wearing the same khakis, white shirt and pink ties. Jack's face was tight with nerves, his hands clasped in front of him. The organ music started, the people in the church rose and the back doors opened. Savannah turned and saw Meri pause for a second before she started down the aisle. The former beauty queen was resplendent in a simple white sheath that skimmed along her lithe frame. She had her blond hair partially up, and covered with a veil that trailed along the back of the dress. She clutched a bouquet of white daisies, tied with a thick pink ribbon.

As Meri made her way down the aisle, Savannah swiveled her attention back to Jack. His eyes were wide and the smile on his face could have lit up the moon. Love was etched on every inch of his face.

Her gaze skipped over to Mac, expecting to see him standing there stoic and calm, the quintessential best man, but instead, he was looking at Savannah. She couldn't read the look in his eyes, didn't want to speculate, because a part of her wanted so badly to see that same bright light of love on Mac's face. Instead, she turned away and focused only on the bride and groom.

Moments later, the wedding was over. Della was drying her tears; Bobby was pretending he hadn't cried. The guests made their way out of the church and across the street to a park that had been decorated for the reception. Lights had been strung between the trees, some tucked into hanging mason jars with flowers weaving in and around the power cords, making them seem as if they were part of the landscape. Long white tables were decorated with simple bud vases holding bright pink and white flowers. Wooden chairs flanked the tables, topped with big pink ribbon bows that trailed along the grass. A dance floor had been set up by the gazebo, which held a local three-piece band Savannah had heard before and really enjoyed. It was elegant and simple and perfect. For a second, Savannah wished this was her wedding.

Then she remembered she was here only as a guest of Mac's, not as his fianceé or his bride or anything more than…a friend, she supposed. No need to get wrapped up in any romantic fantasies.

But when the band launched into "At Last," and the bridal party began walking in, her heart leaped at the sight of Mac. Damn, he really was a handsome man. And when he smiled…she could hardly form a coherent thought.

He broke away from his brothers and crossed to her. Her heart stuttered in her chest, and for a second she forgot to breathe. "Did I tell you that you look incredible?"

She laughed. "Yes, several times."

"That's because you are so stunningly beautiful, I forget what I've said." He put out a hand. "Want to dance?"

She nodded, and he took her hand, then pulled her to the dance floor, where they mingled with Jack and Meri, Luke and Peyton, and their parents. Mac put his arm around her waist, clasped her opposite hand, then deftly waltzed her around the floor. The music flowed like a river between them, and their steps matched with little effort, as if she'd been born to dance with him. She caught the dark, deep scent of his cologne, and fought the urge to nestle her cheek against his. The heat from his body warmed hers, and the familiar stirrings of desire ran through her veins. She wanted this song to last forever, to stay exactly where she was, in Mac's arms.

God, what was wrong with her? This wasn't anything more than a simple dance. It didn't foreshadow anything longer than the three minutes the band played.

"How'd you get so good at dancing?" she asked, because if she didn't make some kind of conversation, she knew she was going to kiss his neck, kiss his lips…and that would lead to her wanting to do much, much more. "I don't think the Boy Scouts offered that as a badge."

He chuckled. "No, they didn't. When I was in college I enrolled in dance lessons for a couple months. Figured it was a good way to meet girls, then sweep them off their feet."

"And did it work?"

"I don't know," he said, then took her hand and spun her out and back into his chest. He leaned down until his cheek was beside hers. She inhaled the tempting scent of his cologne and closed her eyes for a moment. "Is it working?"

Hell, yes, it was. Everything he did worked on her, as if she was under a permanent Mac spell. "Are you trying to sweep me off my feet?"

He turned her back into his arms. She fitted against his chest, smooth and easy, like she had always been in that warm, inviting space. "Yes, I am."

Mac Barlow, the king of mixed messages. Damn him. Why couldn't he just come out and say what he was feeling? She stopped dancing and stepped back. "What is this about, Mac? Because last I checked, we were not a thing. We were a one-time mistake and nothing more."

"You think what happened at the beach house was a mistake?"

Before she could answer him, the song ended and the other dancers began to disperse. Just as Savannah was about to speak, a burly man came up behind Mac and wrapped him in a bear hug. "How's my favorite nephew?"

Mac turned around. "Uncle Tank! Good to see you."

"You, too."

Mac made the introductions, but Savannah barely listened. She was still mulling what had happened on the dance floor. Either way, a relationship with Mac wasn't possible. She lived here, worked here, and Mac's life was hundreds of miles away in Boston. He'd said maybe he would stay in Stone Gap, but none of that was definite, and right now, Savannah just wanted a clear, defined path. No more of his muddled messages.

Tank grinned at Mac. "Now, where's that crabby brother of mine?"

"Standing with Colton." Mac pointed across the dance floor, where his father stood beside a tall man who looked a lot like Mac, but had lighter hair.

"Well, I'll be," Tank said. "Miracles never cease to happen, do they?" Tank clapped Mac on the shoulder, then thumbed toward Bobby. "I'm going to go see your dad. I don't know why we stopped talking years ago, but I figure it's about time we started again. I'm not getting any younger, and he's not getting any handsomer."

Mac laughed, then said goodbye to his uncle, who crossed to Mac's father and Colton. He watched for a second as Bobby and Tank talked. Tank, in his usual burly, over-the-top style, reached out and drew Bobby into a one-armed hug and gave him a knuckle rub on the head. That was all it took to end the years apart.

"Brothers never change," Mac said. Then he turned back to Savannah. "Sorry about that." He put out his hands. "Want to dance again?"

She wanted nothing more than to step into his arms and be swept away. But her heart knew this wasn't going to last, and being here with him was as painful as severing a limb. She couldn't put on a happy face anymore, not when her heart was breaking. "No, Mac. I can't."

She walked off the dance floor and over to one of the tables. It wasn't time to eat yet, so most of the guests were still milling about. Savannah would have given anything for an excuse not to talk to Mac right now, not while her head and her heart were on this rollercoaster.

Mac pulled out the chair beside her. "We can sit if you're tired—"

"I mean I can't keep pretending that we have… something between us," she said, the pent-up words bursting from her in a rapid stream. "Because we don't. I thought we did, and when we made love, I thought we had something really special, but I was fooling myself."

Mac sighed and ran a hand through his hair. "What do you want from me, Savannah? I'm trying here."

"I know you are. But it's not enough. I want that." She pointed to Jack and Meri, their faces close together as they danced. Love practically radiated from their pores, filled every inch of space between them. "I want someone whose face lights up like the sun when he looks at me. Someone who isn't afraid to risk everything for the slim chance of finding that kind of happiness. I want it all, Mac, and I won't settle for less."

"Savannah—"

She put up a hand. "Please, don't say anything. I'm just going to go. I have work to do, and…I'm sorry. Give Jack and Meri my apologies."

Then she turned on her heel and fled the ball like Cinderella at midnight. Except there was no prince coming after her, and no fairy godmother to grant her heart's desire. Just a rotting pumpkin stuffed with realities that she'd waited too long to face.

Mac stayed at the wedding for another hour, pretending to be social, but his mind lingered on Savannah. He watched his brothers with the women they loved, and jealousy ran through him like a fiery river. They had taken the leap, risked their hearts, changed their lives, and this was where they got—

Blissfully happy.

Whereas he was standing here alone with a mental plan to ride back to Boston tomorrow, back to the work he thought had made him happy. But that was all it was—work, not a life.

He looked around the wedding. Meri was laughing at something Peyton had said, the two women watching the men they loved out of the corner of their eyes. Colton was sitting at a table with several of the cousins, engaged in some deep conversation about something sports related, given the snippets Mac could overhear. His mother, father and Uncle Tank surrounded the punch bowl, laughing and talking as if no time had passed between them. This was his family, for all its warts and imperfections, and he loved them. A part of him didn't want to leave for Boston at all in the morn-

ing. He thought again about what he had said to Savannah in the car.

What if I didn't leave?

What if he did stay? Moved his business here, like
he'd mentioned. It would be harder to operate from
Stone Gap, because they would be so far from the central hubs where most of the corporate world operated,
but it wouldn't be impossible.

The bigger problem was this growing sense of dis-
satisfaction in Mac's chest. He didn't want to go back
to Boston, because he didn't want to go back to the
status quo. He thought of the businesses he had yet to
sell, the few he'd been keeping on the backburner, ostensibly as part of a bigger package to sell when com-
bined with Hillstrand Solar. Maybe there was another
option, one that would give him a renewed purpose,
a bigger challenge. An idea that had been percolating
in his head all week, spurred by something Savannah
had said, began to coalesce.

Either way, there was something else, something
more important he needed to do than anything work
related. Mac crossed to Jack, who was standing by the
cake with Luke. "Hey, brother, I'm going to go."

"What? The reception isn't over yet."

"I know, but I have—"

"If you say work to do," Jack said, wagging a finger
at him, "I will tie you to a stake and keep you here until
the very last grain of rice has been thrown."

Mac chuckled. "No, not work. I have to go see Savannah."

Jack glanced around. "Did she leave?"

Even the memory of her running out earlier stung
him. He should have handled that better. Hell, he

should have handled everything this week better. She was right about him. When it came to work he could do his job with his eyes closed, but when it came to a relationship he was all thumbs. "Yeah."

"What'd you do this time?" Luke asked.

"Hey, maybe I didn't do anything." At Luke's raised brow, Mac let out a sigh. "Okay, she said she wanted forever, and I told her all I wanted was something temporary."

Luke smacked Mac in the head. "How the hell do you function in the world with so few brain cells?"

"Hey!" Mac rubbed at the spot. "That was a little unnecessary, don't you think?"

"Luke is right," Jack said. "Savannah Hillstrand is a permanent girl. Any fool could see that. And any man who lets her get away doesn't deserve her."

"You know," Luke said to Jack in a conspiratorial whisper. "There is a single Barlow brother left. We could give Colton—"

"Don't you dare say it." Mac glared at his brother.

Jack elbowed Luke. "Told you he was in love with her."

In love with her? After a few days? That was impossible. No, Mac was merely worried about her. Nothing more. He wanted to make sure she was okay. And that she had everything she needed for running the company. That was all.

Except the memory of her in his arms when they danced lingered. He heard the band shift into another slow song and swore his arms ached without Savannah.

"Too bad Mac didn't get the memo about being in love, Jack." Luke grinned, then put a hand on Mac's shoulder and turned him toward the exit. "Now, go get her. But don't drive too fast. That car—"

"Already has a baseball-sized dent," Mac said, then laughed as Luke's face went pale. "I'm joking. I treated it with kid gloves." He gave his brother a gentle slug, then headed out of the park and back to the Thunderbird. It roared to life, and he put it in gear, then hit the road.

Chapter Fourteen

Savannah sat on the porch of the beach house in the dress she had worn to the wedding and told herself she was happy, even as tears streamed down her face. One last project, she decided, then she would button up the beach house for the rest of the season, heck, the rest of forever, while she went to work and concentrated solely on the company. That was her life, and where she would pour her energies.

Even if the thought of doing so filled her with a sadness that ran all the way to her toes.

She pulled her hammer and some nails out of the trunk of her car, then got some scrap wood out of the shed. She tucked the hammer into her tool belt, leaving her hands free to get the birdhouse out of its temporary home on the shed and bring it back across the yard to reinstall it where it belonged.

But as she picked up the birdhouse, she realized there was no sound coming from inside the box. Not a chirp, not a flutter. Nothing. Savannah held her breath, then peeked inside. A yawning cavern of darkness and a mounded circle of twigs, but no birds.

The baby birds had moved on. They'd finished learning to fly and had left the nest. For some reason that made her cry all over again.

That was how Mac found her, sitting on the ground beside the broken pole that used to hold the birdhouse, the empty wooden box in her hands, while tears streamed down her face. A complete, blubbering mess over a bunch of baby birds.

He knelt down beside her, his face filled with concern. She was glad he was there and mad at him at the same time. She wanted him to leave, wanted him to stay. Wanted him to quit getting her hopes up, then breaking her heart.

"What's wrong, Savannah?"

"They're gone. They left." That made her cry again. God, she was a blathering idiot. What was wrong with her? It was just an empty birdhouse.

But no, it was something more. It was the realization that her father was gone, that he would never be back. Never again put an arm around her shoulders and tell her she could do anything she set her mind to. Never again teach her how to swim or ride a bike or surprise her with a gag gift at Christmas. He was gone, and the baby birds were gone, and her life was not at all what she had wanted it to be, and there was nothing she could do to change that.

"I'll never see them again," she said.

"The birds? Oh, but that's natural. And they'll come

back," he said. "You told me that. Maybe not tomorrow, but next season. And if you put up a bird feeder, they'll come to eat, every day, and you can see them when you are here."

"I won't be here. I'll be at work." She shook her head and put the birdhouse on the ground. "I'm closing up the house. I don't know when I'm coming back to it."

"But I thought you wanted to finish fixing it."

She spun toward him. God, didn't he understand? Didn't he see? "I can't do both, Mac. I can't run the business and fix the house and save those birds and make everything all right. I can only do one thing, and that's keep Hillstrand Solar running." Her voice caught and her throat ached. "I can't let him down. I just can't."

Promise me.

She'd tried so hard to keep that promise. Given that business every bit of herself. And, yes, it was working, but she was so desperately unhappy. The tool belt weighed down her waist, a heavy reminder that what made her happy was closed off to her. She couldn't have both. She had to choose, and the only right choice was the one she had promised she'd make.

Mac settled on the grass beside her. "You aren't letting your father down, Savannah."

"Yes, I am. I'm not doing any of the things I promised, or at least I'm not doing them well. The business is limping along, yes, and it's getting better but it needs…" She shook her head and choked back a sob. "It needs someone who knows what to do. Someone who has passion for it. Who loves being there every day."

"And you don't?"

She bit her lip. The tears stung her eyes, even when

she swiped them away. The truth was there, waiting for her to admit it. But if she did, then what? What would happen to her father's company? To the promise she had made?

Mac caught a tear on his finger and whisked it away. "What are you so afraid of, Savannah?"

"I'm not afraid." But she was. Deep in her bones terrified that she was making the wrong choice, but she saw no other alternative.

"Then why won't you let go?"

Let go and what? Sell the business to Mac, so he could scatter the pieces to the four corners of the world? "Because I made a promise. I told him I would keep it running. I wouldn't let the company die like he did."

"That doesn't mean you have to do it yourself."

She turned toward Mac. His words settled into her. She *didn't* have to do it herself. All these months, she'd thought the promise she made had meant that she, and she alone, would helm Hillstrand Solar. She would shoulder her father's responsibilities, just as he had. "But if I don't, who will?"

"Me."

She scoffed and shook her head. "You just want to sell it. And all those people will lose their jobs. And then my father's dream will die."

"Trust me, Savannah." He took her hand in both of his. "Trust me."

She wanted to, so badly. Wanted to let Mac be the answer to the company's problems. Wanted to believe what she felt in his hands, in her heart. "What if you take it over, and you run it for a few weeks, then you get tired of being in one place, running one business, and you sell it?"

"I won't do anything without talking to you first. It's still your company, yours and your mother's, and nothing will happen without you giving it the okay. Plus, I realized today that you were right, the companies I've been holding on to would work well with Hillstrand. As a cohesive unit, not one big package to sell. I could expand Hillstrand's reach, create an entire green building enterprise. Take what your father did and give it wings, essentially."

She could see the excitement in Mac's face, the anticipation for this new challenge. "I like that. I think he'd like it, too."

Mac tipped her chin until she was looking at him. With his thumb he brushed away the tears lingering on her cheeks. "Let me do that, and you do what you love instead. Fix up this house. Then fix up another one. I've seen you at work, when we installed the panels, fixed that porch, and I've seen the results of your efforts. That's where your passion is, Savannah. Not in that office."

He was right, but admitting that scared the pants off her. "I...I don't know."

He let her go, then put his hands on his knees and looked out at the ocean lapping gently at the sandy shore. Seagulls cried as they dived for their dinner and fought over scraps. A slight breeze danced in the trees and tickled the grass. "You're afraid. And I get that. It can be hard to let go of the tether that's holding you in place."

"It's not a tether. It's a promise."

"No, you're wrong." He let out a long breath. "You never went a hundred percent with your remodeling and reconstruction company. You'd fix a house, then go back and work for your dad for a little while. Fix another, work again at the plant. It wasn't a hobby, exactly, but it wasn't a full-time business, either."

"I had so many responsibilities and..." Her voice trailed off. *What are you afraid of?* Mac was right. She had been afraid. Terrified even. She'd yo-yoed for years between remodeling and Hillstrand Solar, never fully committing to either. No wonder her father had put the business in her hands. She realized now that he had done it not to make her run the company for him, but to force her to make a choice, make a decision. "You're right. I did use the company like a safety net. I saw how much my father struggled in his early years, the times when he almost lost everything—when our family almost lost our home—and I worried that if I went into business full-time, I could end up that way, too."

"That's always a possibility. But life is about risk." He took her hands and raised her until she stood toe to toe with him. "I've made a career out of taking risks. And I've been damned good at it. Until I met you."

She scoffed. "Running Hillstrand Solar for a week wasn't much of a risk."

"I'm not talking about the business." His thumbs ran over the backs of her hands, sending a little spark through Savannah's veins. "I'm talking about falling in love with you."

She opened her mouth. Closed it again. "You're... Wait...what?"

"I fell in love with you the second I saw you with that tool belt, ripping up those floorboards like a woman on a mission." He fingered the tool belt now, slung low on her hips, hanging over her dress. "I don't think there is another woman in the world who can make this look as sexy as you do."

He was in love with her? "But you said yourself, this was only temporary."

"Because I'm an idiot. As my brothers lovingly pointed out to me today." He rubbed at his temple. "You make me want to be more than I've ever been before. Make me want to try harder, and that, in turn, makes me scared as hell that I'm going to screw up."

"You?" She shook her head. "You're like King Midas. Everything you touch turns to gold."

"But you know what happened to King Midas, right? He was cursed and when he touched the things he loved, they turned to gold and he lost them." Mac's ocean-blue eyes met hers. She saw a steadiness in his gaze, an honesty. "Because he was too focused on the money, instead of what was important."

She wanted to believe him with every ounce of her soul, but still she hesitated, afraid of this, too. Of taking yet another leap into the unknown. "And what was that?"

"That the people in your life matter more than anything you can achieve. You do that, Savannah, with every single person at your father's company." Mac smiled. "You know their grandkids' names, remember their birthdays, and they, in turn, love you like you're their own daughter. You walk into that building, and it's a family."

She shrugged. "It's how my father ran things. I guess I learned that from him."

"And I missed that lesson somewhere along the way."

"No, you didn't, Mac." She smiled. "You did it with

Charlie and his car lot. With the way you connected with the employees that worked for my father."

"But not with you." He brushed the bangs off her forehead, then let his touch linger along her jaw. She leaned into that touch, craving it, craving him. "Every time we got close, I shut the door and retreated to my own safety net. Work."

She laughed a little. "How is that the two of us do the same thing? Retreat into what we know instead of taking a leap?"

"Because those leaps are scary. You could fall. Get hurt."

She glanced down at the birdhouse. Three baby birds had been in there, as fragile as twigs, but now they were somewhere else, gathering their own food, taking off under their own power. "Just like the baby birds did. But every year, they take the leap."

"They do. And they survive and return to start their own families."

"It's scary."

"It is. But I watched my brother get married today to the woman he loves, and I realized that I was missing out. That I could accumulate companies and wealth and motorcycles, and none of it mattered at the end of the day when I came home to an empty house. That's why I work so much, because when I'm sitting at the computer, I don't notice that there is no one sitting beside me." He drew in a breath and clasped her hands tighter. "The only person I want sitting beside me from this day forward, is you."

She looked into his eyes and saw what she had seen in Jack's face. She saw a love that spilled out of Mac, a love for her. It was the same way she felt when she looked at him. As if her heart was pouring out of her with every breath. "I fell in love with you when you ran out into the storm to rescue the birds. You were so…gentle and worried and sweet. And I ran out after you because I wanted to tell you how I felt, but then I got scared and I didn't say a word."

"Then I ruined our afternoon together by talking about work." He cradled her jaw, and traced her lip with his finger. "If you can put up with a reformed workaholic who still might need to read a *Relationships for Dummies* book, then I'd really like to make you a contract offer."

She laughed. "A contract offer?"

"It's the most important deal I've ever put on the table." He dropped to one knee and kept hold of her left hand. "Will you marry me, Savannah Hillstrand?"

The fear loomed in her chest again. "Marry you? But we haven't known each other that long and…"

"And it's a risk. A leap into the unknown. But I can't think of anyone else I'd rather make that leap with than you."

She clasped his hand, and thought how good it felt against hers, how right. "It's going to be scary."

"Then let's make sure we build a strong foundation. Starting right now." He picked up the birdhouse and handed it to her. "Those birds are going to need some place to start a family next year."

"They will." A smile filled her face, and filled her heart. "They will indeed."

Together, they fastened the birdhouse on top of the pole. Mac held the new bracing in place while Savannah hammered the nails into the wood. Then they stepped back and assessed their work. The birdhouse sat securely in its perch again, ready for a new chapter.

"It should hold for a good long time," she said.

"That's what I'm counting on." He curled his hand around hers, and together they went down to the beach, where the tide washed in and out, starting things fresh over and over again.

There was a sound behind them and Savannah turned at the same time Mac turned, cheek to cheek again, just like they had that first day on the beach. This time she leaned into him, let her cheek touch his. "Look at the birdhouse," she whispered.

One of the bluebirds stood at the entrance to the birdhouse, peering inside. It hopped out, then onto the roof and lingered there, as if saying, *This is mine. This is where I will start my new life.*

"There's going to be a new family there next year," he said.

Savannah raised her gaze to the beach house, and in her mind she saw the changes that would come in the next twelve months. The new paint, the new floors and walls. And the new future with Mac at her side. "Yes, there is. And I can't wait."

He drew her into his arms and brought his lips to hers. "Neither can I," he whispered, then kissed Savannah as the sun set and the world was washed with gold.

* * * * *

Don't miss the next installment in
New York Times *bestselling author*
Shirley Jump's series
THE BARLOW BROTHERS.

Sadie looked down at her hands, damp hair hanging forward across her cheek.

"I'm not the same girl you asked that question of all those years ago," she said, her voice soft.

"You think I don't know that?" he asked. "Look at me, Sadie." She did as he asked, and Dylan took a long moment just absorbing everything she was now. Slowly, obviously, he looked over every inch of her, from her hair—shorter now than when they'd met by a good foot—down over her body, past every added curve or line, every soft patch and every muscle, all the way to her feet.

Did she really not know? Not realize how much she'd grown up since then—and how every year had only made her a better person? Who would want the twenty-year-old Sadie compared to the one who sat before him now?

"You are so much more now than you were then," he murmured, knowing she'd hear him anyway. "You're stronger, more beautiful, more alive. . .more than I ever dreamed any woman could be."

A PROPOSAL
WORTH MILLIONS

BY
SOPHIE PEMBROKE

Published in Great Britain 2015
by Mills & Boon, an imprint of Harlequin (UK) Limited,
Eton House, 18-24 Paradise Road, Richmond, Surrey, TW9 1SR

© 2015 Sophie Pembroke

ISBN: 978-0-263-25172-2

23-1015

Harlequin (UK) Limited's policy is to use papers that are natural, renewable and recyclable products and made from wood grown in sustainable forests. The logging and manufacturing processes conform to the legal environmental regulations of the country of origin.

Printed and bound in Spain
by CPI, Barcelona

Sophie Pembroke has been reading and writing romance ever since she read her first Mills & Boon® romance at university, so getting to write them for a living is a dream come true!

Sophie lives in a little Hertfordshire market town in the UK with her scientist husband and her incredibly imaginative six-year-old daughter. She writes stories about friends, family and falling in love, usually while drinking too much tea and eating homemade cakes. She also keeps a blog at www.sophiepembroke.com.

For Pete and Kate, for a truly wonderful,
memorable holiday.

CHAPTER ONE

SADIE SULLIVAN BLINKED into the sunshine and waved goodbye to the rental car pulling away from the Azure Hotel. If she squinted, she could just make out Finn's tiny face pressed up against the rear window, and his little hand waving back. Her father, in the driver's seat, was obviously concentrating on the road, but Sadie spotted the glint of her mother's ash-blonde hair beside Finn, and knew she'd be holding him in place, making sure his seat belt was secure.

He was in good hands. She had to remember that. Even if her heart ached at the thought of being separated from her little boy.

The car turned the last corner at the end of the drive and disappeared out of sight, behind the row of juniper trees, onto the road that led up the coast then back inland towards the main roads and Izmir airport. Sadie sucked in a deep breath and wiped the back of her hand across her eyes, quickly, in case anyone was watching. The last thing she needed right now was talk about the boss breaking down in tears. Professionalism, that was the key.

'It's one week, Sullivan,' she muttered to herself. 'Get over yourself. In seven days you'll be in England with him, getting ready to bring him back. Enjoy the peace until then.'

Except next time it might be for longer. A whole term, even. And what if he didn't want to come home to her in the holidays? No, she wasn't thinking about that. Whatever her father said about British schools, about having family around, Finn's place was with her. The local schools were great, and Finn's Turkish was really coming along. He'd be fine.

She swallowed, and stepped back into the coolness of the Azure lobby. Even in late September Kuşadası still enjoyed the warmth of the Turkish climate. In a few weeks, she knew, the locals would start pulling on sweaters and mumbling about the chill in the air—while she, and the few remaining tourists in town at the end of the season, would still be down at the beach, enjoying the sun.

This time next year Finn would have started school. The only question left to answer definitively was, where?

'Did Finn and your parents leave for the airport okay?' Esma asked, looking up from the reception desk, her long red nails still resting on her keyboard.

Sadie nodded, not trusting herself to speak just yet.

'He's so excited about having a holiday with his grandparents,' Sadie's second in command carried on, regardless. 'And the timing is just perfect, too.'

Sadie kept nodding. Then she blinked. 'It is?'

Esma tilted her head to study her, and Sadie tried to pull herself into her best boss posture and expression. She had the suit, the hair, the make-up—all the things she usually hid behind when she didn't quite know what to do. That armour had got her through her husband's death, through taking on his ridiculously ambitious business project that she didn't have the first clue about. Why on earth would it fail her now, at the prospect of a mere week without her son?

It obviously worked, because Esma shrugged and pushed the work diary across the reception desk towards her.

'I just meant with that potential investor arriving this week. Without Finn to worry about, you will have more time to spend winning him over, yes?'

'Yes, of course,' Sadie responded automatically, her eyes fixed on the red letters spelling 'Investor Visit' written across the next five days. How could she have forgotten?

Her priority for the week. The only thing she had time to worry about, at all, was this investor and all his lovely money.

She hadn't wanted to resort to outside help, but things were getting beyond desperate, even if only she and Neal knew the true extent of the Azure's problems. When their hunt for local investors had failed, Neal had suggested seeking investment from abroad—with similar results. But he'd had a last-chance possibility at the ready when she'd asked where on earth they went next. A business acquaintance, he'd said, who had interests in the hotel industry, and might just be interested enough to send an employee over to check out the Azure.

Sadie had been doubtful, but she was also running out of options. She trusted Neal—he was more than her accountant, he had been one of her late husband Adem's best friends. And she had no doubt that Neal would have asked his acquaintance to go easy on her. Everyone always did.

She's a widow. They always shook their head sadly as they said the word 'widow'. *Lost her husband in a car crash, tragically young.*

These days, that was often the only thing people knew about her at all. Well, that and the fact that she was sad-

dled with a white elephant of a hotel renovation that
might never be finished at the rate things were going.

Sadie was almost sure there used to be more to know
about her once.

Behind the reception desk Esma's eyes were wide and
worried, so Sadie reinforced her 'in control of everything' smile. She had to shake off the negativity. She
loved the Azure, just like Adem had, and just like Finn
did. It was her home, and she would make it a success—
one way or another.

She'd made promises. Commitments. And she had
every intention of fulfilling them.

She just might have to accept a little help along the way.

'Did Neal call with the name of the guy the company
is sending over yet?' Sadie asked. 'And we have a car
collecting him from the airport, correct?'

'Yes, at four o'clock,' Esma confirmed. 'I sent Alim.'

'Good.' Alim was reliable, and his English was great—
far better than her Turkish, even after four years of living in the country and working hard to learn. Finn was
a much quicker study than her, it turned out.

And just like that, she'd forgotten all her business worries again and was back to fretting about her son. Part of
being a mother, she supposed.

She checked her watch. It was already gone five.

'Has Alim texted to say they're on their way?' Sadie
asked.

'Almost an hour ago. They should be here any moment.' Esma bit her lip. 'It will all be fine, Sadie,' she
added after a moment. But it sounded more like a question than reassurance.

Sadie smiled broadly. 'Of course it will! I'm certain of
it,' she lied. Then something occurred to her. Esma had
only answered half her question. 'And the name?' she

pressed. 'Neal gave it to you, yes?' How embarrassing would it be to greet this guy with no idea what to call him?

Behind the desk, Esma squirmed, shuffling an irrelevant stack of papers between her hands, her gaze fixed firmly on her nails. Something heavy settled in Sadie's stomach at the sight. Something heavier even than her guilt about Finn being away all week. Something more like the magnitude of the fears and nightmares that kept her awake at night, wondering how on earth she would achieve everything she'd promised her husband and son.

'Esma? What's his name?'

Her face pale, Esma finally looked up to meet Sadie's gaze. 'Neal said it might be better if you…' She trailed off.

'If I what?' Sadie asked. 'Didn't know the name of the person who might hold the future of this place in his hands? Why on earth would he—? Unless…'

Behind her, she heard the swoosh of the automatic doors and the clunk of a heavy suitcase on the marble floors. Her heart beat in double time, and that heavy feeling spread up through her chest, constricting her breathing and threatening her poor, laboured heart.

Sadie turned, and suddenly it was thirteen years ago. She could almost sense Adem beside her—younger, more nervous, but alive—hopping from foot to foot as he introduced his new girlfriend to his two best friends. Neal Stephens and Dylan Jacobs.

Except Adem was dead, Neal was in England—where she couldn't yell at him yet—and only Dylan stood in the lobby of her hotel. Dylan, who was supposed to be thousands of miles away in Australia, where he belonged. Instead, he was at the Azure, as self-assured and cocky as ever. And every inch as handsome.

No wonder Neal hadn't told her. She'd have been on

the first flight out with Finn, and he knew it. He might not know everything, but Neal had to at least have noticed that she'd made a concerted effort *not* to see Dylan since the funeral.

But now she couldn't run. She had commitments to keep—and she needed Dylan Jacobs of all people to help her do that.

Sadie plastered on a smile, stepped forward, and held out a hand that only shook a bit.

'Dylan! How wonderful to see you again,' she said, and prayed it didn't sound like the lie it was.

Dylan's chest tightened automatically at the sight of her. An hour's drive from the airport and hours on the plane before that, and he still wasn't ready. In fact, as he stepped forward to take Sadie's hand he realised he might never be ready. Not for this.

Five minutes ago he'd been moments away from calling the whole visit off. Sitting in the car, as they'd come up the long, winding hotel driveway, he'd almost told the driver to turn around and take him back to the airport. That the whole trip was a mistake.

But Dylan Jacobs never shied away from an opportunity. And, besides, it was Sadie. So instead he'd checked his phone again—emails first, then messages, then voicemails then other alerts—his habitual order. Anything to distract him from thinking about Sadie.

He hadn't seen her in two years. Two long years since the funeral. Hadn't even heard a peep from her—let alone a response to his card, telling her to call, if she ever needed anything.

And now, apparently, she needed everything and she was calling in that promise.

He just wished she'd done it in person, instead of via

Neal. Wished he could have spoken to her, heard her voice, sensed her mood.

Wished he had a better idea what he was walking into here.

She's coping, Neal had said. *Better than a lot of people would. But...she lost Adem, Dyl. Of course she's not the same. And she needs you. The Azure is all she has left of her husband, and you can help her save it.*

So in a rapid flurry of emails Dylan had been booked on the next plane into Izmir and now there he was. At Adem's dream hotel. With Adem's dream woman.

Glancing at the sign above the hotel doors, Dylan had winced at the name. The Azure. Why did it have to be that name? There were a hundred perfectly decent generic hotel names on offer. Why on earth had Adem picked that one?

A half-forgotten memory had flashed through his brain. Adem's excited phone call, telling him all about his next big project, how he and Sadie were moving to Turkey to save some ramshackle old hotel that had once belonged to his Turkish mother's grandfather or something. What he remembered most was the sharp sting that had hit his chest at the name—and the utter irrationality of it.

It's just a name. It doesn't mean anything, he'd reminded himself.

But symbolism was a bitch, and to Dylan the Azure would always mean loss. The loss of his father, his freedom, so many years ago. Loss of hope. Lost chances and opportunities.

Except maybe, just maybe, this time it could be different. So much had changed... And this was a different hotel, thousands of miles and more than two decades away from the Azure where the man who had raised him had walked out on his entire family and never looked back.

This was Sadie's hotel now.

He'd never told Adem the whole story of his father, and had certainly never mentioned the name of the hotel. If he had, his friend would probably have changed it, just to make Dylan feel more comfortable. That was the sort of man Adem had been, the good, caring, thoughtful sort.

The sort of man who had deserved the love of a woman like Sadie.

Unbidden, images of the last time he'd seen her had filled Dylan's vision. Dressed all in black, instead of the bright colours she'd always loved, standing beside that coffin in a cold, rainy, English graveyard. She'd been gripping her tiny son's hand, he remembered, and he'd known instinctively that if she'd had her way Finn wouldn't have been there, wouldn't have had to witness any of it. He'd wondered who had insisted he take part, and how lost Sadie must have been to let them win.

Lost. That was the right word for it. She'd looked small and tired and sad...but most of all she'd looked lost. As if without Adem she'd had no compass any more, no path.

It had broken Dylan's heart to see her that way. But standing outside her hotel...he had just wondered who she would be now.

And then it was time to find out.

Heart racing, he climbed the steps to the hotel entrance and let the automatic doors sweep back to allow him in. He squinted in the relative cool darkness of the lobby, compared to the bright sunlight outside. But when his vision cleared the first thing he saw was Sadie— standing at the reception desk, her back turned to him so he couldn't make out her face. But there was never any doubt in his mind that it was her, despite the plain grey suit and shorter hair.

So many memories were buttoned up in that suit—of the friend he'd lost and the woman he'd never even had a chance with—that his chest tightened just at the sight of her.

He braced himself as she turned, but it wasn't enough. Nowhere near enough to prepare him for the shock and horror that flashed across her familiar face, before she threw up a pleasant, smiling mask to cover it.

She didn't know I was coming. Oh, he was going to *kill* Neal. Painfully, and probably slowly.

Reflex carried him through the moment, the old defences leaping back into place as she smiled and held out her hand. Her hand. Like they really were new business acquaintances, instead of old friends.

'Dylan! How wonderful to see you again,' she said, still smiling through the obvious lie. And Dylan wished that, for once, he'd ignored the opportunity and headed back to the airport like his gut had told him to.

But it was too late now.

Ignoring the sting of her lie, Dylan took her cool fingers between his own, tugging her closer until he could wrap his other arm around her slim waist, his fingers sliding up from hers to circle her wrist and keep her close. Just the touch of her sent his senses into overdrive, and he swallowed hard before speaking.

'It's so good to see you, Sadie.' And that, at least, was the truth. Dylan could feel his world move back into balance at the sight of her and the feel of her in his arms… well, it just told him what he'd known for years. That the feelings for his best friend's girl he'd tried so hard to bury had never been hidden all that deep at all.

He really was going to kill Neal for this.

Sadie pulled back, still smiling, apparently unaware of how his world had just shifted alignment again, the same way it had thirteen years ago when Adem had said, 'Dyl, this is Sadie. She's…special,' and Sadie's cheeks had turned pink as she'd smiled.

A real smile, that had been. Not at all like the one she gave him now.

'Let's get you checked in,' Sadie said, and Dylan nodded.

Even though he knew the most sensible thing to do would be to run, as far and as fast as he could, away from the Azure Hotel.

Maybe his dad had had the right idea after all.

Sadie's hands shook as she climbed the stairs to her tiny office—the one that used to be Adem's—and reached for the door handle. Instinctively, she checked back over her shoulder to make sure Dylan hadn't followed her. But, no, the stairs were clear and she was alone at last, and able to process what had already been a difficult day.

Hopefully by now Dylan would be happily ensconced in the best suite the Azure had to offer—which was probably still nowhere near the standard he was used to. He hadn't let her escape without making her promise to meet him for dinner, though. Of course, she'd said yes—she was hardly in a position to say no, now, was she? She just hoped he had no idea how much she'd wanted to.

Stepping into her office, she slumped into her desk chair and reached for the phone, her fingers still trembling. Dialling the familiar number, she let it ring, waiting for Neal to pick up. He'd be there, she was sure, waiting by the phone. After all, he had to know she'd be calling.

'I'm sorry,' Neal said, the moment he answered.

'So you bloody well should be. What were you think-

ing? Why didn't you tell me? Never mind, I think I know.'
Which didn't make her any happier about the subterfuge.
Not one bit.

'You'd have said no,' Neal explained anyway. 'But,
Sadie, he really wants to help. And you need him.'

'I *don't* need a pity save.' Sadie could feel the heat
of her anger rising again and let it come. Neal deserved
it. 'I'm not some bank that's too big to fail. I don't need
Dylan Jacobs to sweep in and—'

'Yes,' Neal said, calm but firm. 'You do. And you
know it.'

Yes, she did. But she wished that wasn't true.

'Why did it have to be him, though?' she whined.

'Who else do we know with millions of pounds, a tendency to jump at random opportunities and a soft spot
for your family?' Neal teased lightly.

'True.' Didn't mean she had to like it, though.
Although Neal was right about the jumping-at-
opportunities thing. Dylan was the ultimate opportunist
and once he'd jumped it was never long before he
was ready to move on to the next big thing. This
wasn't a long-term project for him, Sadie realised.
This was Dylan swooping in just long enough to give
her a hand, then he'd be moving on. She needed to
remember that.

'Is this really a problem?' Neal asked. 'I mean, I knew
your pride would be a bit bent out of shape, but you told
me you wanted to save the Azure, come hell or high water.'

She had said that. 'Which is this, exactly?'

There was a pause on the other end of the line, and
Sadie began to regret the joke. The last thing she needed
on top of Dylan Jacobs in her hotel was Neal showing up
to find out what was going on.

'Why does he bother you so much?' He sounded honestly curious, like he was trying to riddle out the mystery of Sadie and Dylan. The same way Neal always approached everything—like a puzzle to be solved. It was one of the things Sadie liked most about him. He'd taken the problem of her failing hotel and had started looking for answers, rather than pointing out things she'd done wrong. 'It can't be that he reminds you of Adem too much or you'd have kicked me to the kerb after the funeral, too. So what is it?'

Sadie sighed. There was just no way to explain this that Neal would ever understand. His riddle would have to go unsolved. 'I don't know. We just…we never really managed to see eye to eye. On anything.'

Except for that one night, when they'd seen each other far too clearly. When she'd finally realised the threat that Dylan Jacobs had posed to her carefully ordered and settled life.

The threat of possibility.

'He's a good man,' Neal told her. 'He really does want to help.'

'I know.' That was the worst part. Dylan wasn't here to cause trouble, or make her life difficult, or unhappy. She knew him well enough to be sure of that. He was there to help, probably out of some misguided sense of obligation to a man who was already two years dead, and the friendship they'd shared. She could respect that. 'And I need him. I should have called him myself.' She thought of the sympathy card sitting with a few others in a drawer in her bedroom. The one with a single lily on the front and stark, slashing black handwriting inside.

I'm so sorry, Sadie. Whatever you need, call me.
Any time.
D x.

She hadn't, obviously.

'So we're okay?' Neal asked.

'Yeah, Neal. We're fine.' It was only her own sanity she was worried about. 'I'll call you later in the week, let you know how things go.'

'Okay.' Neal still sounded uncertain, but he hung up anyway when she said goodbye.

Sadie leant back in her chair, tipping her head to stare at the ceiling. All she needed to do was find a way to work with Dylan until he moved on to the next big thing—and from past experience that wouldn't take long. Jobs, businesses, women—none of them had ever outlasted his short boredom threshold. Why would the Azure be any different? The only thing Sadie had ever known to be constant in Dylan's life was his friendship with Adem and Neal. That was all this was about—a feeling of obligation to his friend, and the wife and child he'd left behind. She didn't need him, she needed his money and his business.

A niggle of guilt wriggled in her middle at the realisation that she was basically using her husband's best friend for his money, milking his own sense of loss at Adem's death. But if it was the only way to save the Azure…

She'd convince him that the Azure was worth saving, and he'd stump up the money out of obligation.

Then they could both move on.

CHAPTER TWO

DYLAN WAITED A while before calling Neal to yell at him. After all, he figured he owed Sadie a fair crack at their mutual friend first.

In the meantime, the wait gave him the opportunity to settle into his suite, his frequent flyer business traveller mind assessing the space the way he always did in a new hotel room. Bed: king-size—always a good start. The linens were crisp and white, and part of his weary brain and body wanted to curl up in them right away and sleep until dinner. But he was there to do a job, and that job required him to be awake, so he pushed on.

The room itself was a good size, but Dylan figured this was probably the biggest the hotel had, so he'd have to explore some of the smaller, ordinary rooms before making a judgement on room size. Wandering through to the bathroom, he clocked fluffy towels, good tiling and lighting, and a shower he very much looked forward to trying out later. If that shower head was as effective as it looked, and the water pressure as good as Dylan hoped, his aching muscles would appreciate the pummelling before bed.

Back in the main room, Dylan ran his fingers across the small table and chairs by the window in the bedroom then strolled into the lounge area through the open arch of a doorway. Again, the size was good, the sofas looked comfy enough, and the coffee table was stacked with magazines and brochures detailing things to do in the area. He flicked through them quickly before deciding the mini-bar and desk were far more interesting.

Crouching down, he yanked open the fridge door and nodded his approval. A decently stocked mini-bar—even if he never used it—was a must in Dylan's book. Then he dropped into the swivel chair by the desk, tugged his phone from his pocket and checked for the complementary WiFi the girl at the desk had assured him was part of his room package. To his amazement, it worked first time and with minimal fuss over the password.

He smiled to himself. He shouldn't be so surprised. After all, this was Adem's place, for all that Sadie was running it now. And Adem had always been vocal about the individual's right to easy-access WiFi at all times and in all places. Something else he and Dylan had always agreed on.

Twirling around in his chair, Dylan split his attention between checking his mail again and surveying the room as a whole—and spotted something he hadn't noticed before. Getting to his feet, he crossed the room, pulled aside the curtains and stepped out onto the suite's small balcony.

Now this was worth travelling all those miles for. Breathing in deeply, Dylan savoured the warm sun on his face and forearms, and stared out. He could see now why Adem had been so evangelical about the place, right from the start, quite apart from his family connection to the hotel.

The view was magnificent. Down below, the Aegean Sea lapped against the rocks, bright and blue and entrancing, sending up puffs of white spray with every wave. Above the rocks, scrubby bushes and juniper trees twisted up towards the clear azure sky, all the way up the peak where the hotel sat. Overhead, a bird called out as it passed, and Dylan thought for the first time all year, since he spent the holidays with his sister and her family, that he might actually be able to just switch off and enjoy the moment.

Except he still had to deal with Sadie—and find out how bad things at the Azure really were for Neal to have sent him here when she so obviously didn't want his help.

Eventually, he figured enough time had passed that even Sadie would have finished yelling at the hapless accountant and, leaving the sunny warmth of the balcony behind him, Dylan headed back inside to sit at the desk and call Neal.

After just a couple of rings Neal answered the phone with a sigh.

'You can't possibly be surprised by this call,' Dylan pointed out.

'I know, I know.' Neal sounded stressed, in a way Dylan wasn't used to hearing from his old friend. That alone put his nerves on high alert. 'Trust me, I've already heard it all from her.'

Her. Sadie. The memory of her expression, the shock and horror that had flashed across her face at the first sight of him, rankled all over again.

'I bet you have,' Dylan said. 'So? Is she going to kick me out on my ear or let me help?' It wasn't what he'd expected to ask—he'd expected there to be a lot more yelling first, apart from anything else. But now he had Neal on the phone it seemed like the only thing that really mattered.

'She'll let you help.'

'Because she's desperate.'

'Pretty much.'

'Great.' Dylan put as much sarcasm as he could muster into the word. 'I just love being a last resort.'

Neal let out another, world-weary sigh. 'You know Sadie, Dyl. She's proud. And she thinks it's her responsibility to fulfil Adem's dreams all on her own.'

'She let *you* help.' Which, Dylan had to admit, still irked him a bit.

'Yeah, but I'm less smug than you.'

Smug? 'I'm not—'

'Yes. Yes, you are. And you need not to be this week, okay?' Neal wasn't joking any more, Dylan could tell. And that worried him more than anything else that had happened that day.

But, to be honest, being too smug and alienating Sadie wasn't really what Dylan was concerned about. He was far more worried about being obvious than smug. Worried that Sadie still thought she knew more about his feelings than she could reasonably expect to after so many years—and might refuse to let him help because of it.

'Things are that bad here?' he asked.

Neal huffed impatiently, a far more familiar sound than his concern. 'Didn't you read the info I sent over?'

'Of course I did.' Well, he'd scanned through it on the plane, which was practically the same thing. It wasn't that Dylan wasn't interested in the stats for the Azure Hotel, it was just that he had a lot of other projects on his plate, plus new opportunities coming in. Besides... he hadn't really been able to imagine any of it until he was actually here.

'She needs more than your money, Dyl. She needs your business brain.'

And, okay, yes, it was bad timing, but it wasn't really

his fault that his brain's automatic response to a comment like that was a feeling of smug pride, right? 'Doesn't everyone?'

'Okay, that? That's exactly what I don't want you to do this week.'

The puff of pride disintegrated as fast as it had appeared. 'Fine. So I'm here in a business advisor capacity only?'

'No, she needs your money, too,' Neal said. 'She's insanely committed to Adem's dream of making the Azure a successful hotel. Doesn't matter that he's not there to see it—she's going to make it happen anyway.'

Only Sadie. Other people walked out on commitments every day—families, marriages, financial and business obligations—and never looked back. Only Sadie would remain committed to a dead man's schemes. And only because she had loved Adem so much.

Dylan sighed. 'That's not going to be easy.' He knew that much from the information Neal had sent him—and the fact Sadie had agreed to let him help at all. If she'd thought she could do it herself, she would have. Sadie was nothing if not bloody-minded and determined.

'Probably not,' Neal allowed. 'But it might save Adem's dream. And Sadie.'

And so, of course, he would do it, without question. He just hoped no one ever pressed him to say exactly which of those motivations was strongest for him.

'I'm having dinner with her tonight.' He tugged a sheet of writing paper branded with the Azure logo closer to him and grabbed a pen. 'Where do I start?'

'She needs this to be business,' Neal said. 'Not a pity save, even if that's what it is.'

It was more than that, Dylan knew. This wasn't just pity. He couldn't bear to see Sadie struggling, so he'd do whatever it took to save her. He suspected that Neal knew that too.

'So how do I convince her it's not?'

'By letting her pitch the Azure and Kuşadasi to you as a real investment opportunity. As something you'd want to put money into even if she wasn't involved. Let her present her proposal for the place, then decide if you will invest.'

Suddenly, a plan began to form, right at the back of Dylan's brain, where he always got his most inspired ideas.

'I can do that,' he said, and smiled.

Standing in front of her wardrobe, Sadie shifted her weight from one foot to the other, squinted, then sighed and gave up. Nothing she could do right now changed the clothes hanging there for her to choose from. If Neal had told her Dylan was coming, she'd have had time to go shopping. Not that she would have done. The last thing she wanted to do was give Dylan Jacobs the impression that his presence was new-clothes-worthy.

Either way, her options now were limited.

She flicked through the hangers again, dismissing each outfit in turn. Black suit? Too conservative for dinner with someone who was, business opportunities aside, an old friend. Navy shift dress? Might have worked, if it didn't have hummus smeared down the front of it, courtesy of Finn. She tossed it in the laundry hamper. Grey shift dress? She supposed it could work. The neckline was demure, the fit okay... It was just boring and made her look even greyer than she felt.

Hadn't she once had more interesting clothes? The sort with colour and pop and stuff? She was sure that once upon a time she'd dressed to fit her happy and in-love mood. Maybe that was the problem. When Adem had died he'd taken all her colour and brightness with him—and it even showed in her wardrobe.

Trapping her lower lip between her teeth, Sadie reached right to the back of the closet and felt slippery satin slide through her fingers as she tugged one more dress to the front. *The* dress. The bright red, sexy dress her sister had talked her into buying on their last shopping trip to London before she and Adem had left for Turkey. She'd never yet found the courage to wear it, for all of Rachel's suggestions that it would be the perfect dress to wear if she wanted to convince Adem they should give Finn a little brother or sister.

She let it fall from her grasp. Definitely *not* the right dress for tonight.

Instead, she pulled out her standard black function dress—the one she'd worn for every single event since she'd arrived in Kuşadasi, and the dress she'd known she'd end up wearing all along, if she was honest with herself. It was well cut, didn't reveal too much, looked more dressy than a work dress, but still had the aura of business about it.

Sadie sank to sit on her bed, her hands clutching at the fabric of the dress. Business. She had to focus on that. This was her last and only chance—she couldn't afford to think of Dylan as Adem's twenty-two-year-old university buddy, or the best man who'd brought Adem home from his stag night with an almighty hangover, a blow-up sheep and no recollection of where they'd spent the last two days. Dylan wasn't that person any more.

She swallowed, blinking away sudden tears of guilt and loss at the memory of her husband. Because that was the problem. She wasn't thinking of *that* Dylan at all. Instead, she couldn't help remembering another one, sitting up too late in a bar after someone else's wedding, talking too much and too deeply.

Despite herself, she couldn't help remembering the man who had once asked her if she'd ever imagined what might have happened if he'd met her first, instead of Adem.

Rushing to her feet, too fast, Sadie shook off the memory with the resulting light-headedness. She loved her husband—now, then and always. And she planned to preserve his memory for their son by saving the hotel. Business, that's all any of it was for her now. And she was sure that was all it was for Dylan too.

She knew business now, and she needed to show Dylan that—needed him to see that she wasn't the same girl she had been then either. She'd grown up, learned and changed. She could save the Azure all by herself—she just needed his money.

Nodding to herself, Sadie pulled on her black dress and added her work jacket and heels. A business-casual compromise, she decided. It was perfect.

Heading down to the bar, Sadie was pleased to realise she'd beaten Dylan there, despite her clothing dilemma delay. After a moment's thought she ordered them both a glass of a local white wine—showcasing the specialties of the region had to be a good way to convince Dylan that Kuşadasi was worth his time and interest. Following her theme, she also asked the bartender to check in with the chef on the menu. He returned in short order, carrying both wine and a daily menu. Sadie scanned it quickly and told him to instruct the chef to serve them both the best local food on offer, once they made it through to the restaurant.

She settled back onto her bar stool and took a sip of her wine, feeling in control for the first time that day. Dylan may have caught her off balance when he'd arrived, but it took more than that to rattle Sadie Sullivan. She had everything in hand now—and it was the upper one.

Then he appeared in the doorway, looking far too good in his navy suit and open-collared shirt, and she struggled to swallow her wine without spluttering. Dylan, Sadie was sure, hadn't bothered agonising over what to wear at all. He'd just thrown on what he liked and looked… *perfect* in it.

It was strange; she didn't remember him being quite so attractive. Oh, he'd always been good looking, but it had been in a single-guy-about-town, flirt-with-the-girls-and-take-them-home way. Whereas Adem had always been more steady, less striking—but so gorgeous when he'd smiled at her. It had felt like he'd saved all his best looks just for her, and she'd loved that.

But now Dylan looked more grown up, more reliable, like he'd grown into his looks and out of his bad habits. Sadie shook her head lightly—it was an illusion. She knew from Neal's more recent stories that Dylan was just as much of a playboy as ever.

'You look beautiful.' Reaching her stool, Dylan bent to kiss her cheek, and Sadie ignored the thrill it sent down her spine.

'And you're just as much of a flirt as ever,' she chastised him, earning the reward of a positively rakish grin that made it hard not to laugh. 'Have a seat,' she said, waving at the stool next to her. 'Drink wine.'

He did as he was told for once, fishing his smartphone from his pocket and placing it on the bar before he reached for his glass.

'This is good,' Dylan said, after the first mouthful. 'Local?'

She nodded. 'Everything you're going to taste tonight is from the area. Just another host of reasons why you want to be investing in Kuşadasi and the Azure.'

'Down to business so soon?' His smile was a little lop-sided this time, like he knew something she didn't, but since he was already swiping a finger across his phone screen to check his emails Sadie didn't think he should complain about talking business in a bar.

'Isn't that what you're here for?' Best to be blunt, she decided. History aside, this was a business dinner—for both of them.

'Of course.' Dylan leant against the wooden back of the bar stool, his arms folded behind his head. 'Go on, then. I'm ready to be convinced.'

'About the food?' Sadie asked, suddenly thrown off balance. Surely he didn't expect her to convince him to invest a ridiculous amount of money based purely on one sip of wine and the promise of dinner?

'About this hotel. You're right, this is a business trip. As much as I'd personally be happy to hand over what-ever money you need, I have shareholders and board members who might not be so keen. So I need you to convince me that the Azure is a sound investment be-fore I can agree to come on board.' His tone was per-fectly matter-of-fact, even as he admitted he'd give her a pity save if he could. A very small part of Sadie wished it was that easy.

But no. This was exactly what she'd wanted—no pity save, no charity for the poor widow. Business.

She just hadn't expected him to agree so fast—or for it to be a requirement for him too.

But she could do this. She could show him. She had a

plan—Adem's plan for the Azure—and she intended to follow it to the letter. All she needed to do was convince Dylan it was a good plan.

'Right, then,' she said, briskly. 'Where do you want to start?'

CHAPTER THREE

THE MOMENT THEY were settled at their table—obviously the best seat in the house—Sadie launched into what had to be a rehearsed sales pitch. Dylan tried to pay attention as she listed the details of room numbers and styles, amenities and so on, but in truth very little of it went in. He couldn't keep his eyes off her—and apparently he'd lost the ability to stare and listen at the same time.

Sadie was beautiful as ever, he'd known that since he arrived at the Azure. Before, even. Sadie was Sadie, and her beauty was an intrinsic part of her—and had very little to do with what she actually looked like at all. But now, soaking her in over the candlelit table, he had a chance to catalogue the changes. She was more fragile now, he decided, more closed off. Somehow more off limits than she'd ever been, even after she'd married Adem. Now she was The Widow, and he couldn't seem to help but let those two words—and the tragedy they encompassed—define her in his mind.

Her spark seemed dimmed, and it hurt him to see it. Maybe this week could be useful in more than one way. He'd help her with her hotel, of course. But how could he not try to bring that spark back too? To make sure she was really okay here, alone with a crumbling hotel, a small boy and her memories.

Just as a friend. Obviously. Because there was no way she'd let him close enough for anything else now, if she never had before. Besides, given the position she was in, he wouldn't risk it. Not if it would just make things worse for her. All he had to offer was the money she needed and business support maybe. Then he would be on his way. He wasn't Adem and he never had been.

Dylan knew himself too well—at least as well as Neal, Adem and Sadie always had. He was too like his father to ever settle to one life, one set of possibilities—not when the next big thing could be just past the horizon. So this was temporary, and that was fine with him.

It just meant he only had one week to find the promise in the Azure Hotel and come up with a plan to make it good. He needed to get started on that, pronto. *Priorities, Dylan.*

Their starters arrived without him ever seeing a menu, but as he examined the seafood platter he decided he didn't mind at all. If all else failed, at least he could honestly say the food and drink at the Azure were good. It was a start.

'Did Adem make you memorise all that?' he asked, as Sadie reached the end of her spiel and reached for a calamari ring.

'No,' she said. 'Well, just some of it.'

'But it's all his plan, right?' He'd known Adem since they'd been eighteen. He'd recognised his friend's touch before Sadie had reached the second bullet point.

'How can you possibly…? We worked on it together. Of course.'

'Of course. But this was his dream.' He followed her lead with the calamari, hoping it tasted as good as it looked. One piece of rubbery calamari could ruin a whole meal. But, no, it had the perfect mixture of crunch in the batter and melting seafood. He reached for another.

'His heritage.' She shrugged, her shoulders slim and delicate now she'd taken her jacket off, and more tanned than he remembered. 'He wanted a future here for our family.'

Family. *Stop thinking about her shoulders, Jacobs, and focus on what really matters to her.* 'Where *is* Finn, anyway?'

A shadow crossed her face, and he almost regretted asking. 'He's staying with my parents for the week. I'm flying over to England to collect him after you leave.'

'Because I was going to be here?' That stung. He may not have seen much of the boy since he'd been born, but that didn't make him any less of an honorary uncle.

Sadie gave him a look—the sort she used to give him in the pub when they'd been twenty-two and he'd been acting like an idiot. 'To be honest, I didn't know *you* were the one coming, which I think you must have guessed. Besides, that wasn't it. He's due to start school next year, and my parents wanted to spend some time with him outside the holidays before then.'

There was something else, hiding behind the lightness of her tone, but he couldn't put his finger on it, and it was still too early to press too hard for information—frustrating as that was. He had to have patience. Eventually she'd open up to him again.

A waiter cleared their starter platters, even as another brought their main course—some sort of delicious, spicy, lamb stew thing that Dylan vowed to find out the name of before he left. But right then he had bigger priorities than his stomach.

'Okay, so, I've heard all the grand plans,' he said between mouthfuls. 'How far have you actually got with them?'

Sadie put down her fork and ticked the items off on her fingers as she spoke. 'The lobby, restaurant and bar are finished, as you've seen. So is the spa. Of the bedrooms, the top floor with the penthouse suite—your suite—and the other family suites is done, and the first floor of luxury doubles.'

'So that leaves you, what?' He tried to recall the floor numbers from the lift. 'Another four floors to go? Plus any other reception and function rooms?'

She nodded. 'We had a timescale planned but…'

'The money ran out.' Not a surprise. He'd seen it often enough, even in projects less plagued by tragedy and uncertainty.

'Yes. So we opened anyway, to try and get enough funds to keep going. But at least one of the floors is uninhabitable as it stands, so occupancy is never very high.'

'What about the outside space?' That had to be a selling point in a climate like this.

'The outside pool needs retiling and the path down to the beach needs some work. Fortunately the inside pool is attached to the spa, so got done in the first wave, before…' She trailed off, and he knew exactly what she wasn't saying. Some days, he thought that if he didn't say it, it might not be true, too.

'There's a lot left to do,' he finished for her, cutting short the moment.

'That's why we need your money.'

His fork hit china and he looked down to see he'd eaten the whole bowl without tasting anything beyond that first delicious mouthful. What a waste. He put his cutlery down. 'Dinner would be worth investing in alone. That was truly delicious.'

She blushed, just a little. 'I'm glad you enjoyed it. Somehow I suspect one meal isn't quite enough to win over your shareholders, though.'

'Maybe not. Okay, listen. I'm going to tell you a bit about my company, and you can decide if you want us involved. If you do…then we can discuss what else I need to see and do, what questions I need answered, before I can take a proposal to the board.' She'd been straight with him, as far as he could tell. Time for him to do the same.

'Okay.' Eyes wide, her nerves were back, he realised, pleased to still be able to read her so well.

'My company isn't generally interested in long-term investment. Mostly what we do is take on a failing business, tear it down or build it up until it's successful, then sell it on.'

'In that case, I'd think the Azure would be perfect. We have "failing business" written all over us.' She reached for her wine—a local red, he assumed—and took a gulp.

'The key is, the business has to have the *potential* to be a huge success,' he clarified. 'In the right hands.'

'Yours, you mean.' She sounded more sceptical than Dylan felt was truly necessary.

'Or whoever we put in charge. In this case…we'd need to be sure that you could turn this place around on your own, with just money and guidance from us.' Make it clear upfront that he wouldn't be staying around—not that he imagined she wanted him to.

'I see.' This time her tone gave nothing away at all, and he found himself talking just to fill the silence that followed.

'Unless, of course, you're in favour of taking a bulldozer to the place, putting someone else in charge of the rebuild and taking a back seat until the money starts rolling in?' He knew she wouldn't say yes, but part of him couldn't help but hope she would. It would be the easy way out—but since when had Sadie ever taken that?

She shook her head. 'Sorry. This is personal for me. I made a commitment to make this hotel a success. For Adem.'

'I guessed you'd say that. Don't suppose you'd consider changing the name either?'

'No,' she said, giving him a curious look. 'Why? What's wrong with the name it has?'

'No reason.' She stared and waited. He sighed. He should have known that wasn't a good enough answer for her. 'I had a bad experience at an Azure Hotel once.'

Her wide grin made the admission worthwhile. 'Let me guess. Some woman's poor husband showed up at the wrong moment?'

Of course that's what she would think. And, really, who could blame her? 'You know me.' But not all his secrets—which was probably for the best. For both of them.

'Okay, so if we're not going to knock this place down, what do I need to show you to convince you we're worth your time, money and effort?'

Honestly, he could probably make the decision based purely on the numbers. But that would have him flying back to Sydney tomorrow, instead of spending time with Sadie. He had to give her a real chance to convince him.

'Here's my proposal. I want a proper tour of the hotel. Then I need to see the local area—get a feel for the economy and tourist potential. Numbers are all well and good, but you need to visit a place to get a real feeling for it.' All true, up to a point. 'Then we'll sit down together and see if I can help you save this place.'

She nodded. 'Okay. Do you want me to set you up with the local tour company we use?'

Where would be the fun in that? 'No. I think this will

work much better if you show me yourself.' Not to mention give him a clearer idea of how Sadie was really coping after her husband's death. Multitasking was the key to any successful business, after all.

Sadie nodded her agreement, and Dylan sat back to anticipate dessert, hoping his smile wasn't too smug. Everything was going to plan.

After a restless night, full of dreams that were half memory, half fantasy, Sadie met Dylan in the lobby the next morning, dressed in her best black suit and determined to impress with her business skills. His proposal had been more than fair. Neal must have told him what dire straits they were in at the Azure, but still Dylan had agreed to spend time on the ground, studying and evaluating everything himself, before he made his decision.

Sadie suspected that had more to do with friendship than good business sense. Still, he'd made it very clear over dinner what he needed from her—professionalism—and she intended to give it to him in spades.

Except Dylan, when he arrived, was dressed in light trousers and a pale blue shirt with the sleeves rolled up, sunglasses tucked in his pocket, making her feel instantly overdressed—even though *she* was the one who was appropriately attired. *How does he* always *manage that?*

'Right, let's get going,' he said, as he approached. 'Lots to see today!'

'Before we start our tour,' she said, stalling him, 'I realised there was something I forgot to show you yesterday, and I'd hate you to miss it.'

Striding across the lobby, she led him to the windows at the far side of the elevators. Dylan wasn't the sort to stop and sniff the roses, unless someone reminded him to, and she couldn't have him missing the most magnificent thing about the Azure, just because he forgot to look.

'Oh, really? What's that?' Dylan asked, following, his eyes on the screen of his smartphone.

'Our view.' Sadie stared out across the bright blue waters, the sea almost the same colour as the sky, white foam echoing the wispy clouds overhead. They were high enough to see for miles, out along the coast and out to sea. Her heart tightened the way it always did when she looked out over the water and coast beyond the Azure. Whatever had happened here, she was lucky to have had the chance to live in such a beautiful country. She had to remember that.

'There's a path from the back door that leads straight down to the beach,' she murmured, but Dylan's eyes remained fixed on the view, just as she'd known they would.

It was this view that Adem had used to convince her, back when buying a crumbling hotel had just been a pipe dream.

Look at it, he'd said. *Who wouldn't want to be here?*

And in that moment she hadn't been able to imagine anywhere she'd rather be than in the Azure Hotel, making Adem's dreams a reality.

Dylan looked similarly entranced, his phone forgotten in his hand. Sadie allowed herself a small smile. Perhaps this would be easier than she'd thought.

'Of course, the view would still be there, even if you knocked this old place down and rebuilt it,' he said, turning his back on the view, but his tone told her he was joking. Mostly. 'You could put in a whole glass wall in the lobby, and rooms with a sea view could have folding glass doors and balconies. Really make the most of the asset—and change the name while you're at it…'

Sadie rolled her eyes. Some woman—or her husband—had really done a number on him in an Azure Hotel, hadn't she? Funny that Adem or Neal had never told her that story, when they'd shared so many others.

Was that why he couldn't see it? The romance of this place? This old building was more than just its stones and its view. It was the heart of the place.

'Time for the rest of our tour, then. But I want you to remember—this is all business.' Sure, he'd said it himself the night before, but it couldn't hurt to hammer the point home. 'I want you to treat me and the Azure like you would any other business proposition. We're here to impress you, our client. So, what do you want to see first?'

'I'm the client, huh? My wish is your command. Sounds good.' Giving her a lopsided smile, Dylan stared around him, obviously thinking. 'Let's start with the bedrooms.'

'The suites? Or the luxury doubles?' Which would be best? He'd already seen the best suite in the place—he was staying in it. So maybe the doubles…

'The uninhabitable ones,' Dylan said, cutting short any hopes of impressing him that morning. Sadie silently cursed her loose tongue over dinner. It had to be the fault of the wine.

'Right this way,' she said, her smile fading the moment she turned away to press the 'Call Lift' button.

The bedrooms were worse than she remembered. A lot worse.

'Lot of work needed here,' Dylan said, winning the prize for understatement of the year. Sadie sighed as she took in the broken tiles, missing bed, ripped wallpaper and strange black marks on the carpetless floor.

'Yes,' she agreed. 'And a lot of money to do it.' If there were anything guaranteed to send Dylan running…and she'd brought him straight there. Why had she even given him the choice?

But Dylan just shrugged and smiled. 'But I've seen worse. Okay. Now let's see the ones you've done up.'

Sadie wanted to ask what sort of hotels he'd been staying in, to have seen worse, but instead she decided to grab the life belt with both hands and swim for the shore. 'Luxury doubles coming up,' she said, with a smile that made her face ache.

At least she knew they had carpets.

By the time they were done viewing the hotel, Sadie was exhausted from excessive smiling and from scraping around in her brain for the answers to Dylan's incredibly detailed questions. At least she could never complain that he wasn't taking this business proposal seriously. For all his tourist clothes, he'd been professional to the hilt, asking questions she'd never even imagined she'd need to know the answers to.

Back in the lobby, she looked over her scribbled list of things to look up for him. It was up to two pages already, and he'd only been there less than a day.

'I'd better get back to the office and type up my notes from this morning,' she said. 'I should have answers for you by this evening…'

'Oh, I'm not done with my tour yet, Mrs Sullivan.' He flashed a smile. 'I want to see the town next.' He looked her up and down, and Sadie resisted the urge to hide behind her clipboard. 'Why don't you go and get changed into something more suitable for sightseeing?'

Something more suitable… What had happened to this being all business? What was he imagining—a Hawaiian shirt and a bumbag? But she had said he was in charge, so she bit her tongue. Hard. 'Give me ten minutes.'

He nodded, but since he was already frowning at the screen of his phone she wasn't sure he noticed her leave.

As she dashed up to her room she ran through the morning again in her head. Dylan had seemed somewhat underwhelmed by the hotel as a whole, with far more questions than praise, but Kuşadasi was bound to impress. The local economy and the blossoming tourist trade was what made the Azure a safe bet. She just had to make sure he saw that.

Dylan was so like Adem, in so many ways, she thought as she slipped into a light sundress. Adem had always worked on gut instinct, trusting his feelings to lead him to the right decisions. And instinct mattered to Dylan too—so that was what she needed to win over.

Hadn't he made it clear his business specialised in short-term, in-and-out projects? All she needed to do was hold his attention long enough to get him to invest. Then the Azure would take off, she'd be able to pay him back or buy him out in no time, and it would be back to just her and Finn again.

Grabbing her sunglasses and bag, Sadie took a deep breath and headed down to wow Dylan Jacobs. Whether he liked it or not.

CHAPTER FOUR

It almost felt like a date, Dylan thought as they sped down the Turkish roads towards the town centre. The Azure Hotel wasn't quite close enough to walk in—another point against it—but with Sadie sitting beside him in a pale cotton sundress, her dark hair loose to her shoulders, he found it hard to be objective.

Because this—being alone with her, exploring a new place, relaxing in her company—was everything he'd dreamed about once, in the secret places of his mind he'd never fully admit to. Back in the days when he'd let himself think about a world without his best friend, or one where he'd met Sadie first.

He hadn't let the fantasies into his mind often—he'd learned early in life there was no point wishing the world to be any different than it was unless you were willing to do something to change it. And he hadn't been willing, not in the slightest. If even imagining it had felt like betrayal, the idea of acting on those fantasies had been beyond contemplation.

Adem had been the right guy for Sadie—he'd always known that. Known he couldn't offer her half as much, so he'd never considered trying—not that he'd have risked or betrayed his friendships that way anyway. A woman like Sadie needed love, commitment—she deserved for-ever. And he didn't have that in him.

But now, with Sadie in the driver's seat, sunglasses on and legs bare under that sundress, he could feel those imagined possibilities rising again. And just for a moment he let himself believe that she wanted him here—for more than just his money.

A light turned red and they pulled to a stop, the jerk breaking the moment, and reality sank back in. If this were a date he'd planned, he'd know where he was going. Sadie would be smiling at him, not looking tense and nervous and sad. The familiar guilt wouldn't be sitting in his chest—smaller than when Adem had been alive, sure, but still ever present.

Plus he'd probably be driving.

The lights changed again, and Sadie manoeuvred ex-pertly past waiting cars and swung into a suddenly va-cant parking spot by the marina that Dylan hadn't even noticed. He had plenty of experience driving abroad him-self, but for once he was glad to be driven. It was nice to see Sadie so in control in this place.

'Come and look at the ocean,' she said, sliding out of her seat and into the sunshine. 'It'll give you a feel for the place.'

They stood by the railings together, staring out at the Aegean, and Dylan felt a comfortable warmth settle into his bones—one he wasn't sure was entirely due to the sunshine. He was enjoying Sadie's company just a little too much. He'd always found her presence relaxing, to a point, but before he'd never allowed himself to indulge in that feeling too much. Here and now, though, it felt all too natural.

He shut his eyes against the sparkle of the sun on the

water. Business. That was what he was here for, and that was what he needed to concentrate on. He couldn't afford to forget himself here—he needed to keep on top of his other projects while he was away, as well as work on the Azure proposal with Sadie. Already that morning he'd had enough emails from his assistant back in Sydney to remind him that things never worked quite as smoothly when he was away. He had to stay on top of everything.

Eyes open again, he shut his mind to the view and the warmth of the sun, and turned his attention instead to the practical aspects of the place. A marina, filled with top-end private yachts—and further up, cruise ships. Suddenly he understood exactly why Sadie had parked where she had.

'So, this is your subtle way of telling me that Kuşadasi is a popular cruise-ship destination?' he said, turning his back on the marina to lean against the railing and study her instead.

She gave him a perfectly innocent smile. 'Pure coincidence, I assure you. But as it happens, yes, it is! Tourism is the heart blood of this place. The ships stop here regularly, filled with people ready to explore the town— and spend their money on souvenirs.'

Which all sounded good until you studied the logic behind it. 'But how many of them make it up the hill to the Azure?'

'That's not the point.'

'Of course it is. If the bulk of the tourists visiting this place are only here for the day, what do they need with a hotel?' She winced at his words, but recovered quickly. He had to admire her tenacity, even if her argument was weak.

'The cruise ships are only a small part of the tourist industry here—and, actually, they're the gateway to a whole new market. Some of the people who visit for a day might never have even considered Turkey as a holiday destination before—but after a few hours here they may well decide to come back for a longer stay. Or to tell their friends that it was a great place to visit. Or even look into buying holiday apartments or hotel time shares here.'

A slim possibility. People who liked cruises—like his mother and her third husband—tended to take more cruises, in Dylan's experience. But who knew? Maybe she was right. He'd need more figures before he could make a value judgement.

'Okay, then,' Dylan said, pushing away from the railings. 'So what is it about this town that will make them come back?'

'The history,' Sadie replied promptly. 'The shopping. The atmosphere. The food. The views. Everything.'

'So show me everything.'

'That could take a while.'

Dylan shrugged. 'We've got all day. So, what's next?'

Sadie looked around her then nodded to herself. 'Let's take a walk.'

That date-like feeling returned as they walked along the seafront towards a small island, linked to the mainland by a walkway. Dylan resisted the urge to take her arm or hold her hand, but the fact it even needed to be resisted unsettled him. Not just because this was *Sadie* but because he'd never really thought of himself as a hand-holding-in-the-sunshine kind of guy. He tended to work better after dark.

Sadie turned and led him along the walkway leading out into the sea towards the island, and Dylan distracted himself by reading the signs of fishing tours on offer and checking out the tourist trap stalls set up along the way, selling bracelets and temporary tattoos.

'What is this place?' he asked, nodding to the island up ahead. Covered with trees, it appeared to have a fortified wall running around it and plenty of people wandering the path along the edge of the island.

'Pigeon Island,' Sadie replied promptly. 'You see over there, above the trees? That's the fortress of Kuşadasi—built in the thirteenth century. It was there to protect the Ottoman Empire from pirates—including Barbarossa himself.'

'I didn't realise I was here for a history lesson, as well as a tourism one.'

'There's a lot of history here,' Sadie pointed out. 'And a lot of tourism to be had from history. Wait until you see the *caravanserai*.'

'I look forward to it.' History wasn't really his thing, but Sadie seemed so excited about taking him there he was hardly going to mention it. Maybe it would be more interesting than he thought, looking back instead of forward for once.

'There's a seafood restaurant and café and stuff inside,' Sadie said, as they reached the path around the island, 'although I thought we'd head back into town for lunch. But I wanted you to see this first.'

She stopped, staring back the way they had come, and Dylan found himself copying her. He had to admit, Kuşadasi from this angle was quite a sight, with its busy harbour and seafront. He could see what Adem had loved about the place.

'Does Turkey feel like home now?' he asked, watching Sadie as she soaked up the view.

She turned to him, surprised eyebrows raised. 'I suppose. I mean, we've been here for a few years now. We're pretty settled. I can get by with the language—although Finn's better at it than me.'

'That's not the same as home.' At least, from what little Dylan knew about it.

'Well, no. But, then, I never really expected that *anywhere* would be home again after Adem.'

One quiet admission, and the whole mood changed. He was wrong, Dylan realised, and had been all along. This was nothing like a date at all.

He looked away, down at the water, and tried to imagine what kept her there in Kuşadasi. It couldn't just be history and sheer stubbornness, could it? Especially given how strange and lonely it must be for her there every day in Adem's place, without him beside her.

She shook off the mood, her hair swinging from side to side as she did so, and smiled up at him. 'What about you? Where's home for you these days? Neal says you're operating mostly out of Sydney?' Changing the subject. Smart woman.

'Mostly, yeah. My mum left Britain and moved back home to Australia when she remarried again, and my sister is out there too now, so it makes sense.' And this time, finally, he had faith that they might both stay there now they'd each found some happiness in their lives. He felt lighter, just knowing they were settled.

'Do you see them often?' Sadie asked.

Dylan shrugged. 'It's a big country. We catch up now and then.'

'Between business trips.' Was that accusation in her tone? Because he wasn't going to feel bad for running a successful business, even if it meant always being ready to jump at a new opportunity and run with it—often in the opposite direction from his family.

'Pretty much. Between the office in Sydney and the one in London, I probably spend more time in the air than in my apartments in either city.'

He'd meant it as a joke, but even as the words came out he realised he'd never thought of it like that before. All those years trying to get his family settled, and he'd never stopped to notice that he didn't have the same grounding at all. He'd just assumed his business—solid, profitable and reliable—was enough to give that security. But in truth he was no more settled than Sadie was, in this country she'd never chosen for herself.

Maybe they were both drifting.

'We're both very lucky to live in such beautiful places, though,' Sadie said.

He tried to return her smile. 'Yes, I suppose we are. So, why don't you show me some more of the beauty of this place?'

'Okay.' She stepped away, back towards the promenade to the mainland. 'Let's go and take in the town.'

Home.

Sadie considered Dylan's question again as she led him into the town of Kuşadasi proper. She took him by the longer back route to give him a true feel for the place. In comfortable silence they walked through narrow cobbled streets filled with shops. Half their wares were hung outside—brightly coloured belly-dancing costumes and leather slippers butting up against shops selling highly patterned rugs, or with rails of scarves and baskets of soaps on tables in the street. The smell of cooking meat and other dishes filled the air as the local restaurants prepared for lunch, the scent familiar and warming to Sadie.

As they walked she could see Dylan taking everything in—reaching out to run his fingers over the walls, his eyes darting from one shop display to the next. Had she been so fascinated when she'd first visited? It seemed so long ago she could barely remember.

Would this place ever truly be home? Could it? Or would it always just be the place where she'd lost the love of her life?

When she thought of home she thought of her family—and so, by default, of the pretty English village where she'd grown up, just outside Oxford. She remembered playing in the woods with her sister Rachel, or taking walks on the weekend with their parents and stopping for lunch in a country pub. And she thought of later meeting Adem and his friends in Oxford, when she'd travelled in every day for her first proper job after training in a small, independent spa and beauty salon there. She thought of the first flat she and Adem had rented together in London, after they'd been married.

She didn't think of the Azure. Not because she didn't love it but because it seemed so alien to all those other things. Like a permanent working holiday.

She loved Turkey, Kuşadasi, the Azure. And maybe Dylan was right in an odd, roundabout way. If she wanted to stay there, she needed to find a way to make it feel like home.

They emerged from a side passage out onto the bigger main street, with larger stores and the occasional street vendor stall. Here, after the charm of the old town streets, Kuşadasi looked more modern, ready to compete in the world tourist market. It was important to show Dylan that they had both here.

Suddenly, Dylan stopped walking. 'Hang on a minute.' Turning, he walked back a few paces to a stall they'd just passed. Curious, Sadie followed—not close enough to hear his conversation with the stallholder but near enough to see what had caught his attention.

She rolled her eyes. A sign advertising 'Genuine Fake Watches'. Of course. In some ways Dylan really was just like Adem—they had the same absurd sense of humour and the same reluctance to let a joke lie untold.

Still, she smiled to see that Dylan wasn't pointing out the error to the stallholder, and instead seemed to be striking up a friendly conversation with him as he took a photo on his phone and examined the watches. Another way he was like her husband, she supposed—that same easy nature that made him friends everywhere he went. She'd never had that, really, and couldn't help but envy it.

'Enjoying yourself?' she asked, as he returned.

Dylan grinned. 'Immensely. What's next?'

She'd planned to take him to the *caravanserai*—she just knew his magpie mind would love all the tiny shops and stalls there, too, and it was a huge tourist attraction with plenty of history. But it was getting late and her stomach rumbled, nudging her towards the perfect way to remember why she was so lucky to live in Kuşadasi— her favourite restaurant.

'I think lunch,' she said, watching as Dylan slipped his own no doubt authentic and ridiculously expensive watch into his pocket and replaced it with the genuine fake he had just bought.

'Fantastic. I can show off my new toy.' He shook his wrist and, despite herself, Sadie laughed, feeling perfectly at home for the first time in years.

From the way Sadie was greeted at the door of the restaurant with a hug from an enthusiastic waitress, Dylan assumed she was something of a regular. Despite the queue of people ahead of them, they were led directly to a table right in the centre of the glass-roofed portion of the restaurant, with vines growing overhead to dull the power of the sun as it shone down.

He couldn't catch the entire conversation between

Sadie and the waitress, but he did notice it was conducted half in English, half in Turkish, with the waitress particularly shifting from one to the other with no sense of hesitation at all.

'Adem's second cousin,' Sadie explained. 'Or third. I forget. Most of the Turkish side of his family moved over to England at the same time his mum did, as a child, but one cousin or uncle stayed behind.' She handed him a menu. 'So, what do you fancy?'

'I get to order for myself today, then?' he teased, and she flashed him a smile, looking more comfortable than she had since they'd left the Azure that morning.

'I think I can trust you not to choose the burger and chips. But if you're fishing for a recommendation…'

'No, no. I think I can manage to choose my own food, thanks.'

She shrugged. 'Sorry. I think it's the mother thing. Finn always wants to debate all the options on the children's menu before he makes his choice.'

The mother thing. It still felt weird, identifying Sadie as a mother. Maybe because he'd spent far more time with her before Finn's birth than since. Just another reminder that she was a different woman now from the one he'd fallen so hard for in Oxford all those years before.

'So, what do you fancy?' she asked, folding her own menu and putting it to one side. Dylan got the feeling she had it memorised.

'The sea bass, I think.' He put his own menu down and within seconds their waitress was back to take their orders.

'Can I have the chicken salad today, please?' Sadie asked, smiling up at her friend. 'With extra flatbread on the side.'

'Of course. And for you, sir?'

As he looked up Dylan spotted the specials board behind the waitress. 'Actually, I think I'll have the lamb
kofta off the specials, please.'

Sadie frowned at him as the waitress disappeared with
their menus. 'I thought you wanted sea bass?'

He shrugged. 'Something better came along.'

She didn't look convinced, but rather than press the
point she pulled a notepad from her bag and opened it
to a clean page. Apparently they were back to business.

'So, while we have a quiet moment—what do you
think so far?'

'Of Kuşadasi? It's charming,' he said.

'Not just the town.' Frustration creased a small line
between Sadie's eyebrows. Despite himself, Dylan found
it unbearably cute. 'Of everything. The tourist potential
here, my plans for the hotel…the whole lot. Consider it
a mid-visit review.'

'I've only been here less than a day,' Dylan pointed
out.

'Really? It seems longer.' She flashed him a smile to
show it was a joke, but Dylan suspected she meant it.
After all, he was feeling it too—that feeling that he'd
been there forever. That they'd never been apart in the
first place.

A very dangerous feeling, that. Maybe Sadie was right.
It was time to focus on business again.

Leaning back in his chair, he considered how to put
his comments in a way that she might actually listen to
rather than get annoyed by.

'Your plans…they're the same ones Adem mapped
out when you moved here, right? And that was, what?
Three years ago?'

She nodded. 'About that, yes. And, yes, they're his
plans. He put a lot of time, energy and research into de-

veloping them. I was lucky. When he… When it all fell to me, I already had a blueprint to follow right there. I don't know if I'd have managed otherwise.'

'I think you would have done.' In fact, he rather thought she might have to. 'The thing is…are you sure that sticking to Adem's plans is the wisest idea?'

Her shoulders stiffened, and Dylan muffled a sigh. He should have known there wasn't a way to broach this subject without causing offence.

'You knew Adem as well as I did, almost anyway,' she said. 'Do you really think he wouldn't have triple-checked those plans before putting them into action?'

'Not at all.' In fact, he was pretty sure that Adem would have taken outside counsel, considered all the possibilities, and covered every single base before he'd committed to the Azure at all. Despite his enthusiastic nature and tendency to jump at opportunities, Adem had always been thorough. 'But what I mean is, the best plans need to be flexible. Adem knew that. Things change in business all the time—and quickly. Three years is a long time. The world economy, the tourist trade, even this place, aren't the same as they were then. That's why you need to review plans regularly and adjust course where necessary.'

'I thought you were here to provide investment, not business advice.' Her words came out stiffer than her frame.

Time to put his cards on the table. 'Sadie, I'm here to provide whatever it is you need—to survive here, to save your hotel, or just to be happy. But you have to trust me in order to get it.'

CHAPTER FIVE

TRUST HIM. WHAT A strange concept.

In the years since Adem had died Sadie had grown very good at relying on and trusting nobody but herself. After all, who else could she trust to care as much about Finn and the future of the Azure? Neal had helped, of course, but he'd always deferred to Adem's plan.

She should have known it wouldn't be as simple with Dylan.

Their food arrived and she picked at her salad and flatbread, loving the crunch against the soft gooeyness of the freshly baked bread. Eventually, though, she had to admit that she couldn't hide her silence behind food forever—and Dylan was clearly waiting for her to talk first. Either that or whatever information kept flashing up on his phone really was more interesting than lunch with her.

Actually, that was probably it. Still, she had to try and keep his attention.

With a sigh, she put the piece of bread she'd just torn down on her side plate.

'Look, I know what you mean—about the market changing, and all that.' Dylan looked up as she started to speak. She'd caught him just as he forked another mouthful of lamb between his lips, so at least she knew he wouldn't interrupt her for a moment or two. 'But sometimes you have to stick with a plan for a while to see its full potential. You have to give it time to work.'

There was silence again for a moment while Dylan chewed. Then he said, 'What if you don't have that kind of time?'

And wasn't that the nightmare scenario that kept her awake at night? But it was also why he was supposed to be here—to buy her the time she needed to make things work. He just had to give her that chance.

'You know, just because you're always chasing after the next big thing, that doesn't mean it's always the right thing to do.' Frustration leaked out in her tone. 'Jumping at every new trend or idea would just make us look unsteady and inconsistent. Some people like someone who can see things through—like Adem would have done with this plan. He'd have given it a chance to succeed, I know he would.'

Dylan winced at her words and Sadie realised that her comments could possibly be construed as more of a personal attack than a professional one. But it was too late to take them back now.

'Okay, I admit Adem was always better at committing than I was,' Dylan said. 'To a plan, or anything else for that matter. But he always knew when changes needed to be made, too. That's what made him such a good businessman.'

The most frustrating part was that he was probably right. In this one area Dylan had known Adem better than she could have—they'd worked together straight out of university, until Dylan had left to start his own business abroad, and Adem, newly married and planning a family, had declined to join him after a long talk with her. But until then they'd been the company's dream team, working completely in sync. Dylan was the one person in the world who truly knew what Adem would have done in her situation, and that irritated her.

'So what? You're going to give me a list of changes for the Azure and just enough pocket money to do them, then disappear for six months and let me get on with it?' she asked. 'But what happens next? I bet I can guess. You come back and move the goalposts again—because the market's changed or whatever—and give me a whole new list of changes.' She shook her head. She wouldn't do it. 'I can't work that way, Dylan. I can't *live* that way either. It's not fair to ask me to.'

'I never would,' Dylan shot back. His fork lay forgotten on his plate now, and the intensity in his gaze as he leant across the table was almost intimidating. 'That's not what I'm saying at all. All I mean is…let's go through Adem's plans together, see what needs tweaking or updating. I'm not throwing the baby out with the bathwater here, Sadie. I'm certain that Adem's plans are solid—or were three years ago. But just because you've made one plan doesn't mean you can't adapt or improve it when a better idea comes along.'

'Like switching from sea bass to lamb.' He made it all sound so simple and sensible.

Dylan smiled, relief spreading out across his face. 'Something like that.'

'Okay. I'll think about it.' And that was all the commitment she planned to make to this man.

'That's all I ask.'

They finished eating in silence. Sadie settled up the bill and they were back out on the street before Dylan asked where they were going next.

'The *caravanserai*,' Sadie said, with a faint smile.

'Another tourist site with a lot of history. I think you'll like this one.'

'I'm sure I will.'

The *caravanserai*, a fortified marketplace dating back to the seventeenth century, loomed up above them, its crenellations making it look more like a castle than a shopping centre.

'So, what is this place?' Dylan asked, squinting up at the tall walls.

'These days, part marketplace, part hotel and entertainment venue.' Sadie strolled through the marble arch, the splash of the fountains and the greenery surrounding the inner courtyard helping her relax, just like they always did. 'But back in the day it was a protected place for merchants and such passing through the town—they could be sure they and their merchandise would be safe behind these walls.'

'So I can see.' Dylan placed a hand against the stone wall. 'Solid.'

'Come on. Come and look at some local wares.'

There were fewer goods on offer now that the *caravanserai* was mainly a hotel, but Sadie suspected Dylan would enjoy what there was. She gave him a quick tour of the ground floor, slipping through stone archways into shady stores hung with rugs and other fabrics. Once she was sure he had his bearings, she left him examining some beautifully painted bowls and pottery and escaped back out to the courtyard and the refreshing sound of the falling water from the white fountain in the centre.

She needed a moment to think, a moment alone, without Dylan's presence scrambling her senses. She wasn't sure if it was because she associated him so closely with Adem, or because it felt at once so strange and yet so natural to have him there in Turkey with her, but either way it confused her. She couldn't think straight when he was smiling at her, talking apparent sense that only her personal knowledge of his history and her gut instinct could counter.

She settled down to sit on the edge of the fountain, letting the coolness of the marble sooth her palms, and circled her neck a few times to try and relieve the tension that had spread there over lunch.

Of course, it was possible she'd only grown so defensive with him because he'd been criticising Adem's plan—because it had felt like betraying the man himself, even if she knew intellectually Adem would never have seen it that way. But Adem's plan was the only thing she had left to tell her what her husband would have wanted for her, for their son, and for their dream hotel.

In the absence of anything else she'd clung to it like a life raft. Except it hadn't worked—and she had to face the fact that, whatever Dylan said, that failure was more on her than the plan. She had no doubt that if Adem had been there, with all his charm and enthusiasm, he'd have made it work—and they'd never have been in the position of having to beg Dylan Jacobs for help at all.

If they needed a new plan, then she needed help. She hadn't trained for this, hadn't ever planned to take it on. She could run her spa business with military precision and a profit every quarter—she knew what it needed and what worked. But a whole hotel? She was lost. And she was going to have to confess that to Dylan—not a conversation she relished.

But if she couldn't trust herself to come up with a plan to save the Azure, could she really trust Dylan? Wasn't he just another short-term sticking plaster? Oh, he meant well, she was sure enough of that. But he didn't see things through. Everyone knew that. Why would the Azure be any different for him?

Suddenly, a shadow appeared on the stone floor in front of her—dark and lengthening in the afternoon sun. Sadie looked up to see Dylan standing over her, a contrite expression on his face and a paper-wrapped parcel in his hands.

'For you,' he said, handing her the package.

'Why?' she asked, unwrapping the paper. 'I mean, thank you. But you shouldn't have.' The wrapping fell aside to reveal a beautiful silk scarf—one from the rack she'd shown him inside, but not one she'd ever have looked at for herself. Not because she didn't love it, or because it wouldn't suit her. The bright, vibrant colours were exactly the sort that her sister Rachel was always telling her she should wear, but she rarely did these days.

It was too bright, too bold for her. But, holding it, she wished more than anything she still had the guts to wear it.

'It's just a token,' Dylan said. 'An apology, I guess.'

Sadie shook her head, wrapping the scarf back up loosely in its paper. 'You don't have to apologise to me.'

'I feel like I do. I didn't mean to offend you, at lunch I mean.' He sighed and sat down beside her at the fountain. In an instant all the cool serenity Sadie usually found there vanished. 'You know I'd never badmouth Adem—you do know that, right? I know it's not the same as for you but…you know what he meant to me too.'

'I do.' Guilt trickled down inside her chest. Dylan and Adem had been best friends before she'd even met them. Miles might have separated them, but she knew Adem had stayed in close contact with both Neal and Dylan until the day he'd died. She didn't hold the monopoly on grief over his death.

'I'm not just doing this for him, though—helping you, I mean.' Dylan twisted to look her straight in the eye, and Sadie found it strangely difficult to look away. What was it about this man that was so captivating, so compelling? 'But you have to know I wouldn't give up on this—not on something that was so important to my best friend.'

'I know that,' Sadie said, but she knew it lacked the conviction of her previous agreement.

Yes, Dylan would want to do this for Adem. But she also knew that all he could really offer was a short-term solution at best. The money would keep them afloat, give them another chance, and his thoughts on the plans for the future of the hotel would be invaluable, she was sure. But it was going to take more than that to save the Azure. She needed to find a way to do that herself, once Dylan's money had been spent and the man himself had moved on. She couldn't rely on him to be there for anything more than cash and brief excitement at the start of a new project.

With a sigh Dylan reached across and took the scarf from her lap, unwrapping the paper again. Then, gently, he placed it around her throat, knotting it loosely at the front. The soft silk felt luxurious against her skin, and she couldn't help but smile at the bright pop of colours around her neck. Then she raised her chin, and her gaze crashed into his, heating her cheeks until she was sure she was bright pink. His fingers straightened the fabric of the scarf, brushing against her throat, and her skin tingled under his touch.

How long had it been since she'd felt a tingle like that? She could say exactly, to the day.

Not since her husband had died.

Sadie swallowed, hard, and shuffled back along her stone seat.

'I know I'm not Adem,' Dylan said, his voice softer now. 'And you know me, I don't do long term or commitment, not in my personal life. But if I say I'll take on a work project, I see it through to the end, whatever happens. You can trust me on that.'

Sadie nodded, knowing it was true as far as it went. But it wasn't the whole truth. 'Which is why you only ever take on short-term projects,' she pointed out, as gently as she could.

'Yeah. I suppose it is.' Dylan looked down at his hands, and a coolness spread across Sadie again now he wasn't staring at her.

He looked so forlorn that Sadie felt obliged to try and build him up again. After all, he *was* doing his best, and that had to be worth something. Besides, she needed him.

'Okay,' she said, 'we're in this together, then—if you can convince your stakeholders to invest.'

He glanced up again, a faint smile on his lips. 'I'll be as persuasive as I can with whatever proposal we come up with. So what's next?'

'I don't know about you, but I need some coffee.' She got to her feet, smoothing down the skirt of her sundress and adjusting the scarf. The bright colours looked just right against the pale dress somehow. 'Proper Turkish coffee.' She offered him a hand to pull him up.

'Sounds like just the tonic,' he replied, his fingers closing around hers.

Sadie hoped so. With the strange way she was feeling today she needed some sort of medicine. Or a slap upside the head.

Sadie chose a small coffee shop overlooking the marina. Dylan sat back and let her order while he took in the view. Still, the aroma of thick, burnt coffee beans took him back through the years—to epic coffee-fests with Adem and Neal at university, when they'd drink buckets of the stuff to get through revision or a particularly tough assignment. Or later, lounging around in Sadie and Adem's first flat in London, when they had all just been starting out—and burning the candle at both ends working full time and studying for MBAs or accountancy qualifications at night. They'd passed whole weekends just drinking coffee until it had been time to switch to beer.

'So,' Sadie said, as the waiter disappeared to fetch their coffee, 'you think I need to change direction with my plans.'

Yeah, he should have known that conversation wasn't over. The scarf apology seemed to have worked in the short term, but it didn't really change anything. Her plans were still stuck in the past.

'I think you need to consider new opportunities as they present themselves.' That sounded better, right? 'Adem always knew how to keep an eye out for a new opportunity—and when to jump at it.'

She pulled a face, her mouth twisting up into a grimace that would have been ugly on anyone else. Apparently his new approach didn't sound all that much better after all. 'I suppose you taught him that.'

Dylan frowned. What, exactly, was that supposed to mean? Stupid to pretend he didn't know. And she was right—she'd seen him jump at the chance of new work, new women, new places, new everything too often not to be. Dylan Jacobs didn't stick at anything—except success. And even then he'd found a way to make it fit his own natural tendencies towards the short term.

His sister Cassie always claimed he was just making sure to run first—before he could be left or hurt. Dylan had never had the heart to tell her that he was more afraid of hurting than *being* hurt. He might be his father's son in many ways, but he had a better handle on his own failings. If he couldn't give forever—and he couldn't—it was better never to promise more than just for now.

It had worked so far, anyway.

Sadie was still waiting for an answer. 'Maybe. We both learnt a lot from working together.'

No response. The waiter returned, carrying two tiny cups of thick, black sludge and little sugar pellets to sweeten it. Dylan busied himself stirring some into his coffee while he tried to figure out what he'd said now.

And then, when it became clear he wasn't going to work it out alone, he asked, 'Okay, what did I say this time?'

Sadie looked up from twirling her spoon anti-clockwise in her coffee and shook her head. 'Nothing. Really.' She faked a smile—and Dylan had seen enough of her real ones to be sure this one was fake. 'But we're letting our history colour our business discussions again, don't you think?'

Were they? Not really, Dylan decided. Which meant that whatever discussion she was having with herself in her head probably was. God, he really wished he knew what she was thinking.

'That's kind of inevitable, don't you think?' he asked. 'We've known each other a long time, after all.'

'I've barely seen you in the last five years,' Sadie pointed out.

'Which only makes it worse. We've got a lot of catching up to do.' Instinctively, he reached out to place his hand on hers, where it rested beside her coffee cup. 'And, Sadie, just because we haven't seen each other, that doesn't mean we're not still friends. That we're not still connected.'

She had to feel it too, that connection, tying them together through the years, however far he strayed. Surely
she did, otherwise, he was all on his own out on this limb.
He might not be able to stay, but it felt like he'd never
truly left her either.

Sadie pulled her hand away, and Dylan's heart sank
an inch or two.

'What would you like to do for dinner tonight?' she
asked, not looking at him. 'I could book a table for you
somewhere in town, if you'd like.'

For you. Not us. Yeah, that wasn't going to work for
him.

Clearly the history thing was still bothering her. But
as much as he wanted this to be all business, the truth
was he wouldn't be there at all if it wasn't for their past.
So maybe they needed to address that history head-on
so they could move forward. On to a new business relationship, even if that was all it could ever be. At least
he'd be able to help her.

He just had to find a way to get her to open up and talk
to him about those five years he'd missed. And maybe,
just maybe, what had happened before then.

Unfortunately, Dylan only knew one way to get those
kinds of results. It worked with most of his clients' stum-
bling blocks—and it had always, always worked with
Adem. Like the night he'd shown up pale and troubled,
ring box in hand, trying to pluck up the courage to propose to Sadie, even though they had been far too young.
Dylan had applied his usual technique, talked it out, and
convinced Adem to do it—ignoring any cracking of his
own heart as he'd done so.

The method was foolproof. It had precedent. No reason
at all to think it wouldn't work with Sadie, too.

He needed to get her drunk.

Dylan drained his coffee, trying not to wince at the still-bitter taste. 'Town sounds good. But don't bother booking anywhere. I think tonight you need to show me the Kuşadasi nightlife.'

CHAPTER SIX

THE SAME WARDROBE, the same clothes—still nothing to wear. Sadie sighed and dropped to sit on her bed and study the contents of her closet from afar. What was she supposed to wear for a night out on the town anyway? She wasn't sure she'd ever had one in Kuşadasi—since they'd arrived she and Adem had always been too busy with the hotel. Tonight would be the blind leading the blind.

Except, of course, Dylan was probably the expert at wild nights out in towns and cities across the globe. If she was lucky, maybe she could wait until he inevitably started chatting up some blonde at the bar then slip away home without him even noticing. That would be good. Sort of.

But even that incredibly depressing plan still required her to get dressed.

Eventually she settled on her smartest pair of jeans, a black top that had enough drape at the front to look vaguely dressy, and a pair of heels. She'd just have to rely on the make-up and jewellery she'd picked out to do the rest.

Sadie checked her watch—she still had half an hour before she needed to meet Dylan. The calculation of the time difference between Turkey and England was so automatic these days it was barely seconds before she'd fired up the laptop ready to Skype Finn, glad to see that her parents' computer was already online.

Finn knew the sound of the Skype call well enough that Sadie wasn't surprised when the video picture resolved to show his cheeky face already there, ready to chat. His cheeks were red and his hair a little sweaty around the hairline, as if he'd been doing a lot of racing around. From the shouts and laughs in the background Sadie guessed that his cousins were visiting, too. Good. He had little enough interaction with other children in Turkey; she'd hate to think of him getting lonely over in England, too.

'Hi, Mum!' Finn waved excitedly across the internet. 'Wow! You look really pretty tonight.'

Guilt poured over her in a rush, threatening to wash away her carefully applied eyeliner and lipstick. 'Thanks, little man,' she said, the words coming out weak. She shouldn't be dressing up for Dylan, shouldn't let her son see her looking pretty for another man, even if he was only a friend. She should be with Finn, sorting their future.

That's what I'm doing, part of her brain argued back. She needed Dylan to save the Azure.

When had it all grown so complicated?

'Are you having fun with Grandma and Granddad?' she asked. 'What are you up to?'

'Lots. CJ and Phoebe are here with Auntie Rachel. We've been playing in the garden, and next we're going to build the biggest Lego fort in the world ever!' Finn's eyes brightened with excitement, and Sadie felt a wave of love rush over her, the way she always did when she saw him happy. Whatever else seemed crazy in her life at the moment, Finn at least was as wonderful, perfect and precious as always.

'Sounds fun.' She was just about to ask him something else when the sound of two high-pitched voices yelling Finn's name cut her off.

'Sorry, Mum. Gotta go. CJ needs me for the fort. Otherwise Phoebe will make it a pink princess castle again.' Finn's words came out in a rush as he moved further away from the screen. 'Bye, Mum!'

'Love you,' Sadie called after him, but all she could see was the back of his head, disappearing through the door to the other room. Well. Who was she to try and compete with a Lego fort, anyway?

Before she could end the call her sister Rachel appeared on the screen, settling into the chair Finn had just vacated. 'Sorry. They're just having so much fun together. It's lovely.'

'That's okay,' Sadie said with a smile. 'I'm just glad he's not missing me.'

'Liar.' Rachel grinned back. 'At least part of you wishes he was pining away without you. Go on, admit it.'

'Maybe a very small part.'

Rachel nodded. 'You wouldn't be human otherwise.' She squinted at the screen, and Sadie tried not to duck away under her sister's scrutiny. 'He's right, though. You *do* look pretty. What's going on there worth dolling up for?'

She groaned inwardly. She should have called *before* she'd got ready. She couldn't lie to Rachel—she'd tried often enough over the years, but her sister always saw through it. But how to tell the truth?

'I've got a potential investor visiting,' she said in the end. 'He wants to see the Kuşadası nightlife. Does this look okay for bar-hopping? It's been so long I can't remember.'

'Stand up and give me a twirl,' Rachel instructed, and

Sadie did as she was told. 'It's perfect. So…this potential investor. Is he cute?'

Sadie sat back down with a bump. Cute wasn't exactly the word she'd use to describe Dylan. Heartstoppingly gorgeous but totally untouchable? Closer to the mark. Still, she wasn't saying that to Rachel.

'I suppose so,' she said, as neutrally as she could.

'And is there…dare I risk to hope it? Is there fizz?'

Fizz. The word they'd used as teenagers to describe that intangible connection, that feeling that you just had to touch that other person, be close to them, feel their smile on your face or you'd just bubble over and explode. Did Dylan have fizz? Silly question. He'd always had fizz. That was the problem. And when he'd placed that scarf around her neck and his fingers had brushed her skin…

'There *is* fizz!' Rachel announced gleefully. 'Don't try and deny it. I can tell these things. Psychic sister skills.'

Sadie shook her head. 'It doesn't matter if there is or isn't fizz. The investor…it's Dylan. You remember Adem's best man? He's just here because he wants to help out with the Azure, but he needs to convince his stakeholders we're a good investment so I'm trying to give him enough plus points to present a great proposal to them.'

'Dylan? Of course I remember Dylan. If I hadn't been already married at your wedding…'

'Then you could have lined up behind the other bridesmaids for a shot at him.'

'He was more than cute, Sadie,' Rachel pointed out. As if she hadn't noticed.

'He's an old friend.'

'So? There's fizz.'

'He's *Adem's* old friend,' Sadie stressed, hoping her

sister would just figure it out without her having to spell it out.

'Which means Adem trusted this guy,' Rachel countered. 'Which means you can too.'

'With my hotel, maybe. Not with any fizz.' Even if she *was* ready to throw herself back into romance with a one-night stand or something, Dylan Jacobs would not be a good choice. And if she was even *thinking* about anything longer term, he'd be the worst choice in the world. He'd said it himself, he didn't do commitment. And she couldn't be in the market for anything less. She had her son to think of.

But Rachel clearly didn't get that. 'Why not?'

'Rachel…'

Her sister sighed, the sound huffing across the computer speakers. 'It's been two years, Sadie. Adem wouldn't want you sitting out there all alone, you know that. He'd understand.'

'Maybe,' Sadie allowed. Her husband had been loving, generous and wonderful. He probably would want her to be happy again with someone else. On the other hand… 'But I'm sure he wouldn't want me with Dylan Jacobs either.' He'd want her settled and stable—not things on offer from Dylan, even if he was interested.

'Why on earth not?'

'He's not that sort of guy, Rach. Besides…' She trailed off, not wanting to put the thought into words.

'Now we're getting to it. Tell me.'

Sadie took a deep breath, and confessed. 'If I admit to feeling…fizz with Dylan now, isn't that the same as admitting I felt it when Adem was alive, too?'

'Oh, Sadie.' Sympathy oozed out of Rachel's words and expression. 'Fizz, attraction…it's just that. We all feel it from time to time, with all sorts of people. It's what we do with it that counts. Sometimes we ignore it, and sometimes we act on it and see what happens next.' She paused. 'You didn't, right? Act on it with Dylan, I mean, before?'

'No!' An easy truth. But it didn't stop the niggling guilt reminding her that she'd thought about it.

'Then don't beat yourself up about it. Go out with the guy tonight. Relax. Enjoy a little fizz…'

Sadie groaned. 'I'm going to pretend you're talking about prosecco.'

'Ha! Whatever helps you loosen up a bit.'

'I'd better go.' Sadie checked her watch to be sure. 'Tell Finn I love him. And that I'll call tomorrow.'

'Will do,' Rachel said with a nod. 'Now, go and have fun.'

With a weak smile Sadie clicked the 'end call' button. A whole evening watching Dylan flirt with barmaids and blondes. She had a feeling that fun was the last thing she should expect tonight to be. Maybe more some sort of weird torture technique devised purely to drive her insane.

'And yet I'm going anyway,' she murmured to herself as she gathered up her light jacket and handbag. 'The things I do for this hotel…'

Tipping his chair back against the wall behind him, Dylan watched Sadie's slim form as she made her way across the bar from the bathrooms, wondering if she'd notice he'd replenished their drinks in her absence. Operation Drunk Conversation was now officially two drinks in, and he still felt a little uneasy about it. Apparently Bar Street was the place to go and get drunk in Kuşadası, although with its range of Irish and British bars, as well as some Turkish ones, Dylan wasn't

sure this was necessarily the local colour he'd be trying
to sell to the stakeholders. On the other hand, it clearly
brought in plenty of tourists—and money. It almost reminded him of their student days.

She looked younger in jeans and heels, he decided.
Almost like she had back in London as a twenty-some-
thing. She'd filled out a little since then, he supposed, but
only in the best ways. Her slender curves enticed him as
she swerved through the crowds to reach him. His head
filled with music, the way it had the first time he'd ever
met her—the Beatles' 'Sexy Sadie' playing on a loop
through his mind.

'You're still alone. I'm amazed.' Sadie slipped into her
seat and took a sip of her wine without commenting on
the level in the glass.

'Why amazed?'

'Well, five minutes always used to be more than
enough time for you to find a girl to flirt with when we
used to go out.' There was no bitterness or censure in her
voice, more amusement, but Dylan felt the words like
paper cuts all the same. Probably because they were true.

'Times have changed.'

'Not that much,' Sadie said. 'Neal keeps me updated
on your exploits, you know.'

He bit back a curse. But, on the other hand, she'd
given him the in he'd been waiting for—the first refer-
ence to the good old days. 'I was just thinking how much
younger you look in jeans, actually. Like you used to,
back in London. I half expected Adem to appear and put
his arm around you.'

Sadie's smile turned a little sad. 'Would that he could.'

'Yeah. It must be hard, being here without him. The
memories, I mean.'

'We never came here, actually,' Sadie said, looking

around her curiously at the crowded bar. 'But you meant Turkey itself. The Azure.'

'I did, yeah,' Dylan agreed. Dare he push it yet? Just a little? 'No one would have blamed you for selling up and leaving, you know.' He needed to understand why she hadn't. What made her commitment to this place so strong? What was it about Sadie that made her so able to commit and stick? And what was missing in him?

'It wouldn't make any difference where we were anyway,' Sadie said, which didn't answer the question he hadn't asked, but Dylan supposed he couldn't really blame her for that. 'I see Adem every day when I look at Finn—and, to be honest, I love that reminder.'

Of course she did. He'd never seen any couple as in love as Adem and Sadie. He didn't really need her to answer—he knew. The Azure was her way of holding onto the love of her life. Just because he'd never felt like that about someone didn't mean he couldn't see it in others.

'I'm glad you have that.' The truth, even if it carried a little pain with it. 'I'm sorry. I should have visited more. Spent more time with Finn.'

'Yes, you should,' she said, mock-sternly. 'Why didn't you?'

Did she really not know why? After that night at Kim and Logan's wedding he'd been sure his motives for staying away had been more than clear—and that she'd be grateful he had. Unless she didn't remember? She *had* been pretty drunk. So had he, of course, or it never, ever would have happened in the first place.

Misgivings began to creep up on him when he thought again about his plan. The two of them, drunk alone together, hadn't ended well in the past. But he didn't know another way to get her to loosen up around him.

'Work, mostly,' he lied, realising she was still waiting

for an answer. 'But I'm ready to fix that now.' He raised his glass. 'To absent friends.'

'Absent friends,' Sadie echoed. Lifting her own glass, she drank deeply, unconsciously giving him exactly what he wanted. It was too late for misgivings now anyway. It was time to put the plan into action.

'Hey, do you remember the time Neal got locked out of that hotel wearing nothing but a corset and stockings?'

Sadie burst into laughter, putting her glass down too hard on the table so wine sloshed over the edge. 'Of course I do—it was my corset! What I don't remember is how he persuaded me to lend it to him.'

'You've always been a soft touch for Neal,' Dylan said. 'Besides, he had a very good story. I should know, I made it up.'

She slapped his arm. 'You deviant. Tell me the whole story, then—the truth this time.'

It was going to work, Dylan could tell. By morning they'd have exorcised all their ghosts and memories and be able to move on. To be the friends and business partners Sadie needed them to be.

And nothing more.

He took a glug of his beer and started the story.

'Well, there was this girl, see…'

Several bars later Sadie could feel the alcohol starting to get to her—in that pleasant, slightly buzzy way that meant it was time to stop before another drink seemed like a really good idea. Otherwise tomorrow would be no fun at all. *Now* she remembered why she didn't do this any more.

'I need to call it a night.' She pushed her still half-full glass across the table away from her.

'Not a bad idea.' Dylan drained the last of his pint. 'You always were the sensible one.'

'Somebody had to be.'

She gave him a friendly grin and he returned it, his smile all at once totally familiar and yet somehow new. It made that buzzy feeling in her limbs turn a little more liquid, like honey.

They'd talked all evening, almost without pause. She'd worried, when he'd suggested this night out, that it would be awkward, the conversation stilted. But instead they'd fallen into old patterns, chatting about the past in the way only friends who'd done their most significant growing up together could. The conversation had covered everything from the day they'd met until the last time they had all been together before Adem had died.

Everything except one night—the night of Kim and Logan's wedding.

Did he even remember? And, if so, how much? Curiosity was burning inside her with the need to know. Had *she* remembered wrong? It had been so long ago she was starting to doubt her own memories. They'd both been pretty drunk that night...

But she wasn't drunk tonight. Just tipsy enough to be a little daring.

'What's the plan for tomorrow?' Dylan asked, getting to his feet and grabbing his jacket. 'I've got a business call first thing, then I'm all yours for the day.'

Tomorrow. Had she even made a plan for tomorrow? 'I thought maybe the beach?'

'Lying prone in the sun sounds like the perfect way to deal with my inevitable hangover.' He groaned as they headed for the door. 'I am officially too old for this.'

Sadie smiled. 'I never thought I'd hear you admit to that.'

'We all have to grow up some time,' Dylan said with a shrug, and somehow it felt like he was saying far more than just the words.

Outside, the autumn evening air had turned a little chilly, and Sadie shivered as they walked along the seafront, looking out for an empty cab.

'Cold?' Dylan asked. Then, without waiting for an answer, he slung an arm around her shoulder for warmth. A friendly gesture, Sadie knew. That was all it was—and nothing he and Neal hadn't done often enough in the past. But suddenly, here and now, as the fabric of his jacket brushed her bare neck she felt it. Fizz. Undeniable, impossible to ignore, fizz.

It was no good; she needed to know. And she was just drunk enough to ask.

'I've never asked you. Do you remember Kim and Logan's wedding?'

Dylan squinted out towards the ocean. 'That was the one up in Scotland, right? Where we all stayed in that weird hotel down the road and kept the bar open all night.'

'And Adem and Neal got into a drinking competition and passed out on the sofas in the next room.'

'I remember,' Dylan said, and even the words sounded loaded. 'You and Adem had been together, what? About a year?'

'Something like that. Do you remember what you asked me that night?'

He was standing so close, his arm around her shoulders, that she could feel his muscles stiffen. Oh, yeah, he remembered. 'Do you? We never… You never mentioned it again, so I always figured you must have forgotten. We weren't exactly sober that night.'

She'd gone too far to back out now. 'You asked me if

I'd ever wondered what might have happened if I'd met you first instead of Adem.'

'Yeah.' He let out a long breath. 'You said you hadn't.'

'And I truly hadn't, until that moment.'

The words hung there between them, the implication both clear and terrifying. They'd stopped walking without Sadie even realising, and suddenly a taxi pulled up beside them, the driver rolling down the window to ask where they wanted to go.

'The Azure, please,' Sadie said, shuffling along the back seat to let Dylan in beside her.

They rode in silence for a long moment before Dylan asked, 'And after?'

'After?' She knew what he was asking, but she needed a moment before she answered.

'After that moment. Did you...?'

She looked away. 'I wondered.'

'Huh.' Dylan slumped back against the car seat, as if all the tension had flowed out of his body with her words. Then he shook his head, laughing a little—Sadie got the impression it was at himself, rather than her. 'And then, of course, I tried to kiss you like a total idiot and—'

'Wait. What? I don't remember that bit.' And surely, surely that was the part she *would* remember, however much she'd had to drink.

'Don't you?' Dylan smiled, the expression shaded in the darkness of the cab. 'It was after we'd lugged Adem and Neal up to our rooms. You gave me a hug goodnight and...' He shrugged, trailing off. 'You pushed me away, of course.'

'I can't believe I don't remember that.'

'I'm glad you didn't,' Dylan said. 'Not my finest hour. I felt absolutely awful the next day—and was very glad one of us had been sober enough to be sensible.'

Sadie turned away, searching her memory for the lost moment and coming up blank. How different might their world have been if she'd remembered the next day? If she'd confessed to Adem? A thousand different paths spiralled from that moment, all but one untaken. And she wouldn't want to change it, she realised, not really. She wouldn't give up the years she'd had with Adem, or having Finn, for anything in the world. Things had worked out exactly as they were supposed to.

But that didn't stop her imagining what it might have felt like. And, God, did that bring a bucketload of guilt with it, right there.

Before she'd had time to work her way through half her emotions, they were back at the Azure. She paid up in a daze and walked inside, heading for the lift with Dylan beside her.

'You okay?' he asked, as the doors opened.

She nodded, and stepped inside, pressing the button for her floor on autopilot. 'Fine. So, tomorrow. Meet you in the lobby at ten?'

'Perfect.' He leant across her to press the penthouse button as they started to move. 'Sadie—'

'Don't worry about it,' she said, too fast. 'It's all in the past now.'

The lift dinged as it reached her floor, and she stepped towards the doors before they were even open.

Suddenly there was a hand at her waist, spinning her round, and Dylan was closer than she'd imagined, so close she could feel the heat of him.

'I might be about to be an idiot again,' he said.

Sadie swallowed, her mouth too dry. God, she wanted it. Wanted to feel his lips on hers, to see what she'd missed all those years ago. But the guilt that filled her had sobered her up and was already moving her feet backwards as the lift doors opened.

'Goodnight, Dylan.' She pulled away, stepping out, watching the frustration and fear crossing his face as the doors closed behind him and the lift whisked him away.

CHAPTER SEVEN

DYLAN WOKE UP the next morning to the sound of his phone alarm buzzing, far too early, and his head throbbing in time with the beeps. As if he needed the physical reminder of last night's exploits to give him a bad feeling about the day ahead.

He fumbled for the phone and switched off the alarm, his poor, tired brain trying to catch up with the day. He had a conference call. He had to deal with Sadie. He really needed a shower.

Deciding that the last might help with the previous two items, he hauled himself out of bed and into the bathroom, thoughts flying at him as fast as the water from the wonderfully powerful showerhead.

If he was feeling bad this morning, chances were that Sadie was feeling worse. And not just physically. He knew her tendency to beat herself up about things that weren't her fault, or weren't even all that wrong in the first place, and he had a feeling this morning would be a doozy.

Still, as bad as he felt for making her life more difficult than it already was—or at least more morally and emotionally complicated—he couldn't help but smile, remembering that for the first time since he'd met her he knew he wasn't in this alone. Not completely.

Switching off the water, he dried, dressed and managed to make it through the conference call—hopefully without any obvious signs of his hangover or his preoccupation. As he hung up, scribbling a last few notes to himself for later, he checked the clock. Still twenty minutes before he was due to meet Sadie. Should he work, nap or…?

He picked up his phone and hit the familiar key combination to call Neal. Yeah, it was early in Britain, but Neal had always been an early bird anyway. Except after nights out with him and Adem.

'How's it going?' Neal asked, in lieu of an actual greeting. 'You signed over your life savings to her yet?'

If he thought that would work… 'Nah. I got her drunk and told her the whole story about you and her corset instead.'

'Cheers. I'll look forward to that coming up next time we have a business meeting,' Neal said. 'But, seriously, how is she?'

'Probably hungover but otherwise fine.' He hoped.

Neal sighed. 'What did you do?'

'Nothing.' Much.

She'd try and pull back now, he could feel it. Try and put that distance they'd crossed last night back between them. Unless he could convince her not to.

'Although…' Dylan said, and Neal groaned.

'Here we go. Tell me.'

'I might have questioned Adem's plan for the Azure a bit. It needs updating.'

'So what? You're going to stay in Turkey and develop a better one?' Neal sounded sceptical.

'I'm going to work with her to develop one before I leave,' Dylan corrected him. She didn't have time to pull back. He only had a few more days to help her; they had to keep working. She'd see that, right?

Maybe the best thing was for them both to pretend that last night had never happened, just like last time. At least, once the headache faded.

'Are you, now?' Dylan didn't like the sudden raised interest level in Neal's voice.

'I am. What about it?'

'Just sounds like more involvement than you'd planned on,' Neal said. 'A lot more.'

Since Dylan's original plan had been get in, get out, send Sadie cash afterwards and never have to think about the Azure again, Neal had a point. He hadn't wanted to torment himself more than necessary by staying in her presence when she was more available than ever but still every bit as untouchable.

But all that had changed with two words. *I wondered.*

'She needs more help than I expected,' Dylan said, hoping his friend would accept the excuse.

'She needs every bit of help she can get,' Neal agreed with a sigh. 'I'm glad you're there.'

'So am I.'

Yes, he was still leaving in three days. And, yes, he knew he'd never be Adem, never be the love of Sadie's life. He wasn't imagining some perfect golden future for them together or anything.

But just knowing that she'd thought about it—about them—too? Well, that gave him hope.

And sometimes that was all a guy needed to get through the day.

The first thing Sadie registered when she woke up was her dry mouth. Next came the crushing weight of what felt like a boulder on her chest.

Last night had been everything she'd planned to avoid. How was she supposed to go back to All-Business Sadie after admitting that she'd imagined them together? And for the last twelve years…

After learning he'd tried to kiss her, too.

After almost letting him kiss her last night.

She pulled the pillow over her head and hoped it muffled her agonised groan.

And now she had to spend a whole day on the beach with him. In swimwear.

It all just went to prove that there really *was* a special hell for women who ogled their husband's best friend.

Escaping from her pillowy cage, she took deep breaths and tried to let the morning air soothe her—and her hangover. She needed to be calm and reasonable about this. As she had been about everything else she'd dealt with since Adem had died. She—and the Azure—needed Dylan. They needed his money, his investment and, much as she hated to admit it, his business brain, too. So she needed to find a way to make this right.

And, hopefully, considerably less awkward.

As she kicked off the covers and contemplated, Rachel's words from the night before floated back through her distracted brain. In some ways her sister had been right—as usual. Adem wouldn't want her to be alone or lonely. Which wasn't to say he'd want her to be rushing into the arms of another man either, but Sadie knew he wouldn't expect her to be alone forever.

She had, though. For the last two years the very idea of being with someone else had felt completely alien, the sort of thing that could only happen to other people. Adem had been the love of her life. Where was there to go from there really?

But last night, for the first time, the idea of moving on had seemed like a possibility. The thought of kissing another man had, for once, not filled her with revulsion or even confusion.

She'd wanted to kiss Dylan. And that was absolutely terrifying.

Because even if she was ready to *maybe* think about *possibly* moving on and *perhaps* just *thinking* about dating again, Dylan Jacobs was not the man to move on with.

If she had been after a fling or a one-night stand, something to get her back in the dating game, then maybe. But she wasn't a one-night stand sort of girl, never had been. And now…she had responsibilities. Commitments that had to come before a little personal pleasure.

She had Finn.

She wouldn't be another notch on Dylan's bedpost—and with a guy like Dylan she knew that was all she could ever be.

No, last night had taught her something far more important than the fact he'd tried to kiss her once. It had taught her that they still had history, and friendship, even with Adem gone. Sadie wanted Dylan to stay part of her life—and part of Finn's. She wanted her son to learn about his father from the people who had loved him most—and that had to include Dylan.

Another reason, if she'd needed one, why she couldn't risk anything more with him. She knew him, too well perhaps. One night in his bed and he'd hit the road, not coming back until he was good and certain that she wasn't getting any ideas about things between them going anywhere.

Better to keep things simple. Maybe they couldn't be just business—but they could definitely be just friends.

Now she just needed a way to get that across to Dylan.

Lying back against her cool sheets with the covers off,

she let the breeze from the open window caress her skin as she considered her options. This wasn't a conversation she wanted to have with him while she was wearing a bikini. She needed to stall a little before they got to the beach. Then he could sunbathe, nap, explore, ignore her the rest of the day, whatever he wanted. As long as he understood how things were going to be.

Sadie smiled to herself as the perfect solution presented itself. And it might just solve both of their hangovers, too.

It was hard to tell what Sadie was thinking or feeling when Dylan met her in the lobby. Her eyes were hidden behind oversized dark glasses, her hair pulled back from her face, and she wore a light skirt and tee shirt. From the large straw bag she carried, with towels peeking out the top and a bottle of suntan lotion in the front pocket, he assumed they were still on for the beach. Beyond that, he had no idea how the day might play out—and she didn't seem inclined to tell him.

'Ready to go?' she asked, the moment he approached. When he nodded, she spun on her heel and headed out, slipping behind the wheel of her car and waiting for him to join her.

They drove in silence for about ten minutes, while Dylan thought up a dozen conversation starters in his head. But every time he turned to use one of them Sadie's cool indifference to his presence stopped him.

He had to let her go first.

The first rumblings of doubt started in his mind when Sadie pulled in at a tumbledown farmhouse on the side of the road. There was no sign of anyone else around, but she jumped out of the car all the same and waited for him to follow.

A terrace sat outside the house itself, covered with vines and greenery, right next to the road. Sadie climbed the rickety wooden steps up to it and, after a moment, Dylan did the same.

'Um, did we add something to today's itinerary?' he asked, as they stood alone on the terrace.

'Trust me,' Sadie replied. 'We need this.'

What he really needed was a few more hours of sleep and some mega-painkillers, but she'd asked for his trust, so he'd give it to her.

After a moment the door to the farmhouse opened and a man walked out, smiling widely at Sadie, hands open in welcome. Sadie grinned back, and the two of them spoke in Turkish for a moment or two. Dylan didn't even try to guess what they were saying.

The man motioned to a nearby table, bare wood with benches to match, right at the edge of the terrace with a great view of the passing cars and the dusty fields beyond. But Sadie sat without question, so Dylan did the same.

'So this is…?' he asked.

Before Sadie could answer, a woman in an apron appeared, her dark hair coiled at the back of her head, and placed a strange metal pot, two glass teacups and a basket of bread on the table.

'Breakfast,' Sadie answered, reaching for the bread. 'Told you we needed it.'

Dylan started to relax. Maybe the woman had a point after all. He hadn't managed to make it down to the restaurant that morning, and his stomach definitely needed food.

The dishes kept coming, carried out by the man and the woman while Sadie explained about Turkish tea and waited for it to brew before pouring it. Dylan salivated at the sight of sweet, thick honey for the bread, bowls of olives, scrambled eggs with chorizo, chunks of salty feta cheese and a huge fruit platter. It might not be the full English he'd usually rely on to finish off a hangover, but Dylan had a feeling it would be more than up to the task.

They ate mostly in silence, Dylan savouring every mouthful of the delicious and obviously freshly cooked food. And as they ate, Dylan's hangover wasn't the only thing that started to recede. Somehow, without talking about it or even acknowledging it was there, the tension that had been pulled tight between them since they'd met in the lobby that morning started to loosen, just enough for him to relax.

The powers of good food truly were transformative.

As Sadie mopped up the last of the chorizo and eggs with the end of the bread, Dylan poured out the final dregs of the tea, knowing that things were about to change.

It was time for The Talk.

God, he hated The Talk.

Steeling himself, he waited for her to begin.

'Okay. So, I thought we needed that before we could deal with…' Sadie trailed off.

'Last night,' Dylan finished for her. No point beating around the bush now. 'Good call.'

Sadie picked up her paper napkin and began twisting it between her fingers. 'Here's the thing. I figure you wanted to go out last night to remind me that we're not just business. We have history.'

'I guess, a bit. Perhaps.' It hadn't been much of a plan, but it still discomfited Dylan a bit to have it seen through so easily.

'And you're right,' Sadie went on, apparently unconcerned by his manipulations. 'I get it. We're friends—and I don't want to lose that.'

'I'm glad to hear it.' Ah, so this was the way it was. She was actually giving him the old 'I don't want to ruin our friendship with sex' talk. He'd never been on this side of it before.

It kind of sucked.

But her friendship mattered to him—no, just having her in his life mattered to him. Any way that worked for her. So he'd go along with it, despite the stinging pain that had taken up residence in his chest. Because what else did he have to offer her, really?

'I want you to be part of Finn's life.' She leant across the table, shifting plates and bowls out of her way. Dylan rescued the remains of the honey, which were perilously close to her elbow. 'I want him to know about his dad from the people who really knew and loved him—and that includes you.'

She sounded so earnest, so determined that he couldn't even find it in himself to be mad or frustrated. Because, of course, it was all about Adem in the end. He should never have imagined that it could be otherwise.

'But as for the rest of it,' Sadie said, sitting back again, the distance between them yawning open, 'there's no point dwelling on the past. Right?'

'I've always tried not to,' he said mildly. Tried not to think about how different his life might have been if his father hadn't walked out and left them, if he hadn't spent his youth protecting his mother and sister, taking care of them, finding the money for the household bills each week. How different *he* might be. Life was what it was—no point pretending otherwise.

Except, of course, that was exactly what he was doing every time he thought about Sadie and imagined what could have been, maybe. What they could have had if he'd been the one she'd run into with a full cup of coffee one rainy Oxford day instead of Adem.

Stupid, really. It wouldn't have made any difference. They'd have flirted perhaps. Maybe even dated for a bit. But if she thought he wasn't the settling-down sort now, it was nothing compared to how he'd been at twenty-one. He'd have sabotaged things within a month—and Sadie would probably have cried on Adem's shoulder, and they'd have fallen in love anyway.

Just the way it was supposed to be.

'I'm ready to face the future now, I think.' Bravery shone out of Sadie's face, and Dylan tried to shake away his melancholy thoughts and listen. 'I'm really ready to build a new future out here for me and my son—not just keep living Adem's dream and his plan.'

Did she really think that counted as moving on? She'd still be here, in the place Adem had chosen for them. She might think this was a big step forward, but to Dylan it still looked like clinging to the past.

The past was all well and good, but living there wasn't going to help Sadie find her spark again. For that, she needed to move on to her own dreams. And he was there to help her do that.

'So, what does that mean?' he asked.

'It means I'm ready to listen to your plans, instead of insisting on following Adem's,' Sadie said. 'You tell me what we need to do at the Azure, and we'll do it. Whatever it takes to save this place for Finn.'

For Finn. That was why she thought she was doing this. Interesting.

'Great.' It wasn't moving on, not really. But it might be the best he got from her, and at least it gave him a way to help her. It could be worse. 'Then let's get to the beach.'

'The beach?' Her nose crinkled up adorably, and Dylan looked away to stop himself staring at it.

'I always do my best brainstorming when I'm relaxing,' he said, faking a smile.

CHAPTER EIGHT

LADIES' BEACH WAS comfortingly familiar to Sadie. As they walked from the car down onto the soft sand she took deep breaths and let the salt air fill her lungs, while the sound of gulls and families playing in the sand and surf echoed in her ears. But even as she let the comfort of the seaside wash over her, the feeling that something was missing ached in her middle.

She missed Finn. He loved the beach so much—especially this one. They could play for hours, searching for shells to decorate sandcastles or jumping over the waves as they lapped against the shore. When they'd first moved here they'd spent almost every weekend at the beach the whole summer.

'It's a nice beach,' Dylan commented, his trainers dangling from his fingers as he walked barefoot beside her.

'Nice?' Sadie said disbelievingly. She took another look around her at the perfect yellow sand and bright blue water. 'It's perfect.'

Dylan chuckled. 'Okay, yeah. It's pretty gorgeous. I can see why this, at least, is a big draw for the tourists. Finn must love it here.'

'He does.' The heavy weight of a pebble of guilt joined the ache in her middle. When was the last time she'd brought Finn down to the beach? Things had just been so busy... 'We haven't made it down here together for a while, though.'

She flinched with surprise as Dylan's hand came up to rest against the small of her back, rubbing comfort through her tee shirt and steering her around a hole some enterprising young child had clearly spent some hours digging. She needed to pay more attention to where she was going. But Dylan's hand stayed at her back and the warmth of it, so much more heated than the bright sun overhead, was too much of a distraction in itself.

Friends, she reminded herself. That was what they'd agreed. And beyond one drunken attempt at a kiss she had no evidence at all he wanted anything more. A hand on the back was not seduction—however much it felt like it right now.

'When we get the Azure back on track, you'll be able to hire more help,' Dylan said, apparently oblivious to the effect his touch was having on her. 'Give you more time with Finn.'

'That would be perfect.' Finn deserved so much more than an overworked, stressed mother. She needed to be both parents to him now, and that meant being there all the time. A reduced workload would definitely help with that.

She just hoped it wouldn't be too reduced. After all, what else was she going to do once Finn was in bed or at school? And once Dylan was gone. All the times when she was alone again. She would need something to distract her then, and work was perfect.

Sadie almost laughed at herself. From one extreme to another—it seemed she'd always find something to worry about. They had to actually save the Azure first anyway, and that by no means felt like a sure thing.

Everything was so much harder without Adem there

to help—even if it was just someone else to help build sandcastles or explore seaweed clumps.

Suddenly Dylan stopped walking, right in the middle of an open patch of sand unmarred by castles or holes and a decent distance from any of the other beachgoers.

'This looks like the perfect spot,' he said, dropping his bag and towel to the sand.

'To brainstorm?' Sadie asked, one eyebrow raised.

He flashed her a smile. 'To sleep off the remains of my hangover.'

'I suppose that *is* the first step to saving my hotel,' Sadie said, only half sarcastically. After all, it was going to take Dylan on top form to help the Azure.

'Definitely.'

Without warning, he reached for the hem of his tee shirt and pulled it over his head, revealing more muscles and hair than she'd expected—and definitely more skin than she felt comfortable with as a friend. Sadie's mouth dried up and she swallowed painfully as she tried not to stare. God, but the man was gorgeous. She'd known that, of course, objectively. But she'd never spent much time with such upfront and undeniable proof, certainly not in the last decade.

Dylan had always been good looking, but now he'd grown into his looks completely. He wasn't a play*boy* any more, Sadie decided. He was all man.

She needed to get out of there. 'I'm going to go and swim.'

'Okay.' Dylan looked up from laying out his towel and grabbed for her wrist before she could turn away. His proximity and the feel of his skin on hers sent every sense she had into overdrive. How did anyone ever manage to be just friends with someone who looked like Dylan Jacobs? She needed some sort of handbook.

'Sadie,' he said, staring down into her eyes, his gaze so compelling she couldn't even think of looking away. 'I will find a way to save the Azure. You know that, right?'

Sadie swallowed again, her throat dry and raspy. 'I believe you.'

His mouth twisted up into a half-smile. 'Millions wouldn't, right?'

'This is business,' Sadie said with a shrug. Something she would do well to remember. 'And you know business. If anyone can save the Azure, it's you.'

'Only for you,' he murmured.

It was too much. 'Right. Swimming.' Sadie pulled her hand away from his and tugged down her skirt and pulled off her tee shirt, leaving her in just her sensible purple tankini. Then, with what she hoped was a friendly smile, she headed straight for the water.

She couldn't afford to be swayed by fizz, or touch, or the way he looked at her. Dylan looked at every woman he met that way, she was sure. He was a walking chemistry experiment for the female half of the human race. She couldn't read any more into that.

Money and business advice was all he had to offer her, and only for the short term. Once he got bored he'd be on the move again. She really needed to remember that.

Settling onto his towel, Dylan propped himself up on one elbow in the sand and watched Sadie's tankini-clad form sashaying towards the sea. He doubted she knew she was doing it, but her hips swayed as she walked all the same, her feet sinking into the sand. All those slender curves she kept so well hidden under dark suits and shapeless jackets were on display now and, friends or not, he wasn't going to miss a minute of watching them.

Friends. She'd sounded so certain over breakfast that friendship was all she wanted from him. After the night before, and her escape from the lift, he'd almost believed her. Until he'd touched her wrist on the beach and watched the colour flood her cheeks as their skin had met. Until he'd watched her watching him and known that whatever she thought she wanted, her body had other ideas.

Bad ideas, admittedly. She was a single mother with more responsibilities than money and a rigid sense of commitment that was in complete opposition to his own. But she wanted him. Maybe even half as much as he had always wanted her.

He couldn't give her what he knew she needed—what she'd always wanted since they'd met. Sadie was the kind of woman you settled down for, that you built a life with. Another reason why Adem had been perfect for her. Despite his own fears and apprehensions, he'd put aside every reason not to and jumped at the chance to have Sadie with him for life.

Even if that had turned out to be far shorter than any of them had imagined.

No, Dylan wasn't the man to replace Adem in her life, if anyone even could. He couldn't commit to forever, and he knew that Sadie deserved nothing less. And even if he wanted to try…what would it do to her, not to mention Finn, when he failed? It wasn't worth the risk.

But he could offer her something else. After all the sorrow and stress in her life over the last couple of years, he could see shoots of new growth in her—the first hints of spring ready to return to Sadie's world. She was ready to get out there again, to blossom into a new life.

He could be a friend and business partner in that new life. But right now, in this brief time of transition, maybe he could be something more. Something temporary. A first step, perhaps. Something that would waken that new Sadie completely.

It might be the worst idea he'd ever had—and if he told Neal what he had planned he had no doubt his old friend would be on the first plane out there to stop him. But it had been over a decade now—thirteen years of watching her, wanting her and wondering about her. Who could really blame him for wanting to taste that forbidden fruit, just once, now he knew how much she wanted it too?

Just one night. How bad a sin would that be, really? As long as he was honest and upfront with her, and they both knew what they were getting out of it. They were adults now. If Sadie knew exactly what he was offering, she could make her own decision.

It just might take a while for her to talk herself into it, knowing Sadie.

He watched her lean legs disappearing into the water and shifted to keep a better eye on her as she dived under the waves. She looked so at home out there, like a sea nymph returning to her natural environment after being cooped up on land for too long. She looked free in a way she hadn't since he'd arrived in Turkey.

Dylan wanted to make her look that way on land. Preferably in a bed.

Eventually, Sadie emerged again from the waves, slicking her dark hair back from her face with her hands. With water droplets shining off her skin in the sun, she began walking back towards him, and Dylan found himself putting a lot of effort into keeping his body calm and relaxed in the face of such a sight. God, she was beautiful.

The sound of his ringing phone was an almost welcome distraction. Fumbling in the pocket of his rucksack, he pulled it out and answered, only half listening to what his assistant had to say as Sadie arrived, rolled her eyes at him, and began towelling off with a spare towel.

By the time he ended the call Dylan wasn't entirely sure what he'd agreed to, but he trusted his assistant to email him all the pertinent details. He'd deal with them later, when there were fewer distractions around.

'Honestly. Who brings work to the beach?' Wrapping a flimsy scarf thing around her waist, Sadie dropped to sit on the towel beside him.

'You brought me,' Dylan pointed out. 'This week, that's practically the same thing.'

Sadie laughed, high and bright, a sound he'd almost thought lost. She was so much more relaxed out here; he could tell it from the lines of her shoulders, the absence of the crease between her eyebrows that he'd thought was permanent. This was the Sadie he remembered.

'Seriously, though,' she said, 'what's so important that it can't wait a few hours? Why not just let it ring—or, better yet, turn it off?'

Dylan shrugged—and realised she was watching his shoulders rise and fall. Interesting. 'Guess I don't want to risk missing an opportunity. I've missed too many in my life already.'

He'd been talking about the years spent taking responsibility for his family, saying no to chances and opportunities because they'd needed him. But as the words hung in the air between them he realised she thought he meant something else entirely. And maybe, he admitted to himself, maybe he did. *Did you ever wonder what might have happened if you'd met me first, instead of Adem?*

I wondered.

Sadie looked down at her hands, damp hair hanging forward across her cheek. 'I'm not the same girl you asked that question all those years ago,' she said, her voice soft.

'You think I don't know that?' he asked. 'Look at me, Sadie.' She did as he asked, and Dylan took a long moment just absorbing everything she was now. Slowly, obviously, he looked over every inch of her, from her hair—shorter now than when they'd met by a good foot—down over her body, past every added curve or line, every soft patch and every muscle, all the way to her feet.

Did she really not know? Not realise how much she'd grown up since then—and how every year had only made her a better person? Who would want the twenty-year-old Sadie compared to the one who sat before him now?

'You are so much more now than you were then,' he murmured, knowing she'd hear him anyway. 'You're stronger, more beautiful, more alive…more than I ever dreamt any woman could be.'

Sadie stared down at him, captivated by his gaze as confusion, guilt and hope fought for space in her head. Did he really think that?

Yes. The answer came fast and true as she looked into his eyes. This wasn't Dylan making a move, the way he did with all those other women. This wasn't a seduction attempt. It was him stating a fact—something that was true and obvious to him, even if she found it hard to believe.

The knowledge that he believed it warmed her damp skin far more than the sun overhead. And his gaze on her body…well, that felt even hotter.

She broke, forcing her gaze away from his, and reached for a dry towel to lay out on the sand. Whatever this was between them, she wasn't ready to deal with it just yet. She needed time to process his words—to examine them, pick them apart and find some sense in them, somewhere. And that was all but impossible when he was lying there next to her in nothing but a pair of swim shorts.

'You should go for a swim,' she said, not looking at him. 'The water's glorious.'

'You looked very happy, splashing about out there.' He didn't make any move towards the water, though.

'I love it,' Sadie admitted. A truth for a truth perhaps. 'The sea always makes me feel…free somehow.' Like all her promises and commitments, all her obligations and the weight of her worries might just float away on the tide.

'I can see the appeal.' With a groan, Dylan hauled himself to his feet, brushing off the stray grains of sand that clung to his legs. 'Okay. I'll go for a swim.' He flashed her a smile. 'Just for you.'

'Great. Enjoy.' Sadie sat down on her fresh towel with a bump, staring after him as he walked towards the water's edge, the sun turning his skin golden across his broad back and trim waist.

She needed to think, she reminded herself, not ogle. With an act of willpower much harder than it should have been, she lay down and closed her eyes. There was no way she could think sensibly about that strange moment with Dylan while she could still see him. His very presence was distracting.

Unfortunately, she'd failed to account for her late night and exercise in her plan. The next thing she knew, cool droplets of water were dripping onto her and a sun-warm towel was being laid across her body. Her eyes flew open to find out why.

'Sorry.' Dylan tossed his head back, sending more

water droplets flying. 'But it's pretty warm out here. I was afraid you'd burn.'

Personally, Sadie thought his presence might be more of a threat of that than the sun, but she wasn't telling him that.

'Thanks.' She sat up. 'Good swim? How long was I asleep?'

Dylan shrugged, fished in his bag for his phone and checked the time. 'Half an hour or so, I guess? It's nearly two.'

'Wow. We missed lunch. Are you hungry?' It wasn't like they hadn't had a substantial breakfast to keep them going, but all of a sudden her stomach was grumbling.

'You know, amazingly, I am.'

'Come on, then. There's a great seafood place just off the beach. And it's in the shade.'

Together, they packed up their small camp. Sadie pulled on her skirt and top over her tankini, and breathed a sigh of relief as Dylan put his shirt back on too. Half-naked Dylan on the beach was one thing—sitting at lunch was another entirely.

They headed up towards the boardwalk that ran along the edge of the beach. Brushing dry sand from their feet, they put their shoes back on and Sadie led him past the first few restaurants and cafés to the one she had in mind.

'Finn loves the seafood platters here,' she said, as they waited to be shown to a table. 'You'd think a four-year-old would balk at calamari and battered prawns and such, but he loves them.'

'It's sounding pretty good to me too,' Dylan said. 'Perfect for a light lunch after a morning on the beach.'

Sadie smiled up at him. 'Then that's what we'll have.'

Their table was at the front of the restaurant, and the glass doors that spanned the length of the space had been thrown open. Sadie sat back and listened to the waves, enjoying the cool shade on her hot body as they waited for their food. Her skin felt almost too sensitive now, like it was still being touched all over. She glanced across the table at Dylan and found his eyes already on her.

Maybe that was why.

It wasn't until they were tucking into their seafood platter that Sadie spotted the small flaw in her plan. 'I was going to take you out for seafood tonight,' she said, remembering suddenly her booking at the restaurant on the marina that had such good reviews. It was fancier than this place, and probably had less sand on the floor, but she'd be willing to bet their seafood platter wouldn't have been as good as the one they were enjoying anyway. 'Guess I'd better come up with something else after this. What do you fancy?'

Dylan paused with a prawn halfway to his mouth, looking at her just a moment too long to be entirely comfortable.

'Actually, I've got plans for tonight.'

Oh. How stupid to assume that he'd want to spend the whole day with her and have dinner too. Just because he had the previous day.

'Plans for us,' Dylan clarified, and relief warred with anxiety within her.

'Oh?' she said, as lightly as she could. 'I thought *I* was supposed to be showing *you* the town.'

'And you've been doing a great job,' he said. 'But now it's my turn.'

'Where are we going?' Sadie asked, because she couldn't really ask 'Is this a date?' without sounding incredibly idiotic if it wasn't—and terrified if it was.

'It's a surprise.' Dylan's smile was almost wolfish, and it sent a shiver across the surface of her skin. 'Just dress fancy, be in the lobby at eight, and leave everything else to me.'

Leave everything to him? If Dylan was in charge she shouldn't be worried about it being a date.

She should be scared—or prepared—for it to be a seduction.

CHAPTER NINE

BACK AT THE AZURE, Dylan hung behind as they arrived in the lobby, waiting for Sadie to disappear before he put his last-minute plan into action.

It only took a moment to realise that Sadie was doing exactly the same thing. The woman was incurably curious.

'Go on,' he said, making a shooing motion with his hands. 'You go get yourself all dolled up for tonight.'

'You're sure?' Sadie remained hovering next to the reception desk, her hands clasped in front of her. Behind the desk, the woman on Reception rolled her eyes in amusement. 'You don't need me to call and book anything? What about a taxi?'

'I have it all in hand,' Dylan assured her. Which was only partially a lie—he knew exactly what he needed to do to get it in hand. Sadie just had to leave the area first. 'And if I don't, the lovely...' He waved at the girl behind the desk.

'Esma,' she filled in promptly.

'Esma here can help me. So go. Get ready.' For a moment he thought she was about to object again, then she nodded sharply and started to head for the lifts.

He should let her go. Anything else would just make her more curious, more determined to find out his plans. But still...

'And, Sadie?' he called after her. She paused and turned back to face him. 'Don't wear black tonight.'

Sadie's frustrated expression was its own reward.

Once he was sure she'd really gone, and the lift lights had ticked up to the higher floors, Dylan turned to Esma.

'Okay, here's the thing. I have a plan, but I need a little help.'

'Whatever you need, sir,' Esma replied cheerfully, and he wondered if she'd been ordered to give him anything he wanted, just to make sure he invested. Probably, he decided. No one who worked with people all day was ever naturally that cheery by late afternoon.

'Great,' he said. 'Here's what I need…'

A few phone calls later and it was done. Cars booked—thanks to Sadie's reminder about taxis—and the best table reserved at the restaurant of the swankiest and newest hotel in Kuşadası. As an afterthought, he'd also booked a room. Not—despite the voice at the back of his head telling him what a great idea it would be—to try and convince Sadie that friendship wasn't enough.

No, if Sadie was serious about coming up with a new plan, and doing whatever it took to save the Azure, then she needed to know what she was up against. And so did he. The Paradise Grand Hotel was the place to go for that. By the time she'd taken a good look at the place and its rooms and restaurant, Sadie would know exactly how much work they had ahead of them.

Letting himself into his suite, he headed straight for the shower, whistling as he went. Everything was coming together nicely.

It wasn't until he was lathering up, water sluicing down around him, that it occurred to Dylan that *Sadie* might think the evening could be something other than just business.

And would that really be so bad?

They'd made it past the memories of last night and through the strange, close moments on the beach. If he wasn't mistaken, there had been a definite...softening in Sadie's attitude to him since he'd confessed to the almost-kiss she apparently couldn't remember.

Maybe this *was* more than just business. Maybe it could even be a second chance at something he'd never really had a first chance at.

But no. Tonight wasn't the night.

Even if he did want to try and win one night with her, one glorious stolen moment, it couldn't be tonight. Before anything at all could happen between them, they had to hammer out the work side of things. Mixing business and pleasure never ended well, in his experience.

But once their plan for the Azure was secure, he'd have a whole new proposal to put to Sadie.

He couldn't just take his usual, casual approach to a hook-up—because Sadie wasn't like his usual conquests. They had history, for a start. And she'd been clear on the friendship front, for good reasons. Her place was here in Turkey, with Finn and her memories, much as he wished he might be able to persuade her to move on from that. He couldn't compete with the commitments she'd made—and even if he could, would he really want to? So he'd be upfront about what he could offer—and it wasn't forever. He was a short-term fix at best—in business or otherwise. That had to be clear before he could take things further, otherwise it wouldn't be fair—on either of them.

Tonight would be all business.

Decision made, Dylan shut off the shower and told himself that putting on his best suit for the evening was all about the destination, not the company.

* * *

Don't wear black. What kind of fashion advice was that? And who was Dylan Jacobs to tell her what she should or shouldn't wear anyway?

Except…if tonight was about them for once, instead of business, maybe this was just his way of hinting at that. Letting her know she was off duty tonight; that she could retire the black suit, relax and just enjoy being there with him.

She had to admit it did sound appealing.

Eventually, she picked out a navy halterneck cocktail dress that showed off her slightly pink shoulders, and slid it over her showered and lotioned skin. It was fancier than anything she'd have worn to the restaurant at the Azure or to a bar, but not too over the top. And he had said to dress up…

With a decisive nod, Sadie picked out her highest silver heels and added a little eyeliner to her usual make-up.

When she finally made her way down to the lobby, she was glad she'd made the effort. Hanging off the arm of Dylan Jacobs could be enough to make a girl feel positively plain by comparison at the best of times, but the suit he'd chosen for the evening only made things worse. Charcoal grey and perfectly cut, it accentuated all the wonderful things about his body that she'd tried not to stare at on the beach that morning. With a crisp, white shirt open at the neck he looked the epitome of relaxed elegance.

Sadie stood up a little straighter and hoped she didn't fall over in the unfamiliar heels.

'You look fantastic,' Dylan said, leaning in to kiss her cheek. 'And navy—'

'It's not black,' Sadie interrupted quickly. 'That was your only stipulation.'

'Is definitely your colour—that was all I was going to say.' Dylan flashed her a smile as he took her arm. 'Come on, the car is waiting.'

'Okay,' Sadie said, once they were both settled in the back seat of the car. 'I'm dolled up, we're in the car—*now* will you tell me where we're going?'

'What's the best, most luxurious and prestigious hotel in Kuşadasi?'

'The new Paradise Grand,' Sadie answered promptly, then frowned. 'Wait. Why are we going there?'

'To check out the competition,' Dylan said. 'If you're really ready to go with a new plan to save the Azure, you need to know exactly what you're up against.'

She should have worn a black suit.

Hopefully the car was dark enough that he couldn't see her embarrassed blush. What had she been thinking, imagining this could be anything more than just business? Wasn't that what they'd agreed? And what she'd insisted on from the start?

This was why he was here, in Turkey. Anything else was completely incidental. She had to remember that.

'Here we are,' Dylan said a while later, as the car pulled to a halt. Jumping out, he headed round to open her door before the driver could, and she took his hand as she stepped out of the car.

At least now she knew what she was really there for, she could give it her full attention.

The new Paradise Grand Hotel was on the outskirts of town, a little further than most tourists would like—but there the similarities with the Azure ended. Sadie was pretty sure that any guest would put up with the mildly inconvenient location in return for the splendour the Paradise Grand offered.

The hotel building rose out of a garden of palm leaves

and greenery, all glass and steel and white stone. Her hand on Dylan's arm, Sadie climbed the steps and the automatic doors opened with a swoosh.

Inside, the lobby was every bit as impressive as the exterior. The centre of the building was open all the way to the glass roof—some twenty storeys up—and every floor had a balcony overlooking the majesty of the central foyer. An ostentatious fountain burbled in the middle, surrounded by more local flora. Sadie swallowed as the chattering sounds of what had to be a full-occupancy hotel filled her ears.

Yeah, nothing like the Azure at all.

They were led through to the elevators by one of the several concierges, then up to the restaurant on the top floor. Their table, Sadie was hardly even surprised to note at this point, was right by the window, looking out over the town of Kuşadasi and the ocean beyond.

She wondered if she could see the Azure from there...

'So, what do you think?' Dylan asked, after the waiter had taken their wine order and left them to peruse the menu.

Sadie shook her head. 'The Azure is nothing like this.' And, quite honestly, she wouldn't want it to be. Yes, the Paradise Grand was impressive, and luxurious—but it wasn't her dream. Or Adem's.

'That's because this place is brand-new,' Dylan said. 'Shiny as the day it came out of the box. That's what some customers want.'

'But not all.'

'No, not all.' He leant back in his seat, looking out over the admittedly glorious view. 'But before you decide what your customers want, you need to know what *you* want. If it isn't this, fine. But what is it? What do you want the Azure to be? What makes it special to you? What's the big dream?'

Wasn't that the million Turkish lire question? The one she knew she *should* know the answer to already.

But she didn't. Because it had always been Adem's dream, not hers. She'd gone along with it, listened, been supportive, helped where she could…but she couldn't say what the goal was or the vision, because he'd held all that in his head. All she had were the plans he'd left behind and they'd already established that they weren't enough.

'Adem wanted…' she started, but Dylan shook his head.

'I'm not interested in what Adem wanted for the place. If you truly want to save it, to give it a new future against competition like this, it has to be *your* dream. Not his.'

Sadie stared at him, knowing he was right but still not knowing the answers.

How could she admit to him that her commitment to the Azure had more to do with memories of the past than the future?

Watching her, sitting across the table in that beautiful dress, her shoulders bare and her skin golden in the candlelight, Dylan wished heartily that this could be what it must look like to outsiders—a romantic meal for two. But he was in Turkey to do a job—to help her. And he couldn't let his personal wants get in the way of her very urgent business needs.

Not yet, anyway.

Still, seeing her struggle to answer what should have been the first question he'd asked on arrival, he wished more than anything that wasn't the case.

'I…I don't know,' Sadie finally admitted, the frustration in her expression showing him exactly how much those words had cost her.

'Okay. Try this,' he said. 'Imagine yourself at the Azure in five years' time. How does it look? What's its best features?'

'Five years…' Sadie's eyelids fluttered closed as she considered. 'Finn would be ten.'

Finn. He'd asked her to think about the business, and she'd instantly thought of her son. Dylan frowned. What was he missing here?

'Sadie,' he said, and her eyes flew open again. His gaze locked onto hers, and he knew this was his best chance to get at the truth. 'Tell me honestly. Why do you want to save the Azure?'

'For Finn,' she said, the words coming so quickly he knew she hadn't had to think about them at all. 'Because it's the only thing left of his father that I can give him. It's Adem's legacy.'

A noble reason, but Dylan knew it wouldn't be enough. She had to want it for herself, too. 'What about you?'

'I…I love the spa. That was always *my* place, *my* dream. But the hotel…it was all Adem.' He'd suspected as much, but from the relief that shone out of Sadie's face he had a feeling this was the first time she'd admitted to herself that, in truth, she didn't really want to be there. 'To be honest, without him there, some days it's hard to remember why I stay at all.'

'Sadie…' Dylan's heart clenched at the loss and confusion in her voice. No wonder the place was crumbling all around her. A project as big as the Azure needed love, not just obligation. It needed passion, not just vague enthusiasm. It needed what Adem had felt for it, and Sadie obviously didn't.

'I shouldn't have said that.' Sadie shook her head, as

if she could wipe away the words with the movement. The waiter arrived with their wine, and she took a large gulp the moment he'd tasted it and it had been poured.

'Are you ready to—?' the waiter started.

'Another few minutes, please.' Neither of them had so much as looked at the menu yet. Besides, he wasn't going to let Sadie use ordering food as an excuse to drop this line of conversation. Not when there was so much more to say.

As the waiter backed unobtrusively away, Dylan fixed Sadie with a determined look. 'You were saying?'

She took a deep breath before answering. He wondered if that was a sign that what was coming was a lie. He wasn't used to Sadie lying—or perhaps he'd just never noticed her lies before.

'The Azure is a wonderful hotel,' she said. 'It has huge potential, plenty of history and an awful lot going for it businesswise. But more than that, it's our future—mine and Finn's, I mean. It's my son's inheritance. And I'm committed to saving it.'

'Even though it's not your dream?' She didn't understand. Sometimes commitment wasn't enough. Sometimes commitment made people miserable, made them yell and scream and cry—until they just gave up on it and walked away, like his father had done.

He really didn't want to see that happen to Sadie.

'Only little girls believe that dreams will come true.' There was a scathing note in Sadie's voice, but Dylan ignored it. Because he knew different.

Sadie had believed in dreams once. He'd seen it in her eyes the day she'd shown him her engagement ring for the first time, and again on her wedding day. The first time she'd held out her baby son to meet him. She'd believed in happily ever after, in possibilities and greatness, even if she'd wanted them all with another man.

Finally, he'd found something about new Sadie he didn't like as much as old Sadie.

He sighed. How to make her understand? 'Look. I could give you all the money your current business plan calls for. I could help you come up with a new plan and fund that instead. I could bulldoze the Azure and rebuild it from the ground up, if you decided that was what you wanted. But none of it will make a bit of difference if you don't want it enough.'

'I just told you I—'

'Commitment and obligation aren't enough,' he interrupted her. 'You're not a multinational conglomerate, and you're not trying to build a heartless, soulless place like the Paradise Grand. The Azure is about charm, heart and home—those are its selling points. The personal touch. And if it's not home to you, if you don't love it...' He shook his head.

'So you're saying you won't help me.' Sadie straightened her cutlery beside her napkin and avoided his gaze.

'I'm not saying that,' he said. 'But I want you to really think about what it is you want, whether the Azure truly is your home, before we go any further with this.'

It was a risk—both personally and professionally. He was testing her commitments to the past and, knowing how she'd felt about Adem, it was entirely possible she was going to send him packing. So, yeah, big risk.

But he knew it was also the right thing to do. The only thing.

As the tension stretched between them he reached for his menu and opened it.

'Come on, let's order. That very discreet and professional waiter over there has been hovering for at least the last ten minutes.'

Sadie nodded, and turned to the first page of her own menu, but he wasn't sure she was actually reading it at all. Instead, she looked completely lost in thought.

Dylan just hoped that they were good thoughts.

Sadie ate her meal in silence and, for once, Dylan seemed content to let her. Maybe he knew she had too much to think about to make conversation at the same time. Or maybe he was just preoccupied with whatever message had flashed up on his phone. Either way, he didn't seem particularly interested in her.

So much for her thoughts that tonight might be more than just business. She really should have known better.

The worst part was admitting that, for a moment, she'd hoped it could be something more. That maybe, just maybe, this might be a chance for her to start moving on. To follow Rachel's advice and get back out there. A totally out of character, one-night stand to reboot her chances at romance. Just this once.

Dylan was the king of short-term flings. If she wanted something short and sweet to kick-start her new life, he'd be perfect. As long as they could be upfront about what it was and wasn't, and could keep it separate from business.

But it seemed that *nothing* trumped business for Dylan.

As she finished up her last mouthful of dessert— which was, she had to admit, delicious—Sadie pushed the plate aside and prepared to call time on an altogether depressing evening. Not only had she completely misread Dylan's intentions, the more time she spent at the Paradise Grand, the more convinced she became that the Azure could never be anything like this.

'Do you have a car booked back to the Azure,' she asked, 'or shall I get the concierge to call us a taxi while we pay for dinner? They can take a while on busy nights.'

Dylan looked up from his phone and grinned. 'Sorry, am I ignoring you?'

Sadie shook her head. 'I'm just thinking about getting back to work.'

'Actually, there's one more thing I want to see here first.' He slipped his phone back into his jacket pocket and smiled again, slower this time. Sexier. With his full attention on her, Sadie couldn't stop the warmth that seemed to cover her skin under his gaze. Really, who could blame a girl for getting ideas when he looked at her like that?

'What's that?' she asked, but Dylan was already standing.

'Let me settle up here,' he said, eyes dark with promise. 'Then you'll find out.' He flashed her one last smile as he signalled the waiter over, and Sadie swallowed despite her suddenly dry throat.

Get a grip, Sadie, she told herself firmly. She was imagining things. He'd made it perfectly clear that tonight was about business only. Nothing he did next would convince her otherwise.

Or so she thought, until he led her out of the restaurant to the elevator, stopping at the twelfth floor and pulling out a room key card.

'You got us a room?' she asked, as he slipped the key card into the lock and, with a flash of green, the door fell open. He stood aside to let her in, and Sadie entered, staring around her. 'A room with champagne. And rose petals. And chocolates.'

Okay, maybe she hadn't been entirely imagining the vibes. After all, who booked a hotel suite complete with

built-in seduction supplies if they didn't have plans other
than business for the night?

In a split second Sadie made her decision. Even the
fear and anxiety burning through her veins couldn't compete with the rising tension between them. For twelve
years she'd wondered what it would feel like to kiss Dylan
Jacobs—and since the moment in the elevator after their
night on the town that curiosity had grown beyond all
reasonable proportions.

He wanted her. What more proof did she need than
rose petals on the coverlet and champagne chilling beside the huge king-sized bed? Maybe he'd just wanted to
get business out of the way before they moved on to the
more…personal part of the evening. She could understand that, even if she wished he'd shared his plans with
her earlier. Except she'd never have concentrated on work
if she'd known she had this waiting for her.

And, God, why was she still thinking?

Sucking in a breath, she turned, only to find Dylan
right behind her. Her hands came up automatically to
rest against his chest and she looked up to see heat in his
eyes. No doubt at all, he wanted this too.

'You booked us a room.' Her voice barely sounded
like hers—it was too breathy, too sultry.

Dylan nodded, his gaze fixed on hers like she held all
the power here for once. Sadie kind of liked it.

Seizing the moment, she stretched up onto her toes,
bringing her mouth just millimetres away from his, savouring every moment. 'Good idea,' she murmured, and
leaned in to kiss him.

From the moment their lips touched, bliss filled Sadie.
Every inch of her body fizzed from finally, finally kissing Dylan Jacobs. And she knew, in her heart, that this
was right—that she could move on, that there was a fu-

ture for her beyond always being a widow. That she was still a woman, too.

Until Dylan stepped back, breaking the kiss, his hands on her upper arms holding her away.

'Sadie…no, I'm sorry…'

Normally, the sight of Dylan lost for words would have amused her. As it was, it just enraged her.

He'd ruined her fizz.

'If you tell me you booked this room to compare it to the Azure…'

'I didn't ask for the champagne and stuff!' He waved an arm around wildly, encompassing the room. 'They must have…misunderstood.'

'Just like me.' Sadie bit the words out, too furious to say more.

'No! I… It's just, this needs to be business first between us, Sadie.'

Because everything was, for him, wasn't it? Nothing mattered more than the next project, the next shining opportunity. Certainly not her.

'Of course.' With a deep breath, Sadie gathered the tattered remains of her dignity around her, and gave thanks that she hadn't wasted her best red dress on this disaster of an evening. 'Well, I think I've seen all I need to here. If you'll excuse me…'

She didn't care if he had a car booked or plans to look through some slideshow on the Azure's future. Sadie was going to the bar, drinking one more glass of wine to wipe away this evening, then getting a cab back home, where she would go straight to bed. No champagne, no rose petals, no Dylan. Alone.

'Sadie, wait.' He tried to grab her arm again, but she dodged him.

'I'll see you in the lobby in the morning as normal,'

she said. Maybe if she pretended nothing had happened tonight, he'd forget—like she had, apparently, after that wedding so many years ago. 'We've got plenty of work ahead of us.'

And that was all. Just work.

CHAPTER TEN

THIS NEEDS TO be business...

Sadie woke with the same words echoing in her head that she'd fallen asleep to, and a familiar burn of embarrassment coursing through her body.

What on earth had she been thinking, trying to kiss Dylan? Maybe she could just blame the wine.

Lying back against her pillows, she ran through the night before in her head. The part before everything had gone crazy and wrong. There had to be something she could salvage from her utter humiliation.

The business message had certainly got through loud and clear. So, how did she show him that she was back to work mode today, and that last night had been a minor blip? What had he told her she needed to do to live up to the luxuries of the Paradise Grand?

The other hotel had certainly been impressive, she had to admit, and the food *almost* as good as the Azure's. But it didn't feel homely or comfortable...

Suddenly, Dylan's words came back to her.

'The Azure is about charm, heart and home—those are its selling points. The personal touch. And if it's not home to you, if you don't love it...'

Maybe he had a point.

In fact, she decided as she headed for the shower, even

if last night hadn't been exactly what she'd been hoping for, maybe it had given her something more. Not another notch on Dylan's bedpost, which in the cold morning light she could only agree was a good thing. She'd lost her mind, briefly, but she was back in control now. This was all a business proposal—not a fantasy romance or a glimpse of possibilities that never really were.

Instead, he'd given her a way to prove to him, once and for all, that he should invest. All he wanted to know was that this place truly was her home, her passion.

And she knew exactly how to do that.

Suddenly, the day didn't seem quite so hopeless.

She met him in the lobby as usual, knowing he'd clocked her casual dress immediately. His eyebrows rose, just a touch, as he smiled a greeting at her. Was that nervousness she saw behind his eyes?

'So, boss lady, what's the plan for today?' Boss lady. He really wanted to make sure she didn't forget this was business, didn't he? Well, that was just fine by her.

'Have you eaten breakfast?' she asked, too focussed on her plan for small talk.

'Sort of.' His forehead crinkled up a little in confusion. 'Some fruit and cereal. I wasn't all that hungry after last night's feast. Why?'

'Perfect,' she said, ignoring the question. 'You don't want a heavy stomach for today's activities.'

'Now I'm really intrigued,' Dylan admitted.

Sadie flashed him a bright, fake smile. 'Good. Then follow me.'

He'd seen the whole hotel on their tour on the first day, so by the time she'd led him down the stone stairs and towards the corridor to the spa he'd already figured it out, which shouldn't really have surprised her. He was a bright guy.

'A spa day?' he asked, a hint of incredulity in his voice.

'The spa is one of the Azure's biggest attractions,' she reminded him, as they reached the heavy wooden door that led to her own personal sanctuary. 'It makes sense for you to spend some time here, see what all the fuss is about.' She pushed the door open, the heady scent of oils and steam filling her lungs as she stepped through. 'Besides, you'll need to lock your phone up in the lockers here. It'll do you good to switch off from your other business and concentrate on the Azure for a few hours.'

'I need to stay in touch with the office—' Dylan started, but she cut him off, more determined than ever.

'Not today. You want proof that the Azure is a safe investment? I'm about to give it to you. So I want you paying attention.'

'If you insist.' Dylan sighed, and followed her through the door to the spa reception desk. 'Okay, I'm game. So, what? You're going to give me a massage?'

Sadie wished she could blame the heat in her cheeks on the higher temperature of the spa rooms. Sadly, she knew herself better than that.

'Not me. We have an excellent trained staff here to see to your every need. But I'll show you around first, explain the different rooms to you.' Smiling at the spa receptionist, Andreas, she added, 'Andreas here will take you through to the male changing rooms and lockers, show you where everything is. I'll meet you on the other side.'

Slipping through to the women's changing rooms, Sadie didn't waste time, stripping off to her swimming costume quickly and locking everything up in her personal locker. Wrapping a robe around herself, she headed straight through to the spa, pleased to beat Dylan there by even a few moments. He looked faintly uncomfortable in the fluffy white robe, the towelling material making his shoulders look broader than ever. Still, she decided, it was good for him to go outside his comfort zone now and then.

He looked around him and Sadie watched his face for reactions as he took in the creamy marble, with hints of brown and rust red, which covered the walls. Above them, a domed and mural-painted roof belied their location underneath the hotel, making them appear to be in some ancient Turkish bath instead. The soothing splash of water from the pools toned nicely with the gentle music playing over the hidden speakers.

'So, where do we start?' Dylan asked.

'With the Turkish bath, of course,' Sadie said.

If that didn't relax him into handing over the cash, nothing would.

'This is the warm room,' Sadie explained, as she paused by a steamed-up glass door and slipped off her robe, hanging it up. 'Traditionally, this is where you would start a proper Turkish bath.'

She pushed the door open and Dylan shucked his own robe and followed her through, silently cursing the steam that rose up and obscured the beautiful curve of her behind in her swimsuit.

It had taken every grain of restraint in his body not to kiss her back the night before—and now she was tormenting him with *this*. A whole day in her barely clad company, trying to *relax*. And she'd made it perfectly clear it was all business. Just the way he'd wanted it.

The woman was a demon.

Inside, the warm room was empty of other people—which Dylan appreciated. Sadie took a seat on the tiled bench seat that ran around the outer edge of the room, and he followed suit, choosing to sit opposite her instead of beside her—something he regretted when he realised the steam hid her almost completely now.

He shuffled round a little closer, until he could make out the outline of her face at least.

'So, what do we do here?' he asked, settling back as the heat rolled over him, the steam already dripping off his skin as well as the wall behind him.

'We sit. We relax.' Sadie sounded different here already, like her words could take their time coming out. Like there was no rush for anything any more.

Dylan fidgeted, switching position to try to get a little more comfortable against the tile. 'That's it?'

'That's it,' Sadie said, apparently very satisfied with that state of affairs.

She'd tilted her head back against the wall, and as far as he could tell her eyes were closed. He watched the beads of water roll down the long line of her neck for a moment. No sign that she found this in any way frustrating. Clearly, she was enjoying the peace and quiet.

He gave it a minute before he decided that was too bad. He had questions.

'So, is this a traditional Turkish spa?'

'Yes and no,' Sadie answered, without moving or opening her eyes. 'I wanted to incorporate some of the aspects of a traditional Turkish bath, but I knew I couldn't compete with the authentic Turkish baths in the town. So, instead, I decided to go with a spa that would feel familiar to the visiting tourists—especially the Western ones—but would still feel a little exotic, too.'

'The best of both worlds.'

'That's the idea.'

Listening to her talk, even absently, about the plans she'd had for this place, it was easy to see exactly what was missing in her plans for the Azure. Here, she'd known instinctively what she wanted to do, what was important to the guests, what would work well. This was her comfort zone. The hotel wasn't.

Tilting his head back to copy Sadie, he stared up at the mosaic-domed roof, picking out patterns through the steam. Then, when that grew boring, he went back to watching Sadie instead.

She looked so much more relaxed here. Like she had swimming in the sea the day before. She truly was a water nymph.

'When was the last time you came down here?' he asked. 'Not just in a suit to check on the business either.'

'Too long,' Sadie admitted, turning her head to smile at him. 'I think everyone needs a day in the spa now and then.'

Her eyes fluttered shut again, and he followed suit, trying to find the same boneless relaxation she seemed to here. Letting the heat seep into his bones and the steam soak his skin, he let his shoulders drop and his mind zone out.

Maybe there was something to this relaxation malarkey after all.

Almost too soon, Sadie stirred beside him. 'Okay, time for the hot room.' She stood, gracefully.

Dylan peeled himself away from the tile with rather less finesse. 'This wasn't hot?'

'This was nothing,' Sadie told him, opening the door.

The hot room felt even hotter after the brief blast of normal spa temperature between the two rooms, but they didn't stay in the second room as long, which he appreciated. As they emerged back into the main spa, Sadie plunged herself into the circular pool in the centre of the room, letting the water sluice over her.

With a shrug, Dylan followed suit.

The ice-cold water hit his overheated skin like a thousand pins, and he rose gasping out of the water to find Sadie already out and perched on a wooden recliner beside it. She, somehow, managed to look refreshed and a little smug. Clearly this was revenge for the night before.

'You could have warned me.' He levered himself back out of the pool and reached for the towel she held out to him,

'Where would be the fun in that?' The impish gleam in her eyes made it hard to even pretend to be mad at her.

'Where indeed?' He sat down on the recliner next to her. 'Well, this has been lovely, but—'

'Oh, we're not done yet,' Sadie interrupted him.

'We're not?' Dylan shook his head, cold water droplets falling from his hair. 'What's next?'

'Traditionally, you'd be scrubbed clean by a bath assistant,' Sadie said. 'But today I think we'll let you off with just the massage. You can meet me in the pool afterwards.'

As a member of the spa staff, neatly dressed in white shorts and polo shirt, appeared to lead him to the massage room, Dylan saw another approach Sadie with a clipboard in hand. In a moment, all the relaxation he'd seen in her disappeared as she frowned at the paper in front of her, shoulders stiff.

'This way, sir,' the staff member said again, and Dylan hurried to catch up.

Left alone to settle face down onto the massage table, with just a small towel covering what was left of his modesty, Dylan tuned out the tasteful music and thought instead about Sadie.

She seemed so in control there in the spa—utterly unlike the uncertainty he saw in her when she talked about the hotel itself. Obviously, that was why she'd brought him there—to demonstrate that there was one place she felt totally at home here in Turkey. Here, she had passion and certainty.

The only problem with that was it just made it all the clearer that she didn't want to be running a hotel. She should be taking charge of a chain of spas, perhaps even in other hotels.

Maybe even in his new and burgeoning hotel chain.

Already the idea was taking hold, making him want to jump at the chance to make it happen. Sadie would have a career she truly dreamed of, and they could work together, seeing each other as often as possible…

But she'd have to leave the Azure. Break her commitment to Adem's dream. And there was the sticking point.

The door opened behind him, and Dylan stirred from his plotting as a familiar scent approached. He listened hard, recognising the pattern of her breath, the touch of her footfall.

Sadie.

Whatever she'd said about not giving him his massage, he had absolutely no doubt about who was standing behind him right now.

'Are you ready, sir?' she whispered, obviously trying to disguise her voice. 'I'm going to start with a simple massage. Let me know if the pressure is okay.'

She didn't want him to know it was her. But how could he not, when the first touch of her oiled fingers against his back made his whole body spark with excitement? Every movement she made was utterly professional—he'd never expect anything less from Sadie. But the feelings it left him with…

He was pretty sure that no massage in history had ever been less relaxing than this one.

* * *

This was torture. Actual cruel and unusual punishment for a crime she didn't fully remember committing.

Keeping her hands as smooth and steady as she could as they moved across the planes of Dylan's back, Sadie kept a running stream of mental curses going in her head. Mostly cursing the poor staff member who'd been sent home sick, leaving them short-handed. But partly cursing herself, too, for saying she'd take care of Dylan's massage.

She was the boss. She could have ordered anyone else to swap with her or take care of it. Instead, she'd decided to put herself through *this*.

She really was a glutton for punishment.

Staying professional, that was the key. It wasn't like she hadn't massaged beautiful people before, even a few famous ones. The trick was to treat them exactly the same way you'd treat anyone else. A body was just a body, when all was said and done, and they all needed the same care, love and attention to work away their worries and their aches.

It was just that *this* body was one she'd been thinking about for far longer than she cared to admit.

Focussing on the muscle groups helped, remembering every lesson she'd ever been taught about effective massage. She knew just where to press and where to hold back. She was *good* at this. She was a professional.

She was absolutely not thinking about what was underneath that very small towel.

Eventually, her time was up, and hopefully Dylan would never ask why he'd only had a back massage instead of a full-body one.

Stepping away, her heart still pumping too fast, Sadie murmured, 'I'll leave you to dress.'

'Thanks, Sadie.' His words were almost slurred, like he was too relaxed to articulate properly, but still they caused every muscle in her body to stiffen.

'How did you know?' she asked.

'I always know when you're near me.' Adjusting his towel to cover him, Dylan levered himself up and swung round to sit on the edge of the table. 'I always have.'

It was too much. The softness in his voice against the heat in his eyes. The implications of his words and the knowledge that just moments before she'd had her hands all over his body. Knowing that they were so close now he could touch her almost without moving. Her blood seemed too much and too hot for her body—hotter than it had ever been in any of the steam rooms.

All too, too much.

Business. That's all this was.

Sadie stepped back, away, and cleared her throat. 'Um, we have someone off sick, so I've been called in to cover. So I'll let you get on with enjoying the pool and so on. It'll be good for you to, uh, keep relaxing.'

Dylan nodded, slowly. 'Or maybe I'll just try the cold plunge pool again.'

'Whatever works.' She refused to think about why he might need the ice water, even for a moment.

'Will I see you for dinner?' he asked.

She wanted to say yes, but she couldn't. The wanting in his eyes…she knew exactly where that could lead, if they let it. And even if she'd thought last night that was what she wanted, seeing it now terrified her. This wasn't what she'd brought him to her spa for, not at all.

Dylan didn't do commitment, and she'd already committed too much. Wasn't that why she'd brought him there in the first place? To show him exactly how much she belonged at the Azure? So what good could come from giving in to those feelings now?

'Not tonight, I'm afraid,' she said, trying to sound apologetic. 'I need to type up my proposal for you, remember? But there's a Turkish night in the restaurant. I've booked you a table.'

'Fantastic.' Sadie ignored the total lack of enthusiasm in his voice. 'What about tomorrow?'

Tomorrow. His next-to-last day. She couldn't leave him alone again, but whatever they did needed to involve a lot more clothes than the last couple of days had. And preferably no easy access to a bed.

'Ephesus.' The word blurted out of her. 'I thought I'd take you to see the ruins at Ephesus.'

'Another big tourist attraction, I suppose.' How was his tone still so even, so steady when her own voice seemed to be getting squeakier by the second?

'The biggest. So, I'll see you in the lobby in the morning. Usual time.'

'If that's what you want.'

It wasn't. What she really wanted was to jump him, right here in the massage room. But what she needed to do was get back to work and put this whole afternoon behind her.

'It is.'

She'd do a shift in the spa, remind herself why she loved it so much. Then she'd spend the evening on Skype with Finn and her parents and dealing with the hotel admin.

She needed to remember all the things that *really* mattered in her world. And forget the feeling of Dylan's cool skin under her hands.

Or else she might go insane.

CHAPTER ELEVEN

DYLAN PACED THE lobby the next morning, waiting for Sadie. Who was late. Very late. For the first time since he'd arrived in Turkey.

Turning as he reached the automatic doors, too late to stop them opening for him, he headed back towards the large windows showcasing that brilliant view of the Aegean Sea. He tried to appreciate the view, but his mind was too preoccupied with wondering how the day was going to play out.

The rules had changed yesterday, that much had been obvious the moment he'd sat up on that massage table and looked into her eyes. The heat and want he'd seen reflected there had echoed his own so perfectly he couldn't help but think it was only a matter of time before they had to do something about it or explode. This wasn't a drunken attempt at a kiss in a lift, or a moment of madness brought on by a romantic hotel room. Sadie Sullivan wanted him, maybe as much as he wanted her. And despite every complication, every reason he knew he shouldn't, Dylan wasn't sure he'd make it out of Kuşadası without doing something about that.

Except she was late, and he didn't know which Sadie was going to turn up today—buttoned-up business Sadie, old friend Sadie, or the Sadie who'd tried to kiss him the other night.

Yes, the rules had changed, to the point that Dylan wasn't even sure what game they were playing any more. If they were playing at all.

Ephesus. That was the plan for today. Ancient ruins, stones and sand and history. A big tourist draw, sure, but he couldn't shake the feeling that wasn't why Sadie was taking him there. More likely she was trying to get him somewhere safe—away from temptation and lost in someone else's history instead of their own.

Pity it would never work.

Besides, he wasn't interested in history today. He wanted to talk to her about the future.

Dylan had spent his solitary evening making plans, researching and brainstorming. He'd been looking for a way to set the hotel chain he'd recently taken over apart from the norm, and a spa range of the calibre of Sadie's could be just what he needed. Sure, it wasn't unique, but it *was* good and profitable, according to his preliminary research. He'd know more when his assistant got back to him with the stats and figures he'd requested.

Then he'd just need to talk to Sadie about it. He liked to hope she'd be excited about the new opportunity, but knowing Sadie he suspected that pulling her away from the old one would be the real challenge.

Turning to head back towards the doors, he caught sight of the Azure logo on the reception desk, and almost smiled. Just a few days ago seeing the name would have been enough to make him scowl. But now… Sadie had changed the way he thought about the Azure. About many things.

The lift dinged and the doors opened, revealing Sadie in a light and breezy sundress, a straw hat perched on her head. 'Sorry I'm late,' she said, without much apology in her voice. 'Let's get going.'

Dylan followed, trying not to read too much into the fact she'd barely looked at him.

In the car, Sadie switched the radio on before she even fastened her seat belt, turning the volume up high enough to make conversation next to impossible. Dylan smiled to himself as he settled into the passenger seat. So, that was the way she wanted to play it. Fine.

He was willing to bet there were no radios at Ephesus. She'd have to talk to him then—for a whole day, trapped inside some ancient ruins.

Of course, she'd probably try to just lecture him on the history of the place. Which was fine by Dylan; he knew she couldn't keep it up forever.

Eventually, they were going to have to talk about the heat between them.

Satisfied, he sat back to enjoy the drive, watching the foreign landscape skimming past the window. He had to admit Turkey was a gorgeous country.

Beside him, Sadie let out a little gasp—just a slight gulp of air, but enough to alarm him. All thoughts of the scenery forgotten, he jerked round to see what the matter was.

On the wheel, Sadie's knuckles were white, her fingers clinging so tight there was no blood left in them. Her face had turned entirely grey. But it was her eyes, wide and unfocussed, that worried him most.

'Sadie? What is it?' No response. The car kept rolling forward in its lane, falling behind the car in front as her foot slackened on the accelerator. 'You need to pull over. Sadie. Sadie!'

The sharpness in his voice finally got through to her

and, blinking, she flipped on the indicator. Dylan placed his hands over hers as she swerved onto the side of the road, ignoring the beeping horns of the cars behind them.

The car stalled to a stop, and Dylan let out a long breath as his heart rate started to stabilise. 'Okay. What just—?'

Before he could finish his sentence the driver's door flew open and Sadie flung herself out of the car, inches away from the passing traffic. Without thinking, Dylan followed suit, jumping out and rushing round to find her already leaning against the rear of the car.

He slowed, approaching her cautiously, like an unpredictable and possibly dangerous wild animal. God only knew what was going on with her, but he knew instinctively that this wasn't part of the game they'd been playing since he'd arrived. This was something else entirely.

She didn't stir as he got closer, so he risked taking her arm, leading her gently to the side of the car furthest from the road.

'Sit down,' he murmured, as softly as he could. 'Come on, Sadie. Sit down here and tell me what the matter is.'

Bonelessly, she slid down to the dry grass, leaning back against the metal of the car. Dylan crouched in front of her, his gaze never leaving her colourless face.

'What is it?' he asked again. 'What just happened?'

'I forgot…' Sadie's said, her voice faint and somehow very far away. 'How could I forget?'

'Forgot what, sweetheart?'

'That we'd have to drive this way. Past this place.'

'This place? Where are we?' Dylan glanced around him but, as far as he could tell, it was just some road. Any road.

Oh. He was an idiot.

'This is where it happened?' he asked.

Sadie nodded, the movement jerky. 'Adem was driving out to some meeting somewhere, I think. A truck lost control along this stretch...'

And his best friend had been squashed under it in his car. He hadn't stood a chance.

'I haven't been this way since it happened,' Sadie said, her gaze still focussed somewhere in the distance. 'When I suggested Ephesus...I wasn't thinking about this. I wasn't thinking about Adem.'

The guilt and pain in her voice made him wince—and feel all the worse because he had a pretty good idea exactly what she *had* been thinking about at that moment.

'We don't have to go on,' he said. 'We can just go back to the hotel. I can drive.'

But Sadie shook her head. 'No. I want... This is the worst of it. I just need to sit here for a moment. Is that...? Will you sit with me?'

'Of course.' He shuffled over to sit beside her and lifted his arm to wrap it around her as she rested her head against his shoulder. He couldn't offer her much right now, but any comfort he could give was hers. Always had been.

'It's crazy, really,' she said, the words slightly muffled by his shirt. 'That one place—one insignificant patch of road—can hold such power over me. There are no ruins here, no markers, no information boards. Just me, knowing that this...this is where he died.'

'We don't have to talk about it.'

'Maybe I do.' Sadie looked up, just enough to catch his gaze, and Dylan almost lost himself in the desolate depths of her eyes. 'I haven't, really. Haven't talked it out, or whatever it is you're supposed to do with the sort of grief that fills you up from the inside out until there's nothing left. I just...got on with things, I suppose.'

He could see it, all too easily. Could picture Sadie just throwing herself into the Azure, into making sure Finn was okay, and never taking any time to grieve herself. For the first time he found himself wondering if *this* was the real reason Neal had asked him to come.

'If you want to talk, I'm always happy to listen,' he said. Whatever she needed, wasn't that what he'd promised himself he was there for? Well, any idiot could see that she needed this.

'I don't know what to say.' Sadie gave a helpless little shrug. 'It's been two years… It seems too late. There was just so much to do. Taking care of Finn, the Azure, all the arrangements… He's buried back in England, near his family, you know? Of course you do. You were there, weren't you? At the funeral?'

'I was.'

'So it really is just me and Finn here.' She sounded like she might float away on a cloud of memories at any moment. Dylan tightened his hold on her shoulders, just enough to remind her to stay.

'And me,' he said.

'You're not permanent, though. You're like…in Monopoly. Just visiting.' She managed a small smile at the ridiculous joke, but he couldn't return it. There was no censure in the accusation, no bitterness at all. But that didn't change the way it stung.

Even if every word of it was true.

'I just don't know how to be everything Finn needs,' Sadie went on. 'Mother, father, his whole family… I don't know how to do that *and* save the Azure. But the hotel is Adem's legacy. It's the only part of him left here with us. So I have to. And I'm so scared that I'll fail.'

Her voice broke a little on the last word, and Dylan pulled her tighter to him. *Whatever she needs.*

'I'm here now,' he said. 'And I will come back, whenever you need me. Me, Neal, your parents, your sister... we're all here to help you. Whatever you need.'

It wasn't enough; he knew that even as he spoke the words. He wanted to promise he'd stay as long as she needed him. But he had a rule, a personal code, never to make promises he couldn't keep.

Everyone knew Dylan Jacobs couldn't do long term—him better than anyone.

'I'm here now,' he repeated, and wished that would be enough.

I'm here now.

Sadie burrowed deeper against the solid bulk of Dylan's shoulder, and ignored the fact that, even then, he couldn't bring himself to say he'd stay.

She was glad. He wasn't her boyfriend, her lover, wasn't anything more than a friend. She wasn't his responsibility. And even if she had been...it would have been a lie to say he'd stay, and they both knew it. Better to keep things honest.

She stared out at the scrubland before them and tried to ignore the sound of cars roaring past behind her. How could she have forgotten that driving to Ephesus would bring them this way? No, scrap that. She knew exactly how. Because all she'd been thinking about had been getting Dylan away from the hotel, fully clothed. Putting temptation out of reach before he fought past any more of her defences.

And yet here she was, clinging to him as if for her sanity, giving up all her secrets.

Maybe she should get some of his in return.

'Why do you hate the name of the Azure?' she asked, more for something else to focus on than any other reason. The fact that it probably led to a funny story with another woman—and a reminder why she couldn't become too reliant on him—was just a lucky bonus.

But Dylan said, 'My father walked out on us in another Azure Hotel. I was ten. We were there with him on some business trip. He just got into the car and drove away.'

'I'm sorry.' Sadie winced. Great way to lighten the mood.

Dylan shrugged, and she felt every muscle move against her cheek. 'It happens. He…he wasn't good at commitment. He stuck out family life as long as he could, then one day he just couldn't take it any more. I've never seen him since.'

'What did you do?' Sadie tried to imagine ten-year-old Dylan standing alone in the foyer of some strange hotel, but in her head the image morphed into two-year-old Finn, watching her cry as she tried to explain that Daddy wasn't coming home.

'I took my mum's purse and bought us three bus tickets back home—for me, Mum and my sister Cassie.'

'You became the man of the house.' She could see it so easily—Dylan just taking over and doing what was needed because there was no one else to do it. He'd been bogged down with commitment since the age of ten. No wonder he avoided it so thoroughly as an adult.

'I was all they had left. Mum didn't deal with it well.' From his tone Sadie could tell that was a huge understatement. 'By the time she could cope again I pretty much had it all in hand.'

Suddenly, a long-ago conversation came back to her. 'I remember Adem joking about all those dreadful part-time jobs you had at university. You were sending money home to your family?' Dylan nodded. 'That's why you shared that awful flat in London with Neal too, right?

Even after you were both earning enough to move somewhere nicer.'

All those puzzling facets of Dylan Jacobs that had never made sense fell into place to make a perfect diamond shape. A whole shine and side to him she'd never even considered.

'I'm like my dad in a lot of ways,' Dylan said, and Sadie frowned.

'Doesn't sound like it to me.'

'No, I am, and I know it.' He shrugged again. 'I've come to terms with it, too. I always want to be free to chase the next big thing, just like him. Difference is, I'd never let myself get tied down in the first place. I don't ever want to let anyone down the way he did.'

'You wouldn't,' Sadie said, knowing the truth of it in her bones.

'Anyway. He'd already abandoned my mum and sister. I couldn't do the same, so I took care of them however I could. Besides, they're not like you. They're hopeless on their own.'

'Oh?' Part of her felt warmed that he didn't consider her helpless and hopeless. But one small part of her brain wondered if he'd stay if he did. She stamped down on that part pretty quickly, before it could take hold.

'Yeah. My mum's on her third marriage, my sister's on her second. Every time something goes wrong I have to fly in and help pick up the pieces.' He shook his head. 'We *really* don't do commitment well in my family.'

Except for his commitment to them, which he seemed to hardly even recognise. 'I think commitment is something you have to practise every day,' she said. 'Every morning you have to make your commitment all over again or else it fades.'

'Maybe you're right.' He looked down at her, his expression thoughtful. 'I mean, you're the most committed person I know, so I guess you must be.'

'The most committed person you know? Is that meant to be a compliment?'

'Most definitely,' he assured her. 'Anyone else would have given up already, chucked in the towel and gone home. But not you. You committed to Adem and you won't let him down, even now he's gone. You're incredible.'

'Or possibly insane.' She shifted a little away, uncomfortable at his praise. Hadn't she let her husband down already, by being so distracted by fantasies of his best friend that she'd forgotten to even think about him today? Dylan being there confused her, made her forget to recommit every morning. He made her think of other paths, other possibilities—just as he had twelve years before.

To Sadie, that felt like a pretty big betrayal in itself.

'There's always that possibility too,' Dylan said. 'But either way...I admire you, endlessly. You should know that.'

Sadie looked away, pushing her hands against the dirt ready to help herself stand.

'Ready to move?' Dylan jumped to his feet. 'We can still go back to the Azure...'

'I want to show you Ephesus,' Sadie said stubbornly. That was the plan after all.

'Fallen-down buildings it is, then.' He reached out a hand to pull her up and she took it tentatively. But once she was on her feet he pulled her close into a hug before she could let go. 'Sadie...your commitment—I meant what I said. It's admirable. But don't let it lock you into unhappiness either, okay? Adem would hate that.'

'I know.' The truth of his words trickled through her, fighting back against the guilt.

Dylan kissed her forehead, warm and comforting. 'Come on, then. Let's go and see some history.'

At least, Sadie thought as they got back in the car, this history belonged to other people. Her own was already too confusing.

CHAPTER TWELVE

SADIE SWUNG THE car into the dusty, rocky car park at Ephesus and smiled brightly at him, as if the scene at the roadside hadn't happened at all. Dylan was almost starting to doubt it had himself; it had been such a strange moment out of time when he had seemed to look deeper into the heart of Sadie than he ever had before.

That sort of revelation should have added some clarity to the situation, he felt. Instead, he was more confused than ever.

He hadn't meant to confess all his family's dark and depressing past to her, but somehow, with her sharing secrets, it had only seemed fair that he give back too. He'd tried to keep it as factual and unemotional as possible, knowing that the last thing she'd needed had been him falling apart too. She'd just needed to know that he'd understood, and that he cared. Hopefully he'd given her that.

But just reliving those moments had stirred up something in him he hadn't expected—something he'd barely had to deal with in years. The small boy left alone in charge of a family seemed so many light years away from where he was now that he never really drew a comparison day to day. He could almost forget the way the horror had slowly crept through him as he'd realised what had happened, and the searing pain that had followed, always when he'd least expected it, over the months to come, when it had struck home again what it had meant for his future.

Dylan shook his head. The moment had passed. No point dwelling any longer on things he couldn't even change twenty-odd years ago, let alone now.

They walked up through a street of stalls and cafés, selling hats and tourist tat, more scarves and costumes. Dylan ignored the sellers, but focussed in on the nearest café. Maybe something to eat and drink would do them good.

'Are you sure you want to do this now?' he asked. 'We could stop and grab a bite to eat before we go in.'

But Sadie was already striding ahead towards the ticket booths. By the time he caught up she had two tickets in her hand, ready to pass through the barriers.

Apparently, nothing was going to stop her today. Least of all him.

'Come on,' she said. 'There's masses to see, and we've already lost time.'

Dylan gave thanks for the bottled water and cereal bars in his backpack, and followed.

The path led them through scrubland littered with broken stones—some plain, some carved, all seriously less impressive than he suspected they would have been once. Information boards told them about the area, what had been here before Ephesus, and what had happened to the geography of the place.

'Did you know, there have been settlements in this area since six thousand BC?' Sadie asked.

'I didn't until I read that same information board.' Was she seriously going to talk history for the rest of the day? He supposed he could understand the need to put some distance between now and that heartbreaking conversation at the side of the road, but still. At some point they were going to have to return to the real world. 'Come on, I want to see the city proper.'

As they continued along the path, recognisable buildings started to appear—ruined and worn, but with walls and doorways and even decoration in places. Sadie stopped to read every single information board—often aloud—to him, despite the fact she must have been here plenty of times before. Dylan was sure it was all fascinating, but he had other things on his mind.

She'd admitted that she hadn't dealt with Adem's death, not really. He should have seen that sooner, or at least been more mindful of it. Was that why she was clinging so hard to the Azure?

And, if so, what would happen when she finally *did* deal with everything? Would she be ready to move on? Maybe even with him, for a time?

They turned off the path into an amphitheatre, and Sadie went skipping down the aisle steps to the stage, standing in the middle and calling out a line from some play or another, listening to the words reverberating around the stones.

Dylan took a seat on the carved steps, right up at the top, and watched her explore. Leaning back, he let the sun hit his face, the warmth soothe his body. Sadie wasn't the only one to have confessed all that morning, of course. He'd expected to feel shame or be pitied or something after telling her all about his family. But instead, next to her emotional outpouring, his ancient pains seemed like nothing. Still, somehow it felt good to have shared them. And it had helped Sadie too, he thought. She seemed lighter after her confessions that morning.

Maybe she really *was* ready to let go at last—not just saying the words to win his support and his money.

And if so…hopefully what he had planned for the night would help her make that leap.

The Library of Celsus might just be her favourite part of Ephesus, Sadie decided as she ran her fingers along the delicately carved stonework. It never ceased to amaze her, just imagining all the learning and history the place must have held once. One of the later buildings, from the Roman period, its magnificence had only lasted one hundred and forty-two years before an earthquake and ensuing fire had destroyed it, leaving only the façade—and even that had perished a couple of hundred years later, in another earthquake.

Strange to think that the beauty she stared at now had been rebuilt by modern hands; that they'd found a way to bring some life back to a pile of rubble. But they had. Maybe she could, too.

Turning, she saw Dylan standing at the bottom of the library steps, staring up at the columns and statues. Smiling, she trotted over to join him. She'd known that Ephesus would be just the distraction they needed—especially after that morning. No business, nothing personal—just ancient history.

'It's pretty incredible, isn't it?' Sadie moved to stand beside him, looking back at the façade again.

'It's certainly impressive,' Dylan agreed.

'So much history… A whole different world really.' Just where she wanted to be today.

Dylan turned to her, eyes obscured by his sunglasses. 'You know, I don't remember you being so much of a history buff when we were younger.'

Sadie shrugged. 'Maybe I wasn't, back when the history around me was so familiar. But here…the history here blows me away. I want to know all of it.'

'Why?' Dylan asked, and she frowned at him. She should have known Mr Next Big Thing wouldn't get the appeal of bygone days. 'No, seriously, I'm curious. Why does it matter so much to you?'

'I guess because…well, it shows us where we came from. Where we've been and how far there still is to go. There's a lot of lessons in history.'

'Perhaps.' Dylan looked away, back at the library again. 'But I'm not so sure it can tell us what happens next.'

'You've never heard of history repeating itself?' she asked.

'Of course. But I like to think that we're more than just the sum of what has happened to us.'

Sadie followed his gaze back to the library façade. Suddenly she could see the cracks, the places it had been repaired, and where parts were still missing, in a way she never had before.

She was also pretty sure they weren't talking about the Ancient Greeks and Romans any more.

Was he right? Were they more than their history?

How could he say that when everything he'd told her that morning—about his dad, his family—had so clearly formed him into exactly the sort of man he was? Of course he didn't believe he could do commitment, coming from a family like that. It had even explained to her why he was so desperate not to miss chances—how many opportunities must he have given up to look after his mother and sister? It was a miracle he'd ever made it to university to meet Adem in the first place.

'Come on,' Dylan said, tugging on her arm. 'Let's keep going or we'll never see everything.'

Side by side, they climbed the paved hill through more terraces and temples and half-reassembled mosaics through the rest of the town.

'I mean, look at the people who lived here,' Dylan said suddenly, and Sadie frowned, trying to cast her mind back to the conversation they'd been having.

'What do you mean?'

'Well, they built this fantastic city, survived invasions and slaughters, were Greek, Roman, Byzantine...then the river silted up, the earthquakes hit, and the place started falling apart. And I bet you they never saw it coming—even though it had all happened before—however well they knew their own history.'

'I guess there are always twists and turns we can't predict,' Sadie admitted. 'And maybe sometimes we just choose to hope for the best instead.' Like she had, hoping for a long, happy life with her husband.

'You know that better than most, huh?' He gave her an apologetic half-smile, even though he hadn't done anything wrong, not really. She just wasn't meant to live happily ever after, it seemed. Not his fault. 'It's just kind of sad to think of all those people watching the harbour silt up, losing their access to the Aegean—the only thing that made this place matter—and realising there was nothing to stay for any more.'

Nothing to stay for... The words pricked at her mind, and she knew she'd been right, back at the library, to think they weren't really talking history any more.

'Is this some convoluted way of telling me that you think my harbour is silting up?' she asked sharply, stopping in the middle of the path and not even caring about the tourists behind who had to swerve suddenly. The anger bubbling up as she reran his words in her head mattered more.

Dylan glanced back at her and stopped walking himself. 'Your harbour?' he asked, voice laced with confusion.

'The Azure,' Sadie snapped. As if he didn't know what she was talking about. 'Look, just lose the metaphor. If you think there's no future for my hotel, that it can't be saved, tell me now.'

'You're wrong.' Dylan shook his head.

'Am I really?' Folding her arms across her chest, Sadie tapped one foot against the ancient stones and waited for him to deny it again.

If he dared.

Had the woman actually lost her mind this time?

Dylan grabbed Sadie's arm and pulled her away from the middle of the path into the shade of a gnarled old tree beside a tumbledown wall. Maybe the heat was getting to her. He fished in his bag for a bottle of water and handed it to her.

'Drink some of this,' he said, sighing when she managed to do so without breaking her glare at him. 'Look, I believe the Azure can be saved, okay? I'm just not sure that you're the person to do it.'

She lowered the bottle from her lips, her expression crestfallen. 'You don't think I can do it.'

He bit back a curse. That was not what he'd meant. God, how many ways could he mess this up? 'I'm very sure that you can. But I'm still not convinced that you really want to.'

'We're back to this?' She shoved the bottle back into his hands and cool droplets dribbled out onto his fingers. 'I've given you a million reasons—'

'And none of them are "because it's the work I know I was born to do".'

'Who has that? No one, Dylan. No one else expects that from their job.'

'You should.' He took a long drink of water. 'The difference between you and most people is that this isn't your only option. And obligation isn't passion, Sadie.'

'Fine.' She shook her head, stepping away from him. The extra distance felt like miles instead of inches. 'If this is too big a project for you, too big a commitment, just say so. I'll find some other way to save the Azure.'

She would too, he knew. Sighing, he rubbed a fist across his tired eyes. How had a simple sightseeing trip grown so complicated?

'I know things have been weird between us this week.' Her tone was softer now, and it only made him more nervous. 'But I swear I'm not asking for anything beyond your business and financial support, if that's what you're worried about. I...I think that maybe there could be something between us, yes. But I'm not trying to tie you down, or drag you away from your other opportunities.'

Something between us... Wasn't that the understatement of the year?

'I never thought you were.' At least he hadn't. Until she'd said that.

'Well...good.' She shifted awkwardly from one foot to the other, and he was pretty sure the faint pink flush on her cheeks wasn't just to do with the sun. 'So. Are you in, or not?'

She wanted an answer now. After days of dancing around everything between them—history, business, attraction—suddenly she needed to know. Of course she did.

'Can we discuss this at dinner?' he asked. If he'd read things right, tonight would be the perfect time to present his whole proposal in one go. A chance for them to maybe think about the future for once, instead of the past.

And he reckoned the odds on her saying yes were much better there than here at the side of the road through an abandoned city.

But Sadie stood her ground. 'No. I need to know now. Will you recommend investing in the Azure to your board?'

When had she got so stubborn? Or had she always been this way? Was it one of the things Adem had loved about her? He could hardly remember. The Sadie that had been had almost entirely given way to the new one, the one he'd spent the last week falling for.

He took a deep breath and dived in.

'I have a proposal for you,' he said, wishing his heart wasn't beating so loudly.

'Another one?'

'Yes. I'll help you save the Azure, if that's what you really want.'

'It is.' The words came fast enough, but did he hear a flicker of doubt behind them?

'You might want to wait and hear me out before you make that decision.'

She shook her head. 'I'm sure.'

'Really? Because I think you want something more. And I can give that to you.' He could see her considering it, the temptation on her face clear.

'What?' she finally asked, a little grudgingly.

And here they were. His one chance to win her away from this place. 'I recently took over a chain of hotels—mostly in the UK. I want to turn them into luxury spa hotels—and I think you'd be the person to help develop the spa aspect of them.'

Temptation gave way to shock as her eyebrows rose, frozen high on her forehead. 'I don't... I don't know what to say.'

Which meant she was considering it, right? Time to press the advantage.

'You'd be home in Britain, with your family,' he said, knowing he was sweetening the deal with every word. He'd spent enough time with her that week that he knew what she wanted—even if she wouldn't admit it. 'Finn would have your parents close too. You'd have support, help—and a generous, regular salary. If you really wanted, we could bring the Azure under the chain umbrella, put a new manager in charge…but it would still be yours and Finn's.' He had no idea how that would even work, or what his lawyers would say about it, but he'd say anything to get her to take the deal.

To have a reason to keep her close, to see her regularly, to have her in his life. However he could get her.

But it was more than that, he insisted silently. It was the right thing for her, too. And an opportunity most people would bite his hand off for.

Not Sadie, though. She still looked torn.

'Just think about it,' he said, and she nodded absently, her lower lip caught between her teeth.

He couldn't resist. The timing was wrong, nothing was as he had planned, they still had business to resolve, but he had to kiss her now. Before he went insane with wanting it.

CHAPTER THIRTEEN

SHE KNEW WHAT he was going to do a split second before he moved, could see it in his eyes, the way they softened and warmed. And, just like last time, Sadie knew she should pull away, back off, escape.

Except she didn't.

His hand came up to her waist and she let it, drawing a breath that burned her lungs at the touch. And when he dipped his head, she raised her chin to meet him, her lips aligning perfectly with his, as if they were meant to be kissed.

As if she'd been waiting her whole life for this.

Had that small, contented noise really come from her mouth? From the way Dylan wrapped his other arm around her, hauling her tight against his body as he deepened the kiss, she suspected it had. And she knew, without a shadow of a doubt, that their whole week together had been building up to this. She didn't know if it was history repeating itself, or the future imposing on her determination to cling onto the past, but this, this moment, this kiss, had always been inevitable.

It was what followed that was completely unclear.

After long, long, perfect moments Dylan pulled back, just enough to allow air between their lips again. His face was still so close that she could see every fleck of colour in his eyes, every hint of worry in his expression. He didn't know what happened next either, and somehow that made her feel a little better.

'So you'll think about it?' Dylan cleared his throat. 'My business proposal, I mean.'

Her eyes fluttering closed, Sadie let out a low laugh. All business, this man. 'Yes. I'll think about it.'

His hands dropped from her waist and she stepped back, sucking in the air that seemed to have disappeared for the length of their kiss.

'We should get back,' Dylan said. 'I have something great planned for tonight, and you're not going to want to miss it.'

Something more spectacular than that kiss? Sadie doubted it. 'There's not much more to see anyway. Just the gift shop. If you think you can live without a magnetic Library of Celsus...'

'I don't think I need anything more to remember this day by,' Dylan said, his gaze fixed on hers. 'I won't be forgetting our time in Ephesus in a hurry.'

'Neither will I,' Sadie admitted.

They made their way slowly back down the hill, inches separating them. Sadie wondered if she should be holding his hand—back when she'd last kissed someone for the first time, that had been the sort of thing you did afterwards. But, then, Dylan had never struck her as a handholding type.

She had too much to think about to make conversation on the drive back to the Azure, or do more than clench her jaw a little tighter when they passed the spot where they'd stopped earlier. Dylan's offer, for one, quite apart from that heartstopping kiss.

Why was he offering her this now? He'd come here to help bail out the Azure, but now it seemed he had other plans entirely. And as much as she appreciated him thinking of her…she couldn't help but wonder if this was just his way of keeping her close without actually having to commit to her in any way.

It was a stupid thought. They'd shared one kiss, that was all. But if they did decide to take things further… what happened next? What *could* happen, when Dylan had made it very clear that he wasn't the sort of man who stuck around?

Maybe she needed to separate the business from the personal—except that was impossible when her late husband's legacy *was* her business, and his best friend's job offer might just be a coded message for, 'Let's be friends with benefits.'

No, that wasn't fair. Whatever there was between her and Dylan, it was more than that, she could feel it. What was between them *mattered*.

But not enough for him to change his whole life philosophy—if she even wanted him to.

She sighed. If she took the job, it would mean abandoning her commitments here. And even if it was what she wanted to do, was it worth the risk to her heart? Dylan Jacobs had held a tiny corner of it for a very long time, she finally admitted to herself, and if she let him take more…well, she might not get it back.

And that was a big risk to take, for anyone.

'You okay?' Dylan asked.

She nodded, then realised she was already parked outside the Azure. When had that happened?

'What's the plan for tonight?' she asked unenthusiastically. She needed a long bath and an early night to think about her options, but it was Dylan's last night.

He flashed her an enigmatic smile as he climbed out of the car. 'Just meet me in the lobby at eight. It's a surprise.'

Just what she needed. More unexpected things happening in her life. 'Can you at least tell me what I should wear?'

'Anything you like.' He leaned back inside the car and pressed a swift kiss to her lips. 'You always look beautiful to me.'

And then he was gone, skipping up the steps to the Azure Hotel and leaving Sadie feeling more confused than ever.

Dylan refused to pace the lobby this time. The car was waiting outside, he was suited and booted in his best dinner suit and a crisp, new white shirt. Everything was going to be perfect.

As soon as Sadie showed up.

She didn't keep him waiting too long. He turned as the elevator let out its familiar ping and watched breathlessly as the doors opened and Sadie stepped out.

'Wow.' He'd been aiming for something more eloquent, but from the pink that hit her cheeks, honesty worked just as well. 'You look spectacular.'

'Thanks.' She looked down at her red cocktail dress and swirled her hips a little, making it rise and fall. The movement made every muscle in Dylan's body tighten.

If he didn't know better, he'd say that Sadie had plans for tonight, too.

'I've been saving it for a special occasion,' she said, taking his arm as they walked out of the hotel together. 'I thought that tonight might fit the bill.'

'I hope so.' Now that he was close enough he could feel the slight tremor in her hands, hear the tiny wobble in her voice. Dress aside, she wasn't as confident as she was making out. It made him feel a little better, actually—

because his confidence was giving way to nerves by the second.

'I, uh, I emailed you the proposal. For the Azure, I mean.' Had she? He hadn't checked. And that in itself told him that his priorities were shifting. 'We could look through it later tonight, if you wanted…'

Dylan shook his head. 'It can wait until tomorrow.' Tonight couldn't be about business, he could sense that. It needed to be about them. But the two were so closely linked…would they really be able to untangle them?

The car he'd hired sped them down to the marina, and he tipped the driver generously when they got out. If everything went to plan, they wouldn't need him until the next morning.

'The marina?' Sadie asked, looking around her at the lights. The whole town seemed lit up in the almost darkness of the autumn evening. 'What are we doing here?'

'I have a friend who has a yacht—and he owed me a favour,' Dylan explained, leading her towards the vessel in question. 'So tonight we shall be dining aboard the *Marie Bell*, catered by one of the finest chefs I've ever met. And, if it's okay with you, I thought we might take her out for a spin out on the Aegean.'

Her gaze shot to his. 'Overnight?'

'Yes. She has two bedrooms, and is fully equipped with anything we might need for an overnight stay, but if you'd rather come back sooner…' He trailed off. 'This can be anything you want, Sadie. I just wanted to give you a special night.'

She nodded slowly, her teeth tugging on her lower lip again in that way that just made him mad to kiss her. 'Okay.'

The yacht was every bit as spectacular as his friend had described, and watching Sadie stand at the prow as they motored out of the marina, staring out at the darkening water, Dylan knew he'd made a good choice in bringing her there. They needed tonight—even if it was all they ever got.

And just in case it was, he intended to make the most of every single moment.

Grabbing a bottle of champagne and two glasses from the bar, he headed out on deck to share it with Sadie.

Sadie stared out at the water, dark and constantly changing under the moonlight. Dinner had been beautiful—all four courses of it—and more than made up for their skipped lunch at Ephesus. The conversation, too, had been light and easy—after Dylan had declared a moratorium on business talk the moment they'd sat down. And neither of them had seemed inclined to discuss the past after the day they'd spent together.

Instead, they'd talked about Finn, about cities Dylan had visited recently, places she'd love to go one day, her sister and parents—anything except what was happening between them, or anything that mattered.

It almost felt like a first date.

But now dinner was over and she had to decide what came next. She could tell Dylan was leaving it up to her—which was probably why he'd removed all their other issues from the evening.

It was just them now.

No hotel, no history—no husband. Not any more.

She shivered, and Dylan wrapped his jacket around her shoulders without a word.

Out here at sea, it was just Sadie and Dylan. And it was up to her to decide what that meant.

But only for tonight.

That, she was sure, was the main reason he'd brought

her so far from the real world. Not just to give her a treat at the end of his visit but because, whatever she decided, once they returned to shore it was all over. He'd move on. They'd be business partners perhaps, or maybe not. She hoped they'd still be friends, whatever happened.

But nothing more.

'You're thinking too hard.' Dylan rested against the rail beside her, leaning back to get a good look at her. The lights from the boat lit his face, but hers must be hidden in shadow, she assumed. Yet still he stared at it. 'You're supposed to be relaxing.'

Sadie turned, her back to the water, and he shifted nearer, until he was half in front of her, so close against her right side that she could feel his muscles against her body, even through two layers of clothes.

No pretending this was anything other than it was now. And not even a hint of a suggestion that they might be using that second bedroom.

Sadie sucked in a breath, the scent of him mixed with the sea air filling her lungs, an intoxicating combination. God, she wanted him so much. It felt good to admit that, after so long.

Maybe she always had. But want and love were very different things—and she'd loved Adem.

Strangely, it was that thought that made it all feel possible. This wasn't love—and never would or could be with a man like Dylan. For him, love was commitment and thus impossible. However he felt about her, he'd never let it move past tonight—so neither would she.

Sleeping with him wasn't the same as betraying Adem's memory, not in the way she'd been afraid it would be. Not unless she never planned to sleep with another man again for the rest of her life. At thirty-two, that seemed a little impractical, even to her.

She could have this. She could have one night and no more. She could give in to that curious want that had plagued her since she'd met this man—and that had only worsened over the last week.

As long as she walked away with her heart intact in the morning. And her heart was buried in England with her husband.

Decision made, Sadie rose up on tiptoe before she could change her mind. Dylan's eyes widened, just a fraction, and his arms tightened around her. But he didn't move closer. He was still leaving this up to her.

Sadie closed her eyes, raised her lips to his, and took what she wanted.

The first kiss was gentle, tentative, like the one in Ephesus. But within moments it changed.

'God, Sadie,' Dylan muttered against her lips, and his arms hauled her up against his body so her bottom rested on the higher rail and she could barely touch the deck with her toes. It should have felt unsafe but with Dylan's arms so tight around her body she knew there was no chance of her falling.

She knew he'd never let her go.

'I can't tell you how long I've waited for this,' he murmured, as she placed kisses across his jaw and down his throat.

'About as long as I have,' she admitted, pressing an extra kiss to the hollow of his collar bone, as thanks for discarding his tie and undoing those top shirt buttons after dinner.

His thigh pressed between her legs, her bright red dress rising up high above her knees, and the pressure almost made her lose her mind.

'Really?' he asked, dipping his head for another kiss. 'You wanted this too?'

'Always,' she admitted. 'I just never thought I could have it.' Or should.

'Because— No. Not tonight.' He kissed her firmly. 'Tonight is just for us. No ghosts, no history, nothing between us.'

Sadie looked up into his eyes, almost black with wanting her, and kissed him in agreement. 'Just us. Just for tonight.' She swallowed, hunting down that last bit of courage she needed. 'So, how about you show me the bedroom you promised me this place had?'

Dylan grinned, a wolfish look on his face. God, what was she letting herself in for? And how would anything after it ever live up to tonight?

'Your wish is my command,' he said, and Sadie knew none of it mattered.

Just for tonight she was going to live in the moment, and enjoy every second of it.

CHAPTER FOURTEEN

DYLAN WOKE TO the feeling of something missing. Forcing his tired eyes to open, he waited for them to focus then frowned at the sight of Sadie already pulling that glorious red dress over her even more spectacular body. Without looking back at the bed, she began hunting around for her shoes, pulling them on as she found them.

Huh. Talk about a rude awakening.

Last night had been everything he'd ever dreamt it might be, and more. He could never have imagined the way they moved together would be so in tune, so perfect. He didn't know what had changed that week but, whatever it was, it had only brought the two of them more in sync.

But apparently that perfect connection was over with the sunrise.

'Morning,' he said, levering himself into a seated position and letting the sheets fall away from his torso.

Sadie jumped at the sound of his voice, which gave him some small satisfaction. 'You're awake.'

'As are you. And dressed, too.'

'Yeah, well…we're back in the marina,' she said. He wanted her to come and sit beside him on the bed, just enjoy these last few moments away from the real world, but the look on her face stopped him short of suggesting it. What was it he saw there? Uncertainty, a hint of fear, maybe a little sadness? Or was he just projecting his own feelings onto her expression?

'Time to get back to the real world, then, huh?'

'I guess so.'

'You should have woken me,' he said, trying to inject lightness into the words, to try and break the strange new tension in the room. 'Before you put all those pesky clothes back on, for preference.'

'I suppose you're usually the one slipping out of a borrowed room the morning after, huh?' Her smile suggested it was meant to be a joke, but the words fell flat between them as Dylan felt his mood worsening.

'You were slipping out on me?'

'No!' Sadie said, too fast. 'I mean, it's not like you wouldn't know where to find me, right?'

Was that the only reason? God, what had happened in her head between him falling asleep boneless and sated and the moment he'd woken up this morning? Dylan had no idea—and he wasn't sure he was going to be allowed to find out.

'So it's back to the Azure, then,' he said. Apparently their moratorium on business was over, too. 'That's what happens next?'

'I think it has to be,' Sadie said. 'I mean, you have a flight to catch this afternoon, and you still haven't checked over the Azure proposal. I think I included everything we've talked about, but if you have any questions it would be good to deal with them sooner rather than later. I'm leaving for England in a couple of days to fetch Finn home, remember.'

Home. So Turkey was still home to her. Good to know.

Dylan reached for his pants. Talking business naked just felt wrong. 'Never mind the Azure proposal right now. Have you thought any more about my proposition?'

he asked, wishing the moment the sentence was out that he'd chosen any word other than 'proposition'.

'I…I'm not sure it would be the best idea.'

'Because of last night?'

'Because of lots of things.' She bit her lower lip, and Dylan had to sit on his hands to stop himself reaching for her and kissing them back to last night again. 'Will you still present the Azure proposal to your board for investment? Even if I'm still in charge?'

'Of course,' he said, the words almost sticking in his throat. 'You've certainly demonstrated the potential of Kuşadasi and even the hotel itself as a viable investment. I'll talk to them as soon as I get back.'

'Great. Thanks.'

Awkward silence stretched between them until Dylan thought he might snap. Grabbing his shirt from the floor, he tossed it over his shoulders before striding across the luxurious cabin towards the bathroom. 'Why don't you go see if you can go scare us up some breakfast?' he suggested over his shoulder. 'I'll be there in a few minutes.'

If it was back to business as usual, he needed a shower, some food and plenty of coffee. Hopefully one of those would fill the yawning gap that seemed to have opened up in his chest.

Sadie kept it together until they reached the hotel, a feat she was rather proud of. It would have been so easy, that morning, to turn over and back into Dylan's arms. To let their one perfect night stretch just a little further. But it would have only prolonged the agony.

Because for all her arguments to herself the night before she had no doubt that letting him go again was going to be excruciatingly painful.

How was she supposed to go back to business, or even to being friends, now that she knew how it felt to have his skin against hers, his body pressing hers down into the bed with glorious pleasure? How was she supposed to even *think* about anything else?

But she had to. Because no matter how miffed he might have looked at being upstaged in the casual morning-after stakes, Dylan didn't want anything else. Oh, he might convince himself that they could be something more—but it wouldn't be a commitment, not from him. He wasn't Adem, and she had to remember that. Keep it at the front of her mind at all times.

Or else she had a horrible feeling she could slide so easily into love with the man.

And that *would* be a betrayal. Maybe not of her wedding vows—she knew that if Adem had lived she would never have taken this step, never have had this chance to explore what could be between her and Dylan—and not even of her husband's memory, not really. Rachel had been right in that at least—Adem would rather see her happy than alone.

But she'd be betraying herself. Betraying what she wanted—no, needed—from her own future. Maybe Dylan had been right when he'd said the Azure wasn't her dream, but he couldn't see that it was a part of something bigger. A chance for her to live her life with her son—and she didn't want that life to be confused and clouded by a man who came, made them love him, but never stayed. She wouldn't do that to Finn—or to herself.

Maybe Dylan would change one day, find something or someone worth committing to. But she couldn't take the chance that the thing or person he found might be her. Not when it would affect Finn too.

And it would, she knew. Her own fluctuating emotions

after one week, one night told her that. She needed to be solid and steady for her son, and Dylan Jacobs made her the opposite of both.

'I'd better pack,' Dylan said, as they stood in the lobby of the Azure, more than a metre of marble floor between them.

Sadie nodded her agreement. 'Your car will be here at two. I'll come down and see you off.'

'You don't have to.' He sounded so distant Sadie had to swallow a large lump in her throat before she could answer.

'Yes, I do.'

'Fine. I'll see you then.' He strode off towards the lifts, without looking back.

Sadie took a deep breath and went to check in with the front desk for any important news or messages, hoping they wouldn't comment on how overdressed she was for the task.

Then she was going up to her room to take a bath and break down in private.

The second hand ticked around the clock face seemingly slower than ever, but still inexorably working its way towards two o'clock. Sadie smoothed down her black suit one more time and tucked her still-damp hair behind her ears. At least the make-up seemed to be holding strong— her eyes weren't nearly as blotchy as they'd been a quarter of an hour ago.

In—she checked the clock again—twelve minutes' time she'd go down to the lobby. That, assuming Dylan arrived early too, would give her ten whole minutes to say goodbye to him.

It wasn't enough, but Sadie was starting to worry that no amount of time would be. She'd been so focussed on the fact that he'd be walking away the next day she hadn't spent enough time considering the fact that she wouldn't be able to—not from the memories and not from her feelings.

Dylan might not be the committing sort, but she was—and she should have remembered that before she'd fallen into bed with him. She'd never been the one-night stand sort, so why on earth had she thought she could start now?

She sighed, and sat back down on the bed. Because she'd wanted it so badly, that was why. She'd wanted that one night—and now she'd had it she couldn't give it back. And, truth be told, she wasn't sure she even wanted to.

A sudden hammering on the door jerked her out of her thoughts. Blinking—and hoping the waterproof mascara was still holding up—she quickly crossed the floor and opened the door.

'Dylan.' She was supposed to have another eleven minutes before she had to face him. What unfairness was this?

Without a word he pushed past her into the room. Sadie shut the door behind her; from the furious expression on his face she had a feeling this conversation wasn't one she wanted to share with the rest of the hotel.

'Okay, I'm leaving in, like, fifteen minutes, but I need to know something first.' He had his hands in his pockets, but from the look of the material they were bunched into fists. 'What happens next?'

'Next?' Sadie gulped. The question she'd been avoiding. 'Well, like we said, it's back to business. We can be business partners, hopefully, and friends for definite. I hope Finn and I will be seeing more of you in the future.' Even if it tore at her heart every time. Dylan was part of Adem's life too, and Finn deserved the chance to know him. She just needed to make sure she guarded her emotions more carefully—something that would certainly be easier with her son present.

'So last night was…?'

'Wonderful,' she admitted, with a small smile. 'But I told you, I never expected anything more. I'm not trying to tie you down or make you commit to anything. Well, anything more than saving my hotel.'

'You make it sound like everything that has happened between us this week was only about you getting my investment.'

'You know that's not true,' Sadie admonished. Whatever he might think of her today, he had to know she wasn't the money-grabbing woman his words suggested.

'Do I?' he asked, one eyebrow raised.

'I bloody well hope so!' Her own temper started to heat and rise to match his. Ten more minutes and they could have avoided this completely, parted civilly. But, no, he had to storm in here and demand the last say, didn't he?

'In that case, I can only assume that you slept with me as some sort of personal experiment,' Dylan said, the words sharp. 'A chance to find out what you could have had. And now you're burying yourself back in your old life, the tired old plan that wasn't working.'

'Sounds to me like you don't like being treated the way you've treated God knows how many women over the years,' Sadie bit back. 'What, it's okay for you to indulge in one night and call it quits, but God forbid a woman tries to do the same to you.'

'That's not what this was!' Dylan yelled. 'What we had—'

'Was a mutual attraction we worked out of our systems last night.' The lie hurt even to speak it, but what other option was there? Ask for more and watch Dylan flounder when he realised he couldn't offer it? She might have hurt his manly pride, but that had to be better than letting him destroy any self-respect she had left.

'It was more than that, and you know it.' His tone was low now, dangerous, daring Sadie to deny it.

She couldn't.

'Even if it was,' she said softly, 'it was never going to be anything more than this week, and it's not fair of you to pretend that it was. I have Finn and the Azure to think about, and you have your business… You're leaving any minute now, for heaven's sake.'

'But I'll come back. I said I'd come back.' He made it sound like a huge commitment. Probably because he had no idea what a real one looked or sounded like.

'And there'll always be a friendly welcome for you here.'

'Friends.' He barked a harsh laugh. 'You really think we can go back to that?'

'I think we have to,' Sadie said pragmatically. 'Because, Dylan, you can't offer me anything else.'

'I offered you a new career. A chance to start over.'

'What I want most is the chance to have a future with my son.' The truth, if not quite all of it.

'And what about me? Are you really going to let your dead husband and this bloody hotel stop you from moving on and being happy?'

She could have laughed at the cruel irony of it. Here he was, the ultimate playboy, asking for more—and she couldn't give it to him, however much she wanted to. Because he didn't even know what it meant.

'Are you honestly telling me you're ready to become a father—to a little boy you've barely met?' The sudden shock on his face was answer enough. 'Exactly. Dylan, you're not Adem, and I never expected you to be. I went into this with my eyes open. But you don't do commitment and I need that in my life—for Finn, as well as myself. We need stability and certainty more than ever now. And you can't give us that.'

You're not Adem.

Wasn't that what it always came down to? In the end, it wouldn't have mattered who'd met her first, who'd loved her most, who could give her what—he wasn't Adem. So he was always going to lose.

'I'm not even second choice to you, am I?' he murmured, watching her eyes widen. Could she sense the fury building inside him? He hoped so. But he also knew he needed to get out of there before it exploded. He'd never hurt her, but if they wanted to remain even business acquaintances there were some things they couldn't come back from. 'I'm no choice at all.'

'Finn is my choice,' Sadie said, but he knew what she meant. She would always choose Adem—even his memory—over moving on with him. Over giving him a chance to see if maybe, just maybe, this time he could stick at something. 'Yours is the next big thing. It always has been, and it always will be. You know that, Dylan.'

'Just like my old man, huh?' He knew it himself, always had. But it still hurt to hear it from her—the one woman he'd thought, for a moment, that he could be something more for. Someone better.

'That's not what—' Sadie started.

'Yes,' he replied. 'You did.'

So, really, what was there left to say?

'My assistant will be in touch about the investment proposal in due course,' he said. 'I'm sure it will go through without a problem.'

Sadie nodded but didn't speak. He supposed she'd got

the only thing she wanted anyway. At least one of them was ending this week happy.

'Goodbye, Sadie.' He turned on his heel and walked out, hoping his car was already waiting downstairs.

He didn't let himself believe that the sound he heard behind him as he shut the door was a sob.

CHAPTER FIFTEEN

SADIE DROPPED HER suitcase onto the spare bed in her parents' back bedroom and began rummaging through it for a cardigan. England might be colder than she'd remembered, but it was still good to be home, however temporarily.

Anything was better than moping around the Azure Hotel alone.

At least she had Finn back now. Once they headed home to Turkey, it would be the two of them against the world again, and everything would be fine. Just one look at his beaming face as he'd waved his 'Mummy' sign, surrounded by pictures of aircraft, when she'd arrived at the airport had told her that she'd done the right thing. When he'd wrapped his little arms around her neck and hugged her tight she'd known there was no other choice she could have made.

Finn was the only thing that mattered now. All she had left.

'Knock-knock.' Her sister Rachel appeared in the open doorway, both hands occupied with cups of tea. 'Mum thought you might need this after your journey.'

'Definitely.' Family, a cup of tea, familiar surroundings…this was all exactly what she needed.

A whoop of excitement from outside caught her attention and she moved to the window, cup of tea in hand. In the back garden Finn and his cousins appeared to be playing some sort of game involving a football, three hula-hoops and a garden chair. Whatever the rules, he seemed to be having fun, even wrapped up in his coat and scarf instead of still being in tee shirt and shorts, as he would have been in Turkey.

'The kids have loved having Finn here to play with,' Rachel said, following her gaze. 'It's been lovely for them to all have some time together.'

'I know.' A flicker of guilt at keeping Finn so far away from his family ran through her. 'And I know Adem's parents enjoyed having him for a sleepover last weekend.' More people they didn't see enough of.

'I bet. It must be even harder for them.'

'They came out to visit in the spring,' Sadie said defensively.

'Not the same as having him round the corner, though, is it?'

No, it wasn't. Sadie sank to sit on the edge of the bed and blew across the top of her tea to cool it. 'Finn asked me if we really had to go back to Turkey,' she admitted. 'He's loved being here so much.'

Rachel winced as she sat beside her. 'Sorry. Didn't mean to make things worse.'

'It's the truth, though, isn't it?'

'But not all of it. If you're truly happy out in Turkey then Finn will be too. You know kids, they're always happiest exactly where they are, never ready to move on to the next thing. Especially if it's bedtime.'

The exact opposite of Dylan. Sadie huffed a tiny laugh into her mug at the thought.

'How are things at the Azure anyway?' Rachel asked.

'Any luck with the investment guy—personal or professional?' She nudged Sadie gently in the ribs.

'Dylan's going to present my proposal to the board, but he thinks they should go for investing.' There. She'd said his name without crying. A definite improvement. And the proposal was good—she'd worked on it with Neal before Dylan's arrival for weeks, and had tweaked it to fit everything she and Dylan had talked about on his visit. It was just what he'd wanted, she hoped.

'And personally?' Rachel pressed. 'Come on, Sade. I saw you all dressed up for him, remember? There was definitely something going on there.'

'Well, if there was, it was for one night only,' Sadie said.

Rachel frowned. 'That idiot walked out on you after one night?'

'Yeah. Well, no. I...I guess I walked out on him.'

'That doesn't sound much like you.'

'It was a pre-emptive strike,' Sadie explained. 'He doesn't do commitment, and it was more important to me that we stay friends and business partners. Apart from anything else, Finn doesn't need any more uncertainty in his life.'

'And how's that working out for you?' Rachel asked doubtfully.

'It's fine,' Sadie lied. 'It's for the best.' She just had to keep telling herself that. And not acknowledge the secret fear that kept her awake at night—that she had gone and fallen head first in love with Dylan Jacobs.

Even she couldn't be that stupid, right?

'He did offer me a different business proposal, though,' she said. Better to get the conversation back on professional terms. 'It would mean working back here in the UK, putting a manager in charge at the Azure.'

'That would be perfect!' Rachel bounced a little on the mattress. 'You and Finn could come home and still keep the Azure! Have you told Mum and Dad yet?'

'I turned him down,' Sadie admitted, with a wince.

Rachel stopped bouncing. 'Because you slept with him?'

'Because…it didn't feel right.' Of course, nothing had felt right since Dylan had left either. But how much harder would this be if she had to see him all the time for work, too? No, much better this way, with her safely tucked away in Turkey and him travelling the world, popping in for the occasional friendly visit. Knowing Dylan, they'd be lucky to see him more than once a year.

Another depressing thought.

'Well, I suppose you know best,' Rachel said, although her tone clearly said otherwise.

'I hope so,' Sadie whispered.

Otherwise it was entirely possible she'd made the biggest mistake of her life, sending Dylan away.

'Well, you're in a foul mood,' Dylan's sister Cassie said. He dropped into the wooden chair beside her, exhausted after an hour or more racing around the scrubland that surrounded her home with her two boys.

'Hey, you should be nicer to the guy who's been keeping up with your two tearaways for the past week.' Not that it was a chore particularly. Keeping two six-and nine-year-old boys entertained took energy and concentration, and worked marvellously as a distraction. Of course, it helped that it was also fun.

Much more fun than dwelling on how things had ended with Sadie anyway.

Cassie handed him a cold beer and he took it gratefully. 'Want to tell me about it?'

'I don't know what you're talking about,' Dylan lied.

'Seriously?' Raising her eyebrows at him, Cassie put her own bottle down and ticked her observations off on her fingers. 'First, you arrive here with no warning. You drag the boys off to play outside whenever they ask you questions about your travels. You haven't been to see Mum, even though you've been here for days. And, most importantly, you've almost drunk all my beer.'

'I'll buy you more beer.'

'That's not the point.' Cassie sighed. 'Go on, I'm listening. Detail your boring work problem and I'll make the necessary sympathetic noises as needed. Unless it isn't work…' She sat up straighter. 'In which case I might be much more interested.'

'It's nothing.' Dylan took a swig of his beer, glad it was a million miles away from the local wine he'd drunk with Sadie in Turkey. The fewer reminders the better right now. He'd spoken to the board, had got them to approve the investment and had handed the whole mess over to his assistant before he'd left for his sister's place in Sydney. He just wanted to move on.

'Which means it's a woman,' Cassie guessed. 'Okay, let me see… She's married to someone else? Or just not interested. Oh, Dylan, did you finally find a woman who *doesn't* want you?'

'Not exactly.' Although, really, wasn't that the truth? Sure, she'd wanted him for one night, but that had been it.

Dylan sent up a silent apology to every woman he'd ever spent just one night with, even if he'd been upfront about it from the start. Being on the opposite end showed him exactly how much it sucked.

'So what happened?' Cassie pulled her feet up under her on her chair, just like she'd done when she'd been little. 'You've got me all curious now. Don't leave me hanging.'

Dylan sighed. Cassie had always been stubborn. There was no way he was getting out of this conversation without giving up at least the basic facts.

'I went to Turkey to see an old friend, to see if I could help her business out. We...connected in a way we hadn't before, that's all.' He shrugged. No big deal, no drama, no hole in his chest filled with a swirling vacuum of rage and confusion and disappointment. Nothing to see at all.

'That's all?' Cassie asked sceptically. 'So, what, you slept with her, left as usual, and now you're, what? Missing her?' She shook her head. 'You're such an idiot.'

'Thanks for the pep talk.' His little sister always did know how to kick a guy when he was down. At least, that was what her first husband had said. Her second hadn't commented on it so far. Dylan liked him a lot more than the first.

'Seriously, Dyl, when are you going to stop running before you even have a chance to see if there could be something there?' Cassie waved her bottle at him accusingly. 'You're always the same. You find someone you like, indulge in a fling or whatever, then walk away before it can go anywhere. And this time it really looks like it could have! I haven't seen you this bummed since that deal in London went wrong.'

'What's the point in staying?' Dylan asked. 'I mean, we all know that I'll be leaving eventually, right? When the next big opportunity comes up, I'll be on my way. Why make that harder than it has to be?' He couldn't even deny the accusations Sadie had thrown at him. He didn't stay—and she wouldn't go. Permanent mismatch.

'That's just horse droppings!'

'You've been watching your language around kids too long.'

'I'd use stronger if I thought it would make you listen!' Cassie sighed, and settled onto the edge of her chair, staring earnestly up at him. 'Did you even think about staying and fighting for her? That's what you do, you know, when you love someone. You stay and figure things out. Every morning you wake up and decide to try harder. That's all there is to it.'

'She told me to leave. She has a son…commitments. There was no place for me there.' Even if it had felt, just for a moment, like he could have fitted into their lives perfectly.

'Honestly, Dyl, if you believe that you're stupider than even I ever thought. Just because Dad left doesn't mean you will. Of course you can settle down, *of course* you can commit, when you find the right thing.'

'And how, exactly, do you know that?' Because he sure didn't.

'Because you've already done it once.' Cassie sat back in her chair, a smug look on her face.

Dylan blinked. 'How do you mean?'

'You did it for me and Mum. You spent years taking care of us, committed to making sure we were okay even when we went out of our way to mess that up.' She smiled gently at him, and Dylan felt some of the truth of her words sink into his bones. 'You never thought about walking away, did you?'

'No. I suppose I didn't.'

'And you've never stopped either. You still check up on us both. You're always there for my boys—and I know you always will be. That's why I named you their guardian in my will.'

'You did?' Why hadn't he known that? Unless Cassie

had thought the idea of it would have freaked him out. Which, before this week, it probably would have.

Cassie nodded. 'Too right. I wouldn't trust anyone else with them.'

'Thanks. I think.'

'And I bet we're not the only ones,' Cassie went on. 'What about your friends? I mean, you said you went out there to help this old friend out. You've always done that, too. Whatever your friends needed, you were there. That's commitment too, you know.'

'I never thought of it that way,' Dylan admitted. All those years, he'd committed to the people who mattered to him—his friends and family.

The truth struck him hard in the chest. Friends and family? Sadie was already both, in his heart.

He was already committed, and he hadn't even noticed.

Now he just needed to convince her of that.

Maybe he wasn't Adem. But maybe he could be what she needed now instead.

And maybe, just maybe, he could be what Finn needed too. After all, he knew better than anyone how fundamental having a father figure in a boy's life could be. Maybe he could even give Finn what he and Cassie had lost when he had been ten.

Cassie took another swig of her beer. 'Little sisters are always right, you know. So, need me to book you a ticket to Turkey?'

But Dylan was already on the phone to the airline.

Sadie hung back from the gravestone, flowers held awkwardly in her hands. Her dad was waiting in the car with Finn, ready to take them back to the airport, so she didn't have long. But coming to the churchyard had seemed like the right thing to do before she left.

But now she was here, staring at a stone that spoke about a beloved father, son, husband and friend, she didn't know what to do next.

Adem wasn't here, not for her. She knew his parents felt better having him close, but for her no motionless, cold stone could ever represent her warm, loving, enthusiastic husband. She felt his presence far more in the heat of a Turkish summer or in the halls and rooms of the Azure.

And maybe that was why she needed to be here. To ask for his blessing, or advice, or something. To tell him that she needed to move on at last.

'I'll always love you,' she said, placing the flowers carefully by the stone. 'But I think you know that anyway.' She'd told him often enough in life.

Sighing, she crouched down in front of the flowers. 'We had a wonderful life together, didn't we? And we made the most precious little boy. But...I don't think you'd want me to stay in this limbo. And I'm starting to think I can't.'

She swallowed, fighting back the tears that pooled in the corners of her eyes. 'I need to move on. I'm not quite sure what to yet, but I don't think that matters as much as being ready to take the chances as they come.'

Just because Dylan wasn't an opportunity it didn't mean there wouldn't be others. In work, as well as in love.

'You always said that your instincts were the most important compass you had,' she went on. 'That if you trusted your instincts nothing much could go wrong. You said...' A choked sob escaped her throat. 'You said that asking me to marry you when we were so young, with no prospects, was the biggest ever test of that. And me saying yes...that was the last time I truly trusted my own instincts instead of yours.

'Well, that changes now. I don't know what's going

to happen next but… Dylan's assistant called. We have the investment we need to save the Azure. So I'm going to make that happen and then I'm going to find someone I trust to manage the place when I'm away. I'll take Finn back often, I promise, and it will be there for him when he's old enough. But in the meantime my instincts tell me we should be here, in England, with our families. And then…well, I guess we'll see. I have faith that the right thing will come along at the right time.' She managed a lopsided smile. 'It always did for you after all. Until the last.'

Adem's life had been too short and their happiness cut off before its time. But the happiness they'd had together would be hers to treasure for always. And she would.

Kissing her fingers, she pressed them against the stone. 'Love you,' she whispered.

Then, wiping her eyes, she turned and headed back towards the car, and her future.

CHAPTER SIXTEEN

SADIE SIGHED WITH relief as the car from the airport turned up the road that led to the Azure Hotel.

'Nearly there,' she told Finn, who snuggled down further on his booster seat, arms wrapped around his favourite teddy. 'Nearly home.'

Home for now, anyway.

The flight had been long and tedious, with a change in Istanbul that had dragged on as they'd waited for a delayed plane. Finn had been brilliant, really, but the journey had been trying for *her,* let alone a four-year-old. Still, with the help of plenty of snacks, a new toy or two saved for the occasion, and a well-timed nap on the last leg, they'd made it.

If nothing else, all the time in transit had given her time to think—to start to form plans, ideas that she hoped would come together as the weeks went on.

She was returning to Turkey prepared for her fresh start, ready to jump at the right opportunities as they presented themselves.

Of course, some sign as to what the right opportunities were would be appreciated, but Sadie figured that was part of trusting her instincts—figuring that out for herself.

'We're here,' she whispered to Finn as the car drew to

a halt. He blinked at her a couple of times then opened his eyes wider.

'The Azure?'

'That's right. You ready to get back to your room and your things? I know Esma's been missing you.'

Sadie opened the door and let him hop out onto the pavement, following as the driver retrieved their bags.

'Thanks,' she said, stopping for a moment to look up at her hotel. *Her* hotel. She liked the sound of that.

The familiar Azure sign shone above the glass doors and she smiled at it as she lowered her gaze…and felt her heart stop.

As Esma rushed out and tried to whisk Finn away, chattering loudly about milkshakes and special sweet bread in the kitchens, Sadie stared at the man standing under the Azure sign.

Dylan Jacobs.

Well, she'd asked for a sign.

'What are you doing here?' She stepped closer, leaving her bags on the pavement as the car pulled away.

'Mum?' Finn asked, looking between her and Dylan. Esma shot Sadie an apologetic look. 'Who's this?'

Dylan crouched down beside Finn and the smile on his face was a new one to Sadie. Friendly, warm and with no edge, no demands. No business.

'You probably don't remember me, but I was one of your dad's best friends.'

'You knew my dad?' Finn's face scrunched up, just a little. 'If you were friends with Dad and Uncle Neal, are you Dylan?'

Dylan held out his hand. 'Dylan Jacobs. At your service.'

Finn shook his hand solemnly, his fingers tiny around Dylan's bigger ones, and Sadie felt her heart contract at the sight. 'Uncle Neal tells me stories about you and Dad sometimes. How come you never come and see us, like he does?'

'I've been…' Dylan trailed off before he could finish the sentence, but Sadie was pretty sure the missing words were 'too busy with work'. Wasn't that always the case? But then he started again.

'I'm sorry, Finn. I should have done. I should have visited more. And I'd like to start now, if that's okay with you.'

'I guess so.' Finn tilted his head to the side. 'Do you like milkshakes?'

'Love them.' Dylan grinned. 'Maybe we can grab one together later? After I speak to your mum?'

Finn nodded. 'Okay.' Esma took his arm again and this time he didn't object as she led him off to the kitchens. Sadie sighed with relief—until she realised that left her alone with Dylan.

Just what she was trying to avoid. 'There's really no need for you to be here,' she said. 'I told your assistant I'd get the forms to him by—'

Dylan shook his head to stop her, standing up from his crouch. 'I'm not here in a professional capacity.'

How she'd missed that voice. Warm and smooth and caressing—even when he was chatting with Finn or when they were talking business. Just seeing him again made her want to reach out and grab him, to hold on and never let him go.

This was why she'd needed not to see him again. When she was near him it was impossible to deny that she'd fallen ridiculously in love with him.

'Then why are you here?' she managed to ask through her muddled thoughts.

Dylan stepped closer, taking a breath so deep she saw his chest move under his shirt. 'I'm here to commit.'

'To what?' Sadie asked, blinking. Because he couldn't possibly mean what she thought he did. Could he?

'To whatever you need to be happy,' Dylan replied. 'If that's me thousands of miles away, then I'll commit to that. If it's still the Azure, I'll work like the devil to make that happen with you. If it's England with Finn, I can make that work too. All I want is a chance. A chance to prove that I can be part of your plan, of your future.'

'That's it?' Was this really the same man who had walked out on her in such a fury?

'That's it,' Dylan confirmed. 'I know I'm not Adem, and I never will be. But I can be more than you think of me. All I want is a chance to be with you, however you need me. To be there for you and Finn. And I know that can't happen all of a sudden—he needs to get used to me, we need to figure out things between us... So, a new proposal, okay? No jumping in feet first, just a slow, measured plan you can back out of any time you want. The sort of plan you like, I promise.'

The ultimate commitment-phobe was offering to commit. The man who *always* leapt at the next big thing was promising to stick to just one plan. Her plan.

Hope blossomed deep in Sadie's chest, like the cherry tree in her parents' back garden in England, flowering with hope and possibility in the spring.

But... She shook her head. 'I'm sorry, Dylan. That won't work for me.'

That was it. With just those few words she'd dashed any hope Dylan had ever had of committing again, he was sure. The heaviness in his chest sank lower and lower until...

He blinked. Was she smiling?

Sadie stepped closer and he let just a little chink of hope back in.

'This time...' she said, reaching up to place her hand against his cheek. 'This time I'm trusting my instincts. I'm taking all the opportunities I can to be truly happy again. And I think I know what that means, at last.'

'You do?' Then he wished to God she'd tell him because he had no idea what was going on.

Sadie nodded. 'I want Finn to have the Azure when he's older, but I don't want to run it myself. Once we've got things set up here and on the road to recovery, I'm hoping you'll help me find a manager we can trust so that Finn and I can move back to England.'

'Of course. Does that mean you've reconsidered my job offer?' Was this business? Or pleasure? Her closeness suggested the latter, but her words didn't. And he'd already been caught out by that before.

'I've reconsidered a lot of things,' she admitted. 'I want to run my own spas, I know that. And if we can work together on that...well, that would be great.'

'That all sounds good,' Dylan said cautiously.

'But that's not all,' Sadie went on. 'I'm afraid I'm greedy. I want more than just my family near, my son happy and a dream business. I want you, too.'

His heart stopped, just for a moment. 'I thought you said—'

'I said that slow and measured wasn't going to work for me any more,' Sadie corrected him. 'I know we can't rush too much officially because of Finn—I need to be sure that he's ready for there to be someone else in my life, and that he's happy for it to be you. So, officially, fine, we go with your plan.'

'But unofficially?' He didn't care. He'd say yes to anything right now if it meant being part of her life. Hers and Finn's.

'Life's too short, I've seen that first hand. You have to take your chances for happiness when they come. So just between you and me… I hope you were serious about wanting to commit…'

'I was,' Dylan assured her.

'Good. Because…' She took a deep breath. 'Dylan Jacobs, will you marry me?'

Pure joy spread through his body at her words. This was one opportunity he had no intention of missing.

Reaching into his pocket, he pulled out the ring box he'd acquired in Sydney and flipped it open between them. 'Great minds?' he said, as Sadie laughed.

'I should have known the slow-and-steady thing was a bluff.' She took the ring from the box and stared at the diamond, mesmerised. 'You never did anything that way in your life.'

'Oh, I don't know,' Dylan said, as he slid the ring onto her finger. 'It took me thirteen years to find the right woman to commit to.'

'But now you're sure?' Sadie asked.

'I'm beyond certain,' Dylan promised, leaning in to kiss all her doubts away. 'You're my next, last and only big thing. Your love is the only thing that matters to me. You, Finn and I are going to be the happiest little family ever, I'm committed to that. And I plan to spend the rest of my life proving it to you.'

Sadie smiled, and kissed him back.

And in that moment Dylan knew, bone deep, that proposing to Sadie was worth more than the chance at any million-dollar business deal, and that marrying her would give him more opportunities for happiness than one man could ever use in a lifetime.

EPILOGUE

CHERRY BLOSSOMS BLEW across the garden from the tree at the far end, and Sadie watched, smiling, as Finn tried to catch them, Dylan swinging him up in his arms to reach higher.

In the kitchen behind her, her parents were putting the finishing touches to a Sunday roast—and didn't need any help at all, thank you. Ordered to relax, Sadie had retired to the garden to enjoy the spring sunshine and just be with her family. At any minute her sister would arrive with her brood, and they'd all be together.

In the six months since Dylan had first arrived at the Azure, life had changed beyond recognition—and into something Sadie had never even hoped for. It hadn't all been easy, and business had intruded more than she'd have liked. But Finn had taken to Dylan instantly—and his awed admiration seemed to be reciprocated. Some nights, when Dylan was staying with them—always in the spare room, as far as Finn was concerned—she'd catch Dylan sneaking into Finn's room just to watch him sleeping. The amazed love in his eyes always made her want to kiss him harder.

They'd finally broached the topic of becoming a real family with Finn the weekend before, despite Sadie's anxieties. His little five-year-old nose had scrunched up at the idea.

'So, Dylan would live with us?' he'd asked.

'When he didn't have to travel for work, yes,' Sadie had answered nervously.

'Good. I like our house. I can walk to Grandma and Granddad's from here, and to school, and Phoebe and CJ can visit me lots.' Dylan had shared a small smile with her at that. When she'd tried to insist on finding a place to rent on her own, maybe in Oxford, he'd pointed out that she'd only have to move again in a few months when they finally let everyone else in on their engagement. The whole point was to be near her family—so together they'd found the perfect house just across the village from her parents'.

It already felt like home should.

'So, you wouldn't mind me marrying your mum?' Dylan had asked, and Sadie had heard the nerves in his voice even if Finn hadn't. He'd come such a long way from the man she remembered as Adem's friend. And he was so much more now, to her and to Finn.

'Will I have to wear a stupid suit?' Finn had asked. 'My friend Riley did when his mum got married.'

'You can wear whatever you like,' Dylan had promised, his relief obvious.

Finn had tipped his head to the side, studied Dylan for a moment, then clambered up into his lap for a hug. 'Then I think it would be pretty great.'

As far as Sadie was concerned, it already was.

A commotion came from behind her and Sadie knew that Rachel had arrived with the kids. Finn came running towards her, cherry blossoms forgotten, Dylan following. As he passed, Sadie grabbed Finn around his waist and pulled him up into her lap.

'Mum!' He wiggled, trying to escape. 'CJ and Phoebe are here!'

'I know,' Sadie said. 'So, how would you like to be the one to tell everyone the big news?'

'The wedding news?' Finn whispered conspiratorially.

Sadie nodded, smiling at Dylan over Finn's head.

'Okay!' He jumped down and ran into the house. 'Guess what, everybody! Mum and Dylan are getting married!'

Dylan held out a hand to pull her to her feet. 'Better put this on, then.' He fished in his pocket for a familiar-looking ring box and handed it to her. 'It'll be good to see it on your hand permanently at last.'

'It'll be good to wear it.' She let him slide the ring into place then reached up to kiss him as her mum's squeals of joy rang out from inside.

'When do you propose to tell them our other news?' Dylan murmured against her mouth, his hand brushing across her middle.

'We've got a few weeks yet,' Sadie whispered back. 'Let's let this one sink in first.' In truth, she was enjoying the secret. 'Besides, I want Finn to know before anyone else. Being a big brother is a big job.'

'That it is.' He kissed her again, and Sadie felt a warmth flow through her that had more to do with love than spring sunshine and cherry blossom.

She was home at last, exactly where she was meant to be, and all her plans for the future looked golden.

* * * * *

5_ST19

MILLS & BOON®

Cherish™

EXPERIENCE THE ULTIMATE RUSH OF FALLING IN LOVE

1015/23